W9-BZU-738

PRAISE FOR RICHARD HERMAN, JR., AND

IRON GATE

"MACKAY AND PONTOWSKI ARE BACK AND BETTER THAN EVER! Herman expertly builds a real bonfire of suspense in the opening pages, then sets it on fire with all the explosive action and excitement you expect from a first-class thriller. His research is impeccable and authentic, and he draws heavily on his own combat flying experiences. An excellent read!"

—Dale Brown

Matthew Zachary Pontowski III—Commanding his A-10 Warthogs to soaring victory took him from a desk job at the Pentagon to a stunning promotion to brigadier general; but beyond the military fast track, he's a widower dedicated to raising his young son. Facing a conflict far from home, Matt flies into a hypercharged time bomb the only way he knows—on his own terms.

Colonel John Author Mackay—He beat the odds as a black teenager in a Washington, D.C., ghetto, and overcame his harsh, scarred looks with his one weapon: a brilliant mind. Now, undercover in a country primed for civil war, he finds the racism and unrest of South Africa igniting his fury. One woman is about to join his mission—and show him the meaning of his past and his roots.

"HERMAN WRAPS TWO ETERNAL BATTLES—GOOD GUYS AGAINST BAD GUYS, HEROES AGAINST BUMBLING SUITS AND BRASS—INTO A ROUSING ADVENTURE."

—*Publishers Weekly*

"HERMAN'S LATEST ... IN A FIRST-RATE SER-
IES. ... VIVID, VIOLENT SCENES OF AERIAL COM-
BAT AND PLAUSIBLE MANEUVERING BEHIND THE
LINES WHERE GEOPOLITICAL FATES ARE DETER-
MINED: A NOTABLY EXCITING ACCOUNT OF A
LOW-INTENSITY CONFLICT THAT'S UNCOMFORT-
ABLY CREDIBLE. ..."

—*Kirkus Reviews*

Hans Beckmann—The neo-Nazi leader of the Afrikaner
Resistance Movement, he rules the Boerstaat north of Cape
Town, an enclave of white supremacist insurgents walled
behind the Iron Gate. His politics of hatred and his vision
of world dominance are backed by the force of his Iron
Guard—and by a deadly arsenal beyond the control of any
enemy. ...

Samantha Darnell—A gutsy camerawoman for an ambi-
tious but struggling news reporter, she keeps her colleague
from committing professional suicide by tracking down hot
leads. But it's Sam who may have just found the story of the
year within the files of the national security advisor—a trail
that leads her into the fires of war ... and into a volatile
affair with Matt Pontowski.

"HERMAN CAPTURES AIR FORCE LIFE AND COM-
BAT TACTICS WELL. ... HE COMMANDS THE
READER'S ATTENTION. ..."

—*Library Journal*

"WHAT TOM CLANCY DID FOR THE NAVY WITH *THE HUNT FOR RED OCTOBER,* RICHARD HERMAN, JR., HAS DONE FOR THE AIR FORCE. . . . IT IS DOUBTFUL THAT ANYONE HAS EVER WRITTEN MORE VIVIDLY OR REALISTICALLY ABOUT THE EXHILARATION OF AERIAL COMBAT. . . ."
—James C. Ruehrmund, Jr., *Richmond* (VA) *News Leader*

William Gibbons Carroll—Brilliant, decorated, and determined, the American national security adviser sees the destabilizing of the Pretoria government—and the Afrikaners' discovery of cold nuclear fusion—as a direct threat to major world powers. Fighting a race against time with his own declining health, he vows to engage U.S. forces in South Africa—even if it's his last act of heroism.

Ziba Chembo—Educated in an English boarding school but working as a housekeeper in her homeland, she can lead Colonel John Mackay to the inner workings of a scientist's development of nuclear weapons. A woman of serenity and dignity, she stands proud and firm in her Zulu heritage—and can fight the *tsotsis* like a street soldier in their violent battle of survival.

"MR. HERMAN . . . KNOWS HIS FLYING."
—Newgate Callendar, *The New York Times Book Review*

Books by Richard Herman, Jr.

Dark Wing
Call to Duty
Firebreak
Force of Eagles
The Warbirds
Iron Gate*

*Published by POCKET BOOKS

For orders other than by individual consumers, Pocket Books grants a discount on the purchase of **10 or more** copies of single titles for special markets or premium use. For further details, please write to the Vice-President of Special Markets, Pocket Books, 1633 Broadway, New York, NY 10019-6785, 8th Floor.

For information on how individual consumers can place orders, please write to Mail Order Department, Simon & Schuster Inc., 200 Old Tappan Road, Old Tappan, NJ 07675.

IRON GATE

RICHARD HERMAN JR.

POCKET STAR BOOKS

New York   London   Toronto   Sydney   Tokyo   Singapore

The sale of this book without its cover is unauthorized. If you purchased this book without a cover, you should be aware that it was reported to the publisher as "unsold and destroyed." Neither the author nor the publisher has received payment for the sale of this "stripped book."

This book is a work of fiction. Names, characters, places and incidents are products of the author's imagination or are used fictitiously. Any resemblance to actual events or locales or persons, living or dead, is entirely coincidental.

A Pocket Star Book published by
POCKET BOOKS, a division of Simon & Schuster Inc.
1230 Avenue of the Americas, New York, NY 10020

Copyright © 1996 by Richard Herman, Jr., Inc.

All rights reserved, including the right to reproduce
this book or portions thereof in any form whatsoever.
For information address Simon & Schuster Inc.,
1230 Avenue of the Americas, New York, NY 10020

ISBN: 0-671-87309-1

First Pocket Books printing May 1997

10 9 8 7 6 5 4 3 2

POCKET STAR BOOKS and colophon are registered
trademarks of Simon & Schuster Inc.

Cover art by Ben Perini

Printed in the U.S.A.

This book is dedicated to the eight brave men
who died in the attempt to rescue
fifty-three American hostages out of Iran
on April 25, 1980.

Our forefathers purified the soil with their blood when they fought the savage forces that held this land in bondage. These forces of darkness were never defeated and now they are attacking the gate of our civilization. But it is a great gate, a gate forged with the strength of iron and the blood of our fathers. When you think of this Iron Gate, think with your blood! Blood and Soil! *Blut und Boden!*

—HANS BECKMANN,
   Blood and Soil:
   My Struggle for the Afrikaner Nation

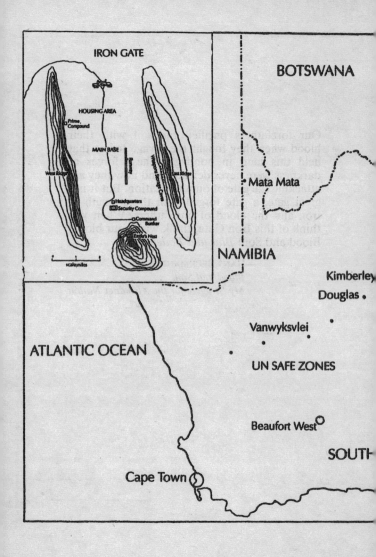

IRON GATE

BOTSWANA

HOUSING AREA

Prime
Compound

MAIN BASE

Weapons Storage Area

West Ridge

East Ridge

Runway

Headquarters
Security Compound

Command
Bunker

Eagle's Nest

NAMIBIA

Mata Mata

Kimberley

Douglas

Vanwyksvlei

ATLANTIC OCEAN

UN SAFE ZONES

scale/miles

Beaufort West

SOUTH

Cape Town

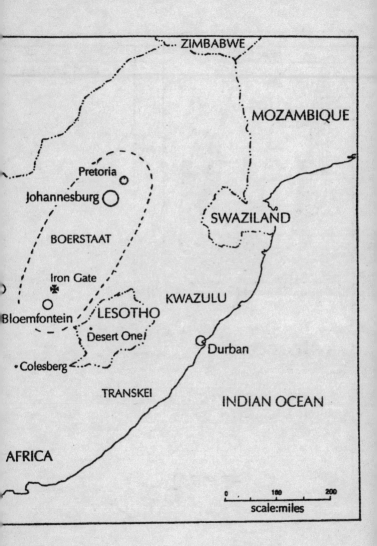

PROLOGUE

Wednesday, July 30
Soweto, South Africa

The two teenaged boys stood at the taxi stand under the black township's only overpass, patiently scanning the passengers in each minivan arriving from Johannesburg. They were in no hurry as this was their first job, one with no deadline to meet, and sooner or later, they would find a man who matched the description they had been given.

And if they killed the wrong man, it was of little consequence. They would simply wait for another. Such was the way of the *tsotsi*, the frightening and vicious township thugs who specialized in street crime.

A minibus packed with black workers from Johannesburg hurtled under the bridge, its driver oblivious to the mass of humanity milling in the street. The crowd parted and formed a narrow lane for the sixteen-passenger van to shoot through as the driver rode the squealing brakes, dragging the minibus to a halt.

The *tsotsis'* lean and smooth faces were impassive when a well-dressed man with lighter than normal skin stepped out of the minibus. They had a target. Without a word, they fell in behind their intended victim as he walked away. They never saw the tall man who was also waiting for the taxi.

John Author MacKay's height of six feet four inches let him see over the crowd and for once, his dark scarred face did not draw attention as he followed the *tsotsis*. A frown

1

crossed his face—they were a complication he didn't need. He moved in and closed the gap when he saw the young thug on the left pull a long thin blade out of his sleeve. It was an assassin's weapon, sharpened on both edges. The teenager on the right took five quick steps, brushed past their victim, stepped in front, and abruptly stopped.

It looked like a harmless incident, typical of life in the crowded township where privacy and solitude were found only around the homes of the rich and powerful. The two *tsotsis* intended to sandwich the man and use their bodies to shield the attack. Only a crumpled body on the ground would mark their work.

Before the boy with the knife could bump into the man and shove the blade into his spine, MacKay grabbed his wrist from behind. He twisted and jerked hard, straightened the boy's arm out and behind him, and hammered his left hand into the back of the rigid elbow. There was a sharp, sickening snap as the elbow came apart and the knife fell to the ground. The boy gasped, pain taking his breath away.

The would-be victim turned at the sound, took it all in in a quick glance, and pushed at the teenager blocking his path. The boy fell back as the man kicked at his knee. But he missed and the toe of his shoe caught the teenager's shin.

The teenager howled in pain, hobbled around, and bumped into MacKay. He looked up and froze at the apparition looming over him. MacKay's high forehead, jug-handled ears, misshapen nose, receding chin, and bad case of pseudofolliculitis barbae created a harsh image that smiling only made worse. MacKay smiled at him.

MacKay pounded the heel of his palm into the teenager's forehead, repeatedly snapping the boy's head back. "This way," the man said and led the way through the maze of shanties behind the taxi rank. MacKay followed, surprised by the man's cool reaction and lack of panic. They turned down a side street, and when the man was certain they were not being followed, walked through the gate in a low wire fence. They halted behind one of the miserable two-room homes that made up most of Soweto.

The man took a deep breath before speaking. "Are you John Arthur?" MacKay nodded. "I understand you are

2

interested in Prime," the man said. Again MacKay nodded. "So are we," the man continued. "But there are problems."

"Financial?" MacKay asked. Now it was the man's turn to nod. MacKay handed him a thick envelope. The man opened it and quickly counted the money. His face glistened with sweat and MacKay was certain it was more than adequate.

"We can help," the man said.

"Are you Inkatha?" MacKay asked.

The man shook his head. "No questions, please."

MacKay pointed at the envelope. "There's more." The man smiled an answer. MacKay had finally made contact.

Thursday, July 31
Voortrekker Monument,
Pretoria, South Africa

The men emerged out of the shadows of the parking lot and passed through the wall that circled the hilltop. On the wall, sixty-four granite wagons in bas-relief formed a laager, the symbol of their defiance. In the valley below, the lights of Pretoria still glowed in the early morning dark. Silently, they climbed the steps leading to the monument. It loomed large above them, a square granite structure blocking the sky, an undefined mass, heavy in the dark. Suddenly, floodlights came on, illuminating the bronze figures of a *voortrekker* woman and two children that guarded the entrance.

As one, the men stopped. They were not a large crowd, maybe four hundred at the most. Fifty years before, they would have numbered in the tens of thousands. But these were the last, the true elders and leaders of their tribe, the ones who would not yield to the future. They were all dressed in dark suits appropriate for a state function or a funeral, as this was. Many were big men, heavyset, and wore beards as befitted their heritage. All carried Bibles, some big and leather bound, cracked with age, others smaller and more portable. The Bibles were worn with use and the lineage of their families; births, baptisms, marriages, and deaths were inscribed inside.

It was a solemn occasion, for they had come to this shrine of their civilization to burn the Bibles and break the covenant they had with the nation and their God. A single man stepped forward to set his Bible down.

A man was watching from the entrance to the main chamber, hidden by the deep shadow cast by the bronze statue. He stepped into the light and picked up the Bible. "Why are you doing this?" he asked. The words were spoken in Afrikaans, the language born out of the Dutch vernacular of medieval Flanders. But Afrikaans had taken on a new hue, changed by the infusion of other languages from Europe, Asia, and Africa.

A low murmur of "Hans Beckmann" worked its way through the crowd. They knew who he was.

The eldest of the men answered. "Because the covenant is broken. God no longer delivers the enemy into our hands so we may triumph over him. We have lost our land, our nation."

"Only part of it," Beckmann said, returning the Bible to its owner. He was not dressed like the others but wore military battle dress and boots. His beret was folded and stuffed under an epaulet and he was unarmed. A webbed canvas belt cinched his jacket against the cold wind. He was clean shaven and his blond hair was cropped short. Being of average height and build, there was nothing outward to distinguish him from most men, but his bearing and voice demanded obedience. He was a man used to command.

"We have lost South Africa, but not our homeland," Beckmann said.

"We are outnumbered no matter where we go," a voice answered, "and the world rules against us."

Beckmann folded his arms across his chest and looked toward Pretoria. "We created this country and we gave it wealth. We brought civilization to this land." The men listened as he repeated the litany at the heart of their beliefs. "I cannot change what has happened but I can restore our heartland."

"How?" a single voice challenged from the rear.

"Give me Prime," Beckmann answered, "and I will carve out the Boerstaat and give you a home, a nation." He waited for those who understood Prime to explain it to the others.

4

It was a long discussion and the first light of dawn was breaking the eastern horizon.

"But Prime is not a weapon," a voice said.

Beckmann stared over their heads. "I can turn it into a powerful weapon."

"But the world is against us," the same voice said. "We will never have a homeland."

"The world understands power. With Prime they will honor our existence and the Boerstaat will be a reality."

"It is a dream," another voice said. "A hopeless dream."

"Apartheid is dead," Beckmann said. "Now we must create the politics of survival. Give me Prime and the Boerstaat will not be a dream. You will have a country to raise your children in."

The sun rose further over the eastern horizon as the men formed a new covenant.

Thursday, July 31
Fredericksburg, Virginia

The old man was standing in the rose garden and addressed the bush in front of him with the same solemnity as he would a prime minister or foreign head of state. After serving in the State Department for twenty-five years, then as ambassador to the former Soviet Union and Japan, and finally as the secretary of state for the late President Pontowski, the tall and elderly statesman wasn't about to change his habits. Besides, the rose bush deserved the respect he was paying it.

His wife, working nearby on an equally beautiful and prized rose, shook her head and snipped a dying blossom, letting it fall to the ground. "Cyrus!" she fumed, determined to get on with deadheading their roses. "Quit daydreaming about smooth-legged young girls. You are past it, you know."

Cyrus Piccard arched one of his bushy white eyebrows at Jessica. After forty-one years of marriage his wife still surprised him. He hadn't been thinking about girls in the least. He was thinking about Matthew Zachary Pontowski III, the grandson of the late president.

Retirement in the elegant colonial house on the outskirts of Fredericksburg was wearing on the old man, and his head, with its heavy mane of gray hair, seemed more bent lately. He needed something to do before he drove Jessica crazy. Again, his wife surprised him. "You want to make one more king, don't you?"

She's right, Piccard admitted to himself. He did want to create another president of the United States.

"Then you had better get on with it," Jessica continued, not needing an answer. "You haven't got much time left."

Piccard's blue eyes came alive and his lanky, slightly potbellied body straightened. Suddenly, his left hand flashed out and with a decisive clip of his small pruning shears, he decapitated the rose. The cut was at exactly the proper angle and height. The blossom tumbled to the ground. Now a new flower would bud and bloom before the end of the season. "Long live the king," he announced.

"Is it Matt?" his wife asked.

"Who else is there?" he replied.

6

CHAPTER
1

Friday, August 8
Johannesburg, South Africa

Colonel John Author MacKay, United States Army, stood
at the curb and waited for the minibus taxi that would take
him to Katlehong, the embattled black township southeast
of Johannesburg. As expected, the metered cabs that served
mostly whites ignored him and sped by. But as it was early
afternoon, the empty minibuses were aggressively trolling
the streets in a vain attempt to hook riders. The drivers
honked and jammed up traffic as they searched for fares
while the pirate cabs boldly challenged the licensed, legal
taxis. It was unregulated competition gone mad.

He split his attention while he waited. One half of his
mind worked the current problem—making contact with
the right taxi—while the other half roamed elsewhere.
Equal opportunity with a vengeance got me here, he decided.

MacKay had come a long way out of the ghetto of
Washington, D.C., where he had been another black teenager caught in the cycle of poverty, crime, and hopelessness
that defined his neighborhood. But he had been blessed
with a strong-willed mother who held her family together
after his father had disappeared. His harsh, scarred looks
had caused him untold grief until high school. Then one
day, he realized that along with his large size, he was well-
coordinated and smart. To be more accurate, a teacher had

him tested and discovered that he possessed an IQ of 140. He was brilliant. He still recalled her words, "Use what you got. Don't waste it."

When a cousin came home on leave from the Army, MacKay had listened to his stories and found his own way out of the ghetto. With the help of the same teacher, he had transferred to another high school, excelled in sports, and made the honor roll. In his junior year, he had applied for West Point, and he wasn't surprised when the Army offered him an appointment—if he could qualify for admission. He did.

That was over twenty years ago, he thought, one part of his attention still on the traffic. Where did the time go? Now he was standing on a street corner in Johannesburg with the alias John Arthur. The choice of name was deliberate because agents had been known to forget their cover names at the most inopportune times. By using a name close to his own, John Author, and since it would take a sharp ear to key on the difference should he fumble, he sidestepped a common occupational hazard that often got agents killed.

An approaching light-blue minibus brought the two halves of his mind back together. A quick glance at the license plate confirmed it was the taxi he had been waiting for. It stopped and he climbed in, ducking to clear his head. There were times when his height was a disadvantage.

"Eight rand, man," the black driver said, demanding the fare be paid up front. In the crazy taxi wars that often resulted in a shootout and dead passengers, getting payment in advance was considered a prudent, if not essential, business practice. But eight rand was twice the normal fare.

"That's inflation for you," MacKay replied. The driver took the fare and nodded. They had successfully exchanged recognition signals. The taxi shot out into traffic as the driver shoved a small pistol back into his waistband. MacKay's bona fides were correct, which was fortunate for the driver because in the close confines of the minivan MacKay could easily have taken the automatic and killed him. MacKay was relieved it hadn't come to that.

The driver turned, now very friendly once the formalities were out of the way, and flashed a smile at MacKay. "Baas, you not African. Where you from?"

MacKay fell into his cover story as a businessman from the United States. "Pittsburgh, Pennsylvania," he answered.

"I didn't know they had niggers there," the driver said.

The old anger flashed through MacKay at the hated word. How often had it been hurled at him by racist whites and the bros? Then he realized the word didn't carry the same power for the driver. "Nigger is a bad word in the States," he explained. "We call ourselves African-Americans."

The driver roared with laughter. "That's dumb, baas. A man can only live in one place." He fell silent, thinking. Finally, he said, "I feel sorry for you. You don't know where you from. I got to know where I from to be happy. You American."

That caught MacKay's attention since he had always thought of himself as an African-American. Yet on the continent of his ancestors, he was only the latter half. MacKay had never spent much time agonizing over questions of identity, but the driver's words had upset him. Then it came to him. The driver was fixed in the present, anchored to his family, clan, and tribe. He had a place he knew as home. MacKay was still searching for his.

The taxi stopped and picked up another passenger. The well-dressed man MacKay had saved from the *tsotsis* in Soweto climbed in and the driver stomped the accelerator. He cut off another minibus as they hurtled down the street. MacKay held on. "Do they all drive like this, Charles?" MacKay asked the newcomer.

"Mr. Arthur doesn't like our Zola Budds," Charles told the driver. The minibuses drove at breakneck speed and were nicknamed Zola Budds after the barefoot woman Olympic runner from South Africa. The two men laughed. "All must appear normal," Charles explained. "We are two passengers riding together. We can talk until we reach Katlehong. BOSS is still a problem."

Charles used the old name for the Directorate of National Intelligence when it had been called BOSS, the Bureau of State Security. MacKay understood the fear blacks still carried for South Africa's intelligence organization. BOSS had been very efficient at identifying politically active Africans and turning them over to the SAP, the South

African Police. Once in the hands of the SAP, an African could expect very rough treatment. While the reports of torture and death had ended with the defeat of apartheid, the fear had lingered on.

A red minibus fell into trail six cars back and held its position.

Charles relaxed into his seat, oblivious to the jerky and reckless ride as the driver raced his way through the traffic. "There are problems," he said. It was MacKay's cue to hand over another envelope stuffed with money.

"Who are you with?" MacKay asked. Charles smiled and shook his head. "I pay for results," MacKay continued. "You haven't produced any."

"One of our people works for a Doctor Slavin who works inside the Pelindaba nuclear reactor plant," Charles said.

MacKay's eyebrows arched. Slavin was an Israeli scientist and the driving force behind project Prime. Without a word, MacKay handed over an envelope.

Charles counted the money. "She will help you," he said.

"She?" MacKay asked, surprised that a black woman would have access to Prime.

"There are things you don't understand about our society," Charles explained. "Maids are a fixture in a white household, much like furniture. It was easy to place her as a maid and nanny in the Slavin household." Charles spoke English with the characteristic lilt of many black clergymen in South Africa. A news reporter had told MacKay that preachers were the people to contact because they knew what was happening in the black community. Another reporter had introduced him to a minister, who in turn had set in motion the series of cutouts and contacts that led him to Charles. It had been a laborious process but he was nearing his goal.

The minibus slammed to a halt for a young woman carrying two large bags. MacKay glanced at her, assuming she was the maid Charles had mentioned. It was only a momentary distraction, for he was watching the red minibus, which had also stopped. But it didn't pick up passengers. He counted eight passengers in the minivan, all young men. The two taxis moved back into the traffic. "Everyone keep looking straight ahead," MacKay said. When he was certain his three companions were obeying, he continued, "We're being followed. It's the red minibus three cars back. It's been on our tail since we picked up Charles."

Their driver let himself be cut off so a clump of heavy traffic would bunch up the two minivans. He checked his rearview mirror. *"Tsotsi,"* was all he said. He accelerated, cutting in and out of traffic.

"Is it BOSS?" MacKay asked.

Charles talked to the driver in Zulu. "I don't think so," he finally answered in English. "Perhaps it is a taxi war." Taxi owners often paid *tsotsis* to eliminate their competition in a very direct way. Other *tsotsis* saw it as another moneymaking opportunity and became insurance brokers, offering "protection insurance" to the taxi companies. This only added another layer to an already confused business with the result that no one took the time to check the sides, or insurance policies, before the shooting started. It was the free enterprise system with a South African twist.

"Is it the same group who tried to nail you in Soweto?" MacKay asked. Charles had passed the incident off as an attempted robbery, but MacKay thought it went much deeper.

"No," Charles said. "That's why we are going to Katlehong. The gangs don't talk to each other and stay in their own territory."

Their driver easily outdistanced the loaded minivan following them. "She runs good, *baas.*" The driver grinned.

MacKay was certain their minibus had a few extra horses under the hood from the way it accelerated, and they soon lost their pursuers in traffic. He turned his attention to the girl and felt old. He was forty-two and she was in her early twenties. She was tall, big-hipped, and someday would be heavyset, probably after childbirth. Her hair was cropped short in the traditional Zulu way. A more pronounced bridge to her nose and slightly lighter than normal skin indicated a European or Asian ancestor in her lineage. She was definitely African and not beautiful in the European sense, yet she had an aura that captured him. She was a young queen, graced by an innate serenity and dignity.

11

Charles waited before making introductions. He knew the effect Ziba Chembo had on people. "Ziba," he finally said, "this is the man I told you about, Mr. John Arthur."

"Mr. Arthur," she repeated, her voice low-pitched and controlled. "The man with two first names." She had a beautiful voice and spoke with an English accent.

MacKay did not reply and, for reasons he did not understand, wanted to tell her his real name, John Author MacKay. He wanted to explain how his mother, almost illiterate, had misspelled his middle name and had written Author instead of Arthur on his birth certificate. He wanted this young woman to know that he would never change it because that would hurt his mother. But he said nothing.

"How can I help you?" Ziba asked.

"We want to find out what is going on inside Pelindaba."

"I'm a housemaid, Mr. Arthur. I work for a man who works at Pelindaba and I never go inside the compound."

"Ziba has a very good education," Charles explained. "She graduated from an English boarding school for girls. But this is the only job she can get. This is her day off and she is going to visit her mother."

"The man you work for," MacKay said, "Doctor Slavin, is a scientist. You must hear things, see documents." Ziba nodded. "What you see and hear may not make sense to you, but they are pieces to a larger puzzle that we can fit together."

"Doctor Slavin and his family are from Israel, Mr. Arthur," Ziba explained. "They are very kind to me. Why should I betray their trust? What does he do that interests you?"

"We think he makes nuclear weapons," MacKay answered.

Charles said, "We know who *they* will use those weapons against." They exchanged words in a language MacKay thought was Zulu. At first, MacKay thought he was trying to cajole the woman into cooperating. Then he realized Charles was establishing a dominance over her and MacKay could almost smell the man's lust. It was the first step in a seduction.

Ziba stared at Charles with a cold look until he looked away. He was outmatched, and she was not an innocent housemaid. "They are not making nuclear weapons," she finally said in English. "Doctor Slavin wants to make electricity. That is all he talks about."

"We know he was at the test site in the Kalahari when it blew up," MacKay said.

"I overheard him discussing it with his wife," Ziba explained. "He said it was an accident, a very small explosion. They learned much from it."

"It leveled two square kilometers of the Kalahari," MacKay replied, "left a smoking crater a hundred meters across, and killed over fifty people. I don't consider that small." She recoiled at his words, shaken by the revelation. MacKay considered his next words as he studied her face. He sensed the intelligence behind her dark eyes and decided to play it straight. "It was a very small thermonuclear explosion, one of the smallest we have ever seen. But it was thermonuclear. Do you know what that means?"

She stiffened, not ready to accept the truth. "Doctor Slavin does not build nuclear weapons. He is very proud of that."

"Then why does he work on nuclear projects?" Charles asked.

"To make electricity," she repeated. "Doctor Slavin is a peaceful man." The doubt in Ziba's voice disappeared. "He is a good man and does not make weapons to kill people."

"Really?" MacKay replied, disbelief in his voice. "There was another explosion at Pelindaba this morning." Her face turned solemn as he continued. "At least twenty people were killed or injured and a building was leveled. It won't be in the papers."

"Was Doctor Slavin hurt?" she asked.

MacKay shook his head as the taxi slammed to a halt. They had reached Ziba's stop.

"What you ask is difficult," Ziba told them. "I must think about it." Charles started to protest but she cut him off with a hard look. She got out and closed the door.

"Baas, look behind," the driver said. He accelerated wildly into the heavy traffic, throwing them about. MacKay twisted around and saw the red minivan right behind them. It was too late. The minivan smashed into the rear of their taxi, knocking it sideways and into a skid.

MacKay dropped to the floor. "Get down!" he shouted at Charles. But the man only held on to the back of the seat in front of him and twisted his head back and forth, his eyes wide with fear. MacKay reached up and pulled him down. The minibus tipped crazily to the left as they skidded, but somehow the driver recovered and kept them upright. They came out of the skid and shot down the dirt path alongside the road, scattering pedestrians. The red minivan hit them again and MacKay heard a dull thud and felt a hard bump. They had hit and run over someone.

Submachine-gun fire raked the back of the minivan. The rear window shattered, sending a shower of glass over MacKay. The driver shrieked in pain and tried to control the minivan as their pursuers rammed them again. The taxi broached sideways and rolled over.

MacKay was vaguely aware of hands dragging him out of the van. He looked up into the face of a *tsotsi*. The boy said something and rolled MacKay over onto his stomach. He felt wire cut into his skin as his wrists were bound together. The teenager stood back and kicked him in the side of his head. Two more kicks and MacKay feigned unconsciousness. The *tsotsis* held a quick council of war, grabbed Charles, and stood him against the minivan. Two pinned his arms while a rag was stuffed into his mouth.

Then MacKay heard a low chant start to build in the crowd. "Necklace . . . necklace." It grew and changed, becoming a hypnotic command for action. The *tsotsis* grinned at each other and waited. Unobserved, MacKay moved his wrists, trying to free them. But any movement only tightened the wire loop holding the other wrist.

An old car tire was rolled into the tight circle that surrounded MacKay and Charles. A low, animal-like wail erupted from the gagged Charles when two men grabbed him and threw him to the ground. The tire was pulled over his body and the *tsotsis* spread-eagled his arms and legs. The gag was jerked free and Charles screamed in terror, making MacKay's skin crawl.

One of the young thugs poured gasoline into the tire's casing and set it on fire. A high-pitched, inhuman shriek split the air and drove nails of terror into MacKay. It was Charles. The flames flared, driving the *tsotsis* away, but not before a vicious kick to the head stunned the doomed man. Charles lay quiet as the flames enveloped his body. Someone threw a seat from the van onto the blaze, pinning him to the ground.

"Necklace! Necklace!" echoed louder as a wild frenzy gripped the crowd. The circle grew wider, forced back by the blaze. Another tire was rolled into the center.

This tire was for MacKay. He scrambled to his feet and ran at the crowd, his head lowered like a battering ram. He speared one man and bulldozed his way through the crowd, kicking and butting. Twice, he stumbled but somehow stayed on his feet. He was almost free when two men clubbed him to the ground. Before they could drag him to his feet, a burst of submachine-gun fire echoed overhead, scattering the crowd. Another burst and the crowd was gone.

MacKay rolled to his right and saw Ziba, sweat pouring down her face, holding an Uzi. She had seen the red minibus chase MacKay's taxi down and had run after them. But it had been a long run and the crowd had held her back until she pulled the Uzi out of her shopping bag and cleared a field of fire.

Ziba flipped the select lever to short burst and raked the *tsotsis* with aimed fire. The professional in MacKay noted the way she stood and handled the weapon. She was good. Then it was over. The eight *tsotsis* and their driver lay in heaps around the burning pyre that had been Charles. She jammed a fresh clip into the Uzi.

Fascinated, MacKay watched as she methodically checked each body. She was action in slow motion. One of the *tsotsis* was still alive and she spoke to him. He snarled an answer and she put a single bullet in his head. She walked over to MacKay and helped him to his feet. Again, with the same deliberate motion, she untwisted the wire that bound his wrists. "Come," was all she said. He followed her, rubbing life back into his hands.

MacKay sat on a kitchen chair stripped to the waist and let the woman clean the scrapes on his face and back. A light rain was falling, beating a tattoo on the tin roof of the two-room, cinder-block hovel Ziba's mother called home. The old woman's hard, gnarled hands were surprisingly gentle as she ran her fingers down his corded neck muscles, prodding and poking. She stood back and studied the muscular development of his chest and shoulders. She spoke three or four words in Zulu. The only word he understood was "Shaka," the name of the chieftain who had united the Zulus in the 1820s and sent his regiments across South Africa, ravaging the countryside and changing the geopolitical map.

Ziba answered from the other room and, again, he caught the name "Shaka." He didn't move, his eyes fixed on the doorway to the other room. Ziba stepped through, washed and changed into a multicolored gown and shawl. The warrior was gone and the queen was back. She stood in the small room, appraising him, before she sat down.

"Why the talk about Shaka?" MacKay asked.

"My mother was paying you a compliment," Ziba answered. "She said you look like Shaka." Legend had it that Shaka possessed a magnificent physique, much like the American's.

"You questioned one of them," MacKay said. "Who were they?"

Ziba gave him a long look he could not interpret. "They were ANC. They wanted Charles."

"Why?" MacKay believed he was owed an answer since he had almost been killed.

"Charles was Inkatha," she answered. Now MacKay understood. The Zulus' political party, Inkatha, and the ANC, African National Congress, were deadly enemies. "There was another thing," Ziba continued, "you couldn't see it, but the way they tied your wrists together is an old BOSS trick. Where did they learn that?"

And where, MacKay thought, did you learn about the BOSS's use of wire as an interrogation technique and how to use an Uzi? He suspected it was at the boarding school for girls that Charles had mentioned. "Are you Inkatha?"

She shook her head. "We only want to get on with our lives." He didn't believe her and she gave him that look again, the one he could not interpret. A heavy silence came down in the room.

Ziba's mother finished with MacKay and studied him for

a moment. She spoke a few words in Zulu and Ziba translated. "She says you should grow a beard. It will help." MacKay scratched his chin, agreeing with her. He had never grown one because of Army regulations and had never considered it out of habit. The older woman stood back and spoke in a low voice. It was a long speech and Ziba listened quietly, not interrupting. Ziba's mother was a woman who expected others to listen.

Finally, Ziba nodded in answer. "My mother says Slavin is not one of us and you are a righteous man. She says I should trust you."

MacKay was still in the ball game.

Wednesday, August 13
Fredericksburg, Virginia

The dream came in two parts, as it always did. Shoshana was running nude down the golden sand of the Grecian beach where they had spent their honeymoon. Her wet skin glistened in the sun and a warm feeling surged through Matt Pontowski. But before she reached him, the dream changed. Now he was coming awake, drifting in the half-world between sleep and full consciousness. Pontowski knew he was dreaming and wanted to prolong it. But another, much stronger, instinct willed him to wake up. Shoshana was now sitting on the edge of his bed. Her hand reached out and her fingers extended to touch his lips. But this time, she was dressed and her eyes were full of worry.

Pontowski came awake with a jerk. His subconscious had sent him a message that something was wrong. He checked his watch—four-thirty in the morning. He sat on the edge of the bed and listened, getting his bearings. He and his son were in the Piccards' home, house guests while he was TDY, temporary duty, to the Pentagon. Silently, he slipped into the hall and checked the room next to his where Little Matt was sleeping. The bed was empty.

For a split second, the old panic gripped Pontowski. It was the fear of any parents when their child is missing. Then, as quickly, the panic was gone. Pontowski padded down the stairs, wearing only a T-shirt and his pajama bottoms. It worried him that Little Matt was still walking in his sleep. He found his seven-year-old son standing by the front door and without a word, he picked up the sleeping child and carried him upstairs. The boy's eyes were closed when he laid him back in bed.

Little Matt stirred, waking up. "Mommy," he half-whispered, confirming Pontowski's guess that his son had been waiting for Shoshana by the door.

"It's okay, good buddy," Pontowski soothed. "I'm here."

"Will you ever go away like Mommy?" Little Matt asked.

Pontowski stroked his son's face. I can see so much of Shoshana in you, he thought. "I'll always be here when you need me," he said.

"Promise?" Little Matt said, turning over and going back to sleep.

"I promise," Pontowski said to the sleeping child. He waited until he was sure Little Matt was sleeping peacefully. A week from Friday, he calculated, pinpointing the next time his son would walk in his sleep. He walked back into his own room and lay down. But sleep wouldn't come. Frustrated, he rolled out of bed, picked up his briefcase, and went down to the kitchen. He could get in at least two hours of reading before he had to dress and head for the Pentagon and another round of briefings.

Pontowski had been appointed as the commander of the 442nd Fighter Wing, but before he could assume command, the Air Force had called him to the Pentagon with two other new wing commanders to be briefed on their commands. Nothing was left to chance and every conceivable subject ranging from wife-beating to environmental pollution was being covered. The two other new commanders were brigadier generals and carried on as if Pontowski, a full colonel in the Reserves, weren't there. It didn't bother him——he had seen it before. He was a reservist and they were regular Air Force and outranked him. But there was another price he paid for having a grandfather who had been a president of the United States. People either assumed a toadlike position to ingratiate themselves or ignored him.

He set the coffeepot to brewing and opened his bulging briefcase. The top document was titled *Sexual Harassment in the Armed Services and the Role of the Wing Commander*.

"Whatever happened to fly and fight," he mumbled to himself.

"Nothing," Cyrus Piccard said as he joined Pontowski at the table, "smells better than freshly brewed coffee in the morning."

"I hope I didn't wake you up," Pontowski said, rising to get the old man a mug.

"No, not at all," Piccard replied. He waited for Pontowski to sit down. "How are the briefings progressing?" he ventured, wanting to talk.

"Boring," Pontowski answered, "but necessary." He ran through the list of topics they were covering. "Running a fighter wing is more like running a business these days."

It was the opening Piccard had been waiting for. "But a commander has to be," he said, sipping his coffee, "shall we say, more attuned to political nuances than your average businessman."

My God, Pontowski thought, he works just like Granddad did when he wanted to tell me something. "True," he said, carrying the conversation in the same direction. "Both the brigadiers going through this dog-and-pony show with me are political animals of the first order."

Piccard studied Matt's profile, struck by the similarity to his famous grandparent. Matthew Zachary Pontowski, better known as Zack to his friends, was the first American of Polish descent to be elected president of the United States, and Piccard had served him faithfully as secretary of state. Like his grandfather, Matthew Zachary Pontowski III carried all the trademarks of his clan: tall and lean, bright blue eyes, a shock of barely controlled light-brown hair, and an aquiline nose. And like his father and grandfather, Matt was a fighter pilot. Eagles, Piccard thought, the Pontowskis are a clan of eagles.

The old man looked into his coffee cup and decided it was time to see if this eagle could fly in the hostile skies of Washington. "You have a political enemy." He waited for Pontowski's reaction, hoping it would be restrained and measured. He got silence.

"I've heard the rumors," Pontowski finally said. "Ann Nevers."

Piccard was impressed. "Indeed," he said. "The esteemed congresswoman from the state of California." Piccard and Nevers were sworn political enemies. Not only did they disagree on every major foreign policy issue, they personally detested each other.

Pontowski shook his head. "What did I do? Piss in her beer?"

"The Honorable Ann Nevers," Piccard replied, falling into the rolling tones of one of his long speeches, "almost lost an election because of your success in the China affair." He was complimenting the younger man on his role in destroying a vicious warlord and helping China avert a civil war. "In this town, it is a capital offense, punishable by death, to cause a senator or representative to lose an election."

"How could a successful foreign policy cause her to lose an election?" Pontowski asked.

"She was looking for an issue to ride to an easy reelection," Piccard replied, "and saw our involvement on the mainland of China as the perfect opportunity to raise the specter of another Vietnam." He paused for effect, ever the orator. "It was in very bad taste for you to have won." Piccard's eyes sparkled as he talked and gained momentum.

Age had not diminished his mental powers, only the physical strength to contend with the contrary and short-sighted individuals who did not see the world in the same light as he did. His political enemies hated him because events proved him right time and time again, and all had been glad to see him retire to his beloved home and rose garden in Fredericksburg. But he and his wife were alone, without children, and Piccard wanted to groom a successor to continue in his path, to follow the obligation for service that he felt so deeply. His choice was sitting across the table.

Like his father and grandfather before him, Pontowski had the required charm and intelligence, with the same vital ingredient of charisma. Jessica Piccard had a simple explanation: It was in the genes. But Matt Pontowski needed time. He always had. His early days as a fighter pilot had been marked by a wild, unruly streak, and only the leadership of Jack Locke, one of the finest fighter pilots to ever fly a high-performance jet, saved him from himself. With maturity came responsibility, and Pontowski discovered he had that rarest of qualities, the ability to lead. Men and women willingly followed Pontowski into combat.

Unfortunately, at least from a political standpoint, Pontowski had not married well. He had married a raven-haired, beautiful, native-born Israeli—a Sabra. But Shoshana had been a perfect wife for Pontowski. She had anchored him to reality and given him a son, Little Matt. Then tragedy had struck when she was killed by assassins hired to get at Pontowski through his family.

Instinctively, Piccard had recast the dice and liked what he saw. Matt Pontowski had the lineage, the charisma, the ability, and now the tragedy for election to high office. But Piccard also knew that Pontowski had to move beyond his sorrow, marry again, and make the commitment to enter public life.

Piccard finished pontificating on foreign policy and Pontowski freshened the old statesman's coffee. "There is a role in all this for you," Piccard concluded.

"I'm not sure," Pontowski said, pulling into himself and thinking of his promise to Little Matt.

Piccard nodded, his eyes closed. "Family obligations cut deep," he said. "Perhaps being true to yourself is the greatest gift you can give to your son."

"Flying and a challenge is what it's all about," he said, staring out the window at the breaking dawn. "God, I dearly love it when . . ." His words trailed off and for a brief moment he was back in the cockpit, caught up in the pure exhilaration and joy of flying. "I'll give it one more try. But if I have to choose between Little Matt and the Air Force . . . well . . . that decision is already made. Besides, I'm sick and tired of all this political horseshit."

Piccard probed a little deeper. "What can you tell me about your wing?"

"It's a Reserve outfit, the 442nd," Pontowski replied. "I assume command August eighteenth."

"What do you do?" Piccard asked.

"We're a fighter wing flying A-10s. The Warthog was designed for close air support and killing tanks, so that's what we train for. But there's an interesting sidebar in our marching orders. We're to prepare for 'intervention in support of international organizations.'"

21

Piccard filed the last away for future reference. "Where did you say your wing is located?" he asked.

"Whiteman Air Force Base," Pontowski answered. "Knob Noster, Missouri."

"Ah," Piccard said, "the heartland of America. A good place to hide." Until you are ready to prove who you really are, he mentally added.

Pontowski looked at the old man, not sure if he liked the idea of hiding.

Thursday, August 21
Alexandria, Virginia

"Bill, wake up," Mary Carroll urged. She glanced at the clock and frowned—the memories always came out of their carefully guarded niches when his defenses were the lowest. Her husband moaned and turned over, on the edge of sleep. "Bill, wake up." This time, her command penetrated his subconscious and his eyes came open.

"Don't turn on the light," he mumbled.

She reached over and touched his face; he was drenched in sweat. "Was it Rwanda?"

"No," he replied, half-asleep. "Somalia."

"Why can't you shake this?" she asked. "You never had trouble handling combat."

"The shrink says it's because I had been trained and was expecting it. Nothing prepared me for the misery of those relief camps."

"But you kept going back."

"Someone had to. No one else was willing to get out of their office and see it for themselves."

"It's not your job and there's nothing you can do to stop it. So go back to sleep."

"It's almost light. I think I'll go for a run." He turned on the light.

Within moments after the lights in the Carroll house came on, the house across the street was alive with activity. The Secret Service agent on duty woke the other two agents and told them William Gibbons Carroll was awake. "Is he going for a run?" Wayne Adams asked. The agent shrugged. He didn't know.

"I hope not," his junior partner, Chuck Stanford, groaned.

"Get your ass out of bed," Adams growled. "This is cushy duty."

"Nothing is cushy at five o'clock in the morning," Stanford grumbled. "Besides, this won't get us promoted." The phone rang. It was Carroll saying he was going for a run in about fifteen minutes. "Shit," Stanford mumbled, pulling on his sweats. Adams ignored Stanford and got ready for a run through the middle-class neighborhood where Carroll lived. The two agents were waiting for Carroll on the sidewalk when he came outside.

Carroll was a slender, dark-complected man of medium height. Dressed in warmups, he could have been a businessman, dentist, or high school coach in his mid-thirties running for exercise. Actually, he was forty-four years old and ran because it gave him a sense of inner calm and a chance to think.

Everything about Carroll was extraordinary; he was a brilliant linguist, foreign affairs analyst, and the most decorated nonflying officer in the history of the Air Force. He had seen action on the ground and earned his medals the hard way—by being shot at. Eventually, he had been promoted to the rank of major general, the youngest two-star since World War II.

The current president had recognized Carroll's ability to accurately interpret the intentions of foreign governments and had taken him into his inner circle as his advisor for national security affairs. Because he was close to the president, Carroll fell under the protective umbrella of the Secret Service, though his neighbors never realized why theirs was one of the safest suburbs of Washington, D.C.

The three men went through their warmup and stretching routine and then, without a word, started to run. From the very first, Carroll set a blistering pace, running five-minute miles. The two agents were hard-pressed to keep up with him but were determined to stay abreast. Their job demanded it. They had finished their third mile when Carroll's right leg gave out and he stumbled, falling to the ground. Within seconds, the backup van following them was on the scene and the national security advisor was bundled inside. The agent-in-charge wanted to take him to Bethesda Naval Hospital, but Carroll insisted they drop him off at his home.

Mary, Carroll's wife, saw the van pull up and was waiting for him at the front door. Adams and Stanford helped Carroll into the kitchen and hovered over him while Mary cleaned and bandaged his scrapes. "What happened?" she asked.

"I stumbled," Carroll replied. "That's all."

A worried look crossed her face. "Your right leg?"

"It's nothing," Carroll answered.

After the two agents had left, Mary leaned against the counter and folded her arms. "Bill, that's the third time. Something is wrong."

"Nothing's wrong," he groused. "I'm just tired."

Mary stared at him. They had married shortly after Carroll had rescued her from an Iranian prison. Theirs was a strong marriage, anchored in middle-class suburbia with two healthy children. "Bill, something is wrong," she repeated. "Go see a doctor."

CHAPTER 2

Friday, October 24
Whiteman Air Force Base, Missouri

Matt Pontowski glanced at the Army officers sitting beside him at the head table. The farewell banquet at the officers' club was dragging, and like him, they were bored. He scanned the other tables, looking for telltale signs of trouble among his pilots. He didn't need a wine-soaked roll being launched across the room with a loud shout of "Incoming!" He allowed himself an inner smile at how it would break the tedium of the speeches that marked the end of the joint exercise his wing had been conducting with the Army.

He shifted his attention to the speaker, the battalion commander, Lieutenant Colonel Gregory Hanson. ". . . excellent results," Hanson was saying, ". . . the 442nd has proven the A-10 is the aircraft the Army needs for forward air control."

The joint exercise *had* gone well, Pontowski told himself, thanks to one pilot. Dwight "Maggot" Stuart had performed a minor miracle in integrating the A-10 and the Army as a team, streamlining tactics and communications into a system that worked well under stress. Automatically, Pontowski looked for Maggot.

He was sitting quietly at a side table, bored as all the others. The pilot was average-looking; normal height, dark hair, and close-set blue eyes. But Pontowski knew what lurked below that bland exterior—a wild man who took it as a personal challenge to preserve the mystique of the fighter pilot. Maggot was a throwback to an earlier age when fighter pilots were expected to be all balls and no forehead.

Unfortunately, senior officers in the Air Force no longer tolerated Maggot's type of behavior, even though the same senior officers had led the pack in their younger days. Pontowski stifled a sigh—times had changed. Too bad, he thought, because Maggot was the consummate fighter pilot. To Pontowski's way of thinking, Maggot's attitude on the ground was related to his success as a fighter pilot in the air. The act of moving the gear handle to the up position on takeoff never changed a pussycat into a tiger.

"Colonel Pontowski," Lieutenant Colonel Hanson said, bringing Pontowski back to the moment. "My officers, to the man and woman"—Hanson was very correct—"would like to thank you and the men and women of your wing for making this exercise such a success." A few more words and he was finished.

Pontowski stood at the podium and closed the banquet as quickly as decorum allowed. The colors were retired and the group dismissed. Pontowski was immediately surrounded by senior officers, all wanting personally to congratulate him. He was used to it. Many officers on the make wanted to ingratiate themselves in the hope that knowing the grandson of a former president would advance their own careers.

Maggot slipped out of the main ballroom and headed for the casual bar, ready for a beer. "Jesus H. Christ," he moaned to no one in particular, "I thought that would never end." The bartender saw him coming and opened a bottle. "Roger that," Maggot said, taking a long pull at the bottle, draining it. He felt better. The bartender opened another beer.

Hanson was the most persistent of the group and wouldn't let Pontowski escape from the ballroom. Finally, he excused himself and sought refuge in the men's room. Hanson followed him, eager to keep the conversation going. "Colonel," Pontowski said, "let's go socialize with the working troops in the casual bar." That didn't work either, and he found himself trapped by the same group of senior officers. But this time a few wives had joined them. Now he had to be charming as well.

A voice rang out over the crowded bar, capturing everyone's attention. "Bartender, a round of tequila for my friends." It was Maggot, and Pontowski recognized the edge of intoxication in his voice. He willed the pilot to be cool as Maggot climbed onto the bar and stood with his head against the ceiling. "A toast," Maggot called.

"To titanium testicles?" a hopeful voice shouted. It was one of Pontowski's pilots, and Hanson's frown matched those on the faces of his women officers.

"Hey, Maaa-gut," another pilot called, egging him on. "How about a toast with social significance?"

"Social significance?" Maggot answered, weaving slightly on his perch. He thought for a moment while Pontowski gritted his teeth. "Right," Maggot said. He raised his glass. "Here's to gun smoke and pussy. One to live for, one to die for. But both smell great." A chorus of boos and yeahs greeted him. "You said 'social significance,'" Maggot protested, climbing off the bar.

A pretty Army captain jammed a finger into Maggot's chest, stopping him cold. "You ever heard of Tailhook, Captain?" Maggot shrugged and pushed past, saying nothing. Pontowski took a deep breath in relief. Maggot was showing restraint.

Hanson turned to Pontowski. The frown was back in place. "She makes a good point, Colonel." He squinted at Pontowski, calculating how to turn the incident to his advantage. "My people know better than to conduct themselves like your captain. Look, you discipline your pilot"— he gestured at Maggot—"and I'll calm my captain down. She won't cause trouble." A little smile crossed his mouth. He was all good-natured friendliness now that Pontowski owed him.

Pontowski wanted to tell Hanson that Maggot had seen more combat than all of his "people" put together and knew what it was like to engage tanks with the odds stacked in the enemy's favor. Instead, he settled for a curt "I'll take care of it." He said good night and left the bar. Now he knew why senior officers left parties early.

* * *

27

"Maggot stepped on it this time," Major Sara Leonard told Pontowski. She consulted her notes, organizing her thoughts. It was the Tuesday morning after the banquet and they were sitting in Pontowski's office in wing headquarters, going over the action items on his calendar.

"His toast in the officers' club Friday night?" Pontowski asked. Sara nodded in reply. "Can John handle this one?" Lieutenant Colonel John Leonard was the commander of Maggot's squadron, the 303rd, and Sara's husband.

She shook her head. "It's serious this time. Two of the women officers at the banquet filed a sexual harassment complaint with the IG yesterday."

"Damn," Pontowski muttered, "the Army strikes again." The battalion commander, Lieutenant Colonel Hanson, had not made good his promise and Pontowski now had the IG, the Inspector General, on his back. Why did it have to be Maggot? he thought. But he knew the answer. "Why can't he grow up?"

"It's the way fighter pilots are," Sara answered.

Pontowski picked up the phone, called the 303rd, and asked for Leonard. As Maggot's commanding officer, Leonard had to be in the loop. The squadron duty officer told him that Lieutenant Colonel Leonard had left the squadron and was on his way to wing headquarters. Pontowski hung up and looked at Sara. Like a good executive officer, she had anticipated her commander's needs and had called for Leonard before she raised the issue with Pontowski. "I'm going to miss you," Pontowski told her.

Sara had submitted her resignation as a full-time Air Force Reserve technician the day before. She was two months pregnant and glowing with good health. Pontowski had tried to convince her to stay on as a regular reservist, since he still needed an executive officer when the 442nd held its monthly unit training assembly. But common sense told her that becoming a mother again at forty-two years of age was a full-time job.

"We'll still be neighbors," she reminded him.

Pontowski smiled at her. "I'll settle for that." Having the Leonards as his next-door neighbors had solved many of his problems as a single parent. Martha Marshall, Sara's mother, was his live-in nanny, and Melissa, Sara's thirteen-year-old daughter from her first marriage, was a ready-made baby-sitter for Little Matt. In fact, Little Matt was becoming more and more of a fixture in the Leonard household. That worried Pontowski because he wanted to make a home for his son. A knock at the door announced John Leonard, Sara's husband of less than two years.

"Sara tells me the IG is after Maggot's ass," he said. Pontowski motioned him to a seat. Leonard was a tall, well-conditioned, thirty-eight-year-old fighter pilot serving fulltime as the 303rd Squadron commander.

Sara read from her notes, filling in the details of the sexual harassment complaint that had been filed against Maggot. She closed her notebook and folded her hands. "There is a loophole," she said.

The two men looked hopefully at her. Maggot was Huckleberry Finn reincarnated as a fighter pilot and totally out of step with the times. But he had two redeeming qualities: No one could fly and fight better than Maggot Stuart, and when things went wrong, he got aggressive. Combat had taught them a hard lesson; that when the shooting started, it was the Maggots who got the job done.

"Technically," Sara explained, "Maggot was not on duty during the banquet. He had not signed in on the computer and was not getting paid. We don't have jurisdiction, because he was in civilian status while at the banquet and not subject to the UCMJ." The UCMJ, or Uniform Code of Military Justice, applied to reservists only when they were on duty.

"That sounds pretty weak to me," Leonard said.

"It will work," Sara replied. "It would help if Maggot claims his freedom of speech is being violated. At the same time, we make a big fuss over his conduct and take corrective action by putting him into counseling. That might satisfy the legal beagles and let them sidestep a jurisdictional battle they will lose."

"Let's see if we can make it fly," Pontowski said, recalling his briefings at the Pentagon. "John, get Maggot into counseling with one of the shrinks. Sara, open the back door to the judge advocate and ask for legal advice on how we can proceed without violating Maggot's First Amendment rights. Meanwhile, I'll maintain I don't have jurisdiction but am taking every positive corrective action I can." He kicked back in his chair. "Doggies," he groaned, "you've got to be a lawyer to run a wing these days. Anything else, Sara?" She shook her head. "I am going to miss you." He grinned, dismissing the two officers.

Outside, Leonard stopped his wife. "Do you think it will work?"

"Probably," she answered. "The Boss wants it to work and the influence he carries definitely helps." She considered her next words. "Personally, I think it's time Maggot grew up."

"He's one of a kind," Leonard said. Sara gave him a look that said it was time for him to get real. "We're lucky we've got him," Leonard protested. "I wish I had a dozen more."

"You're rationalizing," Sara said.

"I know, I know." Leonard moaned. "Maggot saved the Boss's ass in China and now the Boss is returning the favor." It sounded corny and trite when he said it but both knew it was the truth.

"Pontowski won't cover for him again," Sara predicted. "You had better make that clear to Maggot. Very clear."

Saturday, November 8
Johannesburg, South Africa

The small shops across the street from the hotel's patio café were opening when MacKay sat down for breakfast. He watched as clerks swept piles of garbage left by sidewalk vendors from the day before into the street. Arguments broke out when the same vendors returned, spread their wares on the sidewalk, and blocked the entrances to the shops. It was all part of the early morning ritual that marked commercial life in Johannesburg.

MacKay sat next to the low brick wall that fenced the patio and took it all in. As usual, the waiter ignored customers until he saw a tip on the table, and even then, the service was minimal. MacKay decided to try a more direct method in the hope of getting a cup of hot coffee. He caught the waiter's attention and smiled. That encouraged the waiter to adhere to the old standards, and on this particular morning, the service and coffee were excellent.

He scanned the sports section of his newspaper. Buried in one corner was a brief article on American college football that mentioned the traditional Army-Navy game. The memories came flooding back and he could hear the corps chanting when he ran onto the field at Soldier Stadium. It was the best time of his life.

MacKay had thrived at "the Point" and graduated number two in his class. He was five years too late for Vietnam and went through a series of assignments as the U.S. Army rebuilt, recovering from the damage it had suffered during that long war. MacKay had a small part in the transformation as he pursued a career centering on the Infantry, Rangers, and Special Forces. His graduate work was with the SAS, the British Special Air Service regiment, and there he had put the final polish on his training. He became perhaps the Army's leading expert on counterterrorism and special operations. All debate ended after his rescue of three American hostages from the heavily guarded compound of a powerful drug warlord in Burma.

From there it had been a short step into covert intelligence operations, and he had been offered the command of the Army's Intelligence Support Agency, one of the Pentagon's "Boys in the Basement." The ISA went from one success to another under MacKay's leadership, and it soon developed a reputation as a "can-do" organization—a rarity in the field of covert operations.

MacKay's agents could get results, and it came as no surprise when the ISA was tasked for Operation Zenith, the penetration of Pelindaba. Pelindaba was the well-guarded nuclear plant and research facility outside Pretoria, South Africa, and MacKay suspected the ISA had gotten the job only after the CIA had failed. Since MacKay was the only black member of the ISA, it was even more logical that he go into the field with two of his white agents. Just another chance to get my black ass shot off, he told himself.

An African-American couple staying at the hotel entered and sat down at the table next to him. MacKay hid behind his newspaper and studied them: two prosperous, well-dressed, middle-aged blacks on tour. The man was as tall as MacKay and had the same growth of beard. He eavesdropped on their conversation and smothered a smile. Africa was not what they had expected and they were not coping with the experience. After being ignored for fifteen minutes and watching MacKay being served, the woman asked, "How do you get service here?" Her voice was soft and full of hurt.

MacKay felt sorry for them and broke his cover. "You need to get his attention. Tip him first."

"You mean bribe him first," the man grumbled.

MacKay caught the waiter's attention, looked at the couple, and nodded. The waiter received the message and hurried over to serve them. "Thank you," the woman said as Ziba Chembo entered the patio. All conversation stopped as she made her way to MacKay's table and sat down. The two Americans fell into a quiet conversation, speculating about MacKay and Ziba. "Can you blame him?" the woman whispered. "She's striking."

"Regal," the man said. "Very regal."

MacKay forced himself to relax. He had received a vague message two days before to meet Ziba at this hotel, and lacking any other clues, had checked in and waited. It wouldn't do to rush things now, not after waiting three months. But the African tempo of doing business was driving him crazy. His tradecraft demanded they keep their exposure to a minimum when passing information, and a leisurely breakfast did not meet his standards of operational security. But with Ziba sitting next to him, he was more than willing to roll with whatever she had in mind.

"I like your beard," she said after ordering a cup of coffee.

"It really helps with the pseudofolliculitis," he said, doubting that she had ever heard the term for the facial condition, in which whiskers turned inward into an adjacent follicle and created pockets of infection. But she certainly understood the condition.

"Have you ever been to a funeral rally?" she asked, sipping her coffee. He shook his head. "There's one today in Orlando stadium in Soweto," she said. "I think we should go."

The woman sitting next to them interrupted. "Please

forgive me, but I couldn't help but overhear what you said. We would love to go with you. Who's the funeral for?"

MacKay gave an inward groan. This was getting out of hand.

Ziba's face came alive. "It's for the six children who were murdered last week. They were on their way to school. Besides mourning for them, the funeral is a demonstration for peace and solidarity."

"Oh, we read about that," the woman said. "That was terrible. The papers said that whites had hired gangsters from Soweto to do it."

"Latisha, please," the man interrupted, his voice full and rich. "You're imposing on these people." He turned to MacKay and introduced himself. "I'm Lionel Stevens and this is my wife, Latisha. Please forgive the intrusion, but she wants to experience everything while we're here. Will it be safe?"

It was time to discourage them. "You never know," MacKay answered. "There could be serious trouble. Actually, I'm surprised you're touring South Africa at all, what with all the trouble. I thought the State Department was issuing warnings and discouraging tourism."

"They are," Stevens explained. "But all our friends have made the tour and this was our only chance. We wanted to experience it while we still could and came in through Zambia. What brings you here?"

"Winding up an import-export business," MacKay answered, easily falling into his cover story. "I'm getting out of here as soon as I can. You might want to do the same."

"Perhaps you're right," Stevens said, standing. The couple said good-bye and left.

"I still think we should go," Ziba insisted.

Torn by conflicting urges, MacKay gave a slight groan. He wanted a quick turnover of information, but at the same time, the lower region of his abdomen was sending him a strong signal to linger. A vision of Ziba in his bed flitted in front of him. He had not been with a woman for a long time.

Ziba made the decision. "We need to leave now." She stood and walked out. He followed her, mentally promising that his gonads would not do his thinking.

Across the street, a sidewalk vendor watched Ziba use

taxi talk, the system of hand signals that told minibus drivers where they wanted to go, to flag down a taxi. After the taxi had pulled away from the hotel, the vendor found a phone and dialed a number. A man with an Afrikaner accent answered and listened as the vendor said they were headed for the funeral at the soccer stadium in Soweto.

The soccer stadium was only half-full when they arrived and only one TV crew was covering the event. They blended in with the people and found seats at one end of the crowd, near an exit. "We used to fill the stadium to overflowing," Ziba said. "Seventy or eighty thousand people would come."

"How many can the stadium hold?" MacKay asked.

"Sixty thousand," she answered. "You could feel the foundation sway under our weight, with the strength of our spirit." Her face glowed as she recalled the time.

A huge green, black, and gold banner was unfurled across the makeshift stage as six white coffins were carried out and set in a row in front of the stage. Then the singing began, thousands of voices blending into one, carrying a harmony that touched a chord deep in MacKay's soul. He wanted to join in but didn't know how. Ziba started to sing, her voice clear and strong. She carried an arching melody high above the others and her voice soared over the crowd.

Slowly, the stadium filled as the scheduled time for the funeral passed. MacKay sensed the mood of the crowd, warm, friendly, and spontaneous. This was not the harsh, in-your-face attitude that marked American society, but a warm communal spirit. For the first time in years, MacKay was at peace with himself.

A group of young men, maybe two hundred strong, jogged around the field in a group, chanting. It reminded MacKay of his first days at West Point as a Beast when he marched to the calls of a cadet sergeant and his voice joined with his squad, answering back in unison. But this was a *toi-toi* dance and it carried a message of anger and trouble. In the front rank, a leader carried a large wooden cutout of a submachine gun, a symbol of the group's power. Three rows back, MacKay spotted the real thing—an AK-47.

Then MacKay saw Lionel and Latisha Stevens, the couple from the hotel. They walked by in front, looking for seats.

Latisha had changed into a colorful gold and black gown with a matching head scarf. It was a chic African-American creation from New York that highlighted her as a tourist. "What the hell," he mumbled. "They should have known better."

The relatives of the slain children took their places beside the coffins and the preaching began. MacKay was struck by how small the coffins were and felt the anguish of the crowd. The preaching turned into an angry speech, and even though he could not understand the words, MacKay responded to the anger and tension of the crowd. Then a lone voice from deep in the stadium started to sing and the crowd joined in. It was a lullaby and the tension was broken.

The coffins were placed on the back of a truck and a mournful procession formed to make its way out of the stadium to the cemetery. But a *toi-toi* dance started at the head of the procession and a new chant echoed over the crowd, more strident and loud. MacKay's situational awareness kicked in and he sensed danger in the renewed tension sweeping the crowd. Rather than join the mourners, he angled Ziba toward an exit and pulled her into the shadows. Below him, he saw Lionel and Latisha Stevens join the back of the procession. "The idiots," he grumbled. For a moment, he considered rushing into the crowd and cutting them out, herding them to safety.

Instead, he hurried Ziba outside and toward the taxi rank. He held up his forefinger, taxi talk for Johannesburg. But none of the minibuses moved, not willing to brave the crowd filling the street. Behind him, he heard shouting. Then the familiar bark of an AK-47 split the crowd and people surged past, running for cover. MacKay pulled Ziba into a minibus and snapped a command. "Johannesburg. Go!"

The driver shot MacKay a dirty look and motioned them out of his taxi—he didn't want to move and risk challenging the crowd's anger. But a second look at MacKay convinced him that it wasn't worth his life to argue. He gunned the engine and pulled out, pushing through the mass of people. Another taxi cut in front, forcing the driver to slam on the brakes. For a moment, the street was clear of people, as if a curtain had parted to reveal a grim, motionless scene. Latisha was lying in the street, a crumpled mass of gold and black cloth and blood. Lionel was on his knees beside her, bent over, looking down with lifeless eyes. A bullet had shattered the back of his head.

In the background, a tall young man was waving an AK-47 and yelling at his comrades in triumph. Then a rush of people ran by, dropping the curtain on the scene as the minibus shot ahead, racing for safety. "The poor bastards," MacKay said, his face frozen.

"I'm sorry for your American friends . . ."

"The Stevenses weren't my friends," MacKay interrupted.

"The Stevenses were the wrong people," Ziba continued in a low voice so the driver could not hear.

MacKay's mind raced with implications. If Ziba was right, the Stevenses had been mistakenly gunned down because Lionel fit his general description—a tall and bearded American. Why didn't they do it at the café in Johannesburg? Too obvious, he reasoned. Or maybe the gunman was not in position. Besides, I'd be more isolated in Soweto, without a backup. So they haven't got a good make on me, he thought. But who were they? He scratched at his beard, determined to shave it off at the first opportunity. He hated the thought, knowing what it would do to his skin. But he needed to disappear and that would help. "We need to part company," he said.

Ziba reached into her bag and pulled out a thick manila envelope. "The Afrikaners call it Prime," she said, handing the envelope to him. He undid the clasp and scanned the papers and photos inside. Every instinct he possessed shouted that Ziba had delivered up the secrets of Pelindaba. She was much more than a simple maid.

"Why didn't you give this to whoever replaced Charles?" he asked.

"No one has contacted me," she answered.

Another thought came to him. "Why did we go to the funeral?"

Ziba's eyes captured his, intense and full of pain. "So you could meet my people," she said. The pain was also in her voice. All the good and the warmth in the stadium, of individuals joining together and finding strength and their humanity, had been brutally canceled by the violence of the streets.

MacKay wanted to hold her and tell her he understood. But he couldn't find the words. Ziba told the driver to stop, got out, and walked away, not looking back.

Wednesday, November 12
The White House, Washington, D.C.

Elizabeth Gordon gave her hair one last check in the mirror. "Damn, Sam," she moaned. "Why me?" She had discovered another gray hair. She plucked out the offending hair, dropped the mirror in her makeup bag, clipped the remote microphone to her jacket, and turned, ready at last. "How do I look, Sam?"

"Great," Samantha Darnell, Elizabeth Gordon's long-time videographer, answered. She white-balanced the Betacam for outdoor light and maneuvered for an opening shot of Gordon standing in the President's Park with the Oval Office and the west wing of the White House in the background. It was a clear November day and the gentle breeze played with her hair, creating a soft and attractive effect. "The camera never lies," she told Gordon.

It was true. Liz Gordon still had a great body and unlined complexion. But her forty years were starting to show, and soon the network would find another pretty face equally articulate, and fifteen years younger, to replace her. Then she would start the slow slide out the back door, first losing her White House assignment and then being assigned to cover events the higher-powered personalities considered beneath their status. The unfairness of it all ate at Sam, for Elizabeth Gordon was an excellent reporter.

"Okay," Sam said, satisfied with the angle and light, "go for sound." Gordon spoke a few words. "Sound is good. Go."

Gordon fell into her reporter persona. "Today at the White House," she began, "the president broke his hectic schedule to confer with his unofficial advisor, the dean of American statesmen, Cyrus Piccard."

Sam had pressed Gordon to report Piccard's visit to the White House because he was like an ill omen, always appearing on the scene in advance of trouble. It amazed the photographer that the older, more experienced reporters who covered the White House had not made the same connection. Besides, Piccard fit the image of a statesman—tall, dignified, well dressed in an immaculate, dark, pin-striped suit, and always carrying his trademark ebony cane.

"The exact topic of discussion," Gordon continued, "was not mentioned, but a well-placed source in the White House revealed the president was seeking Piccard's advice on appropriate responses to the escalating violence, starvation, and mass migrations in the Third World." She rattled off the ideas Sam had given her, sounding like a knowledgeable observer of international affairs. She stopped in midsentence.

"What's the problem?" Sam asked. "It sounded good."

"It won't make the six o'clock news," Gordon said. "It's a nothing, too intellectual for even a slow news day. I'm dying here." Sam Darnell nodded in agreement. They needed to find a hot topic that would stir the pot or Elizabeth Gordon was out.

Cyrus Piccard stood at the window of Bill Carroll's office, overlooking President's Park. He watched in silence as Gordon and Darnell finished shooting. "I remember her as a charming young girl on her first assignment," Piccard said. "So inexperienced."

"Who's that?" Carroll asked.

"Elizabeth Gordon," Piccard answered.

"She's experienced now," Carroll said. "Liz slept her way to fame. But she got her act together and turned into a damn good reporter. Unfortunately, reputations die hard, and Liz has to live with hers. Being teamed up with Sam Darnell, her photographer, has helped. Sam's got a lot going for her."

"Ah, I see," Piccard said, studying the young woman carrying the camera beside Gordon. He gauged Samantha Darnell to be at least five feet eight inches tall. Her light-brown hair was cut short and she was wearing loose-fitting jeans, a flannel shirt, and a down vest. She walked with an easy stride and made Piccard think of a well-conditioned athlete. "She is very attractive," he allowed, "in a wholesome way."

Carroll joined him at the window and glanced at the women. They fell silent, thinking of other things and the reason for Piccard's visit to the White House. "I understand the president's concern," Piccard said, "about the violence and massive population migrations that are plaguing Mexico and Central America." He spread his hands in a gesture of supplication. "But I simply cannot understand his concern over South Africa."

"South Africa," Carroll replied, "shows every sign of destabilizing. The Pretoria government is talking to the UN Observer Mission about sending in a peacekeeping team in the near future . . . probably around Christmas."

"It's the route of Africa," Piccard said, falling into the sonorous tones of a statesman discoursing on world events. "We have seen it all before. The black liberation movement has replaced the white government . . . the new government's feet of clay are revealed . . . it is hopelessly corrupt and inefficient . . . the economy is looted . . . there is no power sharing . . . tribal warfare breaks out . . . the UN is called in."

Piccard sat down. "It is a quagmire we have avoided in the past and there is no reason for us to become involved. We have *no* national interests there."

"We may have some very important interests there," Carroll told him.

Piccard's bushy eyebrows arched in surprise. "Have they discovered large oil deposits in the Kalahari?" He was a realist who understood the importance of oil to the world economy. It was the only reason he could think of for the United States to become involved in any part of Africa.

"No," Carroll answered. "The whites, specifically the Afrikaners, may have discovered cold nuclear fusion. They call it Prime." He handed Piccard a folder labeled *Zenith Prime.* The old gentleman propped his cane beside his chair and leafed through the pages. He snorted twice.

"Ridiculous," Piccard said, closing the folder. "The Afrikaners are little more than a small white tribe, and even with the help of Israeli scientists, have not made the scientific breakthrough of the millennium." He snorted again. "There is no cheap, unlimited, nonpolluting source of nuclear energy. There is no salvation in a test tube from the tyranny of petroleum. Cold nuclear fusion simply does not exist. That was proven in 1989—those two scientists at the University of Utah, if I remember correctly. What a fiasco that was."

"I'd like to agree with you," Carroll said. "But there is too much evidence . . ."

"Which can all be manufactured for our benefit," Piccard interrupted. He held up a hand. "Please don't go into the technical details. It's all beyond me. The question is, how reliable are your sources?"

Carroll pulled a set of photos out of another folder. "We have the normal satellite and reconnaissance photos." He handed the photos to Piccard. "Excellent coverage. Our most recent information indicates that three accidental explosions have occurred, each one smaller than the preceding. All three were thermonuclear."

"Which could indicate the Afrikaners are developing a nuclear arsenal," Piccard replied.

Carroll shook his head. "We have an agent inside Prime."

"A CIA agent?" Piccard asked, his words heavy with doubt. He had been burned many times by the CIA when he was secretary of state and carried a healthy skepticism about the agency's ability to engage in old-fashioned spying.

"Not this time," Carroll answered. "The Intelligence Support Agency made the penetration." He could tell Piccard was impressed as he handed him another photo. "This is a picture of the cold fusion cell that is producing heat." In the center of the photo was a pile of lead bricks about six feet square. A series of wires and pipes stuck out of the pile at odd angles.

"Not very tidy," Piccard observed.

"Good science doesn't have to be neat," Carroll replied. "It only has to work. Our source also provided us with some numbers, and according to our physicists, it all tracks."

"Numbers," Piccard humphed, "can be created." He lowered his head, thinking. "If what you say is true, other intelligence services will be interested in Prime."

Carroll nodded. "We have identified two and are seeing footprints of a third."

"And the two are?" Piccard asked.

"OPEC and the Japanese," Carroll answered.

Piccard's head came erect at the mention of the Japanese. "This is a new departure for the Japanese."

"As to the third group," Carroll continued, "we have nothing concrete but suspect a European connection." Carroll had returned to the window, slowly squeezing, then relaxing his right fist.

Piccard studied the national security advisor for a moment and decided he did not look well. "Other than the ISA, what resources have we committed?"

"The CIA has an operation going, fairly large, official cover, working out of Cape Town."

"We do not need," the old man growled, "the CIA mounting a large-scale covert operation." The steel was back in his voice. "Let them concentrate on intelligence gathering. If we must become involved, we need a legitimate presence."

"Such as?" Carroll asked.

"I personally favor the traditional approach of more humanitarian aid and—" Piccard paused "—being part of the United Nations peacekeeping team if it is activated."

"Impossible," Carroll replied. "Congress has shut that door with the National Security Revitalization Act."

"My dear boy," Piccard said, "Congress is too astute to tie the hands of our commander in chief if our national interests are truly at stake."

"The act is quite specific," Carroll said. "It forbids us to participate in a UN command without the approval of Congress, which, given the current political climate, will never happen."

"There is a loophole for the president to use if he deems it necessary," Piccard told him. "Congress did not repeal the Emergency War Powers Act of 1965, which allows the president to commit our forces for up to ninety days without consulting Congress *if* Congress is not in session."

"Are you suggesting that . . ."

"You do nothing until Congress goes home for Christmas," Piccard said. "Should my suspicions prove correct that Prime is a fabrication by the Afrikaners to gain international support for their cause, you have the option of gracefully withdrawing at the end of ninety days and blaming Congress. But if the Afrikaners have discovered cold fusion, it allows us the presence to gain access to the process and prevent it from being stolen." He looked up at Carroll. "It will take military force, you know."

Carroll had the advice he was seeking. It was not what he wanted, but he knew it would work. Piccard was an old gentleman of the Virginia Tidewater tradition, refined and gracious, a living anachronism of a bygone age. But underneath the courtly exterior, Piccard was a practitioner of power politics—brutal and ruthless if his country's national interests were at stake. Piccard rose from the couch. "I have taken more than enough of your time. I know you have a full schedule."

Carroll escorted him into the outer office where a waiting military aide would escort him to his limousine. "May I suggest," Piccard said, "that you appoint Matt as the commander of our contingent."

"I'll be damned." Carroll grinned. "You're maneuvering Matt right into the thick of things."

"Of course," Piccard allowed, taking his leave.

Carroll walked back into his office. "Midge," he said to his secretary, "change Captain Smithson's appointment to four this afternoon. I'm going for a run."

"This is the second time you've slipped Smithson," she reminded him. "He has the results of the tests they've been running and wants to see you."

"I can't stand the pompous bastard," Carroll replied.

"He's the best doctor at Bethesda," Midge said to Carroll's back as he pushed through the door into his office. "You shouldn't waste his time." She sighed and made the necessary phone calls. Whatever was wrong with the national security advisor had to be serious if Smithson was making the equivalent of a house call.

Within minutes, the two Secret Service agents who ran with Carroll were waiting outside the White House, doing light warmups. "He's lost the edge," the taller of the two, Wayne Adams, said.

"Yeah," Chuck Stanford replied. "Thank God. He used to really do some killers. For a while, I thought we had the heart attack detail."

"Something's wrong," Adams said. "You see how he favors his right leg since he fell?"

Stanford nodded. He saw Carroll come out of the west wing of the White House and studied his moves. "I hope he's okay. I like the man."

"You two ready to do this?" Carroll asked as he joined them. The two agents nodded and fell in beside him, easily matching his pace. They exchanged glances, for the burning pace that Carroll had once set was gone. A mile later, the national security advisor to the president of the United States collapsed on the Mall.

Within seconds, Wayne Adams had made a radio call and the security net protecting the White House was fully mobilized, reaching out to help the national security advisor. Exactly sixteen minutes later, the helicopter carrying Carroll touched down on the helipad at Bethesda Naval Hospital. Doctor Smithson was waiting and Carroll was rushed into a fully staffed and activated emergency room.

Ten minutes later, Elizabeth Gordon and Sam Darnell were at the hospital, the first of the Washington press corps to react to the breaking story. Gordon ended her report with the line Sam had given her. She turned away from the camera and looked at the entrance to the hospital, giving the lens a beautiful profile shot of her face. "As so often in the past, we can only wait, hoping the miracle of modern medicine can save a man in the prime of his life. A man who is a husband, a father of two young children, and the chief advisor to the president of the United States. And waiting with us is the president."

"It's a good one," Sam said. Gordon smiled. They had the scoop she needed.

Carroll was standing, fully dressed, when Smithson walked into his hospital suite. "You should be in bed, Mr. Carroll," the doctor said, nodding to Carroll's wife, Mary.

"I've got work to do," Carroll said.

Smithson gave in to the inevitability of it all. He had treated Carroll long enough to experience the iron will that characterized the man and instinctively knew what he had to say. It was one of the traits that made him a good doctor. "Mrs. Carroll, may I speak to your husband alone?" The tone in his voice had changed and he was the professional doing what had to be done. Mary turned and left the room. "Please sit down, Mr. Carroll. This won't take long."

"I feel much better," Carroll said, sitting down.

"I don't doubt it," Smithson said. He cut to the heart of the matter, the only way Carroll would want it. "That's the way the early stage of amyotrophic lateral sclerosis works."

Carroll stared at him. "How sure are you?"

"I can't be one hundred percent certain at this point. We ran a CAT scan and an EMG to measure your muscle electrical activity. The results were not encouraging. We need to X-ray your spinal cord and monitor your progress."

"But you're certain enough to tell me now," Carroll said. Smithson nodded. Carroll stood and walked to the door. "I appreciate your frankness," he said, meaning it. He opened the door and stepped into the hall. Smithson saw Carroll touch his wife's cheek.

Smithson looked at his hands. He was 99 percent certain that William Gibbons Carroll had ALS, better known as Lou Gehrig's disease. Although there were a few outstanding exceptions, the average life span after diagnosis was thirty-seven months.

He wondered if he could take a death sentence so well.

CHAPTER
3

Friday, November 14
Owambo, Northern Namibia

The man had been in the bush for three days and he was tired of the hunt. But out of stubborn pride he was going to end it the way he had chosen and not take an easier path. His skin itched and he rubbed at the dirt, exposing his fair skin. He dismissed any thoughts of a hot shower and concentrated on the kraal he had staked out.

It was larger than a normal Ovambo kraal and its wall of crooked tree trunks driven into the ground was in good condition. Inside, he could see the roofs of six thatch and wattle huts. Definitely a chief's kraal, he decided. He came alert when he saw the chief, a dignified and frail old man, emerge through the fence.

The man moved out of his hide and into a shooting position. Slowly, he pulled the Lee-Enfield .303 sniper rifle out of its case and laid the crosshairs of the telescopic sight on the old man's chest. He liked the old British weapon for its balance and smooth action. He chambered a round and waited.

He saw the dust first. Perhaps today, the man thought. A truck came into view, stopped in front of the kraal, and the driver got out. The man shifted the crosshairs to the newcomer. An Ovambo, he decided; high cheekbones, slender build, high forehead, hooked nose with a well-defined bridge. Then he saw the passenger. A European in a sleeveless T-shirt, dirty shorts, and worn hiking boots. It was the priest.

The chief and the priest greeted each other and walked to the back of the truck. The eager villagers crowded around to help uncrate a new electrical generator and a gas-powered water pump. Now the man understood why he was here. That hadn't been explained to him, just the target. He removed the balloon that kept the barrel free of dust and carefully sighted. No wind, he thought, range eight hundred meters. He relaxed and picked up the beat of his heart. Slowly, he squeezed the trigger and between heartbeats, the rifle fired.

The priest's head exploded.

Tuesday, November 18
Iron Gate, near Bloemfontein

The battered and dirty *bakkie* that drove up to the main gate of the base looked like any other pickup truck that had seen hard use on the veld. The gate was a massive, ornate structure of granite and iron at the northern, open end of a valley formed by two steep ridges on the east and west. The valley ran for six miles, and the ridgelines were dotted with surface-to-air missile sites and antiaircraft artillery batteries. The southern end of the valley was blocked by a huge rock outcropping that rose five hundred feet above the valley floor and was capped with a radome. The top of the rock was named Eagle's Nest after Hitler's aerie high above Berchtesgaden, Germany. The base itself was nestled in the valley between the gate and the Eagle's Nest.

The corporal on guard duty waved the truck to a stop and motioned to an inspection stall. Without being asked, the man handed over his ID card and a Lee-Enfield .303 sniper rifle to the two young privates inspecting the pickup. "A nice weapon," the private said, handing him a receipt for the rifle. "I've never seen one before." He ran the man's ID card through a magnetic reader and frowned. "Sir," the private said, returning his ID, "you do not have an exit permit."

"That's not a problem," the driver assured him.

"Please follow the signs to the security compound," the private said. "Welcome to Iron Gate."

The driver drove south, past well-tended houses and rows of neat cottages and manicured lawns. Finally, he reached the main base and stopped in front of the security compound behind the headquarters building. A guard held his door open and escorted him into the guard shack. Inside, he was strip-searched and his anal cavity was examined by a female nurse who seemed to linger longer than necessary over her job.

An adjudant offisier klas 1, a warrant officer, was waiting for the man as he came out of the examination room. The warrant officer was short, dumpy, and had a bull neck. His close-set eyes seldom blinked and missed little.

"Good morning, Chief," the man said. "I'm here to see the Generaal."

Adjudant Offisier Marius Kreiner carefully evaluated the newcomer—a typical Afrikaner with a fair complexion, blue eyes, and a heavy but well-conditioned physique. "Is he expecting you?" Kreiner asked.

"No, but tell him his brother is here."

Kreiner blinked twice and escorted him into the headquarters building. He led the way down a hall and into a waiting room. "The Generaal will be here shortly." He stood silently by the door, never taking his eyes off the man who roamed the room, studying the maps on the wall. It was a professional interest and he lingered over the maps of the base, calculating what it would take to penetrate the perimeter defenses. "Don't even think about it, Erik," a familiar voice said. Erik turned to see his brother, Hans, standing in the doorway. Kreiner looked from one to the other. He had heard the rumors the general had a twin and, up close, he could see the family resemblance of fraternal twins.

"I got this far," Erik said. Neither smiled, and they only looked at each other.

"How?" Hans asked. Erik handed him his identification card. "Is this a fake?" Erik nodded. "It is very good," Hans told him. "Kreiner, take this and find out how my brother managed to get past your security guards with a false ID."

Kreiner took the card and left. Outside, he cursed fluently but silently to himself. One Beckmann was bad enough, but two?

Hans Beckmann slapped his brother on the shoulder and gently pushed his head sideways. It was an old gesture from their youth and the only physical expression of affection that ever passed between them. "What was the job this time?" Hans asked.

"A priest."

"Genuine?"

"Genuine," Erik answered. "He was causing trouble with the Ovambos in northern Namibia."

"Who made the contract?" Hans asked as he poured his brother a beer.

Erik snorted in contempt. "SWAPO . . . who else?" SWAPO, South West Africa People's Organization, had wrested control of Namibia from South Africa in the late 1980s. But like so many revolutionary governments, SWAPO had found it much more difficult to rule than to win a revolution.

"Was the priest organizing a political movement?"

Erik took a long pull at the beer as his brother stretched out in an easy chair. "Worse. He was helping the Ovambos with basic sanitation, irrigation pumps, electricity, that type of thing. Soon they would be questioning why they needed a government that does nothing but collect taxes."

Hans put his hands together and made a steeple with his forefingers. He was reaching a decision. "The kaffirs know how to treat their own people." He smiled and bounced to his feet, suddenly animated. "Once conditions become too bad, they will ask us to save them from themselves. They will gladly give up their precious freedom for peace and security."

Erik shook his head. He knew how his brother worked. "The world has changed. The United Nations with its kaffir-loving ideas will stop you."

"We don't make the situation bad," Hans said. "We let the kaffirs make it bad."

"And," Erik added, "you accelerate the process with gifts

48

of money and guns from their friends. Sorry, not for me. I miss Europe and the IRA is looking for help." Erik liked his brother but he never stayed long. There was always the matter of Hans's voices.

Hans became very serious. "Erik, I am worried. The Europeans know who you are. It would be dangerous for you to leave the country now."

"It's dangerous no matter where I go."

"You can help here. OPEC is backing the Azanians and is hiring mercenaries to train their army."

"My German passport is still good," Erik told him. The two brothers smiled, understanding each other perfectly. Erik would pose as a German mercenary and help the Azanian People's Organization ferment another black revolution in South Africa.

The intercom buzzed. It was Kreiner calling in his report. "We know Meneer Beckmann's identification card is a forgery," Kreiner said, "but we cannot detect it. Even the hologram and magnetic strip are encoded properly." They could hear a tremor in Kreiner's voice.

Hans Beckmann lay back in his chair feeling expansive. He was having a good day. "Solve the problem, Chief. And under the circumstances, no discipline is called for." He broke the connection. "Kreiner is a lifer, a good adjutant offisier but very unimaginative. By the way, where did you get your ID card?"

"Cape Town," Erik answered.

Adjudant Offisier Klas 1 Marius Kreiner shifted his weight from one foot to the other as he waited for Beckmann to acknowledge him. Come on you bastard, he told himself, you know I'm here. Frustrated, he cleared his throat.

"Ah, Kreiner," Beckmann said, looking up from his desk. "What is it?"

"We found a spy—"

"Where?" Beckmann interrupted. The cold fury in his voice caused Kreiner to gulp before he could continue.

"In computer operations . . . a man . . . he came in with the contract workers. He had one of those false IDs like Meneer Beckmann."

Beckmann came to his feet and grabbed his beret. "How long was he inside before he was discovered?"

"Eighteen days," Kreiner answered.

"Where is he?"

"In Interrogation," Kreiner replied as he hurried to match Beckmann's pace. "Because of Meneer Beckmann's false identification card, we are reencoding the magnetic strip on every ID card as a precaution. He turned up when we fed the data on his strip into the computer for validation."

Beckmann was impressed. "Very good, Kreiner."

Kreiner beamed and almost pranced as they descended the steps into the basement of the security compound. He held the door open and they entered what looked like an overlarge hospital examination room. Kreiner handed Beckmann a file and nodded at the young man sitting on the edge of an examination table. "His name is Masahisa Tanaka, a Japanese civilian."

Beckmann studied the man for a moment. He was thin and muscular and sitting absolutely still, held by an inner will and not the handcuffs and shackles binding his wrists and ankles. "Good morning, Mr. Tanaka," Beckmann said. Tanaka did not respond and looked straight ahead. "Please don't be difficult," he continued. "May I ask why you are here?" Still no response. "Perhaps I asked the wrong question. What were you looking for?" The man continued to stare at the wall.

"Strip him," Beckmann said. He read Tanaka's file while a guard cut his clothes away. "You are very young and . . . well, let's not discuss that. I do hope you will cooperate." The man's feet flashed straight out and he drove his toes into the abdomen of the sergeant who had cut off his clothes. The guard curled up in pain and couldn't move.

A smile spread across Beckmann's face but his eyes were icy cold. "I want him talking. Twenty-four hours. Kreiner, we can expect more penetration attempts. Because of our limited resources and the political situation, we are constrained in what we can do. So you must tighten up our internal security. Perhaps some foreign consultants?"

Kreiner flinched at the suggestion. Beckmann gave him

an encouraging look and dropped the file on the desk as he left. He made a mental note to increase the pressure on his counterintelligence agents. They had to ferret out the spies and foreign operatives before they reached Bloemfontein and penetrated Iron Gate. An inner voice told him to speak to Erik about the ID cards.

Adjudant Offisier Kreiner was sweating. It was a natural reaction born out of fear and a deep concern for his own longevity. But he was a soldier, and his stubborn pride demanded that he face the danger in front of him. Hans Beckmann took a quarter turn in the chair behind his desk and looked out the window. He intertwined his fingers and made a steeple. Slowly, he tapped the tips of his forefingers together. "So you have learned nothing."

"I need more time," Kreiner answered. The back of his shirt was dark, stained with perspiration.

"How interesting," Beckmann replied. He turned back to face Kreiner and drilled him with a cold and dispassionate stare. "You are used to dealing with kaffirs, Kreiner. These people, the Japanese, have no sense of inferiority to play on, to exploit. In fact, they believe they are superior."

Kreiner snorted. It was part of the old Afrikaner creed that other races were ordained by God to be inferior, and Kreiner held to that belief like a drowning man clinging to a rotten tree branch in a swirling current. Only the firm knowledge that he was superior to those he interrogated saved him from drowning in the same humiliation he so willingly heaped on others. "He will talk," Kreiner announced.

"Today?" Beckmann asked. He enjoyed watching Kreiner squirm. "Come, demonstrate your superiority to me." The two men walked out of the headquarters building and entered the security compound. Beckmann's leather heels echoed down the hall, a harbinger of his presence.

The interrogation room smelled of antiseptic when they entered and the young man was sitting exactly where Beckmann had last seen him. But now small burns on his nipples and genitals marked where he had been wired for "the telephone" and subjected to repeated shocks. He was not handcuffed or shackled because his ankles and fingers had been broken.

"What has he said?" Beckmann demanded.

"Nothing," came the answer.

"Not even under drugs?"

"We gave him the full course," Kreiner said. "Any more and we will fry his brain. He only babbled incoherently in Japanese. But I did learn his real name—Hiroshi Saito. He has been conditioned to resist interrogation."

A voice whispered to Beckmann. "No!" he roared, turning on Kreiner. "He has not been conditioned. He resists because he believes he is superior!" He whirled to face the young man. The rage drained from his face and his voice returned to normal. "And for that, you are going to die. Today."

Saito's head turned slowly toward Beckmann and he blinked, focusing on Beckmann's face. Saito's lips moved but nothing came out. They moved again and a word in Afrikaans formed. *"Asseblief."* Please.

Beckmann grabbed a chair and sat down. He crossed his legs and leaned back. "The submarine, Kreiner." He cocked his head and took a professional interest in the way Kreiner did it. A large stainless-steel tub was filled with water and pushed to the center of the room while the man's hands were handcuffed behind his back. A nylon rope was passed through a pulley in the ceiling and one end tied to his ankles. On Kreiner's command a guard pulled on the rope and swung Saito to the ceiling, head down over the tub.

Beckmann smiled. "Proceed."

Kreiner grabbed the rope and lowered the man's head into the water, holding him under as he jerked and fought for air. Then Kreiner pulled him up as he coughed and gasped. But it was not a reprieve. Kreiner repeated the procedure again and again, dragging it out for almost an hour. He was disappointed when the man finally drowned and he had learned nothing about the Japanese operation. But he could intensify precautions in Johannesburg.

"Very good, Kreiner," Beckmann said as he stood up.

"What shall we do with the body?" Kreiner said, pleased with Beckmann's approval.

IRON GATE

"A missing agent creates more questions than a dead one," Beckmann told him. "Take it to Cape Town and make it look like he drowned in the ocean. I want the body found." Maybe the Japanese would get the message indirectly. He headed for the stairs but stopped on the first step. "And Kreiner," he said, "that's one."

Kreiner forced a laugh. "Ha, ha. I get it. Very good, Generaal." It was the old Afrikaner joke about the Boer who shot his ox for stumbling the third time. When his wife protested, the Boer had said, "That's one."

Beckmann's heels beat a quick tattoo as he trotted up the stairs. But if it was a joke, why was Kreiner in a dead sweat?

Beckmann ate a leisurely lunch that day and lingered longer than normal over each dish. He grew expansive as he examined the wine and savored the memory of the morning. He thought about the afternoon, which promised to be equally rewarding, and when the time was right, he returned to his headquarters. His staff was assembled and waiting in the conference room, eager with anticipation.

"Time," Beckmann began, "and only time, is our enemy if we are to save our civilization from the black hordes that threaten to engulf us. We must act now, while we can still shape the correlation of events. True, we are few in number but we will prevail!" It was the old battle cry and like all true believers, they responded to Beckmann's words.

"But words mean little without action," he continued. "The next phase of the battle has started. We will feed the fires of black unrest until the kaffirs are sick of the very violence they have created. Then they will turn to anyone who offers them security and the world will see that tribal politics is just another form of racism—the crime they accuse us of.

"But we will not make the same mistakes as before. Instead, we will show the world an island of peace in a sea of chaos. We will welcome our black brothers who wish to live under our rule in prosperity. Of course, the kaffir government will resist, and they will ask the United Nations to send a peacekeeping force to our land. Let them come. We will keep them busy. Very busy." His staff laughed, enjoying the promise.

Beckmann grew serious and swept his hand in a grand gesture at the wall behind him as the lights dimmed. The wall blazed in light and a map of South Africa appeared. The old province boundaries had disappeared and contracted into a large oval that encompassed the central part of the country from Pretoria and Johannesburg in the north to Bloemfontein in the south. "This will be our nation," Beckmann said, his words full of triumph and resolve. "This will be the Boerstaat!"

Beckmann raised his fist in a clenched salute. *"Blut und Boden!"* Blood and soil, he shouted. As one, the men and women came to their feet and echoed his war cry. They would make it happen.

Friday, November 21
The White House, Washington, D.C.

"I think you should go for a one-on-one with Carroll," Sam Darnell insisted. "It's a hot tip."

Elizabeth Gordon looked around the deserted press room and sat down in her cubicle, a worried look on her face. Most of the White House press corps was on the road, following the president on a cross-country junket as he beat the political bushes in a Thanksgiving extravaganza for his party. She shook her head. "The story on Carroll's illness fizzled a week ago. That so-called hot tip is nothing but a wild-assed rumor and nothing is going to rekindle the network's interest. So why beat a dead horse?"

"There might be some life there yet," Sam replied. "Liz, you haven't . . . and . . . ah . . . you might find something else." She almost reminded Gordon that she hadn't been included in the press corps accompanying the president on his last two trips. Supposedly, the seats on the press aircraft were allotted to White House reporters in rotation, and her exclusion twice in a row from the press gang tagging along was ample warning she was out of favor. The damage was compounded because her own network was no longer springing for her and Sam to travel independently, like so many of her colleagues.

She looked at Sam. "I'm on the way out, aren't I?" It

wasn't really a question as much as a simple statement of fact. Sam nodded. "Damn, Sam," Gordon muttered. "What do I do?"

"Start looking. Find an issue before it's hot and work it," Sam counseled. "Be the first to see it coming. Be there before anyone else. You want to be in the hotel when the bombs start dropping." She was referring to the success of the CNN crew who were on-scene and transmitting when the first bombs hit Baghdad during the Persian Gulf War.

"Even if it means leaving the White House?" Gordon asked.

"Even if it means leaving the White House," Sam repeated. "Better to leave on your terms than be kicked out the back door."

"But what's going to be hot?"

"That's why you need to interview Carroll," Sam said. "It's his job to peek into the future."

Carroll agreed to an informal interview in his office after lunch. His coat was off, his collar open, and his desk piled with documents. Sam moved around the office, her camera on, setting the scene and getting the best angle while Carroll and Gordon settled in for the interview. She panned his desk going for an establishing shot, then focused on Carroll's face.

With the preliminaries over, Gordon consulted her prepared list of questions and started the interview. At first, he glossed over the answers, sticking to generalities. But Gordon pursued him for specifics with an unusual relentlessness that impressed the national security advisor. Near the end, she moved onto shaky ground. "Mr. Carroll, since your collapse while running, many of your colleagues have expressed worry about—"

He cut her off. "About my health," he said, ending the question. "I would rather not discuss it, since it is a private matter."

"So your health is not affecting your duties as the president's advisor for national security?"

"If it were, I'd tender my resignation."

Gordon hit him with the bombshell. "Then there is no

truth to the rumor that you've been diagnosed with ALS, Lou Gehrig's disease?"

He looked at Sam and made a cutting motion, ending the interview. She shut off her camera. "Elizabeth, like I said, it is a private matter. I'm going to have to trust you with this, and off the record, yes, I am undergoing medical tests. But right now, I feel fine, and until the tests are final and we know for sure what's wrong, I want to keep it private."

"That's asking a lot, Mr. Carroll."

Carroll nodded. "I know. But if you'll do this, Liz, I promise that I'll let you break the story . . . if I can."

"Fair enough," she answered. "Let's go for a wrap."

When they were finished, Gordon hurried Sam down to the studio in the basement to replay and edit the tape. "Damn, Sam," Gordon said, excitement in her voice. "Carroll's got ALS. It's the story I need and I'm going to break it."

Sam chewed on her lower lip in disapproval. "That's not a good idea. If he has ALS, Carroll's promised you the story. He's good for it. You know that. But if you violate his confidence, every source you've got in the administration will dry up. Don't do it." There was command in Sam's voice.

"But it's all I got," Gordon pleaded.

"But what if he doesn't have ALS?" Sam asked.

"I don't care if I get it right," Gordon snapped, "as long as I get it first."

"It's not the story you want, not right now," Sam told her. Among her other duties, Sam had to keep Gordon from committing professional suicide. "There's got to be something else," she said, running the tape. She stopped the tape and framed Carroll's desk. "Here's something," she said. "Everything on his desk is related to South Africa. Check the labels on the folders . . . AWB . . . UN Peacekeeping Options . . ." She paused for a moment, trying to read the label of a half-buried folder. She hit the zoom and enlarged the frame.

"Hans and Erik Beckmann," Gordon read. "Who are they? I've never heard of them."

"Neither have I," Sam said. "Maybe Jeff has."

Jeff Bissell was one of Gordon's on-again-off-again romances. He was also the aide to Senator Lucknow, who chaired the select committee on intelligence. Gordon smiled. "Poor Jeff. All I have to do is mention something and he spills everything he knows. I'd marry him if he wasn't such a flap mouth."

Gordon and Bissell met for an early lunch the next day, and she was back in the White House press room by twelve-thirty. "Sam, Jeff says South Africa is destabilizing—"

"This is not news," Sam interrupted.

"But there's a twist. Hans and Erik Beckmann are twins, Afrikaners by birth. Hans is a mover and groover in the AWB, whatever that is."

"Afrikaanse Weerstandsbeweging," Sam said. "The Afrikaner Resistance Movement. A neo-Nazi group of thugs."

"Anyway, Hans is the head of a quasimilitia called the Iron Guard that is totally independent of the central government. And brother Erik is a terrorist who hires out to the highest bidder. This all gets interesting because the South Africans had twenty nukes they claim they destroyed in 1994. But the CIA isn't sure what happened to them. Sam, there's one hell of a story there . . . white separatists with their own army . . . nuclear weapons . . . country coming apart. You ever been to South Africa?"

"I've been thinking," Sam said. "What if Carroll left those folders on his desk deliberately? What if he wants us to go rooting around and stirring the pot over there?"

"He's not that clever."

Sunday, December 7
Kansas City, Missouri

Little Matt's eyes were alive with excitement as Pontowski led his son into the Gold Suite. A valet helped them remove their overcoats. "Welcome to Arrowhead Stadium, Colonel Pontowski," the man said. "I hope you enjoy the game. The Chiefs are favored." They walked over to the floor-to-ceiling windows that overlooked the field and joined John and Sara Leonard.

It was Little Matt's first football game and he was jumping with excitement. "We're at the very top," he bubbled, "and you can see everything from up here."

The mayor of Kansas City, Missouri, came over and stuck out his hand. "Colonel!" he boomed, pumping Pontowski's hand and ignoring the Leonards. "We're glad you could join us. It's going to be a great game and the halftime show is fantastic." The mayor recited the events that had been planned to link the game with the observance of Pearl Harbor. "I can't tell you how much your support has added, and the flyby right after the national anthem is a perfect opener. The crowd is going to love it."

Leonard studied the clouds scudding over the stadium. "I don't know," he said. "The weather is not cooperating and the ceiling is pretty low."

A worried look crossed the mayor's face. "I really want that flyby." He was facing a tough election in the spring, and dedicating the game to the Armed Forces, with all the attendant marching units, color guards, bands, and cocktail parties had been his pet project. It was the type of event the citizens of Kansas City loved. "Some important people are counting on it."

Pontowski and Leonard heard the implied political threat underlying his words. But the man had never flown an airplane at 240 knots in tight formation and dodged weather. "You'll get your flyby if it's safe," Leonard assured him, knowing it wouldn't do any good to explain how the weatherman really drove the decision, not the mayor's political ambitions.

Again, the mayor ignored Leonard and fixed a hard look on Pontowski. "I'm sure your boys won't let us down. You support us and we support you, right?" He walked away, leaving the two men alone.

"That's not a man who likes to be told no," Pontowski said.

Little Matt looked up at his father, comparing him with the other dignitaries who had been invited to watch the game. He liked the way his father looked, tall and lean in his uniform. Most of the other men had potbellies and talked too loudly. Not my dad and Colonel Leonard, he thought. He looked up at Sara Leonard and beamed. There was no doubt in his seven-year-old mind that she was the prettiest woman in the room. He grabbed her hand and jabbered with excitement when the first band marched onto the field for the opening ceremonies. Like his father and Leonard, he came to attention when the massed bands played "The Star-Spangled Banner."

The announcer's voice came over the loudspeaker. "Ladies and gentlemen, please direct your attention to the northeast end of the stadium. You can hear the A-10 Thunderbolts from the 303rd Fighter Squadron led by Captain Dwight Stuart as they approach . . ." His voice was drowned out by the four Warthogs that appeared over the edge of the stadium, skimming under the clouds. They were in a perfect fingertip formation, their wings almost touching. From the high vantage point of the Gold Suite, which was above and to the right of the press box, Pontowski looked down on the four aircraft as they flew past. The four jets lifted up as one to clear the flagpoles on the rim of the stadium before disappearing to the southwest.

Pontowski and Leonard exchanged worried looks. "Maggot shouldn't have done that," Leonard grumbled, barely audible over the shouts of approval from the crowd in the box.

The mayor hurried over, again shaking Pontowski's hand, always the practicing politician. "Great show, Colonel. I knew you wouldn't let us down. The reporters in the press box stood up and applauded." He ushered Pontowski, Little Matt, and the Leonards to their seats for the opening kickoff.

The phone call from the Federal Aviation Agency came halfway through the first quarter. The mayor took the call on the phone at his seat and his face turned beet red before he handed the receiver to Pontowski. "It's the aviation safety inspector from the Flight Standards District Office," he said. "He said something about a flying violation because of the flyby." The mayor lowered his voice. "We don't want any problems," he warned.

Pontowski had been expecting the call. He took the phone and listened for a few moments. "Yes, I saw the flyby and your facts are essentially correct." He listened again and motioned for Leonard to join him. "Right," he finally said.

"I'll be right there." He gave the phone back to the mayor. "That was Gene Ponds. He wants to see me right away."

"Who's Gene Ponds?" the mayor demanded.

"A good man," Leonard answered, "just doing his job." Then to Pontowski. "Gene will listen to reason."

"If there's any to listen to," Pontowski added.

"Look," the mayor said, "I told you I don't want any trouble over this. You assured me you would only do the flyby if it was safe. So don't involve me."

Once a politician, Pontowski told himself. "Tango, will you and Sara take care of Little Matt while I put out this fire?"

"We'd love to, but I'll go with you."

"Thanks," Pontowski replied. "But no need for us both to miss the game. Call Maggot and have him meet me at the FAA." He bent over and explained the situation to his son. "Matt, I've got to take care of some Air Force business. But you can stay and watch the game with Colonel and Mrs. Leonard. Okay?"

Sadness filled Little Matt's eyes and Pontowski ruffled his hair. "I'll see you later, good buddy. I'm proud of you." He collected his overcoat and headed for the parking lot. Damn, Pontowski thought, I wanted to see the game with my son, and thanks to Maggot it isn't going to happen.

Pontowski and Maggot arrived back at the stadium twenty minutes into the victory celebration. Little Matt ran over to Pontowski and grabbed his hand, eager to tell him all about the game. Maggot was an instant celebrity with the crowd and an old retired Marine pilot cornered him for a round of good-natured insults.

"What happened with the FAA?" Leonard asked.

"You were right," Pontowski said. "Ponds is a good man. Maggot got caught pushing the weather minimums."

"If the minimums weren't good enough," Leonard said, "they wouldn't be the minimums."

"Ponds bought that argument," Pontowski replied. "But Ponds said that Maggot had better keep his nose clean for the next six months or he'll stomp all over his scrotum."

Pontowski gathered up Little Matt and left with the

Leonards while Maggot and the old Marine continued to entertain the party. "You Air Force pukes," the retired Marine claimed, "ain't got no couth."

Maggot feigned outrage. "You're speaking to the 303rd's couth control officer," he announced. "We're so couth that we can eat oysters without touching our lips or tongue."

"Right," the old Marine answered, his disbelief obvious.

Maggot walked over to the buffet table and rooted through a bowl of oysters, selecting two of the smallest. He walked back to the crowd with his plate. "Sure you want to see this?" he asked the Marine. He nudged one of the oysters to the edge of the plate with the tip of his nose and sniffed hard. The oyster disappeared up a nostril with a soft sucking sound. "Want to see it again?" he asked as a woman ran for the ladies' room. In her haste, she bowled over a reporter from the *Kansas City Star*.

Maggot made page two of the Monday edition.

"Maggot gives a whole new meaning to the term 'triple bang,'" Pontowski told Leonard. They were sitting in his office with the newspaper spread out on his desk. "The reporter dug hard and it's all here: the sexual harassment charge, the low flyby, and the great oyster-sucking scene." He gave a mental sigh. "We can't take this kind of heat. I've got to fire him."

Leonard nodded in agreement. "I know. But it'll hurt morale."

Pontowski looked out the window and considered his options. Leonard was right. Firing Maggot would hurt morale. But given a little time, they would get over that. The irony of it all struck at him—the Maggots were exactly the personality type he needed when the shooting started. But the Maggots were a liability in a peacetime Air Force. "I know," Pontowski muttered. Then, stronger, "Training a fighter jock in peacetime and then going to war is like raising a tiger in captivity and then turning him loose in the jungle. Neither does very well at first until the old skills and attitudes come back. That's why we need to keep a few of the Maggots around. They're the ones who get us through the first ten days alive."

Then another thought came to him. "We'll be okay as long as we don't get caught in a shooting match in the next six months or so."

"Not much chance of that," Leonard conceded.

Damn, Pontowski moaned to himself, am I the only guy who has to stomp on his best people?

CHAPTER
4

The two men walked down the fourth-floor hallway and let themselves into the small office. They were unremarkable in appearance, two European or American businessmen coming to work in a half-deserted office building. "God, it stinks in here," Jason Robby, the older of the two men, said. He threw open a window to the little-used office while his younger partner checked the answering machine. There was a message for MacKay. "Is that Chembo?" Robby asked.

"Yeah," Kevin Grawley, the youngest member of MacKay's Intelligence Support Agency team, answered. "She wants to meet him tonight."

"Better get the message to him," Robby said. "Cape Town is still wetting its knickers over what she gave us last time." He stood in the shadows beside the window and scanned the street. "I'm still coming up dry for contacts. How 'bout you?"

"Nothing since old Charles got the crispy critter treatment with the necklace," Grawley answered.

"Damn," Robby muttered. "Your shadow is still out there."

"He's harmless," Grawley answered. "I can shake him anytime I want. I don't think he's made you, and the Boss never comes here, so he's clean." He stood to leave. "I'll tell him about the message. Besides, he likes her."

"He better put a clamp on the love stud," Robby said. "We don't need him getting his ass shot off because a terminal case of the hornies blew away the last of his good judgment. It won't read well on a death certificate."

Grawley opened the door. "Yeah, I like him, too."

I can't believe I'm doing this, MacKay told himself as he mingled with the crowd outside the Market Theater. Come on, woman, he thought, where are you? You were the one who called.

He breathed easier when he saw Ziba sitting on a low brick wall next to the entrance. They had been out of touch for over a month and his control officer, the CIA station chief in Cape Town, was hounding him for more information. But after the Stevenses were killed at the funeral rally, he had held back, worried that a premature contact would compromise her or his operation. Now he was back in business, and his two ISA operatives, Jason Robby and Kevin Grawley, could stop crawling the walls for lack of activity.

A strong urge swept over him, and he could feel a heat building in his groin. You're acting like a young blood sniffing after pussy, he thought.

Ziba stood and smiled at him. "I have missed you, John Arthur." All his worries vanished, blown away by the sound of her voice and the way she looked at him.

"Have you been here before?" she asked. He shook his head. "This is an important place," she told him. "Much of our struggle for freedom started here. We used the stage to tell our story to the world. There are times when it is more than art." They walked arm in arm around the small square, mingling with the holiday crowd and vendors.

"I thought you had moved," he ventured.

"The Slavins have moved to Bloemfontein," she replied. "I overheard him talk about working at the Boyden Observatory. But I wanted to see you before I left." The sound of police sirens echoed over the crowd and drowned out her words. MacKay closed his eyes and listened. In the distance, he could hear a faint sound that reminded him of surf at a beach. Then he sniffed the air—a trace of smoke, then nothing. Ziba spoke to a man and turned to him. "There's trouble, much trouble around the train station. We need to leave . . . now." In the distance, he heard the unmistakable clatter of a submachine gun.

"Come on," he said. "There's an office near here . . . on Commissioner Street. We'll be safe there." He grabbed her hand and they ran. The streets were deserted and at first they only saw a single person coming toward them—a black teenager. Then more people were running and they heard seven rapid gunshots from a semiautomatic pistol.

"I don't like this," MacKay muttered. But they were almost to Commissioner Street and he pressed ahead. A group of shouting blacks surged into the street and blocked their way. He pulled Ziba into a doorway as a car's headlights swept the street. The glare framed a man on his knees, begging for his life. A teenager jammed a pistol against the back of his head and fired.

"What are my brothers doing?" Ziba moaned.

MacKay threaded his way through the back streets and finally reached the office building. It was dark except for the lights on the fourth floor. "That's the office. Wait here." He headed for the building, using the dark for cover. On impulse, he ducked into an alley and looked back. He was being followed. Damn, he cursed to himself, where did he come from?

What little hope MacKay harbored for his operation evaporated. He fumbled for the keys in his pocket, finding the one to the side door of the office building. He ran, using the darkness and parked cars for cover, anything to prevent a shot. He climbed the steps to the building in two strides and was through the side door, deliberately leaving it unlocked.

Inside, he ripped a fire extinguisher off its mount and jerked out the safety pin. He bounded up the stairwell, his long legs taking five steps at a stride, gaining him precious seconds. Come on you mutha, he thought. Behind him, he heard footsteps. He ran past his floor and stopped on the next landing, twelve steps above. He allowed a tight smile when he heard his pursuer's labored breathing. Come on, you know the floor, he thought. Go on through.

The man went through the stairwell door and into the hallway. MacKay ghosted down the steps and waited beside the door. The door handle turned and he tensed. On the other side of the door, he heard the same labored breathing. He raised the fire extinguisher. The door cracked open and MacKay mashed the trigger, sending a yellowish-white spray into the man's face. MacKay kicked the door open and barreled through, still spraying. The man was rubbing his eyes, twisting wildly from side to side. MacKay bashed the man's head with the fire extinguisher and he collapsed to the floor.

MacKay scooped up the man's Beretta and moved down the hall to his office. He tested the door and it opened enough for him to bob his head around the door jamb to see inside. The body of Jason Robby was slumped in a corner. MacKay slipped inside and felt under Robby's jawbone for a pulse. Nothing. Then he saw the wound. A bullet had punched a hole the size of a pencil into Robby's chest and had mushroomed, blowing out his backbone. The bastard's using Devastators, he thought.

His younger agent, Kevin Grawley, had taken two of the small shaped-charged high-explosive slugs in his stomach and had almost been cut in two. MacKay's face froze as he pulled at the slide of the small Beretta until he had ejected four Devastator rounds. He hit the magazine release and the clip slipped out. A seven-shot clip. All the rounds were accounted for. Methodically he reloaded and walked back down the hall. He stood over the unconscious man as he considered his options.

He had to get out of Johannesburg and reestablish contact with his control. But more important, who had done this? Could he make it look as if he had also been killed in the attack? Could he hide in the death and destruction going on outside?

Slowly, his rage grew. Robby and Grawley had been good men, not killers. He spoke to the man. "Fortunately, you are a gentleman of color and about my size." MacKay rifled the man's pockets, taking his identification. When he was clean, MacKay shoved his own passport, wallet, and keys into the man's pockets. Without a word, he picked the man up and carried him to the office. He stood on a chair, pushed a ceiling tile aside, and felt inside. He pulled out a small box and checked its contents. Everything was there, including the thermite grenades.

For a moment, MacKay considered breaking the man's knees so he would be conscious and immobilized when the grenade went off. He rejected that idea, chambered one Devastator round, and shot the man in the head, blowing away any traces of the beating. "Merry fuckin' Christmas to you, too," he muttered. He pulled the man's shoes off and exchanged them for his own. He stepped into the hall, pulled the pin to the grenade, and rolled it into the office. He had ten seconds to clear the floor. He made it in eight.

Flames were shooting out of the office windows when MacKay found Ziba. "What happened?" she asked.

"An office was firebombed by persons unknown and Jason Robby, Kevin Grawley, and John Arthur were killed in the blast." His voice was a monotone, without emotion.

He felt Ziba's hand slip into his. "Can you tell me your real name now?" she asked.

He hesitated. Then, "John Author MacKay."

"What are you going to do now?"

MacKay studied the apartments in the building across the street. "I don't think the asshole who got Robby and Grawley was working alone. I want to stake out this place and see who shows up. Besides, it's too dangerous to be on the streets now."

Friday, December 19
The White House, Washington, D.C.

Mazie Kamigami Hazelton took a deep breath and picked up the leather folder with her name embossed in gold letters at the bottom. The folder went with her new job as special assistant to the national security advisor and was a symbol, a prop to carry around signifying her importance. She dropped it on her desk and marched out of her new office, a small, windowless cubicle on the second floor of the West Wing, and down the stairs to Bill Carroll's corner office.

Carroll's secretary, Midge Ralston, glanced up at Mazie and smiled. She had known Mazie since she was "the

Frump," an overweight junior staff member on the National Security Council. Over time, Mazie had matured into a brilliant analyst, slimmed down to a petite size four, and married one of Washington's most eligible bachelors, Wentworth Hazelton. But no glamorous exterior could hide the fact that Mazie Kamigami Hazelton possessed one of the finest minds in Washington, D.C.

Midge motioned her inside. "Break a leg," she said. It was Mazie's first day on her new job. Inside, Carroll and Cyrus Piccard were waiting for her.

The old man came to his feet and gave her a courtly nod as they shook hands. He fully approved of Carroll's choice and knew what was hidden behind the petite and beautiful exterior that blended the best of Mazie's Japanese-Hawaiian heritage. "You have been given an impossible task," he said.

Mazie gave him a beautiful smile. "I have been warned."

"Mazie," Carroll said, interrupting them from behind his desk, "cold nuclear fusion will be the number-one item at the cabinet meeting today. This is one of those areas where technical expertise is needed to make policy, and hopefully, you can explain it."

She shook her head. "I can try. How long do I have?"

"I'm an old man," Piccard answered. "I go to sleep after five minutes of anything . . . just like the cabinet."

Mazie laughed. It was a warm laugh, laced with kindness that made her face come alive. "Fusion is the opposite of nuclear fission. In theory, the fission process is simple. A neutron is made to strike the nucleus of an atom, the nucleus splits apart and several more neutrons are released, along with heat and radiation. All this takes place in a reactor or an atomic bomb.

"On the other hand, nuclear fusion is the stuff that powers our sun and the stars. Rather than split atoms, it joins them. Two hydrogen nuclei collide, fuse, and create a new nucleus. The result is a form of helium and radiation. The by-product is an astronomical amount of energy in the form of heat. But it takes a huge amount of heat to make fusion happen—millions of degrees.

"The only places where that kind of heat exists are in the sun, an atomic explosion, or a laboratory device called a tokamat. Cold nuclear fusion is the holy grail of science: The true believers claim that fusion can be made to happen without all the heat in the first place." She was finished.

Carroll nodded. "That took seventy seconds. Very good."

"The laboratory device you mentioned, why don't we use it like a reactor?" Piccard asked.

"A tokamat is self-defeating," Mazie answered. "It takes more energy to develop the heat in the tokamat than is gained from the fusion process going on inside."

"I take it you do not believe in cold fusion," Piccard said.

"In science," Mazie replied, "you don't believe or disbelieve. You prove or disprove. Cold fusion has not been proven."

"Thanks, Mazie," Carroll said, dismissing her. "I want you to come to the cabinet meeting and repeat what you've just said."

After Mazie had left, Piccard leaned back in his chair and waited. Something important was bothering the national security advisor. "Cyrus," Carroll said. "I need your advice." He rose and walked to the window overlooking President's Park. "South Africa is being swept by riots and they have formally requested the United Nations send a peacekeeping team. It gets complicated because the Afrikaners may have discovered cold fusion and are strong enough to act independently of the central government. The CIA seems fixated on finding out what happened to the nuclear weapons the South Africans had before the new government came to power. As usual, we're in a reactive mode, running as hard as we can to catch up. The president wants action. What would you tell him?"

"First," Piccard replied, "exercise the UN peacekeeping option now that Congress is in recess. Second, build a fire underneath the CIA . . . a very big one. Find out what the Afrikaners are up to."

"There's more," Carroll said. "We know that OPEC and the Japanese are running covert operations trying to get at Prime. The CIA claims they've got a make on the third group and are describing it as the neo-Axis. It's a European alliance made up of the old Axis powers."

A deep frown cut Piccard's face. "Germany, Italy, and Austria," he said, "are all dependent on oil imports for their economic survival. Control of Prime would break the stranglehold of OPEC and make them dominant on the Continent. What they didn't achieve by war, they accomplish by economics. The Japanese response to defeat with a vengeance."

"Exactly," Carroll replied. "But we haven't a clue what the neo-Axis is up to."

"I'd look for an Afrikaner connection," Piccard said.

"And the Afrikaners have moved Prime. We don't know where."

"That does complicate the situation," Piccard allowed.

Carroll was still standing in front of the window. He fixed Piccard with a strange look. "And I have ALS," he said. "Lou Gehrig's disease."

Piccard was visibly shaken, and he crossed the room to Carroll. He reached out and rested his right hand on Carroll's left shoulder. "Oh, my dear man, I'm so sorry." There were tears in his eyes. The two men stood there, not saying a word. Piccard sensed Carroll's agony. He wouldn't see his children grow up, walk his daughter down the aisle, or ever hold a grandchild. Those had all been denied to Piccard and he knew the hurt. Is this the price we pay for success? Piccard thought. If so, it was an unfair exchange, very unfair.

"Is that why you asked Mazie to be your special assistant?" Piccard asked.

Carroll nodded. "She can create the continuity my replacement will need until he gets his feet on the ground."

"Does the president know yet?" Piccard asked. Carroll nodded. "Your resignation may be premature," the old man said. "The president understands the value of tragedy in politics." He gathered up his cane and topcoat, ready to leave. "There are some interesting times ahead for you," he said.

"Isn't that an ancient Chinese curse?" Carroll asked. "To live in interesting times?"

"It wasn't a curse," Piccard answered, "but a supplication to the gods against boredom."

Carroll watched him walk down the hall, thankful he had him as an advisor. He turned to his secretary. "Midge, call Chuck and Wayne. Tell them I'm going for a run." Midge made the call and brushed away a tear. She knew her boss was dying.

The two Secret Service agents who ran with Carroll were waiting for him when he came out in his running clothes. "A nice day for a run," Wayne Adams said, enjoying the unusually warm December day.

"Lots of runners out," Chuck Stanford responded. Carroll motioned to the two men and they started to jog, barely more than a walk. The two agents matched his slow pace in silence, each scanning the area, looking for any suspicious activity. Then Carroll picked up the pace and for a few brief moments, the old look was back on his face and he was at peace with the world.

Sunday, December 21
Knob Noster, Missouri

The phone call came at five in the morning. After a dozen rings, it finally penetrated and Pontowski fumbled for the receiver. "Pontowski," he muttered, still half-asleep. It was the command center telling him they had communications traffic that required his immediate attention. "Since when," he grumbled, "do the Reserves handle the hot ones? What the hell are you active-duty pukes hired for?" He listened to the polite answer.

Pontowski banged the receiver down and sat on the edge of the bed, his feet on the cold floor, trying to think. He needed at least two cups of coffee to cut the mental fog that bound him in the early morning. And it was getting worse the older he got. He shrugged on his flight suit and zipped up his flying boots. After splashing some water on his face, he checked on Little Matt. You are a good kid, he thought, gazing at his sleeping son. He went downstairs and knocked on the door of his live-in nanny. "Martha, I've got to go to the base, it's urgent. I know today is your day off, but can you cover for me this morning?"

The door cracked open and Martha Marshall peered out. She was a no-nonsense woman in her middle sixties and brimming with good health. "I should never have let Sara talk me into taking this job," she told him. Martha Marshall was Sara Leonard's widowed mother and had been at loose ends since Sara had married John Leonard and moved to Knob Noster. Martha had jumped at the chance to be a nanny for Little Matt. Not only did the job give her an income, but she lived next door to the Leonards. "I'm too old for this." She gave Pontowski a hard look before relenting. "Oh, of course," she sighed.

"Thanks, Martha, I'll make it up to you."

"I doubt that," she called to his back. "But you can start by getting married."

"Is that an offer?" he answered.

"Not me, you fool."

The communications traffic that was waiting for his attention in the command center was a simple four-line message from the National Military Command Center directing the 442nd to activate Ops Plan Rapid Roger. "What the hell is Rapid Roger?" he asked the on-duty controller.

Even though the captain had sampled Pontowski's early morning personality, she didn't hesitate. "I've never heard of it, Colonel. But I'll find out." She hit pay dirt on the first phone call to the 509th Bomb Wing's plans officer. "Sir," she told the lieutenant colonel, "you had better get right over here and explain it all to Colonel Pontowski." She hung up, faced Pontowski, and took a deep breath. "Not good, sir. Two copies of Rapid Roger were sent to our plans shop over a month ago. A copy was never forwarded to you. I don't know why."

"Lovely," Pontowski grunted. "Command and control by rumor."

"Can I get you some coffee, sir?" the controller asked.

"Point the way," he grumped. "I can get it myself." The caffeine had done part of its work by the time the 509th plans officer scurried into the command center. Without a word, the lieutenant colonel handed the thick document to Pontowski. "Fucking lovely," Pontowski gritted as he scanned appendix C, the operations section of the plan. "We're tasked with a rapid reaction commitment to deploy twenty A-10s within forty-eight hours after notification. And this is the first I've heard of it." He was chewing his words into machine-gun bullets. "Thanks a bunch, Colonel, for not doing your job. Now I'm standing knee deep in muck because you haven't got your shit together."

"Sir," the lieutenant colonel stammered, "your Reserve headquarters, the Tenth Air Force at Bergstrom, should have sent you a copy."

Pontowski flipped to the last page of the document and checked the distribution list. "Not according to this," he said. "We were to get our copy through your plans office, since Air Combat Command is the gaining command. You are part of ACC, right?" He didn't wait for an answer and stomped out of the command center. Regardless of who was to blame, his wing was going to look bad. It was just the way the bureaucracy of command and control worked.

His first action was to initiate a unit recall, hoping most of his reservists would get a telephone call and report for duty within twelve hours. Then he drafted a message to the National Military Command Center explaining the situation. No matter how he phrased it, one outstanding fact could not be avoided: The 442nd was not going to be ready to deploy in forty-eight hours.

Tango Leonard was the first to report in. "What the hell is going down?" he asked. Pontowski told him about the activation message and Rapid Roger. He handed Leonard a copy of the message he had sent to the NMCC. "I don't want to be standing next to you when we get the reply to this," he told Pontowski.

The reply to Pontowski's message arrived six minutes later. Both men were surprised by its brevity. The NMCC wanted to know when the 442nd would be ready to deploy and Pontowski was ordered to report to the NMCC in the Pentagon soonest. "They're probably building a gallows at Ground Zero right now," Pontowski allowed. Ground Zero was the five-acre courtyard that formed the hub at the center of the Pentagon.

Leonard paced the floor, thinking. "Boss, you know how these alerts work. We get ready in forty-eight hours then stand around for a week with our thumbs up our asses waiting to get the execute order. But we might be able to make the forty-eight hours. I'm not saying we'll do it with style and grace, but damn, you've got some fine people here. They proved that in China."

"Get to it," Pontowski said. A knock on the door caught his attention. His new executive officer, First Lieutenant Lori Williams, a tall and willowy twenty-three-year-old African-American, was reporting in. His people were showing up much faster than anticipated.

"Sir," Williams said, "Captain Stuart is outside. He heard about the recall and wants to speak to you."

Pontowski pulled a long face. "Tell Maggot it'll have to wait until I get back. I've got to catch a plane." You're avoiding this, he told himself. It isn't right to keep him hanging. "Lori, scrub that. Tell him to come in."

Maggot walked in and snapped a highly professional salute. His uniform was immaculate, his shoes shined to a high gloss, and he had a fresh haircut. Captain Dwight "Maggot" Stuart had never looked so military. Pontowski waved a salute back and told him to sit down.

"Sir, thanks for seeing me," Maggot began. "I'm hoping you'll reconsider your decision."

"I can't take any more heat," Pontowski replied.

"Colonel," Maggot said, trying not to beg, "I know it's time I quit doing Maggot-type things and grow up. I'm asking for one more chance."

Pontowski glanced at his watch. He was running out of time. "I'm sending your records to ARPC."

Maggot's lips compressed into a thin line and his chin dropped. Pontowski hadn't kicked him out of the Reserves, but by sending his records to ARPC, the Air Reserve Personnel Center, Pontowski had consigned him to the inactive reserve. It was a bureaucratic limbo and he would never fly again. Maggot nodded and stood up. He wouldn't beg. "If you ever need me, sir, call. I'll be there." He saluted and walked out of the office.

Pontowski stared at his desk for a moment. He picked up a glass paperweight and threw it across the room.

CHAPTER
5

The doorman on duty at the Villiard Hotel frowned when the battered old Volvo pulled up and stopped. The car was not up to the Villiard standard and the assistant manager would have more than a small piece of his skin if he didn't send the driver packing. It was his job to man the front line and sort the elite from the tourists and unwanted intruders so the hotel could provide the nation's power brokers with a haven for behind-the-scenes dickering, influence peddling, and if need be, fornicating. Common knowledge held that more deals were wheeled, dealed, and rolled over the American electorate in the Villiard than in the Capitol.

Sam Darnell hopped out of the car and flashed her press card. "Don't park it," she said. "I'll only be a moment. Have you seen Elizabeth Gordon?"

The doorman gave an audible sigh. "I believe Miss Gordon is with Senator Lucknow's assistant, Jeff Bissell."

Shacked up for a matinee, Sam thought. The photographer liked Liz Gordon and accepted her for what she was, but she worried about Gordon's casual approach to sex: "We've got to move on a hot story." The doorman understood and picked up the phone at his station, spoke to the operator, and handed her the receiver. "Liz," Sam said, "the White House has announced we are sending a UN peacekeeping team into South Africa. Congress is going to spit bullets on this one and Ann Nevers wants to talk to you. I'm out front. Hurry." She handed the phone back to the doorman. "Thanks, I owe you." He nodded. It was the way backs were scratched in Washington, D.C.

Elizabeth Gordon made her exit fifteen minutes later, and while her clothes were neat and tidy, her face was flushed. The doorman held the Volvo's door open for her and was glad to see them drive away. Gordon flipped the sunshade down and checked the vanity mirror. "Your makeup case is on the backseat," Sam told her. "You and Jeff sharing confidences or is the relationship on again?"

"A little of both," Gordon allowed. "There is a stirring of congressional support for supporting the UN in Africa."

Congresswoman Ann Nevers was waiting for them in her office in the House of Representatives Office Building. Her view of the Capitol was mute testimony to her political clout and ability to switch party affiliations at the right time. She was almost six feet tall and slightly hunch-shouldered. Her dark hair was attractively streaked with gray and her brown eyes were clear and alert. She could have been a model in her youth and was still pretty. But the years of fighting political games had hardened her attitude and with it, her face. She offered them coffee or tea and sat with them on a sofa.

"I want to spend my remaining years in Congress addressing the problems facing our country," she began, "problems we need to solve now." She stood and paced the antique Persian carpet in front of her overlarge desk. "You know the list. But our attention is deliberately being diverted away by the policies of the current administration. No doubt you've heard the president is committing our troops to serve under a UN commander in South Africa."

Gordon nodded. "I thought the National Security Revitalization Act specifically prohibited that without congressional approval."

"That was our intention when Congress passed the act," Nevers replied. "But there is a clause in the Emergency War Powers Act of 1965 that allows the president to act unilaterally without the consent of Congress, if Congress is not in session. That clause was never repealed and he's using it."

More pacing, her anger in full flow. "This is a middle-aged male thing, you know, a typical macho reaction to male menopause . . . a testosterone hot flash."

"Then you believe the United States should not try to stop the spreading violence in South Africa," Gordon said.

Nevers stared at her for a moment as she considered her answer. Gordon was not living up to her reputation as a mindless pretty face. "Not with a military presence. We learned that lesson in Somalia. As I have often said before, military actions are a smoke screen to divert the public's attention from problems here. We will hold these *new interventionists* accountable. Did you know that Zack Pontowski's grandson has been chosen to command the U.S. contingent?"

"Is that bad?" Gordon answered. "I don't know too much about him, but it was my understanding that he did a good job in China."

"Good job?" Nevers replied, her voice carefully modulated with the right amount of disbelief. "He's the next thing to a mercenary. We'll never see true progress in this country until the Pontowskis are controlled." More pacing. "This is so obvious, using the Pontowski name to develop political support in Congress. Carroll is behind this, I just know it."

Gordon and Sam exchanged glances. Nevers's hostility toward Carroll was well known and Gordon sensed an opening. "It sounds like you're playing the local macho game," she ventured, hoping for an unconscious slip of the tongue.

But Nevers had fielded too many questions from journalists to be trapped. "What game is that?" she asked.

"In this town," Gordon answered, "you are defined by your enemies and respected only for the number of people you've ruined."

Nevers smiled. "Don't be silly, of course not." But Gordon had struck home, for Nevers savored that aspect of political power. "Liz," she said, her voice full of concern, "we've got to stop the Pontowskis and the Carrolls. They represent all that is wrong with our system." She stopped, sensing she had made her case. The interview was at an end and Nevers escorted them out.

In the hall, Gordon said, "She has a good point."

"It was spin control," Sam replied. "She's using you."

The reporter nodded. "And she was too long on generalities and too short on facts. Why all the animosity toward Pontowski? See what you can find out about him."

Monday, December 22
The Pentagon, Arlington, Virginia

When Pontowski arrived at the Pentagon, he was immediately escorted to the NMCC, the National Military Command Center, where the generals asked only two questions: When would the 442nd be ready to deploy? What did he need to make it happen? In short order, he found himself in the command section of E-ring and then in room 3E880, the office of the secretary of defense. The man who greeted him, Doctor John Weaver Elkins, was slender and mild-mannered, and looked more like a librarian than one of the most powerful members of the president's cabinet.

"Matt," Elkins said, "I've been looking forward to meeting you." He motioned for Pontowski to sit down. "I understand you and Bill Carroll are old friends." Carroll was sitting in a comfortable leather chair near the windows that overlooked the Potomac River. Elkins sat down in his own chair and folded his hands. "In a few minutes, we're going into a press conference to introduce you as the commander of the Americans being sent to South Africa. Expect to be hit with some pretty tough questions."

"Like legal justification?" Pontowski asked.

"We've prepared a position paper on that," Elkins answered, handing him a copy to read. "Under the Emergency War Powers Act, the president can commit our troops up to ninety days. We expect Congress to hit us with a barrage of committee hearings when they reconvene. Being a critic is much easier, and safer, than being in the arena making things happen."

"Congress may use its powers under the National Security Revitalization Act to eventually pull you out," Carroll added. "But as long as Congress is not in session, the president is free to act. That's why he's moving fast to protect our national interests."

"And just what are our national interests in South Africa?" Pontowski asked. "A severe shortage of diamonds?"

Elkins laughed. "He's got you, Bill."

Carroll hated what he had to do next. It had been decided by the president not to reveal the real reason for the United States' involvement, and it fell to Carroll to create a believable lie. "We're repaying our European allies for the support they've given us in past operations. They hold a few markers from the Gulf War, Somalia, and Haiti, and it's payback time. We are supporting their interests, not defending ours." Pontowski understood quid pro quo, and while this did seem weak, it was legal. And serving as a peacekeeper was ethical.

"Matt," Elkins explained, "you will be the senior U.S. military officer in the country. However, you will fall under a French general, Charles de Royer, who has been appointed the commander of all UN forces in South Africa. One of your primary duties is to create a command relationship with the UN where an American is not the head honcho. This may be the most important thing you accomplish. Unfortunately, we have very few hard-and-fast guidelines for you."

Which means that I have to play it by ear, Pontowski thought, and get hung out to dry if anything goes wrong. "Like in China?" he asked.

"Like in China," Carroll conceded.

"What about the CIA?" Pontowski asked.

"They have a presence in South Africa," Carroll answered.

"Will they be mounting any covert operations?"

"The agency is out of the covert operations business," Elkins answered.

"Right," Pontowski deadpanned. Elkins did not respond. It was time for the press conference, and he led the way to the auditorium used for press briefings.

Every seat was taken and Elizabeth Gordon was sitting in the front row, her long legs stretched out and carefully crossed for maximum exposure. She thumbed through the notes on Pontowski Sam had passed to her moments before. She was surprised Sam had dug up so much information on such short notice and key phrases leaped out: hell raiser . . . party boy and woman chaser as a young lieutenant . . . always in trouble . . . almost kicked out of the Air Force . . . saved by intervention from White House.

A typical fighter pilot, Gordon thought. She scribbled "political influence" in her notebook. Then she read the rest. As a captain, Pontowski had been involved in a midair collision in which three men had been killed. No other information was available. Gordon wrote "cover-up?" in her notebook. She searched the room for Sam and mouthed the words "good work." The photographer had maneuvered for a position against a side wall to give Gordon the benefit of the best light.

Elkins took the podium and surveyed the crowd. "It must be a slow news day," he said. Laughter rippled around the room as he turned to business. "You have all read the position paper on the president's power to act, so why don't we get right to the questions?"

He was bombarded with a flurry of questions that indicated most of the reporters had not read the position paper and Pontowski admired the easy way Elkins handled them. He was friendly, but with just enough reserve to warn the reporters he did not tolerate fools. Finally, he said, "Why don't I turn this over to the two experts I brought with me, the national security advisor and the man who will be leading the peacekeeping contingent, Colonel Matthew Pontowski." He motioned Carroll and Pontowski to the podium.

The room erupted as the reporters shouted for attention, demanding to be recognized. Carroll ended the shouting by pointing to a man sitting near one of the boom mikes. "Are there plans to send more than just a single wing?" the reporter asked. "Is the CIA involved? Have you established a definite time limit? Is this an open-ended commitment?"

"I'm glad you only asked one question," Carroll replied, causing a few chuckles. "We have made it very clear to the UN that this is not an open-ended commitment, but we have not established a firm time limit as of yet. To do so would be premature. As of now, we intend to send a composite group made up of A-10s from the 442nd Fighter Wing from Whiteman Air Force Base in Missouri and C-130s from the 314th Airlift Wing at Little Rock Air Force Base in Arkansas. We can expand or contract their mission as circumstances warrant."

I wonder what those "circumstances" are? Pontowski thought. He mulled it over and missed Elizabeth Gordon's question, which was directed at him. "I beg your pardon," he said. "Would you please repeat your question?"

"I asked," Gordon replied, certain she had thrown him a curve because of his hesitation, "if you were selected to lead the American contingent because of your political connections?" She deliberately recrossed her legs, letting her skirt ride higher, pushing the limits of journalistic propriety. I hope Sam is catching this, she thought. Show the public what you are.

Pontowski drilled her with a hard look. From the recesses of his memory, he dragged up her name, recalling her coverage of the Persian Gulf War. He was all too aware of the movement of her legs and the expanse of thigh she was showing. An inner alarm sounded, warning him not to dismiss her as a bimbo but to treat her as a dangerous opponent who used sex as a weapon.

His voice was measured and calm when he answered. "Miss Gordon," he said, "there is no way I can answer that with a ten-second sound bite. It is true that many of my family and friends are active in politics. I can't deny that. But I hope that my record speaks for itself and is sufficient justification for my selection. Also, my wing, the 442nd, has an outstanding record and they have earned the right to this assignment."

You opened the subject, Gordon thought, so here it comes. "Speaking of records, Colonel Pontowski, you were in a midair collision in which three other men were killed and you were the only survivor. The cause of the accident was never made public and has led to charges of a cover-up."

"I lost two good friends in that accident," Pontowski said, his voice not betraying his anger. "It is still a very painful memory. As to the charges you mentioned, this is the first I've heard of them. I requested the accident report be released under the Freedom of Information Act and the Air Force granted my request three years ago. Please read the report and I'll be glad to answer any questions you might have. But let's stick to facts, Miss Gordon. We owe the American public that courtesy."

Gordon felt her face flush. "It's my business to deal in facts," she shot back. From the look on his face, she knew she had made a mistake, a very bad mistake. Pontowski had set her up.

His voice was bland. "As I recall, during the Persian Gulf War, you reported B-52 bombers were launched from the aircraft carrier *America.*" A few of the reporters guffawed at the thought of the huge Air Force bombers operating off a Navy carrier. "That must have gotten the Navy's attention," he said, an amused look on his face. The laughter grew louder.

Gordon dropped her gaze and said nothing, letting the questioning pass to another reporter. She wrote "Bastard" in her notebook and stewed until the briefing was over. Outside the auditorium, she stormed down the hall. The bastard, she raged to herself, that conceited, egotistical son of a bitch! Who does he think he is?

"Liz," Sam called. The photographer ran after Gordon, slowed by her camera and tripod. "Slow down."

"I'm going to nail that son of a bitch's hide to the wall," Gordon snapped.

"We'll talk about it later," Sam said. After you've calmed down, she added to herself.

"He insulted me," Gordon said, "and every reporter in there."

The egoism driving Gordon's words angered Sam and she decided it was time to explain a few facts of life to the reporter. "Pontowski is one self-assured SOB for good reason," she said calmly. "So if you want a piece of his hide on the wall, you had better have all your facts nailed down before you go after him. You made a mistake in there."

"I made a mistake! You were the one who found out about the midair collision."

"I never said anything about a cover-up," Sam retorted. "That was your idea."

"He made a fool out of me! Are you defending him?"

"No," Sam replied, "but you brought it on yourself."

"You're fired!" Gordon shouted.

Sam tilted her head to one side and stared at Gordon. "Liz, you went after Pontowski because you listened to Nevers and lost your objectivity. You know better than to trust a politician. Don't you think it's time your brain kicked in?" She spun around and walked away.

Gordon felt like crying. She had blown it again, and the only one telling her the truth was Sam Darnell. "Sam, I'm sorry," she called. Sam stopped and waited. "I'm in trouble here and I don't know what to do." Tears were running down her cheeks as she walked back to Sam.

"It's time to go, Liz."

"You were pretty rough on Liz Gordon," Carroll said when they returned to Elkins's office.

"I wasn't about to let her run over me," Pontowski replied.

"It's a sad fact of life," Elkins said, "that the media and the military will never get along. The military distrusts the press and unfortunately, too many reporters think their words come directly from God on an ecclesiastical hot line."

Carroll looked worried. "Matt, you're playing a different game now. You've got to be constantly looking over your shoulder and checking your backside because everything, and I mean every word, every action you take has political fallout."

"So I've been told," Pontowski said. "I hope this doesn't turn into a goat rope. If there's nothing else, I need to get back to my wing. Any idea when we might get the execute order?"

"Soon," Elkins said. "Probably within seventy-eight hours."

"Can you hold off until after Christmas?"

"We can try," Elkins replied. "But we've got to move fast before Congress reconvenes. They will take the peacekeeping option off the table."

What are the other options? Pontowski wondered.

Tuesday, December 23
Johannesburg, South Africa

A bulky, top-heavy armored personnel carrier rumbled down the center of Commissioner Street at first light. MacKay stood back from the window in the eighth-floor apartment where he and Ziba had been staked out for six days watching his office. "A Hippo," he told her. "Now the police show up."

She joined him and watched as a squad of police moved behind the armored personnel carrier with military precision, checking the burned-out stores and vehicles for any signs of life or resistance. Occasionally, a policeman probed at a body to check for weapons, but they had all been stripped clean. The rioting that had swept through Johannesburg had finally burned itself out.

An Army truck came down the street and parked in front of the office building across the street from MacKay. "Check this out," he mumbled as a squad of soldiers got out and went inside the office building. He focused his binoculars on the window of his old office. His stakeout was about to pay a dividend.

Hans Beckmann stood in front of the train station and studied the destruction around him with a professional interest. He motioned to the Army colonel and walked toward the Civic Center, five blocks to the north. Behind him, a small clutch of reporters and photographers followed along in a tight group.

"It was much worse than we had anticipated," the colonel told Beckmann. "At first, we could do nothing. Then after three days, we were able to go in. Many of the rioters were either sleeping or drunk by then. But there was still much street fighting and it took us forty-eight hours to restore order."

An old white woman wandered toward them in a state of shock. She was still clutching a plastic bag with her Christmas shopping. Hans Beckmann spoke quietly to an officer and he hurried back to the reporters to ensure the old woman was photographed. Betacams whirled and cameras clicked before the group moved on, leaving the old woman behind them, still wandering dazedly in a world she no longer understood.

"How many kaffirs were killed?" Beckmann asked.

"Over two thousand," the colonel told him.

Beckmann fixed the officer with a cold stare. "Not enough. Were any whites killed?"

"At last count, less than fifty. That includes the two CIA agents we were watching . . . a fire in their office . . . an accident."

"I was told there were three agents," Beckmann said.

"The third was a black," the colonel replied. "He was also killed."

"Take me there," Beckmann ordered.

A staff car was brought up and they climbed in. "Take us to Commissioner Street," the colonel ordered.

An Army sergeant led them to the fourth-floor office where the bodies had been discovered. "We had to bag the bodies and remove them," the sergeant said. The office was a charred wreck and little was left that was recognizable. "The kaffir was here, next to the door. We think he was killed first. The two whites were over there. Bad work. Assassinated. The fire made identification difficult. But we had enough. They were all Americans."

"Are you sure about the kaffir?" Beckmann asked.

"His passport had not burned and he had keys to the office."

"His name?"

"John Arthur from Pittsburgh, Pennsylvania."

"The photo on the passport, did it match?" Beckmann asked.

"His face was badly burned," the sergeant answered. "One other thing, the kaffir was wearing shoes I've never seen before. A very light dress shoe with a soft sole, perfect for walking."

Or moving without making a sound, Beckmann thought. He had seen enough. "Turn the bodies over to the Americans," he said, allowing a tight smile. At least one of his counterintelligence operations had been successful. But they will try again, he reasoned. Prime was too tempting a target.

MacKay focused his binoculars on the men coming out of the building. The frustration that had been building in him gave way to a pure, cold anger when he recognized Hans Beckmann. "It was the fuckin' AWB," he told Ziba.

She touched his arm. "It's time to leave."

"You got that right." MacKay swept the apartment, removing any trace that they had been there. Satisfied the apartment was clean, he made a phone call to reestablish contact with his control. He had delayed until the last moment in case the phone line was tapped. He wanted to be long gone if a trace led back to the apartment. But he couldn't get through to Cape Town and hung up.

He thought for a moment and considered his next move. He wasn't on an independent operation and it was time to come in out of the cold. He locked the door behind them and took the back stairs to the parking garage where he had found Jason Robby's blue BMW. "You drive," he told Ziba, "and talk to anyone who stops us." He crawled into the passenger's seat and felt under the dash, searching for the Uzi that Robby sometimes carried. It wasn't there.

"Where are we going?" Ziba asked as she headed for the main road.

"Bloemfontein. That's where you want to go and it's on the way to Cape Town."

They made good time until they reached the outskirts of Johannesburg, where the traffic slowed and finally ground to a halt. Ziba got out to see what was causing the delay. Within moments, she was back. "There are soldiers and a roadblock ahead," she told him.

MacKay got out and saw three white men wearing brown shirts walking down the line of cars toward them. They wore distinctive armbands with a red and black imitation swastika, the symbol for the AWB. One of the brown shirts stopped and spoke to the occupants of a car. Suddenly, he raised his submachine gun and fired into the car, emptying the magazine. He jerked the door open and a black woman fell out and sprawled in the road. The man reloaded and walked toward them.

"Go!" MacKay growled, jumping back into the car. Ziba jockeyed the BMW back and forth to turn around. But before she could break free, they were surrounded by the three men.

"Identification," the shooter said in a bored voice. Ziba fumbled in her purse looking desperately for something that would satisfy the man. She finally handed him her driver's license. It wasn't what he wanted and he dropped it. MacKay saw the slight movement of his submachine gun.

"Hey, hold on," he said, surprising the men with his American accent. He reached into his pocket and handed them the ID he had taken off the hit man who had killed Robby and Grawley.

"American?" a soldier asked.

"The last time I checked," MacKay snapped.

The soldier called a sergeant over and handed him the ID card. "The next time you see an identification like this one," the sergeant said, "do not delay the person. He's Iron Guard." He reached into his shirt pocket and extracted his own card. The soldiers huddled around him and examined the two cards. The sergeant handed the ID back to MacKay.

The sergeant nodded at MacKay and marched off, leaving the three brown shirts standing in the dust. "A fuckin' kaffir in the Iron Guard," one of the soldiers muttered.

Slowly, the shooter saluted. "Go in peace, brother," he said, giving MacKay a cold look that carried a hatred the American had never experienced.

Ziba started the engine and pulled out, heading for the roadblock. "That ID saved our lives," she said.

MacKay studied the card. "He doesn't even look like me," he mumbled.

CHAPTER
6

Friday, December 26
Brandfort, South Africa

MacKay drove the BMW slowly through the town, looking for a service station before they ran out of gas. "Where the hell are we?" he grumbled, cutting through the fatigue that enveloped him like a thick fog.

Ziba reached out and touched his face. "Brandfort. We're almost to Bloemfontein."

"About time," he grumbled. They had been on the road for three days since leaving Johannesburg, dodging roadblocks and marauding gangs of looters. Detours had added over five hundred miles to the journey, and twice he had to steal gas. He had managed to snatch six hours of sleep out of the last seventy-two and was exhausted.

"A hell of a way to spend Christmas," he muttered, his words slurred. "We need gas and I gotta find a place to crash. I'm bushed . . . whacked out." He looked at the closed stores and the Christmas decorations. "It looks peaceful enough here," he said, coasting to a stop in the only open service station in town. A friendly black teenager came out and told them the pumps were closed and they needed permission from the local commando to buy petrol. "What the hell is a commando?" MacKay muttered.

"A commando," Ziba answered, "is a local militia of Afrikaners. That's why there has been no trouble here."

MacKay worked the problem and fished the hit man's ID

card out of his pocket. The boy glanced at the card and went rigid with fear. *"Ja, baas,"* he said, hurrying to the pump. MacKay shook his head, sensing the card was very important and he was missing something. I've got to get this to Cape Town, he thought.

Ziba spoke to the boy, getting directions. "There's a hotel we can stay at . . ." Her words trailed off. MacKay was sound asleep behind the wheel, his mouth open.

A hand on his mouth woke MacKay with a start. Instinct, honed by years of training, took over and he grabbed the offending wrist and rolled away, ready for action. With a little cry of surprise, Ziba fell into his arms. He released her and watched as she massaged her wrist. "You snore" was all she said.

"I don't snore," he grumbled, his male ego wounded.

"You do," she said. "But not loudly." She was smiling. "You make little honks."

MacKay looked around, getting his bearings. He was lying in a bed in a small room, it was dark outside, and his clothes were off. He had a vague memory of someone helping him undress and washing him with a sponge. "Where are we?"

"In Brandfort. I found a hotel."

He reached out and touched her. "Thanks. I was really zonked." She responded to his touch and came into his arms, stroking his face. "You are a powerful man," she murmured. "You will make many children."

"I don't want to lose you," he said.

MacKay woke at first light and rolled up on an elbow. He looked down at the woman sleeping beside him. For once, his face was not a horrific mask but soft and smiling. Her skin glowed and was warm to his touch. She turned to him and threw her arms around his neck as she kissed him and slowly stroked his body. She whispered to him in words he did not understand when they made love and then cuddled into his arms afterward. He fell into a deep sleep.

The sounds of children at play woke MacKay and he sat up when he realized he was alone. He started to pull on his pants but stopped when he saw traces of dried blood on his penis. An overwhelming sadness swept over him as he finished dressing. It was truth-to-tell time. When he went outside, he found Ziba sitting at a table outside their small hotel drinking tea. He sat down. "It's peaceful here," he told her, "especially after Joburg."

"There is much you don't see," she told him. "There is much poverty here and life is very hard. Many young people want to escape . . . like I did . . . before they get too old."

"And how old are you?"

"Twenty-four," she answered.

"Why didn't you tell me I was the first?"

"Zulu girls take their virginity very seriously," she replied. "You wouldn't have believed me."

He knew it was the truth. "I love you, woman." That also was the truth.

"That makes me very happy," she said.

"Ziba, who are you? Who are you working for?"

She looked away. "I was Inkatha. They sent me to school and trained me. But after the elections in 1994, I saw the corruption in Inkatha . . . they are no better than the ANC . . . so I left and went to work for the Slavins. Charles, the man who introduced us, was Inkatha. He found me and asked me to meet with you. The *tsotsi* were after him, not you, and I couldn't let you die like him . . . with the necklace."

"Are you still Inkatha?" he asked. She looked at him and didn't answer. Oh, Lord, woman, he told himself, how I want you. But I've still got a job to do. "Stay with the Slavins in Bloemfontein until I can come get you," he said.

"They gave me a telephone number to call when I got to Bloemfontein," she said. "You can call me there."

"I don't want to leave," he said. "But I've got to go."

Saturday, December 27
Whiteman Air Force Base, Missouri

The execute order directing the wing to deploy to South Africa came down two days after Christmas, and within an hour, the mobility processing line was alive with activity as the 442nd moved out. Pontowski walked through the crowd in the hangar, talking to the men and women who were being manifested on the first cargo aircraft. He was surprised that a number of people with packed bags had shown up who were not on the deployment. "Just in case," as one master sergeant explained.

Back in his office, Lori Williams, his new exec, dropped a new stack of requests on his desk from eighteen people asking to be placed on deployment orders. Her name was on top. "The half of the command post not scheduled to go is threatening to mutilate or cripple the half that is," she told him. Pontowski shook his head in mock resignation and smiled to himself. He had seen it before: Morale and mission were linked hand in hand, and when there was a job to do, his people were there.

Tango Leonard stormed into his office twenty minutes later with a message in his hand. "Did you see this?" he asked. "Some dumb dickhead—"

"Whoa, big fella," Pontowski interrupted. "Dickheads by definition are dumb." The easy words calmed the agitated lieutenant colonel and he handed Pontowski the message. "What the hell," he muttered. The 303rd Fighter Squadron was deploying with only twelve aircraft, not its full complement of twenty. "Lori," he called, "get Langley on the phone." He turned to Tango. "I'll sort this out. Meanwhile, decide who's not going if this holds."

The colonel in charge of the deployment at headquarters Air Combat Command was all sympathy when he explained how the number of aircraft and people being deployed were cut back because airlift was not available. "It's simple," he told Pontowski. "Airlift has been broken since the Gulf War. We wore the transports out and they haven't been replaced."

"Colonel," Pontowski said, "I've got a lot of good people here who are willing to do the job. I hope we're not hanging them out to dry because we can't generate the support they need."

The colonel agreed with him and promised he would work the problem. But he didn't hold out much hope for a change. "We're doing this one on the cheap," he said. "Don't expect too much support."

"That's real encouraging," Pontowski snapped, hanging up.

The first of the C-5s scheduled to carry the wing's heavy equipment and advance party to Africa landed before noon and again, Pontowski roamed the flight line. It was an exercise in logistics, moving people and equipment halfway around the world, and what he saw as normal belied the complexity of the system at work. But it was a system that was strained to the limit. Two hours after landing, the C-5 launched and headed for Puerto Rico.

Martha Marshall led Little Matt through the hubbub and confusion that ruled the squadron building. They found Pontowski as he came out of the deployment briefing with a folder stuffed with charts, flight plans, and instructions under his arm. He thanked Martha and picked up his son. "I've got to go," he told the little boy. "I'll be gone for a while. Can you handle that, good buddy?"

His son nodded gravely, his eyes serious, and threw his arms around Pontowski's neck. "I'll be okay, Daddy," he promised. "Don't worry." It was a familiar routine they both found comforting.

"I never worry about you. But I do miss you."

"Will you be gone long?"

"I don't know. Probably a couple of months."

That satisfied the little boy, and he hopped out of his father's arms, now ready for other things. "Good. We can go fishing this summer."

"You got a deal," Pontowski said. He looked up and saw Martha watching them. Tears were in her eyes.

"I love him, you know," she told Pontowski. A quick frown flickered across her face, then disappeared. "You can't do this again. He needs at least one parent in his life." Then she relented. "Go. We'll be fine."

"Thanks, Martha," he said. "I'll make it up to you."

"Promises," she snorted. "You can start by getting married," she called to his back.

Pontowski waited at the door for John Leonard to say good-bye to Sara. He could see them talking quietly in a corner, and like most of the wives who had come to the base, she smiled bravely. My God, Pontowski thought, this is the second time Sara's said good-bye to her husband when she's expecting. The first time had been years ago when her first husband, Muddy Waters, had left for the Middle East and she was pregnant with Melissa. Muddy didn't make it back.

What gives me the right to demand so much of these people? he wondered.

Tuesday, December 30
The South Atlantic

Pontowski came off the refueling boom of the KC-10 tanker and cycled into the slot on the big tanker's right wing. Below, a few white puffy clouds marred the blue of the South Atlantic Ocean that stretched endlessly in front of them toward the coast of Africa. He watched as his wingman, Jim "Bag" Talbot, moved into the precontact position. The hookup went smoothly and Bag stayed welded to the end of the boom. Pontowski shook his head in wonder and decided that Bag's hangover was not affecting his flying.

The night before, Bag had led the pack that had totally destroyed the tranquility of Jamestown on St. Helena, the island in the South Atlantic where Napoleon had died in exile in 1821. But Pontowski couldn't really blame them for whooping it up after flying three long days, first to Grenada in the Caribbean, then Recife on the horn of Brazil, and finally into the South Atlantic, reaching St. Helena after a five-hour flight.

Pontowski hit the UHF transmit switch on the throttle quadrant. "Bag, you copacetic for piddle packs?" The Warthog did not have a relief tube and the pilots had to use plastic piddle packs to relieve themselves. Pontowski calculated that the dedicated beer drinkers like Bag were putting theirs to full use.

"Six down, three to go," came the answer.

"My gawd!" came over the radio. "The boy's going for a record."

"You're welcome to use our facilities," a female voice from the tanker said.

"Would if I could," Bag answered.

Pontowski smiled. The light banter told him all was well. He checked his instruments and shook his head. They were plowing through the sky at 360 knots true airspeed. Luckily, they had a tailwind of 15 knots. It will be headwind on the way back, he thought. Don't start thinking about that yet, he warned himself. You're not even there.

"Rodeo Flight," the same woman's voice radioed, "my copilot tells me we have crossed the Greenwich Meridian. I'd like to be the first to welcome you to your new command."

The Prime Meridian, Pontowski thought. What genius in the Pentagon came up with that line of longitude to transfer the 442nd to United Nations command? I suppose it makes sense, he reasoned. We take off as part of the U.S. Air Force and land as a UN contingent commanded by a Frenchman. He flipped through the paperwork he had stuffed into the leg pockets of his *G* suit until he found the name of his new commander—General Charles de Royer.

Another quick check of his navigation computer—750 nautical miles before they coasted in at Cape Fria. Then another thousand miles to Cape Town. It was going to be a long, butt-numbing day. He hoped Bag had enough piddle packs.

At Cape Fria, the flight of twelve A-10s and two KC-10s turned south and flew down the coast, enjoying the scenery after the long haul over open water. At first, Pontowski couldn't fathom what was different—his fatigue prevented it. As they neared Cape Town, it came to him. The endless blue skies glowed with a brilliance he had never seen before, and far off to the east, the land was marked with a blood-red horizon. The landscape below him was a dazzling panorama of greens and browns cut with mountain escarpments that challenged the sky.

Neat little towns and farmsteads dotted the countryside, and ahead of him, he could see Table Mountain capped by a wispy beard of cloud streaming out to the north. Bag's voice came over the radio. "Say, Boss. Did you know the name of our base, Ysterplaat, means 'Iron Plank' in Dutch? Crazy name for a base." Bag was silent for a moment. "Let's do the recovery right." Pontowski almost laughed. Like all fighter pilots, Bag wanted to make an entrance. "The place sorta demands it," Bag explained.

Pontowski agreed with him. An overhead recovery was the standard landing pattern for fighters returning from a mission. Up to four aircraft approached the runway in an echelon formation at twelve hundred feet. The lead jet pitched out as they crossed the approach end of the runway and the others followed at five-second intervals, descending to land two thousand feet apart. Not only was it an impressive maneuver, it was the most efficient way to get large numbers of aircraft quickly on the ground. "Okay, Hawgs," Pontowski transmitted. "We're going to arrive looking good. Echelon right for an overhead recovery."

Pontowski flew a shallow dogleg to final and rolled out over Table Bay, three miles short of Ysterplaat Air Base. Table Mountain was off to his right and he had a good view of the waterfront and the town. He was impressed. Ahead of him, he could see the air base, its ramp alive with activity. When his flight of four crossed the approach end of the runway, he made the break, pitching out to the left. It was flawless and Pontowski felt good when he landed and rolled out. His Warthog's crew chief was waiting when he taxied in and marshaled him into a parking spot. Pontowski smiled as he watched the last formation of Warthogs land and taxi in. Not a bad beginning, he thought.

A jeeplike vehicle Pontowski did not recognize pulled alongside his jet and a lone figure wearing a South African BDU, battle dress uniform, climbed out. Pontowski scrambled down the ladder and the man greeted him with a salute. "Welcome to Cape Town, Colonel Pontowski." He spoke English with a heavy but clear Afrikaans accent that made Pontowski think of Holland. "I'm Captain Piet van der Roos, your liaison officer."

Pontowski returned his salute, taking the man in. He judged van der Roos to be in his early thirties. He was of average height and his skin was burned brown from the sun. Van der Roos's uniform hung on his lean body, deep creases etched the corners of his hazel eyes, and his dark-blond hair was cut short. His canvas holster and web belt showed signs of repeated scrubbings and the bulky grips on his nine-millimeter pistol were worn. The captain obviously spent most of his time in the field and was not a staff officer cloistered in some headquarters. The embroidered pilot wings over his left shirt pocket reassured Pontowski that van der Roos also knew something about flying.

"General de Royer," van der Roos said, "has ordered you to report to him immediately." Pontowski arched an eyebrow at the captain's use of the word "ordered." Probably a translation problem, he reasoned. Given Pontowski's position, de Royer probably "requested" they meet immediately. As de Royer was Pontowski's superior officer, a request from him would be treated as an order. But it was much more polite.

"The general," van der Roos said, "specifically used the word 'ordered.'" He motioned for Pontowski to join him in the jeep.

Pontowski stripped off his parachute harness and *G* suit, jammed his flight cap on his head, and crawled into the jeep. Van der Roos drove out of the air base and headed for Constantia, the palatial suburb on the southern side of Cape Town at the base of Table Mountain. "Sir," he said, "General de Royer insists on speaking only French. May I suggest you speak English while I translate."

"Why?" Pontowski demanded. "There's nothing wrong with my French."

Van der Roos glanced at him. "No doubt. But perhaps it will help you understand the general better." Then he grinned. "What do you Americans say? Trust me on this?"

They entered a narrow, tree-lined street with large houses, each surrounded by a high wall. Sentries wearing the blue beret of the United Nations guarded a barricade and checked their identification before letting them proceed. "The residence and headquarters of General Charles de Royer, commander in chief of all UN forces in South Africa," van der Roos announced as they turned into the courtyard of the largest compound.

Inside the main house, van der Roos led Pontowski through a series of rooms, each more opulent than the preceding. From the confusion, it was obvious the French peacekeepers were still arriving. "Nice way to fight a war," Pontowski deadpanned. A wry grin cracked van der Roos's face but disappeared as they entered de Royer's outer offices. The general's aide-de-camp, Colonel Valery Bouchard, directed them to a waiting room to cool their heels. Bouchard was a lean, hard-looking man in his midforties with close-cropped black hair. He wore a single black leather glove on his left hand and walked with a slight limp. The left side of his face was a massive burn scar that showed little sign of reconstructive surgery and his left eye stared straight ahead, never moving. "Is that a glass eyeball?" Pontowski asked.

"I believe so," van der Roos replied. "But who is going to ask him?" An hour later, Bouchard escorted them in to the general.

De Royer was standing by a set of tall windows overlooking a garden, his back to the door. He stood at least six feet ten inches tall, his hair was totally white, and he wore an immaculately tailored tan uniform. The shock came when he turned around. General Charles de Royer had the face of a thirty-year-old man and the coldest blue eyes Pontowski had ever seen. Not a single medal or badge marked the austerity of the general's uniform. Bouchard made the introductions and then retreated to stand by the door.

"Colonel Pontowski, why did you arrive with only twelve aircraft?" de Royer demanded in French. "I was promised twenty."

Pontowski answered in the same language, not waiting for van der Roos to translate. "We only had airlift to support twelve, sir."

De Royer fixed Pontowski with a cold stare. "Captain van der Roos," he said, not taking his eyes off Pontowski, "your function is to act as an interpreter in my headquarters. Does the colonel understand that?"

"Please accept my apologies for speaking French," Pontowski said in English. "I thought it was adequate." Van der Roos translated.

"When will the transport aircraft arrive?" de Royer asked.

"I was told to expect the C-130s on the sixth of January," Pontowski answered after the formality of translating was finished.

"Please tell Colonel Pontowski," the general said, his

voice rigid and flat, "that he now falls under my command and I expect him to respect my position. In the future, he will not wear a flight suit in my headquarters." He waited until van der Roos had translated. "I also expect Colonel Pontowski to respond as a subordinate officer. Explain it to him in a manner that he will understand. I expect my wing to be ready to commence operations on the seventh of January."

He turned and walked back to the window while van der Roos translated. The interview was over and Bouchard held the door open for them to leave. Pontowski spun around and forced a tight control over his anger. He had been stepped on hard and someone at the Pentagon needed to know about it. But who? His orders had been explicit: He took his operational orders from de Royer and his logistical support came through the U.S. Air Force.

Van der Roos said nothing until they were in his jeep and on the road to the air base. "Perhaps you have a sense of the general. Yes?"

"Mais oui," Pontowski replied. He bit off the words. He was a good officer and wouldn't say more.

But van der Roos didn't suffer from the same reservations. "The general is *un trou du cul,"* he said. He had called de Royer an asshole in French. "The only other French cuss word I know is *merde* and it didn't seem adequate."

"That works too," Pontowski replied, "especially since we just stepped in it." The two men exchanged glances. They were going to be good friends.

CHAPTER

7

Monday, January 5
Cape Town, South Africa

Erik Beckmann walked down Burg Street and entered the foyer of the office building next to the bank. He took the stairs and trotted up to the third floor, careful to avoid being seen. He carefully opened the stairwell door and made sure the hall was deserted before taking the few steps to the corner office. A brassy blonde in a black leotard and tights answered the buzzer and held the door open for him. Inside, two girls, both stylishly dressed, stood up. "Is Reggie available?" he asked. Beckmann was in the best whorehouse in Cape Town.

The blonde's lips made a pretty pout and she led him to a back hall. "Last door," she said, leaving him on his own.

Beckmann slipped down the hall and opened the door. "Reggie," he called softly.

A young man came out of a back room and smiled. "Erik, what a surprise. More of the same?" Beckmann nodded and followed him into a brightly lit room. It was a modern computer and photographic laboratory filled with the latest processing and printing equipment.

"The ID card you made for me was an excellent fake," Beckmann said. Reggie smiled at the praise. "It was very easy to penetrate Iron Gate," Beckmann continued. "Unfortunately, you are selling them to others . . . the wrong people. I've got to stop that." The small automatic was in Beckmann's hand.

"No," Reggie whispered, holding up his hand to block the bullet. A loud "phuut" filled the room. Beckmann fired a second time. He walked around the room, methodically destroying the equipment. He fired a single shot into the holographic camera and destroyed its fragile array of lenses. He devoted most of his attention to the computer bank, making sure the programs were erased before disassembling the computers and destroying the circuit boards. Satisfied, he double-checked the room to ensure it was clean of any fingerprints.

Beckmann gave a mental sigh. There was still the problem of the girls. He walked back down the hall.

Richard Davis Standard sat at an outdoor table at the coffee shop on Burg Street looking like any overweight, balding, middle-aged businessman who suffered from high blood pressure and a nagging family. It was an image Standard had perfected over the years, and few would suspect his real role as CIA station chief in South Africa. He glanced at the office building across the street, satisfied with the payoff that had put him on Erik Beckmann's trail, and fumbled with a cigarette. He hated smoking, but his best radio was disguised as a cigarette lighter. "Did he get by you?" he asked.

"I don't think so," a woman's voice answered. "He's still on the third floor. Hold on. Here he comes."

"Don't lose him," Standard said. There's always hope, he thought. Maybe this time "the Boys," his team of four very talented women, could stay on Beckmann's tail. Standard stood, dropped some money on the table, crossed the street, and entered the office building. Like Beckmann, he took the stairs at a brisk pace, hardly feeling the effort, until he reached the third floor. Which office? he wondered as he walked the hall, checking the signs. He stopped in front of the one that announced "Golden Escorts" and listened. Nothing. He knocked and when no one answered, tested the handle. It was locked. He wrapped his left hand around the knob and twisted. The lock snapped and he was in.

"Ah, shit," he groaned. The bodies of three women were on the floor. He keyed his radio. "Beckmann left his calling card at Golden Escorts." He stepped over the bodies and searched the bedrooms. Why? he asked himself. He found the hall and followed it to the lab. He was not surprised to see the other body but he could suddenly taste the coffee he had been drinking. Why blow the guy's face off? He examined the debris Beckmann had scattered around the room.

Again, he keyed his radio. "Get the Boys up here."

Tuesday, January 6
Ysterplaat Air Base, Cape Town

Pontowski was standing on the ramp with de Royer, waiting for the C-130s to arrive. The bevy of officers who made up the general's staff were clustered behind them in a form of close-order drill that made Pontowski think of an amoeba on parade. Only Colonel Bouchard, de Royer's aide, stood apart, keeping his own counsel. His fire-scarred face was turned to the west, scanning the sky. "There," he said, pointing with his gloved hand.

As one, the amoeba turned its head to the west as the first two C-130 Hercules appeared over Table Bay. The squat, high-winged, four-engined turboprop cargo aircraft came down final at traffic pattern altitude in a tight formation, the distinctive sound of their engines filling the sky.

In the distance, a mile in trail, Pontowski could see two more dark-gray Hercules approach from over the bay. With an airman's critical eye, he graded the first formation as they pitched out for an overhead recovery. Perfect, he decided. He chanced a glance at de Royer. There was no reaction from the tall Frenchman. But that was to be expected. De Royer was an Army officer and didn't even wear jump wings. He doesn't know what he's seeing, Pontowski decided.

Lockheed had rolled the first C-130 out of its plant in the mid-1950s, and the Hercules quickly became the unsung workhorse of the U.S. Air Force. It did yeoman labor in Vietnam in the 1960s and early 1970s hauling cargo, troops, and wounded. Because of its rugged construction and outstanding maneuverability, a few were modified into gunships, the fearsome ghost of death called Spectre. Later variants were developed for special operations and could airdrop cargo at high speed and low level under the most appalling conditions.

But the Hercules landing at Ysterplaat were normal trash haulers from the 314th Wing out of Little Rock Air Force Base, Arkansas, and these particular aircraft were older than most of the crews flying them.

The first C-130 touched down on the runway and rolled out to the end as the second came across the runway threshold. The second formation of two was at traffic pattern altitude approaching the break.

The first C-130 to land taxied clear of the runway and past the waiting officers. The pilot nudged the throttles and varied the pitch of the propellers, playing a tune. Pontowski could have sworn he heard the distinctive beat of "The Marseillaise," the French national anthem. Then the escape hatch over the flight deck popped open and a flag was shoved up and unfurled. The Stars and Stripes rippled in the wind as the Hercules taxied past. Then the aircraft stopped and the pilot reversed props, backing the big bird up and turning, pointing the aircraft's nose directly at Pontowski and de Royer. The pilot tapped the brakes, the nose rose into the air as the cargo plane stopped, and then came down, executing a neat little bow.

Pontowski chanced a look at de Royer. The general was looking straight ahead, his face as frozen as ever. But for a moment, Pontowski thought he detected a flash of life in his cold blue eyes.

The second C-130 taxied to a halt and backed into its parking position, this time without the bow. The crews and passengers on board were deplaning and lining up in front as the third and fourth C-130s landed and taxied into their parking slots. A lone figure in a flight suit split off from the group in front of the first C-130 and walked across the ramp. It was a woman. As she neared, Pontowski could read her name tag and make out her rank—Lieutenant Colonel Lydia Kowalski. The star surrounded by a wreath on her pilot wings announced she was a command pilot with years of experience and thousands of hours in the air.

Kowalski was a big, rawboned woman, almost as tall as Pontowski, and her dark hair was pulled back into a severe bun on the back of her neck. Strands of gray laced her hair, crow's feet accentuated her dark eyes, and she walked with an easy gait born of a confidence gained from thousands of hours of flying and countless missions. She stopped in front of de Royer and snapped a sharp salute.

"A most unusual entrance," he said in French, returning her salute. "You are?"

"Lieutenant Colonel Lydia Kowalski, detachment commander for the 314th Wing."

De Royer bisected the woman with his dead-fish stare. "You," de Royer finally said, "are now under my command. I do not approve of this type of display, and in the future, all landings will be normal." He waited for Piet van der Roos to translate, staring over Kowalski's head at the horizon.

"Yes, sir," Kowalski answered, saluting the general. Again, he returned her salute. She executed a perfect about-face and marched back to her waiting crew.

De Royer fixed Pontowski with the same dead-fish look. "Report to my office tomorrow afternoon with your operations officer. Colonel Bouchard will arrange the time." Without waiting for the formality of a reply, the general turned and walked to his waiting staff car. His amoebalike staff split and scurried for their cars.

"A true sack of *merde*," van der Roos said.

"*Mais oui,*" Pontowski agreed as he headed for his office.

Wednesday, January 7
UN Headquarters, Constantia,
Cape Town

Pontowski, Tango Leonard, and Piet van der Roos presented themselves at exactly four o'clock to de Royer's adjutant. Again, they had to wait, but this time, Bouchard offered them coffee or tea. "I apologize for the delay," he said in English.

Pontowski sensed an opening and accepted the offer. He spoke in French, "Colonel Bouchard, may I ask what your background is. You don't fit the image of an aide-de-camp."

Bouchard's face was impassive as he answered. "At one time, I was a company commander in the 2ième Régiment Étranger Parachutiste. General de Royer was my commander. Later, I commanded the regiment."

Pontowski was impressed. The Second Foreign Parachute Regiment was the most famous of the Foreign Legion's nine regiments and considered the equivalent of the U.S. Rangers. "I didn't know the general was a legionnaire," he said.

The intercom buzzed and Bouchard escorted them into de Royer's office. "It is time," the general said, keeping them standing, "to discuss your function in my command. The A-10s are of course needed for a show of force. But the C-130s, which arrived yesterday, are essential because only they can carry out the humanitarian part of our mission. That is why I went to the air base for their arrival."

Pontowski braced himself for a tirade on Kowalski's arrival. But de Royer did not mention it. "It was my understanding that your government was going to send a squadron of twelve C-130s, not four. When may I expect the others?"

"I don't know," Pontowski replied without waiting for a translation. "But I'll find out."

De Royer stared at him while van der Roos translated the entire conversation, including Pontowski's answer. "Do that. Have the C-130s ready to start operations tomorrow. Dismissed." The four officers turned as one to leave. "Colonel Pontowski," the general said, "remain for a moment." He waited until the others had left. "As of now, you are assigned to my headquarters as my air operations officer."

"May I ask why the change?" Pontowski replied, hiding the anger that was building inside.

"As you insist on speaking to me directly, we must give you a reason."

"And I must object," Pontowski said. "My place is with my wing."

"Your place is where I say it is. Further, given your new

position, you will not fly without my permission. Also, I will require a briefing on air operations every morning." He turned to face the window, dismissing Pontowski.

Leonard and van der Roos were waiting for him in Bouchard's office. "I can't believe this," he told them. "I've been kicked upstairs as his air operations officer." A genuine look of surprise crossed the right side of Bouchard's face, but he said nothing. "Tango," Pontowski continued, "you'll have to run the wing."

Leonard sat down. "Holy shit . . . this sounds like what happened in China when Von Drexler tried to do the same thing." The memory of General Mark Von Drexler, the commander of the American Volunteer Group in China, was still painful for both men. Von Drexler had been a brilliant logistician and strategist but had lost his way, seduced by power and freedom of action. The dark inner needs of his egotism had driven him deep into a megalomania that had destroyed him.

"This is a different situation," Pontowski said. "De Royer is not Von Drexler. So let's play it as it goes down—for now. Piet, will you be my aide and translator?"

"But your French is very good, better than mine."

"How true," Bouchard muttered in English.

"But I don't speak Afrikaans," Pontowski explained.

"It would be my pleasure," van der Roos told him. "The first word you must learn is *braaivleis*. A friend is giving one this afternoon."

The "friend" van der Roos had mentioned was the most beautiful woman Pontowski had ever seen. He held back, taking her in, while van der Roos introduced Leonard and Bouchard. She was tall and well-proportioned. Her dark hair was pulled back off her face and gathered on the nape of her neck with a light-blue scarf so it tumbled down her back in wavy disarray. Her high cheekbones and full lips gave her face an exotic look that he couldn't place. She was wearing a man's white shirt with rolled-up sleeves and exposed a generous amount of cleavage that gave no hint of a bra. The bottom buttons on the side of her full denim skirt were undone, showing most of her left leg.

Her dark eyes studied his face as van der Roos introduced him. "Elena, this is my new boss, Colonel Matthew Pontowski. Colonel, Madame Elena Martine, the head of the United Nations Observer Mission to South Africa."

She shook his hand in a very European manner, firm and brisk. "Well, Colonel Pontowski, Charles has told me so little about you. Perhaps it is time for us to become acquainted. Do you prefer to be called Matthew or Matt?"

"Matt is fine, Madame Martine."

"Please, I prefer Elena. Madame makes me sound so old and dreadful." Her laughter destroyed the last of his defenses. "Please, join us and enjoy yourself." She moved on, leaving Pontowski in a slight daze.

"Where did she come from?" Leonard asked, not expecting an answer. He was seriously reconsidering his marriage vows.

"Who is Charles?" Pontowski asked.

"I believe she was referring to General de Royer," Bouchard answered.

"What does Elena do?" Pontowski asked.

"The UN Observer Mission?" van der Roos replied. "It's a holdover from the elections in 1994. No one is exactly sure what they do now. They have a big staff, a bigger budget, villas like this one for business, and they travel around a lot, looking at things. They spend much money, which makes the merchants happy. Come on, I'll show you around and introduce you to the other guests." He led the three men through to the back garden.

Pontowski soon learned that *braaivleis* was Afrikaans for barbecue and most of the guests were from the UN or the diplomatic corps, or were black politicians. The wife of the U.S. ambassador recognized him and ushered him over to her husband, who was locked in an intense conversation with another man. "Dear," she sang out, "look who I found."

"Ah, Matt," the ambassador said. "I was hoping we would meet." He turned to the other man and made the introductions. "General Beckmann, I'd like you to meet Colonel Matthew Pontowski." The two men shook hands.

"My pleasure, Colonel," Beckmann said. "I've heard so

much about you." He stared at Pontowski, his gaze direct and unblinking.

"General Beckmann commands the Iron Guard," the ambassador said.

"So I've heard," Pontowski replied. "I was given to understand the Iron Guard is the AWB's militia."

"We are an independent force for stability," Beckmann replied, as if that explained everything.

Pontowski sensed a rigidity and strength behind the man's bland exterior. "I was hoping to meet some Afrikaners tonight."

Beckmann looked around. "We are in short supply here. We mean nothing to these people." Suddenly, he came to attention and jerked his head in a short nod. "It has been my pleasure, Colonel." He spun around and walked away.

"Whatever got into Hans?" the ambassador's wife asked. "Normally, he is such a gentleman."

Pontowski mouthed the appropriate words and ambled away, still uncomfortable with the brief encounter with Beckmann. Why the hostility? he wondered. Rather than mix, he found a bench on the veranda to sit and take it all in.

Elena joined him for a few moments, ever the perfect hostess. "I see you met Hans Beckmann," she said.

"If you could call it that," he told her.

"He said he wanted to meet you," she replied. "Probably a professional interest." She gave him a dazzling smile. "I must attend to my other guests." He watched her as she moved away. She walked with a long stride and her legs flashed in the torchlight that ringed the garden.

"Your mouth is open, Colonel," a voice said. He turned to see a pretty young woman standing behind him. "Samantha Darnell," she said, introducing herself. "I'm Elizabeth Gordon's videographer."

Great, he thought, the press. I don't need this. He recovered by giving her his best grin. "I hope I wasn't drooling."

"You were close," she said. Silence. Then, "Her mouth is too big."

He gave a low laugh. "Otherwise, she'd be perfect." He

changed the subject and motioned at the party. "This is all very new to us. We only got here a few days ago."

"I know," she said. "I covered your arrival. That was a flashy landing."

"It's called an overhead recovery. There's a reason for it."

"I'm quite sure there is."

He caught the condescending tone in her voice. Civilians, he moaned to himself. He gave her his best smile. "We normally fly in pairs or fours. When we recover, we're usually low on fuel, maybe ten or fifteen minutes remaining at the most, and want to get on the ground fast. Besides, there may be more aircraft right behind us, equally low on fuel. An overhead recovery is the fastest way to get a lot of aircraft quickly on the ground."

Pontowski didn't tell her the tactical reasons and how an overhead pattern minimized exposure time in the landing pattern. If given half a chance, he'd jump into an enemy landing pattern and shoot down any aircraft flying a normal pattern to land. He saw no need to tell a member of the press that his job was to kill people and that he was good at it.

Sam studied him for a moment. He wasn't what she expected, and she wanted him to be a Neanderthal, a goose-stepping moral cretin easy to dislike. Why had she talked to him in the first place? Was it because he was one of the few Americans at the party? She was honest with herself and admitted she didn't know.

Piet van der Roos joined them and Pontowski made the introductions. "Are you enjoying the party?" van der Roos asked.

Sam gave him a radiant smile. "Oh, yes," she said.

I bet you are, Pontowski thought. Probably digging dirt to your heart's content. "Me, too," he answered. "But I was hoping I'd meet more Afrikaners."

"My family owns a vineyard and winery outside Paarl," van der Roos said. "It's been in the family for over two hundred years. It isn't far from here. We could go there for lunch. Perhaps this Saturday?"

"Sounds great," Pontowski told him.

"I'd love to see your home," Sam said.

Great, Pontowski thought. Absolutely great.

Thursday, January 8
The White House, Washington, D.C.

Carroll walked slowly across his office, turned and walked back. Halfway across, his left hand reached out and grabbed the edge of his desk. The national security advisor had almost fallen and was exhausted from the slight exercise. He sat down. Damn! he raged to himself, why do the legs have to be the first to go? He was going to miss running. And he would miss the two Secret Service agents, Wayne Adams and Chuck Stanford, who had run countless miles with him.

He buzzed his secretary. "Midge, please have Chuck and Wayne come to my office. Whenever's convenient." How much time do I have? he thought. Should I resign? Do I need to spend more time with my family? Too many questions I can't answer yet.

He leaned back in his chair and fixed his gaze on his latest purchase hanging on the ornate coat stand in the corner. It was a sturdy, plain brown walking cane. It carried a totally different message than Cyrus Piccard's elegant black ebony, gold-handled cane. Piccard's created an image of old-world grace and charm, an extension of his personality. Carroll's cane was pure hospital, and using it was giving in to Lou Gehrig's disease. "No way," he muttered to himself as he went back to work.

South Africa was at the top of his mental agenda, and he sat motionless, bound by the disease eating away at his nervous system. His powers of analysis and concentration had always been formidable, but now he was working at a much higher level, as if his brain was compensating for the weakness of his body.

What does the future hold for South Africa? he wondered. Will tribalism, greed, and gross incompetence drive it down the same road as most of Africa?

The key is Beckmann, he thought. He removed the leather-edged green pad that covered his desk. A computer video monitor was set under the desktop at an angle and covered with a glass plate. For the next hour, only his fingers moved on the keyboard as he called up file after file of information from the government's computer banks. He had access to everything, including the highly classified System 4, the program that tracked all covert intelligence operations being conducted by the United States.

Carroll turned off the computer and called up his mental map of South Africa. He could alter it at will, creating his own holographic image of the country. He overlaid the mix of races and population densities with economic development. Then he superimposed the transportation infrastructure. Finally, he added in the latest intelligence about Hans Beckmann.

He held this new map of South Africa in his mind. In the center of the map an elongated oval occupied the central part of the country, extending from Bloemfontein in the south to Johannesburg and Pretoria in the north. All that remained of the old nation was anchored on Cape Town, the mother city, with most of Cape Province. Natal Province and Durban formed the homeland for the Zulus, and the rest of the country was carved up into small tribal enclaves. The image flickered in his mind and took on an ethnic and racial hue. The map was tribal.

When he was finished, he sat motionless. He had done what no computer could do; he had gotten into Beckmann's mind. You and the AWB are going to create the Boerstaat, he thought. How can so few people cause so much trouble? Most of the whites in South Africa, including the majority of Afrikaners, are neutral, willing to live with a black majority if the conditions are right. But the conditions are ripe for a revolution, and it's the haters who drive a revolution. And Beckmann is one of the great haters, the spark that can ignite the mixture.

Carroll closed his eyes. He knew the truth about South Africa. So what is the next step? he thought. Pure intelligence gathering could only take them so far. Was it time for a covert operation? His intercom buzzed. "Adams and Stanford are here," Midge said. Carroll told her to send them in.

The two agents stood in front of his desk and shuffled their feet as the national security advisor labored to stand up. "Bad news," Carroll said. "No more running." The two agents nodded as one. "The quacks say that I've got ALS, Lou Gehrig's disease."

Adams and Stanford exchanged glances. They would have to tell their superiors so the Secret Service could adjust its routine and be ready to meet any emergency, but other than that, silence went with their job. They wouldn't even tell their wives.

"Mr. Carroll," Adams said, speaking for the two men, "if it's all the same to you, we want to stay on your detail."

"I appreciate that, but isn't standing post for the president and undercover work what gets you promoted?" Carroll asked.

"Like we give a damn," Stanford said.

"Lunch?" Carroll asked. "My treat." He walked over to the coat rack and picked up the cane. "Another old friend," he said, leading the two agents out the door.

"Say," Stanford said, "I know this neat little place on Columbia . . . if you like great Italian, and got the time."

"Sounds good," Carroll said. He would make the time.

CHAPTER

8

Pontowski made his way down the hall, surprised by the activity in de Royer's headquarters. He had counted on using the peace and quiet of a weekend to settle into his new office and work the hundreds of details necessary to start operations. A file bulging with messages and faxs was on his desk, demanding his attention and confirming his impression that de Royer was a hard taskmaster.

He sat down and sorted the file into three stacks: those he would have to take care of, the ones for Leonard, and those consigned to the trash can. The last message was from the Military Personnel Center at Randolph Air Force Base near San Antonio, Texas. "Damn," he growled. It was the results of the colonels selection board, and Lieutenant Colonel Lydia Kowalski, the C-130 pilot from Little Rock, had been passed over for promotion to colonel.

Pontowski had never experienced the crushing disappointment of being told he had not been promoted, had not been considered good enough for higher rank, that others were more qualified and deserving, and that he had better start looking for a job on the outside. He bowed his head and thought. Less than 40 percent of all lieutenant colonels were promoted to colonel and while Kowalski was undoubtedly fully qualified, she was not the best qualified. Affirmative action was not a player, not when the decisions a colonel made could result in people being killed. But what were the right words to say? He didn't know. He called the wing at Ysterplaat and asked that Kowalski report to his office that morning. He still had to find the words. But at least Tango Leonard had made it.

Lydia Kowalski came out of Pontowski's office and took a deep breath. What the hell, she told herself. The fucking Air Force strikes again. What did I expect? How far can trash haulers, and women, go in this man's Air Force? I should have taken a headquarters assignment and not stayed in operations. You've got to shove paper to get promoted these days.

She walked out of the headquarters mansion determined to take the rest of the day off and find a quiet and remote place to drink. She didn't recognize Sam Darnell, who had arrived for the lunch date at the van der Roos winery with Pontowski and Piet. It might help if I looked like her, Kowalski groused to herself.

Sam was dressed in a white jumpsuit and stylish low-heeled shoes. She had rolled up her sleeves and exposed a fair amount of cleavage. Her hair was pulled back and carefully arranged, the work of a beauty salon. Unconsciously, she had entered into a competition with Elena Martine.

Van der Roos kept glancing in the rearview mirror as he drove, trying to gauge what was going on in the backseat of his Mercedes. Nothing, he decided. Pontowski and Sam were acting totally correct and had said little during the drive to Paarl. Even the black South African private riding shotgun had been more communicative. Van der Roos waited, wondering who would see it first.

Sam was the first. "Oh," she said. "What's that?" She pointed at the impressive, three-spired monument on the side of the mountain overlooking the Paarl valley.

"This," van der Roos said, turning up the road to the monument, "is the *Afrikaanse Taal*. It is a monument to our language, Afrikaans. The two smaller pinnacles represent English and Bantu and are designed to lead into the much taller obelisk."

"It reminds me of a catapult," Sam said, "aiming sky-ward."

"Exactly," van der Roos said. "Afrikaans is the catapult." He parked the car and they walked into the monument while the guard remained behind. "The words embedded in the walkway," van der Roos explained, "mean 'we are serious.'" He fell back, letting the two Americans walk ahead, alone.

Sam stood at the overlook, taking in the magnificent view and the cloud-studded sky. Pontowski joined her, standing a few feet away. The wind whipped at Sam's hair, and in her own way, Samantha Darnell was stunning. She wasn't a classic, sophisticated beauty like Elena Martine, but whole-some and athletic. "I wish I had brought my camera," she said. "It's beautiful up here."

"That's probably why they chose this site," he allowed.

"I'm impressed," she said.

"It is a lesson."

Sam turned and looked at him, surprised by his reaction. "Really? In what way?"

"It shows how Afrikaners think. Ask yourself, Why a monument to a language? Language is the bedrock of any culture, a growing, living thing. But you celebrate it by building libraries or theaters for the performing arts, not monuments on hillsides."

She looked away, reevaluating the man beside her. Much to her surprise, he could think. She hadn't expected that. The military were supposed to be rigid robots, blindly reacting to orders, never questioning. "So what do you see here?"

"The Afrikaners giving the finger to the world."

A surprised "Oh" slipped out and she was angry at herself for squeaking. At least his last response was true to stereo-type.

Piet van der Roos leaned back from the lunch table on the patio of the van der Rooses' Cape Dutch homestead. He listened to the talk and was pleased that his father and Pontowski were getting along. Jan van der Roos was a big, burly man with a full head of white hair and bright blue eyes. His huge hands, worn and calloused, showed the ravages of a lifetime of hard work, and he spoke a heavily accented English with the confidence of a man who knows his place in life. Like most Afrikaners, he had a quick temper, but he was a warm and hospitable host, genuinely glad to have Pontowski and Sam as his guests.

"The lunch was superb," Sam said. "Thank you."

The elder van der Roos raised his wineglass. "A pretty woman and a good wine make any meal a success." Sam blushed at the old-fashioned compliment.

"And this is excellent," Pontowski said, holding his glass to the light and swirling the dark red wine. "It's a shame you don't export it to the States."

"But we do!" Jan boomed. "We have been exporting more and more since the elections in 1994, when the trade sanctions were lifted. I can't meet the demand." He pushed back from the table and stood up. "Come, I'll show you my vineyards." He turned to Sam, "Please come too. I hope it will not bore you."

Sam smiled. "Your gardens and house are so lovely . . . may I look around here?"

Sam's reply pleased the old man. "Of course, of course. My daughter will show you around. Aly has been busy with some tourists in the wine-tasting cellar." He turned Sam over to a young black girl and led Pontowski and Piet to his new Land Rover. "Business has been very good since the elections," he said. "Very good."

"My father is planting more vineyards," Piet explained as they drove through the fields.

"And hiring more boys," the elder van der Roos added. He stopped the Land Rover and they got out. A black foreman and six workers hurried over to meet them. Pontowski listened as Jan spoke in an unfamiliar patois with the workers.

"*Ja baas,*" the grinning foreman said, "it goes well with the vines. Next year, even better." A repeated chorus of "*Ja baas*" rained down. The workers obviously liked and respected the old man.

After a few minutes, they were back in the Land Rover, heading for a new field. "They want raises," Jan said.

"Inflation is very bad," Piet said.

"*Ja*, it is. I will give them all a raise, but not too much money. Better I pay them in food and clothes for their families."

"It is a problem if we pay them too much, too soon," Piet explained to Pontowski. "They want to gamble, get drunk, and won't come to work. Then our production drops."

"Why don't you fire them and hire someone who will come to work when they should?" Pontowski asked.

The elder van der Roos snorted, a bit of his temper showing at the American's lack of understanding. "They are my boys. I can't fire them because of what they are. The young ones are learning and will do much better. Until then, we must go slow and take care of them."

Aly van der Roos was a very pretty, very big, fair-haired young woman. She shared the good-natured temperament of her father, and like his, her hands were hard and calloused from work. She showed Sam around the wine cellars, proud of what her family had accomplished over the years. "We don't get many tourists these days," she said. "Many came right after the elections, but they stopped coming when the troubles started."

They walked outside and into the shade of the oak trees that had been planted over a century before. Most of the tables were deserted except for a small group of German tourists who were working on their tenth bottle of wine and one lone woman sitting off to the side. "She's an American," Aly said. "She's very quiet but is getting very drunk. I'm worried about her."

Sam recognized Lydia Kowalski from earlier that day when they had passed at the UN headquarters. "I know her," Sam said, "I'll talk to her." She walked over and asked if she could sit down. Kowalski looked up, recognized her, and gestured at a chair. She took another drink.

"Are you okay?" Sam asked.

"Just getting drunk," Kowalski said, carefully pronouncing each word.

"It doesn't help," Sam replied.

Kowalski fixed her with an odd look. "Have you ever been drunk?" Before Sam could answer, she changed the subject. "You're here with Pontowski?" Sam nodded. "I saw you arrive but he hasn't seen me. I'm one of the nobodies, you see. We're invisible. Especially to promotion boards." Sam realized Kowalski was very intoxicated and it was best to let her talk. "I'm a trash hauler. Fly C-130s. Haul cargo. Trash haulers don't get promoted." She waved her glass in front of Sam. "Zoomies get promoted, jet jockeys get promoted, golden boys get promoted, not us trash haulers."

"Is Pontowski a golden boy?" Sam asked.

Kowalski nodded, thought about it, then nodded again. "He has sponsors." She started to babble and Sam had trouble following her disjointed sentences. Then she understood. Lydia Kowalski had been passed over for promotion to colonel. She had given everything she had to the Air Force, had risked her life many times, and had given up any hope of a raising a family. "My marriage was a disaster," she told Sam. "I needed a househusband and he wanted to pursue his own career. So I chose the Air Force . . . just like the men do when they have to make the choice."

"Is it Pontowski's fault you were passed over?" Sam asked.

Kowalski's answer surprised her. "No. It's not." The pilot pulled herself up straight. "Don't tell him I'm here. I need to sober up."

Sam motioned for Aly to come over. "We need some coffee," she said. "Everything will be fine." Aly smiled and left. "Lydia, please tell me about Pontowski. What's he really like?"

"He can be a real bastard. But sometimes, I feel sorry for him. His wife was killed . . . terrorists."

"I heard," Sam said.

"It was a hit contract on him," Kowalski said. "They got his wife instead. He's trying to raise his son alone."

Sam probed deeper. "Wasn't he involved in a midair collision?"

"Yeah. Jack Locke was killed. Locke was the best damn pilot who ever strapped on a jet. I was with him on Operation Warlord. That son of a bitch could really fly. So can Pontowski. They were flying a mission during an Operational Readiness Inspection and Locke had a puke from the IG team in his backseat . . . a real shithead named

Raider. Anyway, Locke and Pontowski were going one-on-one and really mixing it up. Raider couldn't take the pressure and panicked. He tried to take control of Locke's jet and crashed into Pontowski's wing. It's all in the accident report. But Pontowski took a lot of heat for it because he survived."

Sam's voice was gentle. "Lydia, I think you like him."

"You either like him or hate his guts. The Warthog drivers will follow him anywhere." She paused. "I'll follow him anywhere, too. And I just met the son of a bitch."

Sam rode in silence during the trip back to Cape Town, thinking about the man beside her. She looked out and saw heavily armed black soldiers, one about every hundred feet, standing beside the road. "Why the soldiers?" she asked.

"They are here to guard the motorway," van der Roos replied. "That shantytown over there"—he pointed to his left—"is Khayelitsha. Over half the people who live there are under sixteen. There is no work and many of the boys have joined gangs. They steal, attack cars, and kill people. They have a saying, 'One settler, one bullet.' When they say 'settler,' they mean anyone who is white."

The black soldier riding shotgun next to van der Roos turned around. "They always chant it in English. When you hear it, run."

"But we're Americans," Sam protested.

"It makes no difference," the soldier replied. "You are white."

The soldier's words stunned Sam. "Do all Africans hate the whites?" she asked.

The guard gave her a big smile. "No, lady. We like the whites. For most of us, the white man is the source of a job. That's all we want." After they had passed Khayelitsha, the guard tensed, his hands clamped around his R-4 assault rifle. "No black will stop here or go to that side of the road."

Van der Roos pointed to the right side of the road, to what looked like a huge campground of tents, trailers, and RVs. "This is our newest settlement. We call it Trektown."

Pontowski saw the difference at once. "But they're white," he said.

"*Ja,*" van der Roos replied. "They are our new *trekboers.*"

"Trekboers?" Sam asked. She had never heard the name before.

"Boer," van der Roos explained, "is the Dutch word for farmer. Trekboers were itinerant farmers who followed their livestock. The trekboers left the Cape in the 1830s on a great trek, a journey or migration, into the interior and were called *voortrekkers*. They fought many battles with the tribes they met. They circled their wagons into a defensive laager to fight. We built a monument to the voortrekkers on a hill outside Pretoria. It is a big square granite structure surrounded by a laager of granite wagons and is a shrine to the Afrikaner spirit."

"Afrikaners do like building monuments," Pontowski said.

"That is true," van der Roos replied. "We want to leave our mark on the land for all to see."

"Why did the trekboers leave the Cape in the first place?" Sam asked.

"To be free of the British who had taken over the Cape," van der Roos replied.

"Were your family voortrekkers?"

"No. We were boers, not trekboers."

"Why are the Afrikaners coming back now?" Pontowski asked.

"For two reasons," van der Roos replied. "To be free of the black governments that are ruling their provinces and for protection. They have heard the chant 'One settler, one bullet.' "

"Trektown," their guard said, "is a laager."

Monday, January 12
Cape Town, South Africa

MacKay made his way down the crowded sidewalk toward the Broadway Industries Centre. After the madness of Johannesburg, the streets of Cape Town were an oasis of calm with people going about their business. Occasionally, some passerby, always white, would glance at him. But it was never with the hostility he had experienced in Johannesburg.

He entered the main foyer, where a middle-aged white security guard stopped him. "What's your business?" the guard demanded.

"I've an appointment with the business attaché," MacKay replied. He was maintaining his cover and acting like a businessman, getting lost in the daily shuffle of commerce. It was all part of his tradecraft as he reestablished contact with his control. It was straightforward and did not require the cosmic gadgets loved by TV and the movies. The hard part was to establish a legitimate cover and then make sure no one penetrated it.

A few minutes later, MacKay was talking to Richard Davis Standard, the business and economic attaché. Standard looked like any middle-aged, overweight businessman dressed in a rumpled suit. But in reality, he was an experienced CIA agent who had seen service in Argentina, Spain, Greece, and Turkey. "Where the hell you been?" he demanded.

"It's tough out there," MacKay answered. "I was lucky to get out of Joburg."

Standard conceded the point. "I heard. Bad business there with Robby and Grawley. That was a nice touch with the shoes on the other body. It even fooled us at first. By the way, who was he?"

"The asshole who shot them," MacKay told him. "I took this off his body." He handed Standard the hit man's ID card and gun. "That ID opens a lot of doors with the AWB. I staked out the office and Hans Beckmann showed up." He let Standard draw the obvious conclusions.

He did. "I'm not surprised. Agents have a habit of turning up dead around Beckmann." Standard drummed the table with his blunt fingers and didn't mention the mangled body of the Japanese agent that the Boys had found. "Beckmann and trouble go together like stink on shit. He showed up here along with his brother, Erik. Now there's another nasty piece of work." He examined the ID card. "We can use this." He dropped it in his desk drawer. "How did you get here?"

"Through Bloemfontein," MacKay answered. "I dropped Ziba off at the Slavins'."

"So the Israeli is at Bloemfontein. We lost track of him in all the confusion and rioting."

"Ziba mentioned something about the Boyden Observatory," MacKay said. "She had a phone number to call." He gave Standard the number.

Standard grunted and placed a phone call to verify the number. "That's not a Bloemfontein number," he told MacKay. "It's at Iron Gate, Beckmann's base, about fifteen miles north of Bloemfontein."

"Damn," MacKay muttered. Ziba was back in the thick of it.

Standard caught MacKay's reaction and again drummed the table. Was MacKay fit to go back into the field? Was he compromised beyond recovery? But MacKay had an agent in place, and that was too good an opportunity to ignore. What the hell, Standard thought, intelligence is like a pool game—it's all recovery and position. The wires to Langley would buzz with the news that they were still on the track of Prime. "Can you reestablish contact with Ziba?" he asked.

"It's already arranged," MacKay told him.

Standard relaxed. Gengha Dung, the CIA's division chief for Sub-Saharan Africa, was going to be one happy lady. She had been nicknamed after Genghis Khan for her dictatorial ways, and Standard's head would not be served up as a sacrificial offering to the DCI, the director of central intelligence, to atone for the failures of her division. "We'll set you up with a new ID and cover," Standard told him. "We'll go full throttle but it will still take a couple of weeks."

MacKay walked to the window. "It seems so normal here."

Standard joined him. "There are problems, especially in the townships. But the situation is different here. Half the population is Cape Colored and the other half split between whites and blacks. The Coloreds have a different attitude than the blacks. They're like cockneys . . . cheerful, witty, with a strong survivalist spirit.

"The government is still very much in control in the Western Cape. The South African Air Force and Navy have a strong presence here and are still loyal. The betting is they will stay that way unless they are ordered to fight the AWB.

It's a different story with the Army. About a third have gone over to the AWB. Luckily, they took little with them." Except for a few nukes, he mentally added.

He walked over to a map. "But the government cannot control the violence and famine that's breaking out in the interior. That's why they called in the UN peacekeepers and relief agencies." He slapped MacKay on a shoulder and walked him to the elevator. "Stay in the Ritz Protea at Sea Point. We'll contact you there."

After MacKay had left, Standard returned to his desk and opened the drawer. He picked up the ID card and carefully examined it. He punched at his intercom and rang up the basement. "Get the Boys," he said. "We've got work to do."

Wednesday, January 14
The White House, Washington, D.C.

The two Secret Service agents walked slowly, following the national security advisor as he walked through President's Park on the south side of the White House. A convoy of three limousines drove up the circular drive from East Executive Avenue to deposit some foreign dignitary at the south portico. "Why does it always happen to the good guys?" Wayne Adams asked. He was the older of the two and considered himself the more philosophical.

"Who knows?" Chuck Stanford answered. "Why do the scumbags always survive? Son of a bitch! I've got a few candidates I'd rather see this happen to instead of him." He thought for a moment. "It's changed him." Carroll stumbled and the two darted forward but stopped when they saw he had regained his balance. "He won't give in to it," Stanford said.

One step at a time, Carroll told himself. Don't let the monkey ride you. Who am I kidding? Wayne and Chuck? They know. So enjoy the walk while you can.

Carroll sat on a bench near the tennis courts. Two junior White House assistants were playing, taking advantage of the break in the weather. Carroll watched them for a moment. They were a vigorous, healthy young couple, both married, but not to each other. He wanted to warn them what would happen if they stepped across the foul line and crawled into the same bed. He allowed a little smile to cross his face. Very few people understood the power structure in the White House.

The earphone in each agent's ear spoke. "How about that," a woman's voice said. "He actually smiled." They weren't the only agents on duty.

Stanford lifted his hand and spoke into his whisper mike under his cuff. "He *is* working, asshole."

"My, we are being protective today," the voice replied, her words silky smooth.

Indeed, the national security advisor was working. On one mental level, he recalled factual data, while on another level, he rearranged the hard facts into combinations, trying to create a reality. But more important, he wanted to peer into the future. Repeatedly, he came up against the impenetrable wall that surrounded the enigma called Prime.

Cold fusion, he mused to himself. Was it only a dream? How was the Israeli scientist doing it? According to the CIA, Slavin was using two isotopes of hydrogen, deuterium and tritium, and forcing their hydrogen nuclei to fuse without exploding or melting down. Carroll was not a physicist so he found it ironic that two substances, which were basically the same, could combine in so many different ways, and the result could be either disastrous or the hope of the future.

But did it work? Was he wasting his time when he should be concentrating on more important issues?

"Sir, are you all right?" It was Adams's voice. Carroll looked up, surprised that it was raining. The two agents were standing over him, holding umbrellas. The couple had left the tennis court and for a brief moment, Carroll wondered if they would ever get safely together. Then he made the connection—people and hydrogen fusing to make new combinations. The two agents helped him stand and he walked, more slowly, back to his office.

"Isn't it ironic," he told them, "that Prime is happening in the country where the same thing is happening to the people." The two agents walked beside him, not understanding what he was talking about, their umbrellas held over his head, keeping him dry.

CHAPTER
9

Pontowski stood up from his desk, walked to the window of his office, and stretched. Outside, moonlight cast a gentle, soothing glow over the gardens and veranda. He watched as a tall figure, de Royer, walked slowly back and forth. His hands were clasped behind his back and his head bent, deep in thought. So you're frustrated too, Pontowski thought.

His own frustration level ratcheted up to a higher level as he considered the problems facing the UN. We've been here almost three weeks and haven't done a damn thing, he told himself. What we need is a concept of operations . . . some idea on how to go about this. He settled back into his chair and grabbed the UN manual on peacekeeping operations.

Twenty minutes later, Bouchard appeared in his doorway. "General de Royer requests you join him in his office." Pontowski stood and they walked quickly down the hall. Bouchard spoke in French. "Madame Martine and the South African minister of defense, Joe Pendulo, are with the general. Be careful what you say. Pendulo remembers everything and understands nothing." Pontowski thanked him and entered de Royer's office.

As usual, the French general was wearing his dead-fish look. Only this time, his cold stare was fixed on Joe Pendulo. What a pleasant change, Pontowski thought, glancing at the minister of defense. Pendulo was a short, wiry Xhosa whose beard was trimmed into a goatee. A diamond ring flashed on each hand, and he wore a gold Rolex watch that hung loose on his wrist, much like a bracelet. His dark silk suit was tailored to his slender frame and his legs were crossed, revealing expensive, hand-stitched shoes and white socks. *What have we got here?* Pontowski wondered.

Elena was sitting in the chair next to Pendulo, looking cool and beautiful in a white linen business suit. The coat was snared at her waist and gave the impression she was not wearing a blouse. It was both businesslike and provocative. *How does she do it,* Pontowski wondered. Her low voice matched the seductive image as she made the introductions. "We are discussing the UN's area of responsibility."

"The stability of my country," Pendulo said, "is being threatened by a small group of white fascists." His voice was in total contrast to his image, and he spoke with an upper-class British accent. "Are you familiar with the AWB?" Pontowski nodded. "Unfortunately, they have an army, the Iron Guard. We want you to destroy it."

"Why don't you use your own forces?" Pontowski asked.

"The leadership of our Defense Forces is entirely white and I cannot guarantee their loyalty if I order them to attack their white brothers. Better they remain in garrison than desert."

"The United Nations cannot do what you ask," Elena told him. "We are here in a peacekeeping function. You are asking us to take an active role in supporting the government against the AWB. That is peace enforcement, which is beyond our charter."

Pontowski expected Pendulo to explode in a temper tantrum. It didn't happen. "What do you intend to do?" the defense minister asked, his voice reasonable and calm.

"It is our intention," de Royer said, "to establish safe zones as we did in Bosnia."

This is the first I've heard about it, Pontowski thought.

Pendulo looked pleased. "That is acceptable to my government. As you know, many of my people are starving because of the instability caused by the AWB and its thugs. Will you use these safe zones for humanitarian relief?"

"That is our intention," de Royer replied.

No sign of emotion crossed Pendulo's face. "Then my government will provide protection, not your forces. If there is trouble, you must coordinate through my office."

What good will that do with the South Africans in garrison? Pontowski thought. But before he could object, Elena answered. "Agreed."

"You," Pontowski told them, "have just taken away our right of self-defense."

"How so?" Pendulo asked.

Pontowski decided to let his anger show. "If anyone starts shooting at us, we can't do squat all about it until we 'coordinate' through your office. We're sitting ducks."

"Then keep your aircraft on the ground," Pendulo replied, as if he were speaking to a child. He stood to leave. "It is late," he said. "I must go." Elena escorted him out and Pontowski gritted his teeth until the door was closed.

"General," Pontowski said, "that little shit is using us. We either do it his way, or we get the livin' crap shot out of us by any thug who wants some target practice. No way am I going to put my people in that kind of situation if—"

"The decision has been made," de Royer interrupted.

"Fuck me in the heart," Pontowski muttered, loud enough for de Royer to hear.

"Colonel," de Royer said, giving no indication that he had heard, "schedule a C-130 to fly a survey team around the country to identify safe zones. Madame Martine will be in charge of the team and you will accompany her. The worst food shortages are in Northern Cape Province, so we will start there."

"And the A-10s?"

"Keep them on the ground. That will be all." He turned to look out the window.

Pontowski stormed out of the office. We've got to get the hell out of here, he told himself.

Wednesday, January 21
Northern Cape Province, South Africa

Pontowski shifted his weight, trying to find a comfortable position on the crew bunk that served as a bench at the back of the C-130's flight deck. He was bored and envied the pilots who were flying the C-130, caught up in the action of the survey mission. He shuffled through the notes on his clipboard and rank-ordered the three airfields they had already surveyed as possible safe zones for UN relief centers. He handed his list to Elena Martine, who was sitting beside him making her own choices. One more to go, he thought. Then we can go home.

"You sure that's it?" Captain Rob Nutting asked over the intercom. He was flying in the left seat of the C-130 as it approached the landing strip on the south side of the town of Mata Mata.

"Yeah, that's it," Lydia Kowalski answered. She was giving Rob Nutting an in-country checkout and was playing copilot to his aircraft commander while he flew Pontowski and the survey team around. So far, he had done an outstanding job. She keyed the intercom and spoke to Elena and Pontowski. "This one doesn't look very promising," she told them. "Too isolated, not enough people. Do you want to land and check it out?"

Elena came forward and studied the land below her. Everything the pilot had said was true. But according to her notes, there was abundant water at this strip and that was a definite plus. "Let's land," she decided.

"Do you have enough runway?" Pontowski asked, not liking what he saw.

"No problem," Nutting assured him. "It's just a bit narrow. We'll do an assault landing on this one."

"Sounds good," Kowalski said. Rob was on top of it.

Pontowski scanned the field with his binoculars and focused on a group of villagers gathered on the left side of the landing strip. "Looks like we've got a reception committee," he said. He and Elena strapped in on the crew bunk while Rob flew a standard pattern and brought the C-130 down final, nose high in the air. "I got some kid standing on the right side of the runway," Kowalski said.

"Got him," Rob told her. "No problem."

The pilot slammed the big cargo plane down on the exact point he was aiming for. Just as he raked the throttles aft, Kowalski saw movement off to the right side. The kid she had seen moments before was running across the runway.

"Look out!" she shouted. But it was too late. Rob had committed to the landing and had lifted the throttles over the detent, throwing the props into reverse. They felt a slight bump.

If a high-speed camera had filmed the landing, it would have recorded the main gear sinking into the surface and pushing up a small wave of dirt in front of the tires. As the wheels emerged from the depression, the dirt flowed back into place, leaving tread marks and some wrinkles to mark the C-130's touchdown point. The camera would have also recorded a ten-year-old boy being sucked under the right gear and disappearing into the depression before being thrown up against the underside of the fuselage like a flattened rag doll.

What the camera could not record was the fear that had driven the boy across the runway. The size and noise of the Hercules had totally overwhelmed him and the only refuge he could see was his father—standing on the other side.

The props threw a cloud of dust and debris out in front as the Hercules howled to a stop. Pontowski and the loadmaster were the first off, checking for damage. All they found were a few wet brown stains on the fuselage aft of the right main gear and a piece of cloth hanging on the gear door. Rob joined them as they finished inspecting the aircraft. "I killed a kid, didn't I?" The anguish in his words matched the look on his face.

Before Pontowski could answer, a group of villagers surrounded them. A man carried the mangled remains of his son and yelled while two women sent a loud keening lament over the crowd.

Elena Martine climbed off the Hercules and headed for the three Americans. A hand reached out and grabbed her shirt, ripping it while another woman pushed her to the ground. The villagers had finally found scapegoats for all their troubles. Pontowski heard Elena scream and pushed through the crowd. But two men blocked his way, yelling and pointing at the dead child. Elena screamed again, and Pontowski bulldozed his way through with Rob and the loadmaster right behind him.

Kowalski heard the shouting, jumped out of her seat, and ran back through the cargo compartment. She reached the rear ramp in time to see Pontowski, Rob, and the loadmaster standing back to back as they were hit and kicked by the angry villagers. They were holding their own but not for long.

She ran back onto the flight deck and jumped in the left seat. "Starting three!" she yelled at the flight engineer as she cranked the right inboard engine. They quickly brought the left inboard engine on line. "Riley," she shouted at the flight engineer, "sit in the right seat and keep 'em revved up." She grabbed her helmet and ran for the rear of the aircraft.

"Follow me," she yelled at the three men from the UN survey team still standing in the cargo compartment. They didn't move. "Come on!" she roared. Still, they made no attempt to follow her. "Screw you!" She pulled her white helmet on, lowered the green visor, and picked up a tie-down chain. She was going it alone.

Lydia Kowalski was a big woman, strong by any standard, and full of resolve. She jumped off the ramp and headed for the villagers, swinging the chain. A man saw her and froze. She had emerged out of the blowing dust like a demon from hell and the C-130's blaring engines were her war cry. The man wanted none of it and started to run. But he slipped and fell into his comrades, yelling incoherently. Now they saw her, and like him, they ran. The riot was over and only the Americans and Elena were left behind with a small body.

"What the hell happened?" Kowalski shouted as she picked Elena up off the ground. She was bruised and dirty, but okay.

Rob pointed at the body. "I hit the kid," he yelled.

"Let's get the hell out of here," Pontowski shouted. "Before they come back."

Thursday, January 22
UN Headquarters, Constantia,
Cape Town

Piet van der Roos was waiting for Pontowski when he came to work an hour later than usual. It had been a long night sorting out the aftermath from the survey mission, and Pontowski had waited for the results of the blood tests before returning to his quarters. Both pilots had tested free of any drugs or alcohol, which, for Pontowski, ended the incident. He had told them it was sad but not their fault. Now the aftershocks of the mission were reaching him.

"Pendulo was on TV last night," van der Roos told him. "He said the UN was responsible for the accident and the pilot will be held accountable. Whites can no longer kill blacks without fear of justice."

"Lovely," Pontowski grumbled. "Absolutely, fucking lovely." He filled a coffee cup and drank. He still needed one more cup to clear the cobwebs of sleep away. "He never asked for our version of what happened."

"Pendulo's turning it into an issue," van der Roos told him. "He wants to control the UN and make it do his bidding."

"What will he do next?"

Van der Roos shook his head. "I don't know. He's a very clever man and wants the presidency."

The answer came just before noon when Bouchard appeared in Pontowski's office. "The general wishes to see you," he said. "It is about the survey mission."

Pontowski took the few steps to de Royer's office and found him, as usual, standing at the window. Doesn't he ever sit down? Pontowski wondered. "I have spoken to Madame Martine," de Royer began, speaking in French. "Minister Pendulo has asked the minister of justice to swear out a warrant for the arrest of Captain Nutting, the pilot on yesterday's mission."

"Martine was there," Pontowski said, "and she knows what happened. Didn't she explain it to Pendulo? I thought that was her job. The kid ran in front of a landing C-130. What the hell did he expect Nutting to do?"

De Royer stared at him, unblinking. "The warrant is for Captain Nutting's arrest," he repeated. He turned to look out the window and Pontowski assumed the meeting was over. De Royer's voice stopped him as he left. "You have a little time," the general said.

"Yes, sir," Pontowski replied. Now what does that mean? he wondered. Then it came to him. De Royer was telling him that he had some time to act before the warrant was served. "I'll be damned," he muttered to himself. He grabbed his hat and ran to his car.

The Operations building at Ysterplaat was all but deserted when Pontowski entered. The duty officer, Gorilla Moreno, looked up from his desk, glad to have someone to talk to. "I need to see Colonel Leonard and Colonel Kowalski—now," Pontowski said. "And get Rob Nutting in here ASAP."

"Colonel Leonard is flying," Gorilla told him. "Colonel Kowalski is in her office and Rob has the day off. I think he went down to Victoria Harbor with a couple of the guys."

"Gorilla, find Nutting. Get every warm body you got and search until you do. But get him here. Quick."

"Yes, sir," Gorilla said as he reached for the phone.

Pontowski found Kowalski in her office wading through the inevitable paperwork that greeted her each morning. "The South Africans are swearing out a warrant for Nutting's arrest," he told her.

"That sucks, Colonel."

"Tell me," Pontowski replied. "There is no way I'm going to let one of my troops end up in a foreign jail over this." He paced the floor, thinking. "Cut leave orders for Nutting. Backdate them four days . . . before the survey mission. Lay on a C-130 to fly him out . . . anywhere but Africa."

"We came through St. Helena," she told him. "It's a British dependency. Will that do?"

"Perfect," Pontowski said. "Lydia, we haven't got much time to bring all this together. Maybe an hour. You better get someone to pack for him."

She gave him a worried look. "I gave him the day off."

"I know. Gorilla is organizing a search for him."

A South African Army major and two MPs, one white and one black, walked into Operations an hour later. First Lieutenant Lori Williams, Leonard's executive officer, was waiting and greeted them with a severe formality far beyond her normal manner. The sight of a tall and pretty black woman wearing the uniform of a U.S. Air Force officer wasn't what they expected.

"I have a warrant for the arrest of one of your pilots," the major said. He handed her a copy of the warrant.

Lori carefully read the warrant, which was in three languages, one of which was English. "I'll present this to my superior," she told them. "Please wait here." She walked slowly down the hall to Kowalski's office. The stall was on.

Outside, Pontowski was waiting by a C-130, his personal radio in his hand. The aircraft was preflighted and the crew on board, ready to go. Even Nutting's suitcase was there. But no Nutting. His radio squawked at him. "Bossman, this is Groundhog. We have a situation that requires your presence in Operations. Over." The command post controller's rigid use of correct communications protocol warned him that someone was monitoring the radios and the warrant had arrived.

"Groundhog, this is Bossman, standby one. I have a problem with maintenance. Break, break. Gorilla Control, this is Bossman. Say status of parts. Over."

Gorilla's voice came over the radio, scratchy but readable. "Bossman, this is Gorilla Control. We have the parts and are delivering them to the aircraft. ETA fifteen minutes. Over."

Good work, Gorilla, Pontowski thought. "Roger, Gorilla Control. Break, break. Groundhog, Bossman is inbound to Operations. ETA five minutes. Over."

"Groundhog copies all. Over and out."

We just might pull this one off, Pontowski told himself. He told the crew to start engines in five minutes and call for clearance. He drove slowly to Operations, arriving six minutes later. In the distance, the C-130's engines were spinning up.

Inside, he was introduced to the waiting major and presented a copy of the arrest warrant. He took his time reading the document. "This does appear to be in order," he said.

"Of course," the major replied.

"Unfortunately, it will have to be presented to our embassy."

"There is no diplomatic immunity involved," the major said. "We have jurisdiction in this matter."

Pontowski paused. He could hear the C-130 taxiing out.

"There is a problem . . . I believe Captain Nutting has left for the States on leave." He turned to Lori. "Lieutenant Williams, please verify the status of Captain Nutting."

Lori was into the game and she made a phone call. "We processed leave orders . . . ah . . . last week. He has signed out but we don't know if he has departed the base yet."

"We will seal the base and search for him," the major said.

"Please do," Pontowski said. "May I suggest you start at his quarters." Lori called for a sergeant to show them the way and ushered the three men out the door.

Gorilla came in with a big grin on his face. "We found him at Victoria Harbor sightseeing. He's on the plane." The sound of a C-130 taking off reached them.

Lydia Kowalski came out of the command post. "They're airborne," she said.

Lori started to laugh. "I have never heard so much rogering, overing, outing, and break-breaking in my life. This was like a Boy Scout camp. But you did skin and grin the man." It was the highest compliment she could pay them.

Friday, January 23
The White House, Washington, D.C.

The intercom on Carroll's desk buzzed. "Congresswoman Nevers is on line one," Midge said.

Carroll picked up the phone, surprised that Nevers was calling him. The animosity between them was deep-seated and extended far beyond any political rivalry. "Carroll here," he said. As expected, he was talking to Nevers's secretary, who put him through to the congresswoman. It was one of the minor irritating games played in Washington to establish who was top dog. But he was long past that.

"Bill," Nevers said, sounding cordial but businesslike. "I'm concerned about a report from South Africa that one of our airplanes was in an accident where a child was killed. I understand the South African government wants to arrest the pilot."

"That's basically correct," he told her. "It was a regretta-

ble but unavoidable accident. A boy ran right in front of a
C-130 when it was landing. There was nothing the pilot
could do."

"Nevertheless," Nevers replied, "it raises many questions
about what we're doing in South Africa."

"There are always questions," Carroll said. "Why don't I
send you all the messages and reports we have on the
accident and you can decide for yourself."

"That would be fine," she said. "As you said, it appears to
be a regrettable but unavoidable accident. One of the facts
of life we have to live with. Thanks for the help." She broke
the connection.

What's that all about, he wondered. She actually sounded
friendly. Has she changed her position on the UN? Probably not. Is she being reasonable for once? Or maybe she
wants to declare a truce.

He lay back in his chair, willing to wait.

It was late afternoon and Carroll was clearing his desk to
go home. Mary had a family reunion planned over the
weekend and many members of his family had flown in.
Midge came to the door of his office and caught his
attention. "CNN is interviewing Nevers on TV," she said.
He nodded and she turned on the TV.

A reporter was standing with Nevers in the hall of the
Capitol. "This is an outstanding example of why we should
not be in South Africa," Nevers said. "Unfortunately, our
pilot was the cause of the accident . . ."

So much for reason and facts, Carroll thought. "Turn it
off," he said. There was no truce.

CHAPTER

10

Thursday, January 29
Cape Town, South Africa

Elizabeth Gordon was oblivious to the perfect summer morning outside the window of their bungalow overlooking Sea Point. "Damn, Sam," she complained, "one of my contacts at Government House slipped and mentioned something called 'Prime' when we were talking about nuclear weapons. I tried to follow up, but it's like running into the Great Wall of China. During the interview with Pendulo yesterday, I pushed as hard as I could without asking, 'Oh, by the way, Mr. Minister, what about the rumors that you have nuclear weapons and are going to bomb the shit out of the AWB?'"

"Maybe you should have," Sam replied. "Sometimes a direct question is the only way."

"Not with that little creep," Gordon replied. "All he wanted to do was get his hand up my skirt."

"Thank goodness you were wearing pants," Sam replied.

"Sam, our coverage is blowing the other reporters here out of the saddle. But if I'm going to stay ahead of them, I need to get out of Cape Town. So I've arranged an interview with Hans Beckmann, the general who runs the Iron Guard. It's on for Monday and I'm leaving tomorrow. That will give me the weekend to look around. No cameras are allowed so I'm going solo." She paused, carefully considering her next words. "How are you getting along with Pontowski?"

Sam shook her head. "There's nothing there, Liz. It was just a chance meeting at a party and an opportunity to do some sightseeing. There might be a good story up in the wine country." She didn't mention the conversation she had had with Lydia Kowalski.

"Look," Gordon persisted, "you've got an in with Pontowski. Use it. Get some coverage of the relief work going on at the base and develop Pontowski as a source. Who knows? He might slip up and say something he shouldn't."

"I don't use people that way," Sam told her.

"You use people or they use you," Gordon replied.

Pontowski opened his car's sunroof and savored the fresh morning air as he made the ten-mile drive from the air base to the UN headquarters in Constantia. He was spending more and more time at the headquarters as the UN got its act together. Several times, he had considered moving from his room in the officers' quarters at Ysterplaat to Constantia. But each time, he had rejected the idea. The traffic slowed as he passed the University of Cape Town. A large number of students were going to classes and he gauged approximately half were black. That's a good beginning, he thought.

He parked his car next to a pearl-white BMW sports coupe with a diplomatic license plate. He trotted up the steps into the main building. "Is that Madame Martine's car?" he asked the guard at the entrance. The guard confirmed his suspicion. She hasn't been around since the fiasco at Mata Mata, he thought. He ran through his mental list of action items for the day as he made his way down the hall. High on the list was the reminder to call his son that evening. He had called the night before and spent fifteen minutes talking. Better than nothing, he told himself. But not being with his son was a void in his existence.

Piet van der Roos was waiting for him. "The general wishes to see you," he said.

"No doubt with Madame Martine," he replied.

Van der Roos gave him a surprised look. "Well, yes . . . how did you know?"

"I know everything." Pontowski grinned. He picked up a folder labeled ROE and entered de Royer's office. He had been waiting for this opportunity. As usual, de Royer was standing at the window, gazing at the garden. An image of a prisoner standing at a cell window yearning for his freedom flickered in front of Pontowski. He did a mental double-take when he glanced at Elena. She was still composed and beautiful, but no amount of makeup could hide the bruises on her right cheek and leg where she had been viciously kicked.

"I convinced Mr. Pendulo," Elena began, speaking in French, "that Captain Nutting was not responsible for the accident at Mata Mata. And of course, Captain Nutting will be welcomed in South Africa when he returns from leave."

That will be one cold day in hell if I have anything to say about it, Pontowski thought. You only get one shot at my troops.

De Royer's cool façade never cracked, but Pontowski sensed he was pleased with the outcome. "Of more importance," de Royer added, "the government has agreed to my plan to set up safe zones in the interior." He turned to a map on the wall. A line of five small red circles marched across Northern Cape Province and into the Orange Free State. All were in the Great Karoo, the thirsty land north of the Nuweveldberge mountain range.

"Vanwyksvlei," the general explained, pointing to the middle safe zone, "is most in need. A ground team is in place and ready to receive supplies. We will commence airlift and convoy operations tomorrow."

"I am very worried that we are moving too fast," Elena said. "Tomorrow's too soon, too rushed."

"We are ready to go," de Royer said. "The team is in place and has set up a distribution center with the local government. Why should we delay further? People are starving."

"It is a matter of security," she told him. "We cannot afford another Mata Mata and I'm not sure if the South Africans will provide protection."

"We can protect ourselves if we change the ROE," Pontowski told her.

"ROE?" Elena asked.

"Rules of Engagement," Pontowski explained. "When Pendulo took away our right to self-defense and you agreed to it, you changed the ROE."

"I really thought you understood," she murmured. "It is a condition of our being here." Then, her voice much stronger, "I cannot change the rules of engagement now."

Who's running the show here? Pontowski thought. Her or de Royer? "Is tomorrow a go?" he asked.

"You know my concerns," she said. "The decision is yours." She rose to leave and extended her hand to Pontowski. "Good morning, Colonel, General." Then she was gone.

De Royer sat down and fixed Pontowski with his usual stare. "We will commence flying relief missions tomorrow," he announced.

"With no change to the ROE?"

"No change," de Royer answered.

"General, that sucks." He was going to push the issue.

"We are still allowed to conduct training," de Royer said. "Speak to my aide. That will be all."

Pontowski left in a quandary. What had Secretary of Defense Elkins told him? He had to "create a command relationship where an American was not the head honcho." No one had suggested it would be so frustrating. Bouchard was waiting for him. "The general said to talk to you about training," Pontowski said, reverting to English.

The right side of Bouchard's face lit up while the left remained frozen. "We have much to discuss."

"Then let's get together tomorrow," Pontowski told him.

When Pontowski returned to Ysterplaat, he went to his quarters and changed into a flight suit, glad to be back to a routine he understood. He made the short walk to Operations and saw a video camera and tripod stacked in a corner. Sam Darnell was back to haunt him. A dark-haired, heavyset captain he had never seen before glanced up from behind the table serving as the ops counter. "Building! Ten-hut." The command echoed down the empty hallways.

Pontowski shook his head. "That's not necessary. You are?"

"Captain Walderman, sir. I just transferred in from the New Orleans Guard."

"Right," Pontowski said, remembering when he had signed off on his application. "You don't look like your photo," he said.

"Well . . . ah . . . I put on some weight."

Tango Leonard walked into the room. "I see you met Waldo. He came in yesterday with the first rotation." Pontowski had set up a schedule by which personnel rotated back to Whiteman every month, and the first replacements had come in the day before.

"Where is everybody?" Pontowski asked.

Leonard looked embarrassed. "There's not much going on, so I gave most of them the day off." He hesitated before continuing. "Boss, I got a problem. Only the C-130s are flying a few sorties. Nobody knows for sure how long we're gonna be here. I mean we're sitting around here with our thumbs up our butts waiting for something to happen."

They walked through the building. Most of the offices were deserted and needed a good cleaning. He had seen it before and knew how closely morale was linked to mission accomplishment. It was time to get the finger out before the malaise spread any further. "Call a staff meeting for thirteen hundred this afternoon. I want every section head and anyone else you can think of to be there. Hogs, Herks, anyone," he repeated for emphasis.

Leonard nodded. "Gotcha. By the way, your friend the photographer is here looking for you. I sent her to the other side of the field to get her out of my hair until you got back. The Froggies have really been busy. You should go over there and see what they're doing."

"She's not my friend," Pontowski muttered, taking his advice. "And no can say 'Froggy' around here."

Lieutenant Colonel Raymond Dureau, the French officer in charge of the UN's relief logistics, reminded Pontowski of a bantam rooster, small, proud, and very combative. He almost strutted as he led Pontowski between two rows of neatly parked white vehicles. "We have forty-two trucks, eighteen armored cars, four medical crash wagons, and two maintenance trucks," Dureau told him. Pontowski was impressed. He had been so focused on air operations that he had missed what the UN was doing elsewhere.

"Your government has also given us the warehouse tents you used in the Gulf War," Dureau said. "But we have only been able to prepare a few loads for delivery by the C-130s."

"What's the holdup?"

"Getting the supplies through customs. We have to bribe the new inspectors the ANC hired to run customs."

Pontowski couldn't believe what he was hearing. "Bribe? Those supplies are for their own people."

"The supplies are for different tribes," Dureau said.

"Why is this the first I've heard about it?"

Before Dureau could answer, he received a message over his personal radio. "Excuse me, Colonel. I am needed in the tents. There is a problem." He snapped a crisp salute and marched off.

Pontowski was about to follow him when he saw Sam walking toward the trucks, her Betacam on her shoulder. He leaned against his car and waited for her to finish shooting. She does move nice, he thought.

"Are you waiting for me, Colonel?" Sam called.

He liked the sound of her voice. "I heard you were looking for me."

Pontowski's radio squawked at him. It was Waldo Walderman. "Colonel, you're needed in the supply tents."

"I'm on my way," Pontowski replied.

"May I come?" Sam asked. "I've never seen the tents." He held the car door open for her.

They had rounded the end of the runway when she asked him to stop so she could get a panoramic shot of the tents. "They're huge," she said. "They look like circus tents—but not as high."

"Those are warehouse tents we first used in the Gulf War," he explained. "Later we used some of them for the Bosnia relief operation." He parked the car in front of the main entrance and they got out. He immediately regretted bringing her when they walked in. Four big men, all well over six feet tall, bearded, and wearing tan uniforms, were gathered in a tight circle around Dureau, dwarfing him.

"They're AWB," Sam whispered, turning her Betacam on.

"Turn the damn camera off!" the oldest of the four shouted.

Sam ignored him and kept on shooting as Pontowski spoke to Dureau. "What's the problem?" he asked.

Relief flooded across the Frenchman's face. "They ordered us to stop loading."

"I didn't say that," the same Afrikaner bellowed. Pontowski pegged him as their leader even though he was not displaying any signs of rank. "I said that only relief supplies can be loaded. Anything that is military in nature is forbidden."

"No problem," Pontowski replied. "We're only in the relief business."

"We will inspect all cargo to make it so," the Afrikaner said. "Without our approval, nothing leaves this tent. We will shoot down any airplane or destroy any truck carrying cargo that has not been cleared by us."

Pontowski's face turned rock hard and he stared at the man, forcing him to look away. "That would be a very bad mistake," he said, his voice low and quiet. But his tone carried a conviction backed with steel and resolve. "A very bad mistake," Pontowski repeated. Sam turned her camera on him, making sure she captured the sound of his voice.

The Afrikaner tried to regain control. "We have authorization from Madame Martine. She insists that the UN remain totally neutral and has ordered you to—"

"Wrong again," Pontowski interrupted, the steel in his voice still cutting. "General de Royer has command here, not Madame Martine. You're wasting my time."

Much to Sam's surprise, the Afrikaner barked a command at his men and they left. She shut off her camera. "I never realized Afrikaners could be so arrogant."

"Some of them are authoritarian, anal retentive, goose-steppers," Pontowski said. "Then it's just a matter of throwing more authority around." His face softened and the hard edge in his voice was gone. "But most of the ones I have met are good, decent people."

"Like Piet and his family," she added.

He smiled, drawing her in. "Like the van der Rooses."

"Colonel," Sam ventured, "I'd like to do a feature on you . . . the senior ranking American officer . . . that sort of thing. I'd have to follow you around. But I'll try not to get in your way."

Pontowski thought about it for a few moments. "I prefer to be called Matt," he said. "What exactly do you have in mind?"

"Some coverage of you at work, maybe a shot of your living quarters."

He grinned at her. "To prove what a luxurious life we lead? Come on, I can show you my quarters now and you won't have to come back later."

They left the tent and drove to the officers' quarters. "Separate entrance," he said. "To impress reporters." He opened a side door and they stepped into a sparsely furnished room. A single bunk was pushed against a wall, opposite a desk and chair. The only concession to luxury was a comfortable easy chair with a reading lamp.

She took in the room and shook her head. "The picture on the desk . . ."

"My son, Little Matt."

"Can I . . ."

"Film the room? Sure, go ahead. But I don't think it's going to make the news." He stepped back while she panned the room with her Betacam.

"This is the human element our editors want," she explained. She finished and lowered the Betacam. "Matt, thanks . . ." She smiled at him.

"Come on," he said, suddenly aware he was alone in his quarters with a very attractive woman. "Let's go to lunch in the mess hall and then I've got a staff meeting. You can get an idea how I work."

He ushered Sam through the chow line and they sat with four young airmen. Much to her surprise, she found the men relaxed and at ease with their commander. Afterward, they bussed their own dishes and walked back to the Operations building.

A group of twenty officers and sergeants were gathered for the staff meeting when Pontowski and Sam arrived. Gorilla almost called the room to attention but a warning gesture from Leonard strangled the words in his throat. "Bad news," Pontowski began. "This government-paid vacation to LaLa Land is over." Sam hit the record button and videotaped the meeting.

"Oh, no," a voice groaned in mock despair from the rear.

"Come on"—Pontowski grinned—"how much longer did you expect to go on sucking at the big blue tit of the Air Force?" The staff meeting wasn't what Sam expected and did not meet her image of a rigid military structure. But there was no doubt who was in charge. "It's time to make some shit happen around here," Pontowski told them.

"About time," a woman's voice called from the rear.

"Well, at least one person is ready to do some work," he said. "Okay, here we go. Tomorrow, we're starting a full-up training schedule. If we're not flying relief missions, then we're flying training sorties. Second, I want to turn this pigsty into a combined operations and intelligence center called the COIC." It sounded like "koe-ik" to Sam's ear. "We're going to have a combined operations where we all work together—C-130s, Warthogs, you name it. If it wears an American flag, it's here. Come on, follow me."

Sam followed the group through the building as Pontowski outlined his ideas. "I'm thinking of turning this room into a main briefing room. Think big, at least sixty seats." They continued to troop through the building as he outlined his plan. Finally they were back where they started. "You've got an idea of what I want," he told them. "So make it happen. Don't be afraid to change things around to make it work. But do it. Get the word out to all the troops: If you're not flying, you're here working on the COIC."

Pontowski's next stop was in scheduling with Kowalski and Leonard. "Sam," he said, "you're welcome to stay if you want. But we've got a lot of boring work to do. We're flying our first relief missions into Vanwyksvlei tomorrow."

"Is there any chance I can get on that flight?" Sam asked. Like all journalists, she was always looking for a story and hoping to be in the right place at the right time.

"I'll have to clear it through the general," Pontowski told her. "Be here at oh seven hundred if you want to go."

The building was alive with activity when Sam walked in the next morning at exactly seven o'clock. Gorilla was already at work, leading a team tearing the room apart. She made her way through the debris until she found Tango Leonard. "Where's the colonel?" she asked.

"At the UN," Leonard answered. "He called and said de Royer nixed your going on the flight. But you're welcome here."

Disappointment showed in her face. "I'll hang around," she said. She spent the morning taping the preparations for the first missions. It was a revelation the amount of hard work that was needed to launch just one sortie, and she was at the C-130 recording the onload of cargo when Pontowski drove up in a staff car.

"Sam, I'm sorry. I tried but the Old Man wouldn't approve of any reporters going on this flight."

She nodded. He looked tired, as if he hadn't slept. "Have you been up all night?" she asked.

"I got about three hours' sleep," he told her. "It gets easier after the system is up and working." A small bus drove up and the crew flying the mission got off. Pontowski introduced Captain Jake Madison, the aircraft commander, and his copilot, Captain Brenda Conklin. "Brenda's a fully qualified aircraft commander," Pontowski explained. Conklin looked more like a very pretty blonde college student than a seasoned trash hauler.

Sam came alert, sensing a story of sexual discrimination. "It's not what you think," Conklin told her. "After a few sorties for familiarization, I'll get an in-country check ride. It happens to everyone."

"It seems very arbitrary," she replied.

"But it works," Pontowski said. Sam recorded more action as the crew went through the preflight, started engines, and taxied out.

"What do we do now?" Sam asked.

"Wait," Pontowski said. From the drawn look on his face, she knew he meant "sweat it out."

"Is waiting the hardest part?" she asked.

Pontowski watched the C-130 as it lifted into the sky. "We train 'em, give 'em the toys to play with, and now we got to trust them to do it all by themselves."

"You'd rather be up there, wouldn't you? With them."

"Any day of the week," he said.

Friday, January 30
Vanwyksvlei, Northern Cape Province

Erik Beckmann sat in the back of the van and listened to the two Africans talk on the radios. This was his first operation with the Azanians and he was appalled by their total lack of radio discipline. Why would anyone back this stupid bunch of kaffirs? he wondered. What decision, or fear, caused OPEC to pour money and arms into the Azanian cause? Did the Arabs think the Azanians were the key to South Africa?

It had been a simple process to sign on with the Azanian Liberation Army after disposing of Reggie in Cape Town. He had flown to Durban and checked in at the George Hotel on Marine Parade overlooking the beach. Then he sat on the front veranda drinking with all the other mercenaries seeking gainful employment until he was approached by the right person. When he was satisfied that he had made contact with the Azanians, he mentioned the right names in the German Red Army Faction to establish his cover. After a large amount of money had been deposited in his Swiss bank account, he was flown to Kimberley. A car had taken him to a large farmstead on the Karoo, where he met the two blacks he was now sitting with in the van outside Vanwyksvlei.

"Do your men understand there must be no shooting?" Beckmann asked. "We need hostages, not bodies." Although the two men reassured him that every single man understood, Beckmann doubted it. Still, they were the tools he needed to give his brother a prolonged hostage situation. Africans, and not the AWB, had to hold the hostages. Eventually, the Iron Guard would free the prisoners and return them safe and sound to the acclaim of the world press. It was simple in concept and difficult in execution because the Azanians lacked the traits needed: patience and discipline.

Bloody stupid kaffirs, he thought. No wonder they need

us. The radio crackled with the news that the C-130 was approaching the landing strip on the western edge of Vanwyksvlei.

"This was the second place we surveyed," Tech Sergeant Riley Stine, the flight engineer, told the two pilots. "We should have called it quits here and never gone on to Mata Mata."

"It won't happen again," Jake Madison reassured him.

Brenda Conklin studied the airstrip and small town spread out to the east. It looked peaceful enough in the afternoon sun, and a small welcoming crowd was clustered on the parking ramp, well back from the runway. She saw a white pickup leading a procession of two flatbed trucks and a forklift across the ramp. "We'll be offloaded and out of here in no time," she told Madison and Riley.

"Not quick enough for me," Riley replied.

Madison greased the landing and taxied clear of the runway as a French soldier wearing the blue beret of the UN held his arms up, showing them where to park. Two other soldiers, also wearing blue berets, were standing by the white pickup. They were the UN ground team responsible for the distribution of the food and medical supplies the C-130 was hauling. "I wish they were carrying guns," Riley groused as they shut down the engines.

"Cock this puppy for a quick engine start," Madison ordered. He got out of his seat to talk to the soldiers. "Everyone stay on board." The memory of Mata Mata and Rob Nutting was still fresh in his mind, and caution was in order.

Erik Beckmann got out of the van and walked to the edge of the low ridge overlooking the town. He raised his binoculars and saw the pallets of cargo coming off the back of the C-130. Not too soon, he told himself. They carry five pallets. Wait until all five are off and the three soldiers have moved away from the aircraft. Divide to conquer. "No!" he shouted, willing the small crowd at the edge of the parking ramp to stand still.

He ran back to the van and climbed inside. "Your men moved too soon!" he yelled at the two Africans. "Damn you!"

Madison saw the crowd start to move and for a long moment, he stood frozen, unable to think. Don't be stupid, he told himself. It won't happen again. He watched the people come at him. Now he could make out their faces. They were not half-starved villagers like those in Mata Mata but young men, fit and well fed. They were chanting words he didn't understand. When they were less than twenty-five yards away, he heard a distinct "Mata-Mata-Mata."

The chant galvanized him into action. "We got trouble!" he yelled at the Frenchmen. "Get on board, we're getting out of here." They ran for the crew entrance as Madison waved his right hand with the forefinger extended in a tight circle above his head—the signal for start engines. Conklin and Riley were ready and the shrill shriek of the auxiliary power unit coming to life split the air. The men leaped up the three steps of the crew entrance and pulled the hatch shut behind them as number three engine started to turn. The ramp at the rear of the aircraft was coming up and the cargo door coming down.

Madison climbed onto the flight deck and settled into the left seat. "Taxi!" he shouted. The big aircraft started to move, heading for the runway. A white pickup truck raced alongside with four men in the back. It pulled out in front of them and blocked the taxi path to the runway. Madison sawed at the small steering wheel on his left and headed for the other exit leading to the runway. But another truck was in front of him, winning that race. Men were running alongside and banging on the fuselage aft of the engines.

"Goddamn it to hell," Madison roared over the intercom. "Have we got enough room to take off from here?"

"Negative," Conklin answered, much calmer.

"Perk," Madison shouted over the intercom at the loadmaster, Staff Sergeant Tanya Perko, "button 'er up."

"Working it," Perko answered. She was chaining closed every entrance that could be opened from the outside.

The pilot cracked the throttles and outran the men who were swatting at the side of the aircraft like ineffectual flies buzzing around an elephant. "Don't let them get at the tires," Conklin told him.

"I'm gonna taxi across the rough," Madison said, turning the Hercules toward the open ground that separated the parking ramp from the runway. But a truck was running parallel to them and cut him off. Madison turned back, toward the center of the ramp. Men scattered in order to avoid the props. Another truck came up on the left side and he turned into it, making it give ground, before he circled back to the right.

"Scanner in the top hatch!" Madison yelled. Riley unstrapped and opened the emergency escape hatch behind his seat. He climbed up and sat on the edge, his feet dangling inside. The navigator, Captain Stan Sims, handed him a headset.

"We're fuckin' surrounded!" Riley shouted. "Keep turning! Fast!"

Erik Beckmann focused his binoculars and watched the C-130 move across the ramp. His lips were compressed into a tight line as the Hercules turned in a wide circle. Again and again, it circled, clearing an area around it. Whenever a truck moved too close, the C-130 headed for it, forcing the truck to give ground. Once, a truck refused to move as the C-130 bore down on it. The driver scampered to safety just as the Hercules turned away. When the tail of the aircraft was pointed directly at the truck, the pilot ran the engines up and the prop blast blew the truck over onto its side, skidding it twenty feet.

Then the aircraft circled again, clearing its arena of any matador willing to challenge or goad it into action. Finally, it sat in the center of the ramp, not moving, a giant bull at bay. The men held back, honoring the circle it claimed as its own.

One of the Azanians joined Beckmann. "Let my men use their weapons," he begged. "They can shoot out the tires."

Beckmann fought down the urge to beat the man senseless. "If we start shooting, the Army will come. Besides, I have seen your men shoot. They spray the air like madmen. We need hostages, not bodies."

"But they are safe inside," the African told him. "If we shoot at the engines or the tires, they cannot move."

Stupid bastard, Beckmann thought. "Tell your men they can shoot if it makes it to the runway and tries to take off. Look, we already have them without firing a single shot. They aren't going anywhere." The man looked confused. Beckmann shook his head, letting his displeasure show. "Soon, they will run out of fuel and the engines will stop. Then we can pry the aircraft open like a tin can. No one will answer their calls for help for two days and by then, we will be gone with our hostages. Now do you understand?"

The Azanian nodded. "Good," Beckmann said. "Bring the officer who was in charge. He disobeyed his orders and moved too soon."

"Ja baas," the Azanian blurted as he hurried back to the van to carry out his orders. Beckmann turned toward the airstrip. The outboard props on the C-130 were stopped and only the two inboard engines were still running. They're conserving fuel, Beckmann told himself. For a moment, he considered using force to end it. No, he thought. Let them send out cries for help on their radios. It is much better to drag it out and show the world that the kaffir government and the UN are inept fools. Better and better. I should have thought of that in the first place. So it takes a little longer. I have the patience and forty-eight hours.

He laughed to himself. Besides, he thought, there is the added pleasure of disciplining the stupid kaffir who bungled the operation to begin with.

Friday, January 30
Ysterplaat Air Base, Cape Town

The command post controller came down from hanging new lights over his control console when he heard the SatCom radio squawk. He picked up the mike and hit the transmit button. "Go ahead, Lifter One. Groundhog reads you three-by." Although the straight-line distance between Ysterplaat and Vanwyksvlei was 275 nautical miles, the command post was patched by fifty thousand miles of skips to a satellite, back to another ground station, back to a second satellite, and finally to the C-130 on the ground at Vanwyksvlei. But the connection was good enough for him to hear every word and press the panic button.

Kowalski was the first through the door and was talking to Brenda Conklin when Leonard came in. "Get the Boss in here quick," she said. "Lifter One is in big trouble."

"I'm here," Pontowski said. Kowalski quickly described the situation. Pontowski's orders came quick and furious. "Tango, get two Hogs overhead Vanwyksvlei ASAP. No, hold on. I want surprise on our side and we don't want to make the situation worse than it is. Tell them to hold at least ten miles away. But if anyone starts shooting at the C-130, they're cleared in hot. Lydia, the Hogs don't have a radio that can reach us here. Get a C-130 with a SatCom there soonest to act as an airborne radio relay. Stay with the Hogs and don't go near the airstrip."

"What's the ROE?" Leonard asked.

"Until I can talk to Pendulo and he tells me otherwise, they're cleared to strafe anybody or anything that shoots at the C-130 or them."

"Got it," Leonard replied as he ran out of the room.

"Boss," Lydia said, "let me take the C-130."

"Do it," Pontowski told her. "You can coordinate the show up there. Go."

Pontowski sat down and thought. He had to pull it all together, but how? "Get me General de Royer on the secure line," he told the controller, "and place a call to Madame Martine at the UN Observer Mission." Within seconds, he was explaining the situation to de Royer. Much to his amazement, de Royer told him to handle the problem and that his aide, Colonel Bouchard, would be over there shortly. He broke the connection.

Martine was next and he asked her to contact the Ministry of Defense and get Pendulo on the line. "Matt," she replied, "he's out of town. I'll try to find him."

"I need somebody to make a decision," Pontowski told her.

"Don't do anything until I get back to you," she said.

Now he ran the numbers through his head: forty-five minutes' flying time to Vanwyksvlei, two-hour loiter time in the area, forty minutes back. That meant a pair of Hogs had to be launching every two hours to maintain a constant cover over Vanwyksvlei. How long was the C-130 good for? In the vicinity of eight to ten hours, if he remembered correctly. He rushed out of the command post to make it happen.

Sam was standing outside. "What's happening?" she asked.

"We've got problems. I'm sorry, but I haven't got time right now."

"Is it okay if I hang around?"

He paused. It was going to get messy. Did he want it all recorded for the public to see? But on the other hand . . .

"Sam, when the C-130 landed at Vanwyksvlei, it was surrounded by a hostile crowd. The crew is trapped inside the aircraft but no one's been hurt and there's been no shooting . . . so far. We're trying to sort it out before anyone gets hurt. You're welcome to stay, but you'll have to stay out of the command post, Intel, or the briefing rooms. Waldo here will take care of you." He turned her over to the A-10 pilot and went looking for Leonard. Outside, he could hear two Warthogs starting engines. Soon they were joined by the sound of a C-130. Good show, he thought.

Pontowski was with Leonard in the command post firming up the launch schedule when Bouchard came in. He was wearing the dark-green battle dress of the French Army and said nothing as he hovered in the background like a grim specter. Elena joined them twenty minutes later. "I can't find Pendulo," she told them.

"So how do we get our people out of this mess?" Pontowski asked.

"The government must respond," she said. "Not us."

"Then they had better get involved or we're going to lose the crew, the UN ground team, and one Hercules."

"I'm sorry, Matt. But we must wait."

"The ground team are my men," Bouchard said. "La Légion Étrangère does not sacrifice its own."

"I didn't know you were legionnaires," Leonard said.

"But of course," Bouchard replied. "As is General de Royer."

Kowalski's voice came over the SatCom. "The Hogs are

on station," she told them, "and we're all up and talking on the UHF. Vehicles are blocking the runway, but other than that, situation is unchanged. The bastards are holding back, afraid of the props."

How long before they start shooting? he thought. That will end the standoff in short order. "Lydia," he asked, "how long can they keep two engines idling?"

"A long time," she answered. "They got lots of gas. I'll work it out and get back to you."

"Colonel Pontowski," Bouchard said, catching his attention. "Perhaps this might be a good time to discuss joint training."

Why now? Pontowski thought, trying to read the meaning behind his words. But there was no clue in the Frenchman's misshapen and grotesque face. "Let's talk in Tango's office," Pontowski said, leading the way.

The moment the door closed, Bouchard came right to the point. "I have a Quick Reaction Force of two hundred men under my command. They are fully trained and can work with the C-130s."

"Are they legionnaires from the 2nd REP?" Pontowski asked. Bouchard confirmed his guess and it all fell into place. De Royer had brought in the Foreign Legion's 2ième Régiment Étranger Parachutiste with the peacekeepers. Now he was going to use it. "What do you have in mind for our first joint training exercise?" Pontowski asked.

An hour later, he was back in Intel, searching for more answers. "What's the threat?" he kept asking. When Intel didn't have the answers, he asked if they had any contacts with the CIA. Again, the answer was negative. Another idea came to him and he went in search of Sam. He found her drinking coffee alone.

"Sam, do you know who the CIA station chief is?"

CHAPTER
11

Saturday, January 31
Cape Town, South Africa

It was just after midnight when Pontowski parked his car in front of the Broadway Industries Centre. The guard at the building's entrance was expecting him and sent him up to the U.S. Consulate on the fourth floor, where Richard Davis Standard was waiting. "What can I do for you, Colonel?" he asked.

At first, Pontowski thought Standard was overweight and sloppy. But something about the man caused him to reconsider. He had an air of strength and sureness that reminded Pontowski of a tiger he had once seen in a zoo. The animal had lain in its cage, looking overfed and lazy, until a teenager had set off a firecracker. The animal had reared and paced back and forth, its muscles rippling under a baggy skin.

"Couldn't this have waited until Monday?" Standard asked.

"Monday will be too late," Pontowski replied. He quickly described the situation on the ground at Vanwyksvlei.

"I'm the business and economic attaché," Standard told him. "I don't see what I can do to help."

"I think you can."

"Who gave you my name?"

"A reporter," Pontowski answered.

"Your reporter has some strange misconceptions about

153

what I do." Pontowski didn't answer. "Of course," Standard continued, "I do talk to different people and hear things. It is possible that you are up against the Azanian Liberation Army. So far they've been mostly a pain in the butt. But lately, there have been reports that OPEC is supplying them with money, arms, and mercenaries to train their army."

"So far," Pontowski said, "no shots have been fired and the C-130 crew hasn't seen any weapons."

Standard paced the floor. "Vanwyksvlei is outside the Azanians' normal area of operations. My best guess is that it's a local political squabble with the Azanians trying to grab the food and supplies."

Pontowski knew that was all he was going to get. But knowing the threat, he could plot his tactics. "Thanks for the help. Sorry I had to disturb you so late."

Standard escorted him to the door. "Colonel, the next time you want to talk to me, call this number." He gave Pontowski a business card for Techtronics International.

Sam had collapsed onto a couch in the COIC, her body aching with fatigue. It amazed her how Pontowski, Leonard, and Kowalski, now that she had returned from the first mission, kept on top of the operation. Not once did they take a break, constantly talking to people, conferring with each other, sorting out the aftermath of the first mission while planning for the next. She stretched and let herself slip into sleep, vaguely wondering where they found the stamina to keep going.

Pontowski tapped her shoulder, waking her. She looked up at his touch and her face flushed, embarrassed that he saw her when she felt so vulnerable. He handed her a mug of steaming coffee. "We're getting ready to launch the rescue mission," he told her. "I thought you might be interested."

She sipped at the coffee and stood up. "Thanks."

Sam walked out to the ramp and waited while two banks of portable floodlights were wheeled into position. She moved around and recorded the action, using the lights to create an eerie effect. A group of forty paratroopers materialized out of the dark and climbed the ramp of the waiting C-130.

She recognized the last man to board, Colonel Valery Bouchard. He resembled a gargoyle from hell, burdened with 150 pounds of equipment. The parachute gave him a humpback and a rucksack bounced underneath his chest-pack emergency chute. A MAT-49 submachine gun was strapped to his right side. But she sensed something different, very dangerous.

It was a strange, surrealistic scene as the engines whined and taxi lights cut through the dark and reflected off the floodlights, sending slivers of light knifing into the night. She maneuvered for position as the C-130 taxied out, followed by four A-10s.

She walked into the COIC and saw Pontowski standing by the door leading into the command post. "What happens now?" she asked.

"We wait," Pontowski replied. She had heard that before, but now she knew what went with it.

Saturday, January 31
Vanwyksvlei, Northern Cape Province

Erik Beckmann crawled out of his sleeping bag, stood up, and stretched. The first light of dawn was cracking the eastern horizon and he could make out the C-130 sitting on the parking apron. But the scene had changed since he went to sleep. He grabbed his binoculars and scanned the area. Only one prop on the C-130 was turning, and the man sitting in the escape hatch on top of the flight deck was using a spotlight to constantly sweep the area.

He climbed into the van and kicked the two Azanians awake. "How long has only one engine been running?" he demanded.

"Since midnight," came the answer.

"And the spotlight?"

"About the same time."

"Why didn't you tell me?" he shouted.

"You were sleeping and it didn't seem important."

A new sound drove him outside. He reached the edge of the ridge in time to see a single A-10 fly down the runway, barely clearing the trucks parked to prevent the C-130 from taking off. It pulled up to five hundred feet and turned hard for another run in. He twisted and saw a second A-10 as it dropped over the one-story buildings on the far side of the airstrip. It buzzed the ramp at twenty-five feet, crossed the runway at ninety degrees, and came directly at him. For a gut-wrenching second, he was immobilized with fear. He dropped to the ground as the big fighter pulled up and turned over his head. The sound was deafening and he covered his ears.

The first A-10 was now crossing the ramp while the second turned in for another run. A C-130 came out of the south and headed for the field. Beckmann came to his feet, his knees still weak, and was thankful that he was not on the field. Then it came to him—they hadn't fired a single shot or dropped a bomb. Beckmann ran to the van, yelling. "Order your men to open fire!"

"But you said . . ."

"We are under attack! Fire!" He ran back to the ridgeline in time to see jumpers streaming out of the back of the C-130. When they reached the end of their twenty-foot static lines, their parachute canopies snapped open. They swung once before landing on the area between the parking ramp and the runway, less than two hundred yards from the C-130.

Erik Beckmann's jaw hardened into stone. Their agent at Cape Town had promised them at least forty-eight hours of noninterference. An A-10 swept down over the ramp and pulled up as its wingman followed two thousand feet in trail. He listened for the sound of gunfire. Nothing. Then another pair of A-10s crossed at a ninety-degree angle. It was a well-orchestrated ballet meant to intimidate the Azanians and it was working.

The parked C-130 was immediately surrounded by a ring of paratroopers as another group ran for the runway. Beckmann watched in disgust as the soldiers pushed the trucks off the runway. The Azanians had not even bothered to remove the wheels. The C-130 that had dropped the paratroopers landed and taxied in as two A-10s flew over. Now the ring of soldiers was fanning out, running for the buildings. He listened for sounds of gunfire. The only sound he heard was another A-10 orbiting the field.

He ran to the van. "Why aren't your men attacking!"

"They are," one of the men answered. Beckmann grabbed him and dragged him out of the van, away from his radio. "What do you hear?" He pushed him to the edge of the ridge. "What do you see?" The only sign of activity on the ramp was a fuel truck moving toward the C-130s. "They broke and ran," he gritted, overlooking his own initial reaction to the A-10s. He pulled out his nine-millimeter automatic pistol and jammed it behind the Azanian's left ear. At least there would be one casualty.

"Ja baas, asseblief baas," Yes, sir, please, sir, the Azanian begged in the only words of Afrikaans he knew.

Slowly, Beckmann lowered his pistol and walked to the van. He ripped the door open and fired, emptying the clip at the man still inside.

Colonel Valery Bouchard stood under the wing of a C-130 and spoke into his radio. Quickly, each of his squads checked in. He dropped the handset into its holder and walked over to the small group clustered around the crew entrance to Madison's C-130. "The area is secure," he told them. "They all ran away." He turned to his three compatriots from the Foreign Legion. "The cargo was ransacked but some of it is still here." He pointed to the buildings.

An A-10 flew by and wagged its wings. "We're in contact with Groundhog at Ysterplaat," Brenda Conklin called from the flight deck. "They want to know our intentions."

The senior member of the UN ground team scratched his beard. "We are here, the cargo is here, the area is secure. Let's do what we came to do. We are ready for the next delivery."

Brenda relayed the message and listened to the reply. "Groundhog says to stand by," she called.

Saturday, January 31
Ysterplaat Air Base, Cape Town

The news that the crew and the C-130 were safe had swept the COIC like wildfire and the hall had reverberated to calls of "Yes!" and "Right on!" and a less appropriate "Shit hot!"

Sam smiled and packed up her gear. She was tired and wanted a hot bath. But before she could leave, Elena Martine and the minister of defense, Joe Pendulo, rushed into the building and demanded to see Pontowski. Things are getting interesting, Sam decided as they disappeared into the command post.

Pendulo dusted off a chair in the command post and sat down. He crossed his legs and fixed Pontowski with a strange look. "You have embarrassed my government," he said.

"Now how did I manage to do that?" Pontowski asked.

Pendulo did not miss the sarcasm. "My government is responsible for ensuring the safety of all its citizens."

"No one in your government responded," Pontowski told him.

Pendulo ignored him. "You also acted without my approval. Technically, you committed an act of war against my country."

"I must protest, Mr. Minister," Elena said. "No act of war—"

"I don't mind repeating myself," Pendulo interrupted. "An act of war was committed."

"No shots were fired," a cold, flat voice said from behind them. It was de Royer. He was standing in the doorway, his head almost touching the lintel. Where did he come from? Pontowski thought. And I didn't know he spoke English. "The airdrop was a training mission and no one was injured," the general said as he dismembered Pendulo with a visual scalpel. His English was flat with no trace of an accent.

Pendulo looked puzzled. "A training mission?"

"Training is a routine part of our operations," de Royer said. The two men stared at each other. It was a contest of wills that Pendulo had to win.

"Return all your people here," Pendulo ordered. "We will inspect your aircraft and equipment to verify that no ammunition was fired. In the meantime, you will fly my inspector general to Vanwyksvlei to verify that no one was injured. We will discuss the matter of UN safe zones later." He strutted out of the command post with Elena right behind him.

"Order everyone out of Vanwyksvlei," de Royer said.

"I think," Pontowski said, "that the jaws of defeat just had victory for lunch."

It was late Saturday night when the last of Pendulo's inspectors left the base. Sam had tried to record them at work, but they had ordered her to turn off her camera. "Why are they so touchy?" she asked Pontowski.

"Because they haven't got a clue what they're doing," he answered.

"Did they find anything?"

Pontowski shook his head. "We showed them that the ammo drums on the Hogs were full and none of them wanted to get within ten feet of Bouchard. The inspectors Pendulo sent to Vanwyksvlei didn't know the UN had pulled out. They wouldn't get off the airplane, much less go into town." He walked outside and looked across the ramp. "Damn," he muttered. "All that for nothing."

It was a moment she wanted to capture and she regretted not having her camera. In the half-light, Pontowski looked much older, aged by fatigue and responsibility. He had slept three or four hours in the last sixty and she knew he was exhausted and bitterly disappointed. The UN had been on the verge of accomplishing something good, but it had been taken away from them by the politicians. Yet she was just as certain he would try again. "Good night," he told her. He turned and headed for his quarters.

He unlocked his door, went inside, and flopped down on the bed, not bothering to take his boots off or turn out the light. He was instantly asleep.

Sam sat in her car and fumbled with her car keys. What is the matter with you? she chastised herself. Stop this. So you like him . . . too much. She beat on the steering wheel. "Damn you, Matt Pontowski." Then, "Well, do something, Samantha."

She glanced at his room and saw the light was still on. Without thinking, she got out of the car and followed his path. She knocked lightly on the door but there was no answer. She tested the handle and pushed the door open. A gentle look crossed her face when she saw him passed out on the bed.

"I suppose somebody's got to take care of you," she whispered. She closed and locked the door behind her.

The sound of running water woke Pontowski. He tried to sit up but fell back into the bed. I don't remember getting undressed, he thought, trying to get his bearings. On the second attempt, he managed to get his feet on the floor. Did I leave the shower running? He came fully awake with a jolt when he saw Sam's vest and boots in a pile by the door. "Oh, no," he moaned.

"You okay?" Sam called from the bathroom.

He stood up, glad that he still had his shorts on. Then he sat back down. He needed a cup of coffee, but the coffeemaker was in the bathroom. "Here," she said. The bathroom door cracked open and a hand appeared, holding a full coffee mug. He took it and the door closed. He took a big gulp and as usual, the caffeine went to work. He pulled on his trousers and sat back down.

"Sam . . . last night . . ."

"You don't remember, do you?"

"I . . . ah . . ."

The bathroom door came open and a fully dressed Sam stepped out. "I put you to bed."

"Where did you . . . ah . . ."

"Sleep?" she asked. "With you. Where else?"

"And . . ."

She gave him an amused look. "Nothing happened. You were out of it."

"Who's going to believe that?" he mumbled.

"You and me, Matt."

He liked the way she said his name.

Monday, February 2
Bloemfontein, South Africa

Liz Gordon stood near the helipad at the Landdrost, Bloemfontein's most luxurious hotel. She was wearing a safari outfit with a short-sleeved bush jacket, matching tan shorts, and hiking boots. She hadn't intended to buy the expensive ensemble, but the manager of the Landdrost had made it quite clear that it would be paid for by her host, along with the lavish suite and all her meals.

The Landdrost had pampered her and catered to her every whim over the weekend and she was feeling very regal as the dark helicopter approached from the west. The pilot circled low in the French-built Gazelle and settled gently to the ground. The copilot jumped out and held the rear door open. She glanced at the silver roundel with a raised gauntlet clenched in a fist. It was the symbol of the Iron Guard—the black fist of steel against a silver background. She ducked her head and ran under the whirling rotor blades.

This was the way she wanted to be treated.

The pilot flew low over the road leading to the base and pulled up to hover just outside the main gate. The gate reminded her of the Porta Negra at Trier, Germany; a massive, black granite structure. After she had seen the gate, they headed into the valley. "This looks more like a town than a military base," she told the pilots.

"It's our home," the copilot answered. The Gazelle touched down on the grass in front of the headquarters building and the pilot cut the turboshaft engine. Again, the copilot helped her as she got out. No one was waiting for her.

"I was expecting to meet General Beckmann," she said. For the first time since arriving at Bloemfontein, she felt she was being ignored, a nobody.

"You have," a voice said behind her. She turned to see the pilot. "Hans Beckmann," he said, taking her hand in his. Gordon wasn't sure if she was captured by his voice or by his eyes.

It was a simple lunch at the home of Stafesersant Michael Shivuto, one of the Iron Guard's black NCOs. Gordon had been surprised when Beckmann took her there and knocked on the door of the black family's home. He had been warmly received by the wife and children and made welcome. Now they were sitting in plastic chairs on the lawn eating sandwiches and drinking tea. "I thought the Iron Guard was lily white," Gordon said.

Beckmann smiled. "Propaganda. We have many blacks in

the Iron Guard. I met Sergeant Michael Shivuto when I was in Koevoet in Southwest Africa. He was one of our best trackers. Too bad you can't meet him, but he is with his men in the field."

"I never heard of Koo Foot," she said.

He smiled at her mispronunciation. "It means 'crowbar' in Afrikaans. In the 1980s the South West Africa People's Organization sent terrorists across the border into Southwest Africa, it's called Namibia now, to kill innocent people. Koevoet was an elite counterinsurgency unit that tracked the terrorists down." He grew very serious. "We lost. If men like Michael Shivuto had stayed behind, SWAPO would have butchered them. We take care of our own."

"Will he ever be an officer?"

Beckmann shook his head. "It's not possible. Maybe his son, Daniel. But not Michael."

"Why?" she asked, intrigued by his open manner and willingness to discuss anything.

"Can you write poetry in Afrikaans?"

"I can't even write poetry in English," she told him.

"But if your daughter was raised speaking Afrikaans, could she write poetry in our language?"

"Perhaps," Gordon allowed. She was beginning to understand his thinking. She looked around, enjoying the quiet garden. Children were running and playing in a playground. "What are those buildings over there?" she asked. "The ones behind the double fence."

"Our intelligence offices. As you can see, it is not a big compound. We can go there if you want, but I'll have to call ahead and tell them to hide all the secrets."

She laughed and shook her head. Maybe Sam was right about asking a direct question, she thought. "What can you tell me about Prime?"

He looked at her expectantly as if she were going to say more. How much does she know? he wondered. "Yes?" he replied, urging her on.

"I heard a rumor . . . that you had nuclear weapons."

Relief masked as understanding crossed his face. "Ah, that. Come. I'll show you." He thanked Sergeant Shivuto's wife and drove Gordon to a man-made cave sunk into the side of the eastern ridge. The massive double blast doors leading into the cave were standing open and he led her inside. Gordon had never been in a nuclear storage bunker, but she recognized its function at once. Along each wall were rows of steel vault doors. "Open any one you want," he said.

She pulled at a small locking wheel and was surprised how easily the massive door swung open. Beckmann switched on a light. Only an empty bomb cradle was inside. "At one time, we had twenty-one nuclear devices. But we destroyed them all before the elections in 1994."

"Why?" she asked.

"Because it was the only responsible course of action," he told her. "Now, what else can I show you?"

"Everything." She laughed.

"Of course."

Dinner, like lunch, was a simple affair in Beckmann's quarters. And as with the base, Gordon missed what was going on beneath the surface. A world-class chef had spent hours preparing the simple and unadorned meal. "I appreciate your taking so much time," she told her host. "I didn't expect you to personally show me around. I wish my partner had been able to photograph this."

"It was my pleasure," he said. "We have videotapes of the base you can have." They went into the lounge for coffee and he showed her old photos of his family that went back to the 1870s. "My family were voortrekkers," he told her. "They fought the English in the Boer War and later the Germans in both world wars." He opened his family Bible and traced his ancestry. "These are the men and women who brought civilization to this land. This is our land, our heritage. This is the reason we want our own nation."

Time for another direct question, Gordon thought. "But won't it be apartheid all over again? Only on a smaller scale?"

"We were wrong in creating apartheid. Now we want to make an island of peace and security in an ocean of chaos. Look at the violence and starvation sweeping my country." His words were etched with pain. "But not where we are building the Boerstaat. Here we can raise our families."

"Tell me about your wife and children." She smiled at the way he blushed.

"I . . . ah . . . have never married. This"—he swept his hand in a large circle—"is my life." He stood up and extended his hand, helping her to her feet. Their fingers held for a moment longer than necessary. "It is time to take you back," he said. She felt a sudden sadness that the day was over.

Gordon sat in the copilot's seat and they flew back alone. The lights of Bloemfontein glowed in the night sky, welcoming them. "This is a beautiful land," he told her. She agreed and wanted to touch him. They flew in silence and he landed the Gazelle on the hotel's helipad with a gentleness that made her think of his touch. He escorted her to her suite and held the door open. "Good night, Elizabeth Gordon," he said.

She looked at him. "Can you stay?" she murmured. To her surprise, he blushed and stammered.

"It's not possible," he finally told her. "Perhaps . . ." he dropped the thought. "Please come back. God speed."

She watched him go, feeling very lonely.

Tuesday, February 3
Cape Town, South Africa

Sam sat at the keyboard of the video editor in the TV studio, fast-forwarding the tape she had recorded at the air base. She stopped the tape and framed Pontowski. He was in the staff meeting outlining his ideas for the COIC. "Watch how they respond to him," Sam said. She ran the tape.

"He does use colorful language," Gordon observed.

"True," Sam admitted. "But he is not offensive." She found the scene in the tents where he confronted the Afrikaners. "He doesn't back down," Sam said. Again, she fast-forwarded the tape. "This is his room. Monks live better."

Gordon listened to Sam and studied her face. She's fallen for the guy, Gordon decided.

"This is when they launched the rescue," Sam said. She framed Bouchard as he climbed on board the C-130 with all his equipment.

"Scary," Gordon muttered.

Sam saved the sequence of the planes taxiing out in the dark for last. It was powerful visual drama as lights pierced the night, casting odd shadows while engines roared and crew chiefs hurried to launch the planes. "He may have gotten four hours sleep out of sixty, but he never blew his cool once. And they rescued the C-130 and the UN ground team without a single casualty on either side."

"You make him sound like some sort of little tin god," Gordon said.

"He's very human, believe me. He's really grouchy and a zombie when he wakes up. It takes about three cups of coffee to get his brain engaged."

"Sam! You didn't?" Gordon chastised. Sam blushed brightly and shook her head. "Look," Gordon continued, "why don't you knock off and go back to the hotel? General Beckmann gave me some videotapes and I want to see them. I'll catch up later for dinner."

After Sam had left, Gordon found a studio technician and went to work. She was going to set the record straight.

Friday, February 6
The White House, Washington, D.C.

The phone message was waiting for Mazie Hazelton when she returned from the NSC staff meeting in the Executive Office Building across the street. Carroll wanted to see her soonest. It was a summons she couldn't ignore, and she hurried down the stairs. Carroll's secretary waved her right in. Cyrus Piccard was with Carroll, sitting in an overstuffed easy chair. His knees were crossed and his head lay against the back. The old statesman was asleep and gently snoring. He let out a honk and woke.

"Mazie, my dear," Piccard said, "so good to see you again." She couldn't help smiling at him and his courtly ways.

"We were talking about Gordon's performance last night on the six o'clock news," Carroll said from behind his desk, "and engaging in some damage control."

Mazie frowned. "We've got our hands full without a distraction like this. The network gave her almost six minutes and she made Matt look like a recovering Neanderthal."

Carroll shook his head. "It's payback time for when he embarrassed her at that news conference."

Piccard humphed. "Matt's references to 'sucking at the big blue tit of the Air Force' or 'making some shit happen around here' don't play well in the heartland of America."

"It's not that bad," Mazie protested.

Piccard gave an expressive sigh. "Unfortunately, many of our countrymen equate profanity with immorality and wickedness."

"It's the comparisons to the Iron Guard that hurt," Carroll said angrily. "She presented us as stumbling fools who run over kids and get chased out of a relief center while the Iron Guard creates stability."

Piccard's chin slumped to his chest and his eyes closed. Mazie smiled indulgently at Carroll, thinking he had fallen asleep again. She was wrong. "When I was very young," Piccard said, "a gentleman denied nothing and apologized for nothing. Perhaps that would be a wise course of action at this time."

"The media, not to mention Congress, will eat us alive," Mazie told him.

"My advice is to ride this one out," Piccard told them. "I'll speak privately to the Lords of the Hill and warn them about Beckmann."

Carroll nodded. Piccard's powers of persuasion and influence with key legislators were well known. "Mazie," Carroll asked as he picked up the phone, "can you give Cyrus some dirt on Beckmann to pass on?"

"You'll have a file today," Mazie told Piccard.

Carroll buzzed his secretary. "Midge, I need to speak to the secretary of defense." He waited for Midge to call John Elkins. "There're many ways to send the public a message of confidence in your people," he told them. Elkins came on the line. "John, have you seen the results of the last promotion boards?" Elkins said that he had. "You might want to speed up the release of the brigadier general promotion list," Carroll suggested.

Elkins thought it was a good idea.

Thursday, February 12
UN Headquarters, Constantia,
Cape Town

Pontowski looked up from his desk when he heard the knock. Piet van der Roos was standing in the doorway of his office, an uncomfortable look on his face. "Samantha Darnell is on the phone," he told Pontowski. "This is the fourth time she's called."

"She still wants to see me?" Pontowski asked. Van der Roos nodded a reply. Do I want to see her? Pontowski thought. She's been calling since Gordon did the number on us on TV. For damn sure I can't trust either of them. What was I thinking of when I let her roam around and shoot at will? "Set up an appointment for this afternoon," he told his aide. "Fifteen minutes. No cameras, no cassette recorders, no notebooks."

Van der Roos was waiting for Sam when she walked through the headquarters entrance. She was wearing a simple but very becoming summer dress and her hair had been carefully arranged. "This way, please." He was rigidly formal, his way of telling her that he also disapproved of Gordon's latest TV exposé.

Pontowski was standing when van der Roos ushered her into his office. He motioned for the aide to remain, not wanting to be alone with Sam. It was a sign of his deep-seated distrust. Sam glanced at the Afrikaner and understood that Pontowski wanted a witness to whatever was said. "Thank you for seeing me," she said.

"Please sit down, Miss Darnell." Van der Roos pushed a chair forward and retreated to stand by the door while they sat.

She took a deep breath. "Matt—"

He cut her off. "It's Colonel." He stared at her, forcing his message across the desk that separated them.

She tried again. "Colonel Pontowski, I want to apologize for what Liz did and assure you that I had nothing to do with that broadcast." He didn't respond and continued to stare at her. He doesn't believe me, she thought. She had to convince him of the truth.

"I showed the tapes to Liz, but she edited them on her own. I wasn't there when she did the voiceover and sent it out. I would have stopped her . . ." Her voice trailed off, withering under his look.

"Miss Darnell, I believe you." Pontowski's voice was toneless and flat. "But I trusted that what you saw would be reported fairly and accurately. Obviously, I was mistaken. It's true I use profanity to communicate. That's the way I work. But I am neither a 'cowboy' nor a 'moral Neanderthal,' as Gordon prefers to call me. I will take my hits when they are justified, but the report was not fair to my people or our mission."

"It was unfair," she admitted.

"At least we agree on that."

"But it was taken out of my hands," she pleaded. "What more can I do?"

"Run a more balanced follow-up story?" He stared at her, unblinking. So attractive, so appealing, he thought. And so dangerous.

"The network won't do that," she replied. "Once they commit to a story, that's it."

He stood up. "I doubt that it would do any good for me to approach Miss Gordon directly." Sam shook her head. "Then we have nothing more to speak of." He turned to face the window. The interview was over. He heard the door close as van der Roos ushered her out. I just did a de Royer on her, he thought, still looking out the window.

CHAPTER
12

Friday, February 13
Iron Gate, near Bloemfontein

Hans Beckmann was not a superstitious man and Friday
the thirteenth meant nothing to him. After dressing and
saying his morning prayers, he had a light breakfast and
spent an hour in his office talking to individual members of
his staff. They had learned through hard experience to be
accurate, brief, and complete. They called it the ABCs of
survival, because Beckmann had an unerring instinct for
finding what had been overlooked or mismanaged. The
results were never pretty.

On this particular morning, it was mostly going well. The
Iron Guard had received a shipment of air defense weapons,
including the German-made twenty-millimeter Twin Gun
antiaircraft system, and the last of the aircraft, Czech-built
Aeros, had been delivered. Intelligence reported that violence in black townships around Johannesburg was increasing on schedule and the internal migrations Beckmann had
predicted were increasing.

Only two items were of some concern, which the kommandant, the lieutenant colonel in charge of intelligence,
promptly pointed out. The UN had, after some delay,
established five safe zones in Northern Cape Province. The
kommandant was worried because he had received assur-
ances the safe zones would be delayed indefinitely. Unfortu-

nately, the UN's C-130s and trucks were moving relief supplies in an increasing volume.

"And the second item?" Beckmann asked.

Now the kommandant looked worried. "Those five safe zones are an arrow pointed directly at Kimberley. If the UN can establish a safe zone around Kimberley—"

"Yes, yes," Beckmann interrupted, "I see. The central government will then be able to spread its influence into the Boerstaat using Kimberley as a base. But I think our friends, the Azanians, will prevent that from happening." The kommandant beat a hasty exit, happy to escape.

Security was next. The major reported they had apprehended a pilot trying to sneak off base just before midnight. He was currently in interrogation. Adjudant Offisier Kreiner was conducting the questioning. Nothing of interest—so far.

His comptroller, the only civilian on the staff, was last, and he also had good news. The Iron Guard had received a large infusion of money from its European supporters to purchase arms and continue its subversion campaign in South Africa. Beckmann paused, calculating how much he would owe them. They were going to be severely disappointed if they expected access to Prime. He expected the Germans would press him very hard on that issue.

The comptroller recommended they hire more mercenaries to provide the technical expertise the Iron Guard lacked. Beckmann thanked him and the comptroller marched out of the office. Beckmann's staff was having a good day.

Adjudant Offisier Kreiner was waiting for Beckmann at the bottom of the stairs leading into interrogation. *"Goeimôre,* Generaal," he said.

"Good morning, Kreiner. Any progress?"

Kreiner licked his lips. "This way, please." He held the door for Beckmann. A man was sitting in a chair, stripped to his shorts. His hands were handcuffed behind him and he was drenched in sweat. "This is Lieutenant Kobie Wolmeres. He was caught trying to leave base without authorization. He claims he was going to see his girlfriend."

"Is this true, Lieutenant?" Beckmann asked.

"Ja, ja," he mumbled.

"But you know the rules," Beckmann said. "Why didn't you bring your friend on base? It is allowed and encouraged."

Kreiner spat disgustedly. "He says he wanted privacy."

Beckmann shook his head. "Kreiner, you overreacted. This is nothing more than a youthful escapade. He should have been fined and returned to his quarters with a warning. We are not barbarians."

"We found this hidden in his shoe." Kreiner handed Beckmann a piece of paper. It was a map of the compound where Prime was housed.

"This is very serious," Beckmann said. He faced the lieutenant. "Perhaps it would be best if you told us all there is," he offered. Silence. "Please proceed, Kreiner." Beckmann moved a straight-back chair into the center of the room and straddled it backward as Kreiner went to work. A rope was lowered from the ceiling and tied to the handcuffs that shackled the lieutenant's wrists behind his back. Kreiner jerked on the other end of the rope and lifted him out of the chair, pulling his arms back and dislocating his shoulders. The lieutenant shrieked in pain. "Very good, Kreiner, I like that." Beckmann's heart raced and his palms were moist as his thighs strained against the chair. Gratification swept over him and he felt alive. "Again, please."

Psychologists claim that both the interrogator and the victim are bound together in a strange alchemy of dependency and domination and share the victim's debasement. Until now, Kreiner had fought against that whirlpool by convincing himself he was superior to his victim. But Kobie Wolmeres was an Afrikaner, and that knowledge dragged Kreiner into an abyss of self-disgust where he became even more vicious.

But Beckmann had descended much lower, and violence that degraded any person fed his tortured ego as nothing else could. Through a perverse logic, having absolute power over another human made him feel virtuous. The ordeal continued until the lieutenant passed out. "Revive him," Beckmann ordered.

Kreiner lowered the unconscious man to the floor and splashed him with water. "We will need a doctor," he said. "Physical interrogation is out of the question now."

A sadness came over Beckmann. "I need answers. You know what to do." He rose from the chair and walked slowly up the stairs.

The pilots came to attention when Beckmann walked into the hangar. "As you were," Beckmann called as the colonel in charge of his air wing came forward. The pilots moved back so he could see the latest addition to the Iron Guard's growing Air Force. "Is it ready to fly?" Beckmann asked pleasantly.

"Of course, Generaal," the colonel replied. They walked around the jet aircraft, a Czechoslovakian-made Aero L-39ZA. It was a small plane, only forty feet long, with a wingspan of thirty-one feet. Fully loaded with fuel and stores, it grossed out at 12,500 pounds. Originally, the L-39 was designed as a trainer, but it was soon modified as a light attack fighter. "We would have preferred our old Mirage F-1s," the colonel said, "or perhaps an Alpha Jet."

"These are better suited for our needs," Beckmann said. "The others are too expensive, take too much maintenance, and spare parts are always a problem. I had to make a decision; a few jets or eighteen of these."

"It is a good airplane," the colonel conceded. "We have made some modifications and should be able to reach five hundred knots for short periods of time. That will surprise the Americans." He stroked the mottled green and brown camouflage paint. "It is highly maneuverable."

Beckmann pulled the colonel aside. "How reliable are your pilots?"

"Kobie, Lieutenant Wolmeres, chases pussy too much. But other than that, my Afrikaners are good reliable fellows. The two Russians and the Cuban, I can't say. I would never have hired them."

"We have more aircraft than pilots," Beckmann told him. "That is why I hired them . . . to fill the void. As for Lieutenant Wolmeres, he will be immediately transferred." The lie came easy, for in a sense, Kobie Wolmeres was being permanently reassigned. Beckmann walked over to one of the Russians and spoke to him in English. "You flew in Afghanistan?" The Russian nodded. "Did you drop nerve gas on the Afghans?" Again, the nod. "Did you ever attack your own people?"

A sad look. *"Da."*

The colonel hurried over to them. "Generaal, a message on the radio. There is an emergency in the compound."

Beckmann sped through family housing and skidded to a halt in front of Sergeant Shivuto's house. A fire truck and a crash wagon were blocking the road in front of him and fire hoses were played out and connected. But there was no fire for them to fight. Beckmann reached into the glove box, pulled out a dosimeter, and attached it to his shirt pocket. The scientist had warned him many times about the possibility of being zapped.

The security at the gate into the compound was as tight as ever and the guards subjected Beckmann to a routine examination. At Beckmann's orders, no one, himself included, was ever taken for granted. He breathed a mental sigh of relief when he saw the Israeli scientist standing with a small group of his assistants outside the main building.

The scientist was dancing from foot to foot and laughing. "We did it, Hans," he shouted when he saw Beckman. "We did it!"

Beckmann reined in his emotions. There had been false alarms before. "What did you do, Itzig?" he asked with a humor he didn't feel.

"Ignition!" came the answer. "We achieved ignition without an explosion!"

Beckmann closed his eyes and took a deep breath. How many times had Slavin explained to him that the key was ignition, the point at which the fusion process starts. "Are you sure it was ignition?"

"Yes, yes, yes." Slavin was beside himself, giving in to his emotions. "Before we had to evacuate, we measured gamma rays of exactly 2.22 million electron volts. That was the proof."

At last, Beckmann thought, the Jew has finally done it. Itzig Slavin had created cold nuclear fusion, the discovery of the millennium, and it was his. "Then why are we standing outside?" Beckmann asked.

"Oh, that," Slavin said. "We couldn't control it and had a meltdown."

"Is the laboratory destroyed?"

"There's a big hole in the floor," Slavin replied, "maybe thirty feet deep, and the apparatus is ruined. But that is nothing. I can rebuild it." He tapped his head with his right forefinger.

"Then why are we outside?" Beckmann repeated.

Slavin gave him a look normally reserved by high school teachers for their thickest students. "It's radioactive, of course."

"When can you go back in?"

"Never," Slavin answered. "We sealed it off to contain the radioactivity when we came up the elevator."

Wonderful, Beckmann thought. Now we have to build a new laboratory and we don't have time to sink a shaft two hundred feet deep. "See if one of the old weapons storage bunkers can be used," he told Slavin.

It was late evening when Beckmann returned to the interrogation room. He found Kreiner sitting at a desk, writing up his report and filling in a death certificate. "Did he talk?" Beckmann asked.

"He babbled like a baby," Kreiner said. "Drugs make it very difficult to separate hallucinations from the truth. But it can be done."

"Who was he working for?"

"The French defense attaché."

"How much money was he paid?"

"He was paid nothing," Kreiner answered.

"Impossible. Why else would he betray his people?"

Kreiner was confused. "I don't know. I asked him that same question . . . it's all on the tapes . . . he said, 'Because you are wrong.' But I think he was hallucinating."

"He was a traitor," Beckmann said with anger. He clenched and released his fist several times, regaining control. Unfortunately, the lieutenant was dead. "I have no use for traitors," he said as he started up the stairs. He stopped on the first step. "And Kreiner," he said, holding the rest of the sentence like a guillotine over Kreiner's head.

Kreiner did a quick panic. He's going to say "two," he thought. It is no longer an old joke. It is a warning.

Beckmann stared at him. "Perhaps a woman next time?"

Kreiner breathed easier, knowing what he had to do.

Thursday, February 26
Cape Town, South Africa

Elizabeth Gordon was tired when she returned to the bungalow she and Sam were renting. It had been a fruitless day chasing down leads and reluctant politicians for interviews, and she was thankful that it was going to change. "Sam," she called. "You here?"

"In the bedroom," Sam answered. "I'm packing."

"Why?" Gordon asked, walking into the bedroom.

"This isn't working out, Liz. So I'm going home. I've booked a flight for tomorrow."

Gordon sat on the edge of the bed. "It's Pontowski, isn't it? You've fallen for him."

Sam stopped packing and sank into a chair. "I like him," she admitted. "But you're part of the problem."

"Really?"

"Liz, you did a smear job on him."

"You seem to forget what he did to me at that press conference," Gordon said angrily. "He deserved it."

Sam shook her head. "He was straight with the facts—which you weren't."

"What he represents is wrong—violence, killing, promoting the military. Don't you remember what Nevers said? We're not going to make true progress in this country until the Pontowskis are controlled. She was right. Anything we do to get rid of him is okay."

"So he's not politically correct. Then say that. But you deliberately distorted the facts to advance a private agenda. What kind of integrity is that?"

Gordon gave her a sad look before answering. "It's done all the time in this business. How else can we hold the bastards accountable?"

"Who's the 'we' and who are 'the bastards'?"Sam asked. "I'm going home."

"Please stay," Gordon pleaded. Her eyes were moist with tears. For all their disagreements, they were good friends. "I can't do it without you. I know I make mistakes . . . get carried away. But there's a story here and I . . . we . . . can tell it."

"The story is drying up," Sam told her.

"Only in Cape Town," Gordon told her. "I told the network I wanted to travel around the country and do a series on what's really going on here. They bought it. We can start at Bloemfontein. I've got a contact there."

"Beckmann?" Sam asked. She didn't expect an answer. "You're doing his PR for him."

Gordon allowed a tight smile. "It took me awhile, but I got his number. He is, without a doubt, the most charismatic man I've ever met. He takes you in with his eyes and voice. I never understood why Hitler could sway the Germans like he did until I met Beckmann. He's a story in himself."

"At least you're sounding like a reporter now," Sam told her.

"I know what he's doing," Gordon replied. "The blacks will always outnumber the whites here. So he's offering the blacks who live in his 'Boerstaat' a second-class citizenship. He buys them off with security, a fairly decent job, and a promise for the future. But they're still serfs, better off than they were before, but still bound to a lord and the land."

Gordon had caught Sam's interest. At heart, Sam was a professional and was willing to pay the price of frustration, disagreement, and even danger that went with the job. "I'll give it one more chance," she told Gordon. "But this time we play it straight."

"We'll tell both sides of the story," Gordon promised. "And who knows, you and Pontowski may work something out."

"Not now," Sam said sadly. "So when do we leave for Bloemfontein?"

"We need to wrap things up here . . . make arrangements. The network wants coverage on the formal state dinner at the president's mansion a week from Saturday. We can leave after that."

Friday, February 27
UN Headquarters, Constantia,
Cape Town

Pontowski looked up at the polite knock on his office door. Piet van der Roos and Bouchard were standing there. "Sir," Bouchard said, "General de Royer requests you join him on the veranda."

Van der Roos mouthed the word "sir" and gave a puzzled look as he handed Pontowski his hat. What's going down now? Pontowski wondered as Bouchard walked ahead to open the door onto the veranda that overlooked the formal gardens.

The three men stepped onto the veranda and donned their hats as a gentle breeze washed over them, promising another pleasant summer day. Pontowski was surprised by the number of people and estimated that most of the headquarters staff was gathered around him. The crowd shuffled back, forming a corridor leading to de Royer, who was standing in front of a UN flag flanked by the tricolor of France and the Stars and Stripes. Bouchard motioned Pontowski forward.

As he approached de Royer, the general came to attention. Instinctively, Pontowski saluted, and de Royer returned the salute. "Ladies and gentlemen," de Royer said in his impeccable English, "I received a message today from the chairman of the Joint Chiefs of Staff of the United States. He has asked me to act in his place and it is with great pleasure that I introduce to you Brigadier General Matthew Pontowski and my new vice-commander."

The announcement stunned Pontowski. He had never expected to make general. In fact, he had been seriously thinking of resigning his commission at the end of this assignment in order to build a more stable life for his son. Then it hit him; he had made flag rank, an almost impossible accomplishment. Less than 2 percent of all colonels made brigadier, and the enormity of it all bore down on him with a weight that surprised him. Few men and women were ever selected to bear such a responsibility, and for the first time in his life, he knew true humility. He stood there speechless as de Royer stepped forward and pinned a star on each shoulder.

De Royer stepped back and extended his hand. "May I be the first to congratulate you on your promotion?" he said in English. They shook hands.

"May I also congratulate you," a familiar voice said. Pontowski turned. Elena Martine was standing there, looking cool and beautiful as always. The ugly bruise on her face had healed and her old confidence had returned, giving her that mix of allure and respectability that fascinated him. She stepped up to him and kissed him on one cheek. Her lips lingered a shade longer than called for and were soft and warm on his skin. The crowd applauded as he made his way through, receiving handshakes and congratulations.

At the door, Bouchard was waiting. He saluted and handed him the message de Royer had mentioned. Pontowski glanced at it and smiled. "I've been frocked," he said.

"What does this 'frocked' mean?" Martine asked.

"Officially, I'm still a colonel, drawing a colonel's pay. But I'm allowed to wear my new rank until the Senate approves the generals' promotion list."

"Oh," she replied, not understanding what it all meant. She smiled and left.

"General Pontowski," Bouchard said, "if you would please follow me." He led the way down a side hall and into the basement, where he spoke into a speaker nested in a heavy steel door. The door was opened from the inside and Bouchard waited for him to enter first. "This is the general's command center," Bouchard explained. "The general will be here shortly." Pontowski looked around, surprised by what he saw. He was standing in the middle of a combined situation room, command post, and communications center. It was functional, efficient, and in total contrast to the opulence of the rest of the headquarters. He had never suspected its existence.

Pontowski studied the big situation maps on the wall as he waited. Five red circles marked the location of the UN safe zones that were now in operation, and blue circles proposed zones for future activation. "We are very force-limited," de Royer said from behind him. He turned, surprised that no one had announced the general's arrival in the command post. Elena was standing beside him.

"As you are now the second in command here," de Royer said, "it is time to put you in the picture." He removed his hat, the distinctive kepi worn by the French, and picking up a pointer, stepped up to the situation map. The room fell silent as he talked, his voice matter-of-fact yet commanding. It was a tour de force, and the general's detailed mastery of the situation in South Africa was obvious. Pontowski was shocked by the amount of killing, rioting, and looting sweeping the country. It was much worse than he had suspected or the papers were reporting.

De Royer concluded with, "The correlation between the location of our safe zones and the fighting is obvious. Our presence stabilizes the area and stops the violence. Unfortunately, we only have two thousand men and women for our entire operation, which limits what we can do. But if I am correct, we can control and suppress violence and rioting once it breaks out by a rapid show of force."

He's going to use the Quick Reaction Force, Pontowski thought. Well, why not? We proved it worked at Vanwyksvlei.

"The unknown factor in the general's plan," Elena said, "is the intentions of the AWB. Will they allow us the freedom to move quickly?"

De Royer drew an oval on the map that extended from Pretoria to Bloemfontein. "The AWB will oppose us here, in the area they claim as the homeland for Afrikaners. I am convinced the AWB is encouraging black violence to make the situation so bad that the blacks, at least those inside the Afrikaner homeland, will beg for protection, more than willing to sacrifice their freedom for security."

"Which explains the rioting and looting around all the big cities," Pontowski added.

De Royer nodded in agreement. "And because of the circumstances, the rest of the world will allow them to do it."

That's a new twist, Pontowski thought. "What circumstances, General?"

"Prime, of course," de Royer answered.

Pontowski was confused. He had never heard of Prime and wanted to ask for clarification. "As far as we know," de Royer continued, before Pontowski could ask the question, "there are at least three foreign operations circling in on Prime. There is a European consortium of Germany, Austria, and Italy directly supporting the AWB with massive infusions of money. Since the AWB has control of Prime, they have what you Americans call 'the inside track.' The Japanese have a small operation trying to penetrate Prime. One of their agents was caught inside Iron Gate, but other than that, we don't know the extent of their operation. Finally, there is OPEC. The Arabs are supporting the Azanian Liberation Army in the hope the Azanians will gain political control of the country and therefore, Prime."

De Royer drilled him with his cold stare. "Of course, I am not counting your country's efforts nor those of my own. So far, these operations have not collided with each other. But they complicate the situation and it is only a matter of time before they do come in conflict. I believe at least one, the Japanese, can be convinced through diplomatic means to withdraw. That is why Madame Martine is here. I believe she can use her contacts to that end. I want you to be my representative and work with her." He picked up his kepi and marched from the room.

I'll be damned, Pontowski thought. I pin on a star and instantly become part of the inner circle, one of the movers and groovers. And de Royer actually showed traces of human life.

Elena reached out and touched the back of his hand, sending a shiver down his spine. "I asked the general if we could work together," she told him. Another shiver, this time more pronounced, shot down his back. She was, without doubt, the most beautiful and enticing woman he had ever met.

The phone was answered on the first ring. "Techtronics International," a woman's voice said.

Pontowski glanced at the business card Richard Standard had given him at the consulate. "Stan Pauley, please," he said, reading the name.

"Pauley," a male voice said. It was Standard.

"I need to see you," Pontowski told him.

A long pause. "Consulate. One-thirty." The line went dead.

"Is this important," Standard asked when Pontowski entered his office, "or are you flexing your new rank?"

"Yes and no," Pontowski answered, wondering how he knew about his promotion. "What's Prime?"

"Why?"

"Well," Pontowski replied sarcastically, "General de Royer knows about it, Elena Martine knows about it, and I haven't got a clue."

Standard groaned. "Can't anybody keep a secret anymore? It's bad for business."

"Is the lack of secrets bad for job security?" Pontowski asked.

Standard didn't see any humor in it. "Prime is the code name for a South African scientific project."

"What's the project about?" He was going to have to pry it out, one question at a time. No answer. Pontowski leaned across the table at him. "Should I ask the same reporter who put me on to you? Or do I run around in public asking questions?"

Standard gave in. "This is classified top secret. We have evidence the Afrikaners have discovered cold nuclear fusion."

Pontowski slowly shook his head. "Sure. Somebody at Langley has been inhaling dope—again."

"There's too much evidence to ignore it," Standard said. "And someone is serious enough to have killed an agent who got too close."

"Ours?" Pontowski asked.

"No. Japanese."

"Now that's interesting," Pontowski said. He told Standard about the meeting in the command center with de Royer and Elena. "De Royer wants me and Elena to use 'diplomatic means' to convince the Japanese to cease and desist."

"Sounds like a good idea," Standard allowed. "Tell them

their man, Hiroshi Saito, was killed and we've got his body. If they want to know who did it, just say the AWB. They'll figure it out."

"The Japanese will appreciate that," Pontowski said. He turned to leave, but Standard's voice stopped him at the door.

"Pontowski, thanks for the heads-up."

The phone call came at seven the next morning and woke Pontowski from a sound sleep. "Be ready in thirty minutes," Elena said. "Don't wear a uniform." The line went dead.

"Was that for real?" he mumbled, shaking his head. As usual, he had a hard time waking up and wasn't sure if the phone call was a dream. He staggered to the bathroom for a shower and shave. The face that stared back at him from the mirror was still more asleep than awake. He rubbed the stubble of his beard, hating the thought of shaving in his comatose condition. He would be lucky not to cut his throat. He scraped at his face and for the first time, noticed the gray in his hair. Where did that come from? he thought. He frowned. The gray had probably been there for some time but he hadn't noticed it. Are you worried that Elena will see it? And how did she get the phone number to my quarters?

Elena was waiting for him in her white BMW when he came out of the officers' quarters. He slipped into the passenger seat on the left-hand side and was surprised by the comfort of the leather-covered seat that matched the contours of his body. "Nice car," he said.

"It's a custom based on the M series," she told him. "The company did it for me." She wore a white cotton shirt with the top three buttons undone and baggy white shorts. Her bare legs flashed as she danced on the pedals and accelerated down the street. He forced himself to think about the road.

She handed him a thermos filled with coffee. He poured himself a cup and took a long drink. It was bitter and strong. "Good stuff," he said. "I need a caffeine jolt to jump-start my brain in the morning." She allowed a slight smile and concentrated on driving. He was amazed at how smoothly she drove as they headed north on Highway N7. He glanced at the speedometer and did a classic double-take when he made the conversion from kilometers to miles per hour. She was driving at 200 kilometers an hour—in excess of 120 miles per hour. He gulped. "Are we in a hurry?"

"Are you afraid," she murmured, "of my driving?"

"Damn right," he answered.

She laughed and slowed until the speedometer settled on 150, 92 miles per hour. "Is that better?" They drove in silence while he let the coffee do its work.

"Where are we going?" he finally asked when he was fully awake.

"I arranged a meeting with the head of the Japanese mission," she said, not taking her eyes off the road. "He agreed to meet this morning and exchange views." She gave him a long look.

"The road," he begged.

Again, she laughed and concentrated on driving. "You don't trust me."

"Damn right," he mumbled, pulling his seat belt tighter. He wished she were wearing hers.

"You didn't tell me you knew Hiro Toragawa," she said. "Mr. Toragawa sends his regards. I am told," she added, "that he honors the memory of your wife."

"I know him," he said. The memories came flooding back. He had worked with the Japanese while he was in China. His wife, Shoshana, had been gunned down by assassins while she was with Toragawa's granddaughter, Miho. Although the killers were after Shoshana, she had died protecting Miho.

Pontowski stared out the window, willing the memories to go away. But they had a power he could not deny. He concentrated on the scenery playing out before them. Slowly, the pain of remembering eased. "When did you talk to Toragawa?" he asked.

"On the telephone this morning," she replied. "I have many contacts through the UN and it was arranged. I explained our problems here."

"You were talking to the right man," Pontowski said. "When it comes to the Japanese, he can make things happen."

"Yes, I know. He is very powerful. He was willing to listen because you are here."

"So I'm your entrance ticket," he said.

"Perhaps," she said. "But you also represent the military strength behind the UN. The Japanese understand and respond to symbols." She hit the brakes and pulled off to the side of the road. "I need to change, since we must observe the conventions with the Japanese." She pulled a wraparound skirt out of the backseat and got out. She buttoned it around her waist before shrugging off her shorts and walking around to Pontowski's side of the car. "You drive," she said, holding his door open. She was already settled into the passenger seat when he climbed into the driver's seat. Her skirt had fallen open, revealing her legs. He could see her panties—a filmy nude-colored lace.

"These are the 'conventions'?" he muttered.

She closed the skirt and buttoned up her shirt. "I keep promising myself to go naked more often," she said. "I hate clothes." She looked at him for a moment. "Drive." He pulled onto the highway and accelerated. The power of the V-12 engine surprised him and they were passing a hundred kilometers per hour in less than five seconds. "Wow," he breathed. It was the most exciting car he had ever driven. They drove in silence, and he found that he was pushing the BMW, wanting to go faster.

"Take the road to Lamberts Bay," she told him. "Then follow the coast road north." He followed her directions and once past the sleepy town of Lamberts Bay, the road paralleled the Atlantic Ocean. At one point, he stopped to take in a magnificent seascape. Elena only looked at him, saying nothing. She directed him to take a side road that twisted and turned for over a mile until they came to a small lake with a rambling white house set on the other side. Vineyards stretched out on both sides of the road. "A safe house," Elena said. "I will make the introductions, but you must do the talking."

He was shocked. "It might have been nice if you had warned me. What the hell am I supposed to say?"

"The usual thing," she said.

A polite young Japanese dressed in dark slacks and a short-sleeved white shirt met them as they got out of the car. "Ah, General Pontowski, Madame Martine, we have been expecting you." His English was perfect and only the calluses on his hands gave him away. Two exact clones joined them as they entered the house. "This way, please," he said, leading them out onto the patio next to the pool. Shade trees waved gently in the breeze and the sound of a small waterfall drifted over them.

A very short, stocky, older man was waiting for them. He gave a bow, little more than a nod of the head. Elena introduced Pontowski and stepped back, a half-amused look on her face. The man bowed them to chairs before he sat down. "How may I be of service?" he asked. His voice was hard and unrelenting. It wasn't the question, or the attitude, Pontowski expected. Elena's amused look vanished.

I'm in over my head on this one, Pontowski warned himself. He decided to plunge straight in. "As you know, my country is committed to supporting the UN in South Africa. Unfortunately, it is a new undertaking for us, and we are worried that our friends and allies might not understand our actions."

"What are these actions you speak of?" the man asked.

Pontowski glanced at Elena. Still no help there. He took the mental equivalent of a deep breath. "By supporting the UN, we may unintentionally harm the activities of our other friends and allies. That is not our intention and we are deeply sorry. Of course, I am speaking of activities that we know nothing about." Only silence answered him. He wasn't getting anywhere.

He tried again. "I must also bring you bad news. One of your countrymen, Hiroshi Saito, has been killed. Our Consulate in Cape Town has his body and asks your permission to return it to Japan."

"The manner of his death?" the man asked.

Pontowski shook his head. "I was only told the AWB is responsible."

"I am most grateful and in your debt," the man said. The tension had been broken. He called out in Japanese and a tea cart was pushed onto the patio with a large selection of pastries and jugs of coffee and tea. A petite woman in a kimono served, and as with her male counterparts, only the calluses on her hands betrayed her real function. There was no doubt in Pontowski's mind that every one of his hosts was an accomplished killer. They made small talk and thirty minutes later, Pontowski and Elena were back in the BMW, headed for Cape Town.

"What the hell was that all about?" he asked, deliberately letting his anger show.

"Stop the car," she replied. "Over there." He pulled off onto a lay-by. She got out of the car, crossed the road, and walked down a path to the beach. He locked the car and followed her down a steep path to a secluded cove. They were alone, and she sat down on the sand and looked out to sea. "I thought you understood," she said. "The decision for the Japanese to withdraw was made by Toragawa. We were only fulfilling the conventions, saving them face, making it appear that the UN's military presence was the motivating factor. Telling them about Saito was brilliant and soothed many ruffled feelings." She gave him a quizzical look. "I thought you had dealt with the Japanese before?"

"It wasn't like this," he answered.

"Wasn't it? The Japanese are amazingly consistent. By the way, do brigadiers make U.S. policy?"

"What are you talking about?"

"By apologizing in advance, you told the Japanese there would be no linkage between what they do in South Africa and overall U.S. policy toward Japan. You gave them carte blanche to stay and do what they want."

"Oh, no," Pontowski groaned. "I didn't mean to do that."

"Well," she said, "you did. But if they withdraw, we will know they did not interpret your remarks as policy."

"It might have been nice," Pontowski muttered, "if we had talked about what I should have said on the way here. We had plenty of time."

She touched his arm. "Oh, Matt," she said, her voice low-pitched and sensual. "I really thought you knew." Shivers were racing down his spine. "I'm going for a swim," she announced. She unbuttoned her skirt and it fell away. Four more buttons and her shirt was off, abandoned on the sand. She was not wearing a bra. With an easy motion, she discarded her sandals and pulled off her panties. "Come," she said, walking slowly down to the water.

Pontowski didn't move. She's beautiful, he thought. And smarter than hell . . . and well connected . . . and worldly. He had never met a woman like her. At one time, he told himself, I would have been on her like a bear on honey. Red warning flags flashed as he watched her step into the water. The words of his grandfather came rushing back, all too clear and full of meaning. "Women, beautiful women, come with the job. But sex has nothing to do with true power and responsibility. Never confuse them. It can be very dangerous."

He had seen that danger in China when his superior, General Von Drexler, driven by megalomania, had given in to the lure of sex. Pontowski had watched the two combine and destroy the brilliant general. Not me, he told himself. He closed his eyes, remembering other beaches: the beach outside Haifa in Israel when he and Shoshana had finally made their peace, the beach in Crete where they had spent their honeymoon, locked in love.

"Are you asleep?" Elena said, breaking his reverie. He looked up. She was standing over him, her bare skin glistening, water dripping on his pants.

He stood. They were almost touching. "Not really," he answered. "I was just waiting to see if the sharks got you."

"Sharks?" she said, her eyes wide in shock.

"Oh, Elena," he murmured, mimicking her. "I really thought you knew." He turned and walked back to the car.

Elena dropped him off at Ysterplaat Air Base. She lowered the BMW's window and leaned out. Her hair was in disarray, held loosely back off her face by a twisted scarf. Her shirt was half-opened and he caught a delicate scent that made him think of sea spray and sand. "Matt," she said, "this is the strangest courtship." She gunned the engine and raced away.

CHAPTER
13

Tuesday, March 3
The White House, Washington, D.C.

Early morning was the best time in the White House, and Carroll was certain ghosts of past presidents roamed the mansion just before dawn. He walked slowly down the quiet halls of the west wing toward his office, hoping he would see at least one apparition. He had a few questions he wanted to ask, especially if it was Matt's grandfather.

His secretary was already at work, preparing his desk. "Good morning, Midge," he said. "Sometimes I think you live here."

"Actually, I sleep under my desk," she told him. They exchanged smiles at the old joke as Carroll started his morning routine. Midge had removed the writing pad from his desk and the computer monitor was turned on. He sat down and called up the President's Daily Brief. For the next hour, he hardly moved, only pecking at the keyboard to scroll the display to a new report.

He finished by reading the CIA's most recent assessment of South Africa. They've got it wrong, he decided. "Midge," he called, "is Mrs. Hazelton in yet?" Less than a minute later, his special assistant was in his office. "Mazie, what's your read on the latest from South Africa?"

"The Japanese have withdrawn," she said, "which tidies up the situation a little. And the NRO sent over some very interesting Keyhole coverage of the AWB's base at Bloemfontein." She handed him the latest spy satellite imagery the National Reconnaissance Office had forwarded to the NSC. "The satellite picked up faint traces of radiation leaking from this area inside the Iron Gate." She pointed to the underground laboratory where Prime had melted down. "It correlates with some earlier satellite coverage from the thirteenth of last month." She handed him a second high-resolution print. "The satellite just happened to be over-head and imaged the base. Look at all the activity around the same area . . . fire trucks, people milling around. Analysts at the CIA claim this was an underground nuclear laboratory."

"Your assessment?" Carroll asked.

"It fits the same general pattern of activity we monitored at Pelindaba before they moved Prime. I think they had a meltdown. The Afrikaners are still working on cold nuclear fusion and making progress."

"That's making some pretty big assumptions," Carroll allowed. "It's more logical to assume some type of nuclear weapons development gone haywire."

Mazie shook her head. "Contrary to what everyone thinks, the Afrikaners did destroy their nuclear weapons in 1994 and the Iron Guard does not have nukes. This has to do with Prime."

Carroll studied his assistant. He wasn't so sure about the nuclear weapons being destroyed. "If they haven't got nukes, what do they have?"

Mazie took a deep breath. "Nerve gas."

Carroll allowed a little smile. "How did you come to that conclusion?"

"When the Iron Guard received a shipment of Aeros from Czechoslovakia that were not nuclear-capable. But those aircraft are configured for chemical warfare."

"So what do you recommend we do?" Carroll asked.

"Jack up the CIA and find out what's going on inside Beckmann's Iron Gate. He's certifiable."

Carroll leaned back in his chair. "Make it happen, Mazie." He thought for a moment. "Would you care to join Chuck, Wayne, and me for lunch?"

"I'd love to," she told him. Mazie liked the two Secret

Service agents, who took it as their personal crusade to look after Carroll and pass on the latest White House gossip.

Wednesday, March 4
Cape Town, South Africa

"You look better," Standard said when MacKay entered his office at the Consulate.

"Yeah, it surprised me, too," MacKay said cautiously. The bandages had just come off and he wasn't sure about the new image he was presenting to the world. During his first week at Cape Town, one of the Boys had suggested plastic surgery was in order to change his appearance. It was not a matter of vanity, as MacKay had accepted his harsh image years before, but of survival.

It had been a relatively minor thing for a local surgeon to straighten MacKay's nose, pin back his jug-handle ears, and change his hairline. To cover his pseudofolliculitis and receding chin, he had let his beard grow again. The change was startling, and MacKay had a new persona.

That was the easiest part. Setting up his business cover had taken much more work. The Boys had spent long hours building a fictitious business. They created a corporation that specialized in security systems and left a paper trail that gave the corporation life and, more important, money.

At the same time, the Boys had to make MacKay an expert in security systems and apply for a business license in South Africa. The last had nearly sunk the entire project until they found the right bureaucrat to bribe. While all this was going on, one of them had traveled to Bloemfontein, rented an office and an apartment, opened bank accounts in the corporation and MacKay's name, and set up a safe house.

The Boys had done it all in seven weeks and were four very exhausted women. But Standard was having his doubts about MacKay. "Do you feel up to this?" he asked.

"Why are you asking?" MacKay answered.

"I'm worried about you. You lost two good men in Johannesburg."

"Tell me about it."

Standard decided it was time to discover if MacKay could still do the job. "You are partially responsible."

MacKay's answer surprised him. "I was totally responsible. I should have called Robby and Grawley the second I knew there was trouble brewing near our office. I started improvising, playing it by ear, and went there by foot. That took thirty minutes, and they were killed during that time. I've run it a hundred times and the results are always the same. I fucked up."

"You're being too hard on yourself," Standard said. "You didn't pull the trigger."

"I could have prevented it," MacKay said, "and I'll live with that for the rest of my life."

Standard made his decision. "You learned something. Don't wing it next time." MacKay nodded. "The company is still on our backs big-time about Prime and wants results, as of yesterday. You're going back to Bloemfontein."

MacKay smiled at him.

Thursday, March 5
Iron Gate, near Bloemfontein

Beckmann's staff was lined up for the early morning parade into his office, and each had carefully prepared and rehearsed the ABCs of his morning briefing. The moment one staffer left Beckmann's office, the next would walk through the door, and for a brief, terrifying period, have his three to five minutes of Beckmann's undivided attention.

The kommandant, a lieutenant colonel, who served as Beckmann's intelligence chief was worried as he waited for his turn, not certain how Beckmann would react to the latest information from Cape Town. The chief of logistics came out of Beckmann's office muttering to himself, his face gray with worry. The kommandant was through the door before it closed.

"*Goeimôre,* Generaal," he said, standing at attention.

"Is there any good news this morning?" Beckmann asked.

"The kaffir government cannot control its own bureaucracy in Pretoria. The corruption is unbelievable and the black bureaucrats are looting the treasury. The ANC should never have replaced the white bureaucracy with their own people. The government has all but ceased functioning."

Beckmann nodded, pleased with what he was hearing. "They did this to themselves without any help from us. What is Cape Town doing about it?"

"The president," the kommandant replied, "is sending his cabinet there to reestablish order. It is the old system under apartheid, where a cabinet minister divides his time between Pretoria and Cape Town."

"Details," Beckmann ordered.

"The cabinet ministers are departing on Sunday's Blue Train, after the president's reception on Saturday night. They will arrive in Pretoria with much fanfare on Monday morning and immediately go to work."

Beckmann leaned back in his chair, his fingers together in a steeple. "So they are using the Blue Train," he murmured. The Blue Train was the luxury service that ran between Pretoria and Cape Town and rivaled the famed Orient Express in its opulence. It was a holdover from the old days of white supremacy and the new government kept it in service because their bureaucrats enjoyed using it. It was a symbol of how things had changed.

Beckmann sprang to his feet and the kommandant almost passed out. "Perfect!" Beckmann shouted. "Thank you, that is very good news." The kommandant breathed easier and beat a hasty retreat.

Beckmann punched at his intercom. "Send the rest of my staff back to work," he told his aide-de-camp. "Have Sergeant Shivuto report immediately." He paced the floor, thinking. This was an opportunity to hurt the central government and embarrass the UN at the same time. He had to isolate the government and cut off its foreign support, especially from the United States. What were the political consequences for the Iron Guard if he failed?

Perhaps his brother, Erik, could persuade the Azanians to attack the UN again and divert attention from the Iron Guard. Yes! That definitely had possibilities he needed to explore. He listened for that inner voice that warned him when he was overreaching. There was only silence.

Sergeant Shivuto entered Beckmann's office exactly fifteen minutes later. Shivuto was an Ovambo, a slender man who stood five feet six inches tall. He had close-set eyes and a big nose that had been broken and never properly set, giving his face an unbalanced look. His uniform was clean and pressed and his boots shined. But that was the exterior. Underneath was a true professional, intelligent, confident, well trained, and loyal.

"Michael, *hoe gaan dit?*" How goes it, Beckmann said in Afrikaans. Shivuto answered in the same language, one of the four he spoke fluently. "Can Koevoet stop a train?" Beckmann asked. Koevoet was the elite black unit Shivuto had created for Beckmann. It was named after the counterinsurgency unit where they had met.

"We are trained and ready for it," Shivuto replied, "but have never done it." The answer satisfied Beckmann. If Shivuto said Koevoet was ready, they were.

"Can your men employ the new twenty-millimeter Twin Gun?"

"We have never seen it," Shivuto answered.

"Start training today and prepare to move out Friday night."

"What is our mission?" Shivuto asked.

"To stop the Blue Train," Beckmann told him. "You will receive the details later."

Shivuto saluted and left.

Saturday, March 7
Cape Town, South Africa

Elizabeth Gordon stood by the honor guard at the entrance to the president's mansion with a remote microphone in her left hand. Her white gown shimmered under the floodlights and her blond hair was arranged in a carefully tangled mane. The gown was perfect for the occasion as one limousine after another arrived to deliver their loads of elegantly dressed dignitaries and their resplendent wives.

Sam Darnell visually cued her as a limousine flying the United Nations flag drew up. "In this strange land of contradictions," Gordon said into her microphone, "the first formal state dinner hosted by the president of South

Africa is being held against a background of violence and death while the appearance here is one of normality, pomp, and ceremony."

Sam zoomed in on the small UN flag on the fender of the limousine. "One cannot help but ask," Gordon continued, "is this merely a façade covering up a crumbling government or is it a sign of stability? Only time will tell."

The honor guard came to attention as the door of the limousine opened and Elena Martine stepped out, flashing a generous exposure of leg for Sam's camera. Pontowski was right behind her in his formal dark-blue mess dress uniform. The simplicity of his uniform was in stark contrast to the glittering uniforms of the African dignitaries around him. His command pilot wings and two rows of miniature medals sent the message that he was professional military—not a pumped-up politician.

Again, Gordon spoke into her microphone. "Madame Elena Martine is the head of the United Nations Observer Mission to South Africa. She is escorted by Brigadier General Matthew Pontowski, who is representing General de Royer, the commander of all United Nations forces in South Africa." Gordon joined the couple as they passed the honor guard arm in arm. They paused for a moment and exchanged the standard pleasantries warranted by the occasion.

Sam zoomed in on the three and framed the two women standing side by side. Elena was understated and elegant while Gordon was dazzling and glamorous. Together, they were the stars of the evening. Sam kept the lens focused on Elena as they walked away, hoping she would at least trip or stumble, anything to break the image. "Sam," Gordon said, handing her the microphone, "I've got to go in now. I wish they allowed cameras inside." She looked at her photographer. "Are you okay?"

"I'm fine," Sam said, lowering her heavy camera. "I'll meet you back at the bungalow." She walked away, wondering why she felt so unhappy.

Inside, Elena preceded Pontowski through the reception line as protocol dictated. But it was very obvious they were a pair. "Matt," she said, taking his arm as they entered the reception hall, "I do believe your little camerawoman, the one you call Sam, is jealous. Have you captured her heart?"

"She's media, Elena. In our country, they don't have hearts."

"But they are certainly beautiful," she replied, throwing a smile in Gordon's direction. The reporter was surrounded by a group of admiring military attachés and Minister of Defense Joe Pendulo.

"How did she wangle an invitation?" Pontowski asked.

"I arranged it," Elena said. She laughed at the confused expression on Pontowski's face. "You must learn how to handle a woman in her prime," she told him. "I'll explain it later."

"Is that a promise?"

"Oh, yes," she whispered.

Gordon returned Elena's smile as she and Pontowski passed by, then turned back to Pendulo. "Mr. Minister, I understand you're leaving for Pretoria tomorrow?"

"Ah, yes," Pendulo answered, speaking with a singsong lilt, the sign that he was in a good mood. "I am taking the Blue Train. It is a very civilized way to travel and gives me the peace and quiet I need to think and plan. Why don't you come with us and experience it for yourself?"

"I would love to," Gordon replied. "But I'm going to Bloemfontein."

"Ah," Pendulo said, "the train stops at Bloemfontein. Now you must come." It was quickly arranged for Gordon and Sam to travel with Pendulo as far as Bloemfontein. She took Pendulo's arm and followed Pontowski and Elena.

Pontowski stood by the big window of Elena's apartment overlooking Bantry Bay. A cold wind had swept in from the South Atlantic carrying the first message of the approaching winter and whipping the waves into whitecaps as they crashed into the rocks under a waning moon. "You have a beautiful view," he said over his shoulder.

There was no answer. He walked over to the fire that was crackling to life in the Swedish fireplace and undid the gold button to his jacket. He pulled his bow tie loose and undid his collar button. "That feels better," he mumbled to himself. He hated the formal uniform and swore he would change it, if he ever got the chance.

He poured himself a cognac and looked around for Elena. She had disappeared and only her delicate silk shawl on the floor marked a trail to the bedroom. He picked it up, draped it across a chair, and walked around the large room, not sure if he liked her austere and modern apartment. But the fire was warm and inviting, a welcome change after the formal state dinner. He sat down in one of the modern chairs that made him think of an infant seat for adults. It was surprisingly comfortable and he laid his head back. God, I'm tired, he thought, drifting off to sleep.

Elena's voice reached him, bringing him back. "Matt."

"How long have I been asleep?"

"Not long," she answered.

Pontowski shook his head to clear the cobwebs. Then he saw her and for a brief moment experienced the certain knowledge that his heart had stopped beating. She was curled up in a large leather-covered beanbag and, except for her earrings and high-heeled pumps, was naked. The surge of blood to an extremity that had been dormant for over a year was reassuring proof that his heart was still functioning.

She uncurled from the beanbag and walked to the bar, her skin glowing in the firelight. She poured two snifters of cognac and handed him one, her fingers lingering for a moment on his hand. A shiver shot up his arm. "You do have this most distressing habit of going to sleep whenever I get undressed." She sighed. "It must be me."

"Not hardly," he said, now fully awake.

She settled back into the beanbag with an easy motion that set a few more of his nerve endings on fire. "Matt, we must talk."

"The lesson on the care and feeding of older women?"

"You must take this seriously. You Americans can be so thick at times." She was looking directly at his crotch.

"It's a condition that comes . . . and goes," he said. "You do make it hard . . . to carry on a casual conversation."

Elena tilted her head to one side and looked him in the face. "Americans," she fumed. "I told you before that I hate clothes. Now concentrate . . ."

"I am," he promised her.

". . . on the subject. A woman like Elizabeth Gordon is very complex. She is capable and determined to be successful. But she is still a woman. At one moment she will be all business, doing what is demanded by her work, doing her best. But at another moment, and with the right man, she wants to be romanced, touched, petted, and made love to. In Gordon's case, it becomes complicated because she uses sex, or the image of sex, to get what she wants."

"What does that make her?" Pontowski muttered.

"Men use money and force to get what they want," Elena replied. "What does that make them? Matt, never confuse money, lavish dinners, or sex for that matter, with power. You must read every situation correctly and never be confused."

"Like now?" he asked. Elena did not respond, letting him sort out his confusion. "By the way," he grumbled, "what does all this have to do with you arranging an invitation for Gordon?"

"Because like most of us, she wants to be included, not excluded. Once included, she becomes a friend and ally. Did you see the crushed look on your little camerawoman's face—"

"She's not *my* camerawoman," Pontowski interrupted.

"—when she was excluded?" Elena finished.

Pontowski's blood pressure skyrocketed into the stratosphere as Elena stood up and walked to the big window. "Come here," she murmured. He was across the room in a few easy strides. She moved close, facing him, almost touching. He felt a bare foot move briefly against his right calf. Her hands moved into his jacket and she pushed it off his shoulders, letting it fall to the floor. He felt her fingers tug at his shirt buttons.

"You're wrong. She is very much yours." Her hands were on his chest, rubbing him. "Like now," she whispered.

The aroma of freshly brewed coffee nudged Pontowski awake. He fought the irritation that always came with the morning and tried to go back to sleep. Then he realized where he was and sat up, looking for his clothes. They weren't in the room, and for a moment, he couldn't remember where he had left them. By the fireplace, he told himself.

Elena padded into the room wearing a man's white shirt and carrying a silver tray with the coffee. "Relief," he muttered.

"They tell me you are a bear in the mornings," she said, sitting down on the side of the bed.

"Who told you that?" he grunted. "It's not true."

She arched an eyebrow at him, poured a cup of coffee, and handed it to him. "And you don't take cream or sugar." Her intelligence was accurate. "Matt, we do need to talk."

"Like last night?"

"I hope you remember what it was about."

He sipped at the coffee, in desperate need of a caffeine jolt. "Elizabeth Gordon," he mumbled.

She crossed her legs and watched the sheet covering his body. She was getting the wrong reaction. "Matt, concentrate."

"I'm trying. It helps when you wear clothes."

"Favorable media coverage is essential if we are to succeed. Gordon does not like you and will be a problem."

"That's an understatement."

"Matt, you must control her or we will fail."

"How do you propose I do that?"

Elena sighed. He wasn't paying attention. "By including her."

"And that will do the trick?" He made no attempt to hide his sarcasm.

"There is also her photographer," Elena said. "The one with the unfortunate name. You must use her."

It all came together for Pontowski. "I get the message. Like you're using me." He stared out the window. "Elena, I'll cooperate with Gordon, but that's as far as it goes."

Elena sighed. Americans were so naive. She reached over and touched his chin. Her touch was warm and soft as she turned his face to hers and kissed him lightly on the lips. "Matt, I am very fond of you." She stood and dropped her shirt to the floor. "Come, let's take a shower. It's Sunday and I want to show you the Cape of Good Hope."

* * *

Elena stood by the wall overlooking the South Atlantic. The wind whipped at her dark hair, captivating Pontowski. My God, he thought, she's so beautiful. She pointed to the south, her hand gracefully sweeping the far horizon. "The next land is Antarctica," she told him. "Over two thousand miles to the south." She pointed to her left, to a spur of land jutting into the ocean. "That is Cape Point. There"—she pointed to her right, to the west, to another point of land— "is the Cape of Good Hope."

Pontowski stood there, possessed by the sight. "Can you imagine," he said quietly, "how Vasco da Gama must have felt when he turned eastward? When he finally made it after all the others had failed and after years of trying?" For a brief moment, he was there, standing on the deck as the little ship came about, turning from south to east, its yards creaking in the wind and the bow plowing through the deep blue water.

"Matt, you're a romantic."

He grinned. "Yeah, I guess so." Then the moment was gone and they walked down the long flight of steps to the parking lot below.

It was dark when they returned to Elena's apartment and the light on her answering machine was flashing, demanding her attention. She hit the playback button and they listened. "This is Captain van der Roos calling for General Pontowski. It is six-forty-five Sunday evening. The general is needed at the air base. It is an emergency."

What happened to my radio? he thought. He checked it and discovered it was turned off. "Oh, no," he moaned. "Elena, I need to get to the base ASAP."

"I'll drive you," she said. For once, he was glad she had a heavy foot.

The base was alive with activity when they drove through the gate. Ground crews had already uploaded two Warthogs with three external fuel tanks, giving the A-10s an extended range, and a full-scale weapons generation was under way for the remaining ten birds. A small group of South African Air Force officers and sergeants were watching the hectic, but very controlled, minuet as dozens of maintenance and weapons personnel performed what looked like a miracle.

They had never seen so many warbirds made ready for combat so quickly.

Tango Leonard was waiting for Pontowski and Elena inside the COIC. "What's going down?" Pontowski asked.

"The Blue Train is under attack," Leonard told them. "It's stopped somewhere south of Bloemfontein. That's all we know. When I couldn't find you, I ordered a load out and called the air crews in. Intelligence is trying to talk to their South African and UN counterparts, but no one's answering the phone since it's Sunday."

"How did you find out?" Pontowski asked.

"Your aide, Piet, called. He was looking for you and trying to find de Royer. Apparently, the general went horseback riding and is out of radio contact. That was an hour ago."

"Damn," Pontowski muttered, disgusted with himself. He had been distracted by lust and not paying attention to business. He should never have been out of radio contact with the command post. He thought for a few moments. "Elena, see what you can find out. Use our phones in the command post." Leonard called the new pilot, Waldo Walderman, over to escort her into the command post. Waldo was more than happy to oblige. Pontowski motioned for Leonard to follow him into Intelligence.

"Technically," Pontowski told Leonard, "this is none of our concern and it's a matter for the South African government. But they're afraid of a mutiny if they order their forces to fight other South Africans. And according to the ROE, we can't do a damn thing anyway."

"We can always do a visual recce," Leonard replied.

"Good thinking," Pontowski told him. "Let's do something, even if it's wrong. Get two Hog drivers in here and a C-130 pilot." Leonard made it happen, and within minutes, two A-10 pilots, Jim "Bag" Talbot and Diego "Gorilla" Moreno, were in Intelligence. Lydia Kowalski was right behind them.

"Brenda Conklin," she told Pontowski, "is getting my crew together and they'll be right in. We brought night-vision goggles and flares with us. Give the word and I'll have Maintenance rig the flare ramp."

"Where the hell did you get flares and a flare ramp?" Leonard asked.

"It's part of our WRM," Kowalski told him. WRM, or war reserve material, was part of every wing's essential go-to-war capability. "We've been stuck with it since the end of the Vietnam War. It was taking up space in a warehouse and our resource manager was more than glad to send it with us."

"Whose idea was that?" Pontowski asked.

"Mine," Kowalski answered.

"Get it loaded," he ordered. Kowalski grabbed a phone and made the call.

Leonard shook his head. "It's almost the twenty-first century and we're using 1950s technology."

"That's what you get when you fight a war on the cheap," Pontowski told him.

Brenda Conklin came in with the C-130 crew. Except for the navigator, all were women. "Okay, troops," Pontowski said, "here we go. We know the Blue Train is stopped and under attack someplace south of Bloemfontein. We're launching a recce package of two Warthogs and one Herk to get a UN presence in the area. Tango, I want you on board the C-130 as the airborne commander. You run the show from up there and use the SatCom radio to downlink with us."

"What about the ROE?" Bag Talbot asked. "Other than look, we can't do squat all up there."

"I'll try to get it changed and relay through Tango," Pontowski replied.

"How we gonna find the train?" Gorilla Moreno asked.

"Follow the railroad tracks," Kowalski muttered.

"With that piece of shit you call a radar?" Gorilla replied.

"Stan can," Brenda told him, pointing at her navigator, Stan Sims.

"If we had Mavericks," Gorilla said, "we could use their IR." The Maverick was a guided antitank missile with a cooled infrared tracking and guidance head. Until the Maverick was launched, a video monitor in the cockpit displayed whatever the Maverick saw. It was a poor man's forward-looking infrared that could see into the night.

"Get a training Maverick with no warhead uploaded," Pontowski said. "Launch in thirty minutes. Work out the details once you're airborne. Get going." He motioned for Leonard to wait while the others filed out.

"You'll have to play this one by ear, Tango. That's why I want you up there. Just don't make the situation worse than it is."

Leonard looked at him, very worried. "Boss, this has all the potential to be a real goat rope."

"Tell me," Pontowski muttered. Then, more hopefully, "Be flexible."

"The key to airpower," Leonard quipped.

Bag and Gorilla clambered down from the crew bus and walked toward their waiting jets. "I feel sorry for that poor bastard flying as Kowalski's navigator," Bag said.

"Why's that?" Gorilla answered.

"Shit-oh-dear, the crew's all wimmen. How'd you like to be in a flyin' whorehouse?"

Gorilla laughed. "Sounds good to me."

Sunday, March 8
Near Colesberg, South Africa

The radio calls sounded crisp and professional as the formation headed north, toward the city of Bloemfontein. Kowalski's C-130 led with the two A-10s loitering along in trail. Below the aircraft, the Great Karoo had struck an alliance with the night and swallowed up most traces of life. But at rare intervals, a cluster of lights contended with the dark, fighting the primeval force of the land. High above, the sky shimmered with unfamiliar constellations and held the promise of a new day.

Leonard stood behind the navigator on board the lead Hercules, impressed with Stan Sims's radar technique. What looked like a faint string of lights etched a path from the top of the scope to its center. "This is the railroad track," the navigator said, tracing the string with a pencil. "These bright returns"—he pointed to a cluster of pinpoint lights—"are buildings. Hold on . . ." he played with the controls. "Tallyho the train." A bright return at the top of the scope was snaking down the string. The navigator stomped the intercom button on the floor. "Found the train," he announced to the crew. "On the nose at twenty miles."

Leonard picked up his night-vision goggles and moved behind Conklin, who was flying in the right-hand seat as copilot. "I don't think those will do much good until we get a lot lower," she told him.

Leonard thought for a moment and called the A-10s. "The train is twelve o'clock at twenty. Anything on your RHAW?" The RHAW, or radar homing and warning gear, warned them of any radar activity, hostile or friendly.

"Negative," Bag answered. "Too far out for the Maverick." The IR on the Maverick was short-ranged, good for six to seven miles at the most.

"Time to earn our flight pay," Kowalski told Leonard. "Let's take 'er down for a look-see."

"Hold on," Leonard said, considering his options. He wasn't ready to put any aircraft at risk for a reconnaissance mission. "Lay down a string of flares and put some good old-fashioned light on the situation. See if you can raise Groundhog on the SatCom and advise them we've found the train."

Kowalski started the descent while Conklin radioed Ysterplaat. Groundhog answered with the inevitable reply of all command posts. "Standby one."

Sunday, March 8
Ysterplaat Air Base, Cape Town

Pontowski and Elena were in the command post talking to de Royer on the telephone when the C-130 reported it was in radar contact with the train. "Any instructions for Colonel Leonard?" the command post controller asked.

"Tell him I'm working the problem." Pontowski spoke into the phone. "General, we found the train. It's a hundred nautical miles south of Bloemfontein. But according to

Pendulo, we have no authority to intervene. So unless there is no change to the ROE, I'm going to tell the A-10s to do one pass, visually check out the train, and return to base."

"Pendulo is on the train," de Royer told them. "My staff was able to contact him by telephone before they found me. Unfortunately, he had lost all control and made no sense. He screamed for help until the connection was broken."

Pendulo feels different when it's his skinny ass getting shot at, Pontowski thought. But there is absolutely no way I'm going to stand around and listen to politicians Monday morning quarterback this and claim we committed an act of war against the South Africans. "How long ago did you lose contact with Pendulo?" he asked.

"Over an hour," de Royer answered.

"And no one in the government has responded?" he asked. Elena told him she couldn't get past the single operator on duty. "Then someone had better make a decision," Pontowski told them. "Because without a change to the ROE, I'm recalling my birds and throwing the entire matter in the government's lap."

"What do you want?" Elena said.

"The right to self-defense," he answered. "Someone shoots at us, we shoot back. Period."

"D'accord," Agreed, de Royer said.

"I can't allow that without talking to Minister Pendulo first," Elena said.

"So be it," de Royer said, his words frozen in ice. "General Pontowski, recall your aircraft immediately. Madame Martine, you can discuss the matter with Monsieur Pendulo's successor next week."

Well, well, Pontowski thought. De Royer is an equal opportunity employer. He treats everyone the same.

A long pause. "I agree," Elena finally said. She put the phone down and walked out of the command post.

"Thank you, General," Pontowski said. But the connection had been broken. He turned to the command post controller. "Tell Colonel Leonard he has the right to self-defense and can return fire if anyone shoots at them."

The controller gave him a thumbs-up as he passed the word to Leonard.

Sunday, March 8
Near Colesberg, South Africa

Bag Talbot watched the flashing red anticollision light on Kowalski's C-130 as she maneuvered for a flare run over the train. He called his wingman, Gorilla Moreno, over to a discrete radio frequency. "I'm surprised they found the train," Bag conceded.

A string of six flares illuminated the sky. Each of the five-foot-long tubes hung from a parachute, and its magnesium core burned with three million candlepower. The laydown was good and the flares drifted downwind, illuminating the train. "Now look at that," Bag said. "The flyin' whorehouse did good."

"Roger on the good," Gorilla replied. They switched back to the C-130's frequency.

"I'm at ten thou," Kowalski transmitted, "in a left-hand racetrack pattern. I'll come around for another flare drop."

"Roger that," Bag answered. "We're at fourteen thousand, in a right-hand racetrack."

On the second pass, Kowalski had the wind drift killed perfectly and the flares kept the train illuminated for a longer time. Below them, the Blue Train was framed in the light and appeared to be undamaged. But its last car had been cut loose and was standing alone, a mile back down the track. "The train is backing up," Conklin said over the radio. "Probably trying to get that car."

"They're under attack," Kowalski replied.

"How can you tell?" Bag asked, very frustrated. He wanted part of the action and all he heard was two women talking about it.

"Old-fashioned binoculars work fine," she answered. "Someone is throwing a lot of smoke down there. The train has stopped moving."

Leonard made his decision. "Tell Bag and Gorilla to go down for a low-level visual recce." Kowalski relayed the order.

Bag's voice came over the UHF radio. "Rog. I have you in

sight. I'll lead, Gorilla, cover." Leonard watched the two red anticollision lights on the Warthogs as they dropped out of the sky. When they were through the C-130's altitude, the trailing light split off—Gorilla maneuvering for separation. It was a tactic they had practiced many times. Gorilla planned to run in behind Bag and cross his track at a thirty-degree angle. If a gunner was foolish enough to launch a missile or shoot at Bag's back as he pulled off the target, Gorilla would call for evasive action and then use his own thirty-millimeter cannon to encourage the shooter to cease and desist in his actions.

A strong feeling that something was wrong, very wrong, hit Leonard. Among fighter pilots, it is called "situational awareness" and Leonard never disregarded it. "Gorilla," he transmitted over the UHF, "strangle your lights. Bag, stay above five thousand feet on the first pass."

"Climbing to five thou," a disappointed Bag said as Gorilla's anticollision light disappeared in the night. Suddenly, the ground erupted in bright flashes as a combination of antiaircraft artillery and shoulder-launched surface-to-air missiles converged on both Bag and the C-130. Only Gorilla was safe, hidden in the night. "Oooh shit!" Bag roared. He pulled off hard to the right and started jinking, that series of short, random, and hard changes in altitude and heading that broke any tracking solution.

Flares popped out behind his Warthog, capturing the seeker head of the SAM missile that was homing on him. The missile curved in on the first flare and disappeared into the night without exploding.

Kowalski rolled ninety degrees to the left, standing her Hercules on its left wing, and pulled the nose to the ground. "Hold on!" she yelled. A string of glowing orange-red tracers reached up from the ground, finding them in the night. The maneuver loaded the Hercules with over two Gs and knocked Leonard to the deck.

The flight deck exploded over Leonard and he felt something warm and heavy on his back as the C-130 rolled out, wings level. Wind noise deafened him and he tried to push himself to his feet. But something was holding him down. He pushed again and the pulpy mass of the flight engineer slipped off and freed him. He came to his feet. Kowalski was flying the aircraft and rubbing at her face, which was a mass of blood. Brenda Conklin was half-standing out of her seat and reaching over Kowalski to pull the fire handles and feather an engine.

"I can't see!" Kowalski shouted over the wind noise. Leonard grabbed a blanket off the crew bunk and mopped at her face. He was surprised to see she was unhurt. "I'm okay," she yelled. "Brenda, how we doing?"

"We took a hit on the left wing. Number one is feathered, fire light out and fuel shut off. What happened to Pat?" Staff Sergeant Patricia Owens was the flight engineer.

Leonard grabbed a flashlight and looked at his feet. The sour taste of bile rose in his throat and he felt dizzy. He gulped for air and dropped the blanket over the body. "She bought it," he yelled. He found a headset and plugged back in to the intercom. That helped with the wind noise and he heard Kowalski talking to the Hogs.

"We've taken battle damage," she transmitted, her voice surprisingly calm and matter-of-fact. She had been in combat before.

"Say altitude," Bag radioed. They didn't need a midair collision and the Warthogs would stay clear of the stricken C-130.

"Straight and level at niner thousand," Kowalski answered.

The last of the flares had drifted over the antiaircraft battery and cast an eerie glow over the landscape. "I got the fucker in sight," Gorilla radioed. "He's under the flares. I'm in." Since Gorilla was running dark with no lights, no gunner could visually track him in the night.

A flash erupted on the ground, much too bright to be his high-explosive shells. "I'm off," Gorilla radioed.

"You got something big," Bag said.

"Probably a fuel tank," Gorilla replied. "The train has stopped short and didn't make the hookup."

"I'll check it out," Bag transmitted. "I'm in. Cover, *por favor.*"

"Got it," Gorilla answered as he positioned to fly cover for Bag. They were two professionals going about their work. Bag was back on the radio. "The train is not moving and the rear car is still separated. No reaction on the ground."

On board the C-130, Leonard had regained control of his raging emotions. "Can you make it to home plate?" he asked Kowalski. Ysterplaat was 430 nautical miles away, and he was thinking of diverting into Bloemfontein. But he wasn't sure of the reception they'd get there.

"Can do," she answered.

"Brenda," Leonard said, "radio Groundhog with our status." He keyed his UHF radio. "Bag, Gorilla. Can you find us and join up?"

"Have you in sight," Bag answered. "Tango, what the hell happened?"

For the first time, Leonard had time to evaluate the damage around him. A single round of AAA had penetrated the left side of the flight deck, gone through the flight engineer, and exited above the navigator's head. Part of the navigator panel had fallen onto Sims and stunned him, but he appeared to be okay.

Kowalski answered, her voice flat and unemotional. "Two hits. Triple A. One outboard on the left wing. Number-one engine feathered. Fire light out and fuel shut off. Second hit on the flight deck. My flight engineer is dead. We're cleaning up the mess."

The two A-10 pilots did not respond. There would be no more talk of flying whorehouses in the wing.

Sunday, March 8
Ysterplaat Air Base, Cape Town

The men and women filed into Intelligence, the room where the mission had started. Bag and Gorilla sat on the floor, their backs against the wall while Conklin and Sims found seats next to the door. The C-130's loadmaster, Tanya Perko, arranged two empty chairs for Leonard and Kowalski to use when they arrived for the debrief. The shadow of Staff Sergeant Patricia Owens, the C-130's flight engineer, hung over them and they waited in silence.

"Room," the wing's intelligence officer called, "ten-hut."

They all stood as Pontowski entered. Leonard and Kowalski were right behind him. She had on a clean flight suit but her hair was still matted with patches of blood.

"Seats, please," Pontowski said. "Colonel Leonard, it's all yours."

As mission commander, it fell to Leonard to conduct the debrief. Intelligence took notes for the OPREP, Operations Report, and the INTSUM, Intelligence Summary, messages they had to send out immediately afterward. The debrief went smoothly as Leonard recapped the mission in chronological order. Occasionally, he called on others to fill in details. The tension kept building as he neared the subject of Sergeant Pat Owens.

"There was absolutely no," Bag said, "activity on my RHAW. Hell, I don't know, maybe they got a visual on us from the flares. They drifted off the train and I got a good look at the Triple A. It came from the hills a half-mile to the west."

"That's the bastard I nailed," Gorilla said, a cold hard satisfaction in his voice. "Got a decent secondary explosion."

"Weapons employed?" the intelligence officer asked.

"GAU-8 cannon," the A-10 pilot answered. He had been through the questions many times before in China. "Eighty-four rounds expended, high explosive/depleted uranium mix, absolute altitude 150 feet, range 2,250 feet, speed 325 knots."

Both Pontowski and Leonard nodded in satisfaction. Gorilla had flown a perfect strafing pass at night, under flares, over strange territory. It was a stellar performance. "One secondary," Gorilla continued. "A fireball consistent with a vehicle's fuel tank."

"I can confirm the secondary," Bag said.

The intel officer turned to Kowalski. "Did you ever see the Triple A that hit you?"

She nodded. "I was in a left bank at the time. We took at least two hits."

"And neither detonated?"

"Negative," she answered. "We were damn lucky."

"Lucky?" the intel officer asked.

Leonard answered. "Yeah, lucky. If either shell had

exploded like it's supposed to, everyone on board would have bought it. The shells must have been old stuff, floating around the international arms market for years and decayed over time."

"But someone on the ground knows how to shoot," Brenda Conklin replied. "Where did he come from?"

"It doesn't matter," Gorilla said. "He's dead."

Lori Williams skidded through the door and rushed up to Pontowski. "Martine is on the phone. She was back in contact with the Blue Train and they said one of our bombs killed six people. But before she could clarify, the connection was broken. General de Royer wants to see you immediately."

"Boss," Leonard said, "we weren't carrying bombs."

CHAPTER
14

Monday, March 9
UN Headquarters, Constantia,
Cape Town

Pontowski ignored de Royer's injunction against flight suits in his headquarters and brought Leonard, Kowalski, and Gorilla with him. The right side of Bouchard's face showed surprise when he saw the small group troop into the office for the meeting. The other half of his face had been cast into marble and never changed expression.

Pontowski was tired and Bouchard's fire-scarred face momentarily broke through his defensive shield and conjured up memories from his past. An image of Shoshana flashed in front of him and he remembered how fire had seared her body and forever changed her. But Bouchard had been through a living hell that far transcended Shoshana's ordeal. What had it done to him?

"The general was expecting you alone," Bouchard told Pontowski in French.

"If the general wants to know what happened," he replied in the same language, "these are the people who were there and can tell him." Bouchard did not reply, escorted them in, and announced their names to refresh the general's memory. Strange, Pontowski thought, how only the right of his mouth moves, not the left. Yet it doesn't affect his speech.

For once, de Royer was sitting and not standing at the window. "I am waiting for Madame Martine to return from

2 1 1

the Ministry of Defense," de Royer said in English. His words were accent-free and he spoke in a curiously flat monotone. "They are demanding a full explanation about the bomb."

"It wasn't ours," Pontowski told him. "The A-10s only had a gun."

Much to his surprise, de Royer only nodded. "This presents us with a new problem," he said. He fixed them with his cold-fish stare. "I assume Colonel Leonard was the mission commander. Please tell me all that happened."

I'll be damned, Pontowski thought. He never questioned what I said, knows how we work, and is going for the facts. He reevaluated the French general, sensing for the first time why he had been selected to head the UN forces in South Africa.

Leonard's recap of the mission was short and complete. "Any questions, sir?" he asked.

De Royer turned to Gorilla. "Captain Moreno, exactly what happened on your attack?" The general had a curious way of speaking. He never seemed to ask a question. He listened while Gorilla described his strafing run on the AAA battery that had shot at Kowalski's C-130. "What caused the large secondary explosion?" the general asked.

"General," Gorilla answered, "when you strafe any target with a mix of thirty-millimeter high explosive and depleted uranium ammo, you get secondaries." The general scowled, not understanding. "If there's anything that can explode," Gorilla told him, "it does. Even bodies."

"I have never seen a demonstration of your Avenger cannon," de Royer replied. The glint was back in his eyes for a moment. "Perhaps that can be rectified." Bouchard interrupted the meeting and announced Elena was waiting outside. "Please show Madame Martine in," de Royer said, still speaking in English.

Elena walked in and sank into the chair Bouchard placed next to the general's desk. "It's a madhouse at the Ministry," she told them. "No one is in charge, able to make a decision, and they are looking for someone to blame. Unfortunately, they are more concerned with the bomb you dropped than with who is attacking the Blue Train." She went on to tell them how the position of the UN had been compromised. A few ministers were demanding the arrest of the pilot, and no one wanted to wake the president with the bad news. "This was the very reason I agreed to Pendulo's rules of engagement in the first place," she said.

"We weren't carrying bombs," Leonard told her.

"I saw bombs being loaded on A-10s," Elena said.

"They never launched," Pontowski replied. "They're still sitting on the ramp where you last saw them."

"Then where did that bomb come from?" she demanded. There was no answer.

"The situation is complicated by Captain Moreno's attack," de Royer said.

"I do not need to remind you, sir," Pontowski said, "that we were given the right to self-defense." Reminding the general was exactly what he had in mind. De Royer did not answer and looked at Elena. What sort of game is he playing? Pontowski wondered.

"Fortunately," Elena said, "we also suffered a casualty on Colonel Kowalski's aircraft—"

Kowalski interrupted, anger flaring. "Excuse me. Since when are casualties fortunate? My aircraft was hit by two antiaircraft artillery rounds. One hit the flight deck." Her words were fast and furious. "It hit Staff Sergeant Patricia Owens, my flight engineer, in the left armpit and exited the top of her head. It punched a hole over my navigator, barely missing him. Sergeant Owens's brains were splattered over me and my copilot. While we handled the emergency, Colonel Leonard had to mop my head so I could see without blood dripping from my hair. My navigator and loadmaster removed Sergeant Owens's body from the flight deck in pieces."

She paused, letting her words sink in. The room was silent. Kowalski's hands were on her hips as she leaned into Elena. "Right now, my loadmaster is drinking herself into a blind drunk because that's the only way she can handle it." She stood, faced de Royer, and came to attention. "Will there be anything else, sir?" The "sir" was crisp and abrupt, almost a shout.

"No," de Royer answered. "You are all excused. General Pontowski, please remain for a moment."

Pontowski was almost certain, but not positive, he heard signs of life in de Royer's voice. He waited as the others left. "Explain to Colonel Kowalski that Madame Martine was correct. It was a 'fortunate casualty' because it validated the subsequent attack by Captain Moreno. Without such proof as to the severity of the attack on the C-130, we would be in an untenable position. As to what happens next, I will speak to the president. I do not expect the South Africans to react and we may be allowed to intervene. Have two A-10s and a C-130 on station at first light and be ready to respond to new tasking."

Pontowski turned to leave. De Royer's voice stopped him. "No disciplinary action is necessary for Lieutenant Colonel Kowalski's outburst."

Without turning around, Pontowski said, "Thank you, sir." He left, wondering where the "thank you" had come from. He hadn't intended to say it.

Monday, March 9
The Blue Train, near Colesberg

Sam Darnell moved down the corridor of the Blue Train, past the luxury suites. The cars were still dark but the first glow of morning twilight gave her enough light to see and move quickly. She videotaped a young black attendant dressed in a blue blazer and gray slacks who was sweeping up the broken glass where bullets had stitched the side of the car. "Are you okay, Marcus?"

"Yes, ma'am," he replied. "The cooks have prepared a breakfast in the dining car." Sam shook her head. Even under the most appalling conditions, the staff was still living up to its reputation. She made her way into the president's car to find Elizabeth Gordon. Heavy curtains were pulled across the windows and the lights were on.

Elizabeth Gordon was in the main room with Pendulo and motioned for Sam to join her. "This is quite a performance," Gordon whispered. Sam sat and rested her video camera on her lap. She aimed it at Pendulo and hit the record button.

Pendulo was stalking up and down, head twisting from side to side. "They are after me!" he screamed. "You must get help now." He turned to one of his aides. "Why isn't the phone working?" No answer. "Go find out. Don't come back until it is working. No, come back immediately." The aide darted out of the car, glad to escape Pendulo's wrath.

"Why aren't my guards here!" he shrieked. Again, no answer.

"Where are they?" Sam asked in a low voice.

"In the car that was cut loose," Gordon answered. "He ordered the engineer to back up, but they start shooting if we move. Are you recording?" Sam nodded an answer. "Watch this." Gordon stood and caught Pendulo's attention. "Mr. Minister, have any more passengers died and how many are wounded?" Pendulo waved a hand at her, dismissing the question. Gordon sat back down. "Did you get all that?"

"I can't be sure," Sam said. Pendulo looked at her video camera, his eyes in a narrow squint. "I think I'm in trouble," Sam whispered.

Pendulo turned to another aide. "Order the engineer to back up immediately. I require my guards."

They waited while the order was relayed forward. After a few minutes, the train shivered with life and started to creep backward. The windows shattered as gunfire raked the side of the train. Sam fell to the floor and crawled to a window. She held her camera up and pointed the lens out a window. She hit the zoom button and swept the scene, hoping to get something. The train stopped moving and the gunfire stopped.

Sam lowered the camera, hit the rewind and then the play button. She looked through the viewfinder to see what she had recorded. She had all of Pendulo's performance, including the expressive wave of dismissal. The guy is a real actor, she thought. Unfortunately, she had caught none of the action outside the train. She looked up and saw Pendulo talking to another aide who was looking directly at her.

She slipped out the door and headed for their suite. She made it as far as the connecting passage leading to her car when a hand grabbed her shoulder, spun her around, and grabbed at the camera. It was Pendulo's aide. Sam instinctively curled over the camera and protected it with her body. Without it, she was lost. "What do you want?" she shouted.

The aide smashed a fist into her face, but Sam only held on to the camera more tightly. She ejected the cassette and dropped it on the floor. "Take it," she said, kicking it to him.

A nasty grin split his face as he scooped up the cassette and shoved it into his belt. He started to swing at Sam's head, but Marcus, the attendant she had recorded earlier, was there. He stepped between them and took the blow full on his shoulder. The two men glared at each other. Pendulo's aide snarled angrily, but Marcus only stood there and stared him down. Finally, the aide retreated down the corridor. Marcus didn't take his eyes off the man.

"Thank you," Sam said to him. "I appreciate your getting involved." Marcus looked at her, not understanding. "I mean," she told him, "you took a big risk defending a white against another . . ." Her voice trailed off at the expression on his face.

"Miss Darnell," Marcus explained, his voice matter-of-fact, "you are a passenger on the Blue Train and in my care. Let me help you to your suite and I'll get some ice for your face."

"My God!" Gordon said when she returned to their suite. It was broad daylight but the curtains were still drawn. "What happened?" Sam was huddled on her bed, an ice pack on her face.

"Pendulo's goon," Sam said. "He wanted the tape."

"Did he get it?" Gordon asked. Sam nodded. "I doubt if we could have used it anyway," Gordon said worriedly. "The track is torn up in front of us. We're not going anywhere."

"We'll get out of here," Sam said. She moved to the window and cracked a curtain. "Look, you can see two A-10s circling." The sight of the two warbirds helped to ease the tension that had bound her. "Liz, something's funny. Whoever is out there could have attacked again last night. So why are they waiting?"

Monday, March 9
Ysterplaat Air Base, Cape Town

Lori Williams, Leonard's executive officer, handed Pontowski a mug of steaming coffee the moment he came through the door of the COIC. Three hours of sleep and a shower had given him a second wind. "Captain van der Roos is waiting for you in Colonel Leonard's office," she told him.

As usual, Waldo Walderman was the duty officer behind the chest-high scheduling counter, and he was posting the crew availability. All the pilots and crew members from Sunday's mission were in crew rest and wouldn't be available until after twelve hundred hours. The most experienced A-10 pilot he had on duty was Skid Malone, and he was paired with Waldo. "Don't get your ass shot off today," Pontowski told him. "It got tough out there yesterday."

"Not to worry, sir," Waldo replied.

Pontowski found van der Roos in Leonard's office. The Afrikaner was wearing his BDUs and drinking coffee. "What's up, Piet?" Pontowski asked.

"Sir, I want to get involved."

"Like Bouchard?"

"Exactly."

"I don't see how."

"I fly helicopters."

"I know that, Piet," Pontowski said. "But there's two problems. First, what will you do if I order you to fly against your own countrymen? I'm thinking of Afrikaners, Piet."

"I don't know what I would do," van der Roos admitted. "But my father says we must fight the people who are destroying our country because we have no place to go. You can go home after this. Many of the English can go to Great Britain or Canada, but for the Afrikaner, this is our home. We must fight for it."

"Second problem," Pontowski said, "what about your government? They'd have to approve it."

"I spoke to my Air Force and the generals have convinced the president to lend the UN four Pumas and eight pilots."

"Let me think about it, Piet." They walked back to the scheduling desk and Pontowski poured himself another cup of coffee.

The phone rang and Waldo answered. "Sir," he was almost shouting, "we got tasking from the UN! General de Royer is on the secure line in the command post."

Pontowski bolted. Just before he went through the door, he turned to van der Roos, his decision made. "Piet, just don't paint the choppers white."

Inside the command post, the controller handed Pontowski a phone. De Royer came right to the point. "I have spoken to the president. He has requested that we intervene and rescue the passengers. Colonel Bouchard will be at the base shortly to plan the operation. You may use whatever force is necessary."

"Why the sudden change of heart on their part?" Pontowski asked.

"I explained the situation to them," de Royer said, breaking the connection.

"You do work fast," Pontowski said into the dead phone. Then it came to him: De Royer had told him what to do, not how to do it.

Pontowski sat in Leonard's pickup truck with van der Roos as two C-130s, call sign Lifter One and Two, taxied out of the chocks, their cargo decks jammed with Bouchard's paratroopers. Pontowski listened to the radio chatter as they took off and headed to the northeast. One hour thirty minutes flying time, he told himself.

Ten minutes later, four Warthogs taxied out. Skid Malone was the lead pilot and Waldo Walderman his wingman as Basher One and Two. Bull Menke and Goat Gross were flying the second element as Basher Three and Four. Waldo gave Pontowski a thumbs-up as they taxied into the quick-check area. Crew chiefs and weapons personnel gave the jets a quick inspection, pulling safety pins from the ordnance hung under the wings, checking the tires, and scanning for loose panels and leaks.

"Less than four hours," van der Roos told him. "That was very quick to plan a mission, load the paratroopers, and take off."

"They're a bunch of hustlers," Pontowski said. Now, with de Royer, he had to wait, the burden of all commanders.

Monday, March 9
Near Colesberg, South Africa

Skid Malone's orders were crisp and clear as his formation of four A-10s approached the area where the Blue Train was last reported. "Basher flight, go tactical. Waldo, take spacing." His wingman moved out two thousand feet to his right and descended a thousand feet. He was stacked up sun and below Skid. That way, Waldo did not have to look into the sun to see Skid. It also worked for Skid, who looked down at the ground and not into the sun when he searched for his wingman. The second pair of two A-10s, Bull and Goat, angled off to the right for separation. They were ready to enter the area.

"Herks in sight," Skid transmitted.

In the rear of Lifter One, the lead C-130 and command ship, the jumpmaster stood between the paratroop doors. "Prepare to stand!" he bellowed in French. "Stand up!" Bouchard stood and looked back over his shoulder. His men were on their feet, twenty to a side. "Hook up!" Forty hands snapped their static lines to the anchor line above their heads. "Check equipment!" Each man jerked and tugged at his equipment, making sure all was secure. When Bouchard was finished, he took the slack out of his static line by making a bight and clenching it tightly in his left fist.

"One-minute warning," the American navigator said over the intercom.

"Stand in the door!" the jumpmaster shouted. The red light was on. Bouchard shuffled forward, his stick behind him. He would be the first out his side, leading his legionnaires. He felt good, and the right side of his face smiled.

The red light flickered to green and Bouchard was out the door as the jumpmaster shouted "Allons! Allons! Allons!" Let's go!

* * *

219

Skid Malone rolled up on his left wing to watch the two C-130s below him as they passed over the Blue Train. Parachutes mushroomed out, swung once, and hit the ground. He keyed his radio and called Waldo. "Blue Force is on the ground."

"No bouncers," Waldo said. The legionnaires had jumped at five hundred feet to minimize their time in the air. If a jumper had experienced a malfunction, he would have hit the ground before his emergency chute deployed.

Skid scanned the nearby hills and saw a few, very faint, extremely rapid flashes. "Lifter One!" he shouted. "Jink! Ground fire!" He was out of position and swore eloquently as he circled for an attack.

Jake Madison, the aircraft commander of Lifter One, heard Skid's call and cranked the yoke to the left, turning his C-130 as hard as he dared without ripping off the wings. Immediately, he cut back to the right and pulled on the yoke, gaining altitude. Then he rolled the Hercules to the left. But it was only a feint, as he rolled back to the right and descended. He danced the C-130 back and forth for another thirty seconds until he was sure they were clear.

"Lifter Two," Madison radioed, calling the second C-130. "Say position."

"Right behind you," came the answer.

"Check for damage," Madison ordered. His own crew checked the C-130 carefully, looking for battle damage. The loadmaster scanned the underside of the wings and raised the cargo door to check the empennage section under the tail. The flight engineer checked the fuel systems and electrical buses while the pilots did a controllability check. Both aircraft were unscathed. "Lifter Two, you're cleared to return to homeplate," Madison transmitted, sending the second C-130 back to Ysterplaat.

Lifter One climbed to twenty-four thousand feet and entered a racetrack pattern, holding fifteen miles south of the Blue Train. A voice with a heavy French accent came over the UHF radio. "Lifter One, Blue Force is on the ground and at the train."

"Roger, Blue Force," Madison replied. He told his navigator to relay their status to Groundhog at Ysterplaat. He directed his copilot to fly the aircraft and grabbed his clipboard. For the next five hours they would orbit overhead and act as an airborne command ship and radio relay.

"Lifter," Skid radioed, "Basher One has activity on the ground."

"Cleared in hot," Madison answered. He almost told Skid to stay well clear of the train, but Skid had heard Pontowski explain the rules of engagement and it was unnecessary.

"Waldo," Skid transmitted, "fly cover." He dropped to the deck and headed for the hillside where he had seen the flashes. He called the leader of the second flight. "Bull, do you have me in sight?" Bull Menke answered in the affirmative. "Sequence in behind me."

Skid saw the train and firewalled the throttles as he dropped to two hundred feet above the ground and displaced to the right of the railroad track. He jinked back and forth in small, random heading changes. But there was no reaction from the ground. "Come on, you son of a bitch!" He yelled. He was deliberately challenging the gunner who had shot at the C-130s and the paratroopers.

Ahead of him and to the right, the twin barrels of an antiaircraft gun slued in his direction. It was a German twenty-millimeter Twin Gun built by Rheinmetall of Dusseldorf, and this time it was loaded with HEI, high-explosive incendiary rounds, and not TP, target-piercing ammunition, like the night before. The gun crew had learned from their mistakes and the loss of six friends when Gorilla's Warthog had destroyed the other gun of their battery.

The gunner punched the A-10's speed and distance into the input panel, used the joystick to acquire the warbird in his open sight, and then transitioned to the optical sight. He placed the reticle on the nose of the aircraft and mashed the joystick down, slaving the gun to the Italian-built P56 fire-control system. The computer did the rest and triggered the gun automatically when it had a firing solution.

Each of the twin barrels fired at a rate of a thousand

rounds per minute and gave out a long burst of rapid, staccato pounding. The gunner held the joystick down, emptying the two 550-round ammo boxes that fed each barrel, and sent an almost solid stream of twenty-millimeter rounds toward the Warthog. It was payback time.

A hard jolt shook the Warthog's airframe, and Skid felt the stick go numb, losing much of its responsiveness. "I'm hit!" he yelled over the UHF. Then, much calmer, "Coming off to the east. Climbing. Control problems, fire on number two and losing hydraulic pressure." Five twenty-millimeter rounds had raked the right wing and one had hit the right engine. But Fairchild's engineers had designed the A-10 to take battle damage and still fly. They had done their job well.

Skid's hands danced around the cockpit in a well-practiced routine, first retarding the right throttle, then pulling the right engine fire-pull handle. His left hand dropped onto the emergency flight-control panel on the left console. He glanced at the panel before throwing the switches for manual reversion, the mode that gave him a minimum amount of control so he could still fly the aircraft.

Waldo joined on him to check for battle damage.

The second pair of Warthogs cut a wide circle around the train at altitude, holding clear until Skid was out of the area. Bull keyed his UHF and called the command C-130. "Lifter One, Basher Three and Four can troll for the Trip A that nailed Skid."

"Basher Three and Four," Madison replied, "hold clear in case I need you to assist Basher One." It was a good decision, and Bull pulled off to the north.

Waldo joined on Skid and scanned the underside of the stricken Warthog. "It looks bad," he radioed. "The underside of your right wing is shot to shit, hydraulic fluid is pouring out, and your right engine is still on fire."

Skid's breathing was labored. "Heading south. This Hog ain't long for the world." His Warthog was sending him unmistakable signs that it was dying. The warbird lumbered south, slowly losing altitude. When it passed through two thousand feet, Skid radioed, "Ejecting."

The canopy snapped back into the airstream, the Aces II ejection seat shot up the rails, and the Warthog pitched over into its final dive as Skid's parachute deployed, separating him from the seat. Less than three seconds after pulling the ejection handle, Skid was drifting toward the ground under a good canopy.

Waldo orbited the chute, marking the location on his navigation computer. "He's on the ground," Waldo radioed when Skid landed. On his second orbit, Waldo saw four small trucks, each packed with men, racing across the open terrain and headed directly for the downed pilot. "Skid's got company coming his way," Waldo told Lifter One.

"They may be friendly," Madison answered.

"I'll check 'em out," Waldo replied. He rolled in on the lead truck and overflew it at low level. The men in the truck waved at him. "They seem friendly enough," Waldo said.

Skid's voice came over the radio. "Skid on Guard. How do you read?" The downed pilot was clear of his chute and transmitting on his PRC-103 Survival Radio.

"Five by," Madison replied. "Four trucks headed your way. East of your position about two miles. They may be friendly."

"Sure," Skid said. "And the check's in the mail. I think I'll hide."

While Skid found a spot to hide, Madison worked the problem of mounting a search-and-rescue mission for Skid and checking on the status of the Blue Train. "I can see a lot of smoke coming from the train," Bull warned him.

Bouchard's voice came over the radio. "Lifter One, this is Blue Force. The train is under attack and we are taking casualties."

Madison was sweating hard. The situation was coming apart and he was in over his head. "Bull, talk to Blue Force directly and support as able. You own the area around the train."

"Shit hot!" Bull yelled to himself. Madison had a clue. He called Bouchard and his wingman, Goat Gross, over to a discrete radio frequency.

Skid's voice came over the radio, low and barely audible. "Those trucks are hostile," he said. "They're hosing down everything in sight." The pilots could hear the rattle of submachine guns in the background.

"I'm in," Waldo radioed. "Say position."

"On the side of the hill to the west of the trucks," Skid told him. "About two-thirds the way up."

"That's mighty close," Waldo said. He selected WD-1 on his weapons panel and the gunsight appeared in his HUD, head-up display. Because of the close distances, bombs or CBUs, cluster bomb units, were out of the question. He was going to perform thirty-millimeter surgery with his cannon. He flew down the shallow valley where the trucks had parked and squeezed off a long burst. Three trucks exploded, and he pulled up to circle for another run. The Warthog was in its element, doing what it did best. Waldo repositioned for another run and nailed the last truck with a short burst. It disappeared in a towering column of smoke and flames.

He pulled off sharply to the right and ruddered the big fighter around, never losing sight of the trucks and the men who were running for their lives. Again, he dropped for a strafing run. Smoke belched from the nose of his Hog. Only Skid was moving when he pulled off. The pudgy, easygoing, compliant, eager-to-help Waldo was a top gun.

"Waldo," Madison radioed, forgetting to use Waldo's call sign Basher Two, "where's Skid?"

"He's up and running over the crest of the hill," Waldo replied. "Look at the son of a bitch go!" He could see the downed pilot sprinting down the backside of the hill, well clear of his pursuers.

"This is turning into a piece of shit," Madison allowed.

Waldo clicked his radio transmit button twice in agreement.

An explosion shattered the quiet and Sam heard a woman screaming in the corridor. She chanced a glance outside as two more explosions rocked the train. A legionnaire ran down the corridor shouting to abandon the train.

Elizabeth Gordon stood frozen, unable to move. "Come on!" Sam yelled, grabbing her camera and gadget bag. A loud explosion shattered the compartment's window, and only the heavy curtain saved them from being shredded by glass splinters. Still, Gordon didn't move. Sam jammed two bottles of Perrier water into her bag and pushed Gordon out the door. Marcus was sitting in the corridor, his face cut by flying glass.

"Help him!" Sam shouted. Gordon ran back into the compartment and returned with a wet towel and a first-aid kit. Together, they helped Marcus to his feet as smoke filled the corridor. The train was on fire. The legionnaire was back and led them to a door.

"Over there," he shouted, pointing to a ravine two hundred yards away. Legionnaires were guiding other passengers into the ravine and setting up a defensive perimeter.

"You're an American!" Sam shouted at the legionnaire.

"Yeah. Go!" He pushed them out of the train as another explosion knocked them to the ground. Then they were up and running.

"Blue Force, say status," Bull Menke radioed. There was no answer from the train.

"Goat," Bull said, "they got problems. Let's go look. I'm in." He firewalled the throttles and nosed over for a high-speed pass over the train. He jinked hard, confident no gunner could visually track him. For insurance against an infrared or radar-guided threat, he popped a sequence of flares and chaff cartridges into his slipstream. There was no reaction.

"Two's in behind you," Goat Gross called. "You're clear." Goat crossed behind Bull at a ninety-degree angle while Bull pulled up and brought the Warthog's nose around to bear behind Goat. It was a classic example of close-in mutual support as they checked the train and trolled for the antiaircraft battery that had gunned Skid out of the sky.

"They've abandoned the train," Goat called as he pulled off. "I didn't see any mortar explosions."

"I think I got a fix on the gun," Bull said. He described the location to his wingman. "We need to take that mutha out." He was fairly confident they were up against a twenty-millimeter twin AAA. And they knew how to kill a twenty. "Trick-fuck," Bull radioed, calling for the tactic they would use. "One's the trick."

"Thank you very much," Goat replied. He was the fuck.

Bull set up a tight orbit three miles from the suspected AAA site, outside the range of a twenty-millimeter gun. He wanted to get the gunner's attention while Goat used terrain masking to maneuver to the far side. On the first circuit of his orbit, Bull darted inside twelve thousand feet, baiting the gunner, then retreating. He waited for the radio call. "Goat's ready," his wingman transmitted.

"Bull's in," the lead replied. He turned into the target on an attack run and jinked hard. When he was well inside two miles, he broke the run off and scampered for safety as a stream of twenty-millimeter bullets reached out for him. The "trick" part of the tactic had worked, and the gun had revealed its exact location by concentrating on the wrong target. "Bull's off."

"Goat's in. I've got the gun. The fuck is on." Goat Gross was in the pop and coming down the chute with the target marching down the projected bomb impact line in his HUD. The AAA gun was still shooting at Bull, who was now out of range, when Goat pickled off two Mark-82 AIRs. The five-hundred-pound bombs missed the target by eight feet. But it was like horseshoes; close counted. "Scratch one Trip A," Goat radioed.

"Bull's bingo." Bull Menke had reached his minimum fuel and had to return to base.

"Goat's bingo plus two hundred." His wingman had two hundred more pounds of fuel than Bull.

"Waldo's bingo minus one." Walderman was cutting into his reserve and had to head back immediately.

"Lifter copies all," Madison told them. "Thanks for the help."

The three Warthogs joined up and headed south while the lone C-130 still orbited south of the Blue Train. Two more A-10s checked in. They were five minutes out and had forty-five minutes of fuel for playtime in the area.

Monday, March 9
Ysterplaat Air Base, Cape Town

Waldo was a sad-looking sight as he stood beside the fuel truck and debriefed the sergeant from Intel. His face was flushed and wet with sweat. His flight suit was plastered to his pudgy body, and he was speaking in a squeaky voice. Behind him, a crew rushed to finish refueling so Munitions could upload six Mark-82 AIRs and six canisters of CBU-58s and crank a new load of thirty-millimeter rounds into the cannon's ammunition drum.

Pontowski frowned and turned to Bull Menke and Goat Gross, who were waiting for their jets to be rearmed. "Waldo is not an inspiring picture," he said. "How did he do?"

"The guy was absolutely cosmic out there," Bull admitted. "I thought he was a toad-sucking ass-kisser the way he hangs around and volunteers for every little pissant detail like he needs a life. On the ground, he's pathetic, but up there . . . it sure beats all."

"Indeed," Pontowski replied. "This is going to be a max effort to keep two Hogs on station. I want you to get turned and launch on the hour. I'll get Waldo a wingman." The two pilots headed back for their jets while Pontowski drove Waldo to the COIC.

Leonard had reported in, fresh out of crew rest, and was in the command post trying to sort out the developing fiasco four hundred nautical miles to the northeast. "I can't get my hands around this sucker," Pontowski told him. The problems the two men were confronting, lack of information and distance from the action, were not unique, and they were merely the latest in a long line of commanders to deal with the fog of combat.

"We need to do a number of things," Pontowski continued. "One, a SAR for Skid." A SAR was a search-and-rescue mission best mounted by a combination of helicopters and fighter escorts controlled by a command aircraft. "Two, we got to launch a pair of Hogs every forty-five minutes to keep a CAP over the train." A CAP was a combat air patrol dedicated to a single mission. "Finally, we need to reestablish contact with Bouchard."

On cue, Jake Madison's copilot on board Lifter One called in a status report. The two men listened as the command post controller copied it down. Lifter One had reestablished radio contact with Blue Force. Bouchard reported that a mortar barrage had destroyed the train and driven the legionnaires, passengers, and train crew into a shallow ravine. The A-10s had suppressed hostile fire and it was currently quiet. But they had many casualties.

Madison's voice came over the radio. "Some asshole on the ground calling himself Minister Pendulo keeps grabbing the radio and ordering me to land and pick him up."

Pontowski picked up the mike. "Disregard Pendulo." He looked at Leonard. "One problem solved." He keyed the mike again. "Say status of Skid."

"We've lost contact," Madison answered. "He last reported he was being chased by four men but he shook them off. He's calling for a pickup at first light tomorrow morning."

"What the hell?" Pontowski grumbled. "There's over six hours of daylight left. What is he thinking of?"

"Skid's one of our SAR experts," Leonard told him. "He knows we need time to set up an extraction. Don't worry, he's a Hasher. They'll never catch him."

"General," the controller said, interrupting them. "General de Royer is on the phone. You're needed at UN headquarters immediately."

"Tell him I'm on my way," Pontowski said, hanging up. "Tango, I've got to go put out another fire. Keep turning the Hogs to cover the train and plan a SAR for first light tomorrow morning."

"We need a helicopter," Leonard said.

"Talk to Piet, he's hanging around here someplace," Pontowski replied. He grabbed his hat and hurried out to his car. What the hell is a Hasher? he wondered.

De Royer was in his command center with Elena, waiting for Pontowski to arrive. He was pacing back and forth in front of the situation map on the wall, and for the first time, anger and frustration had broken through his granite exterior. His French was fast and animated, almost impossible for Pontowski to follow. He turned to Pontowski and waved at the map. "The Legion is not rescued!" he shouted in English.

What's going on? Pontowski asked himself. This was a side to de Royer he had not seen before. He looked to Elena for help as the general turned and faced the map, his hands clasped behind his back. She motioned for Pontowski to join her. "I've never seen him so upset," she said in a low voice.

"You'll have to clue me in," Pontowski said.

"The general thinks we were set up," she told him.

"By who?"

"The Iron Guard."

CHAPTER 15

Monday, March 9
Ysterplaat Air Base, Cape Town

It took Pontowski an hour to drive back from Constantia
after meeting with de Royer and Elena. The heavy traffic did
nothing for his disposition, and he stewed, still angry at the
time he had wasted ricocheting between Constantia and the
base.

The traffic grew heavier as he approached the base.
Capetonians were streaming out to the base to watch the A-
10s' takeoff and recover and had turned the operation into
an impromptu air show. Vendors had set up stands beside
the road and were selling refreshments, T-shirts, and film.
Two military policemen had to clear a path the last hundred
feet for him to enter the gate.

Once inside, the chaos outside the fence changed to the
controlled confusion he understood. The roar of engines
and the hustle of the ground crews turning the A-10s and
uploading munitions broke his anger. This was what he
loved: the hurly-burly of operations, people doing what they
had been trained to do and doing it well.

Jake Madison's C-130, Lifter One, taxied in and parked
next to a Puma helicopter. The three-bladed, twin-engined
helicopter reminded Pontowski of the old HH-3 Jolly Green
Giant. But the Puma was much smaller and could carry
only sixteen passengers.

Pontowski slipped unnoticed into the COIC, and like the

ramp, it was bursting with activity. He checked the scheduling board and glanced at the big clock on the wall. The SAR for Skid was scheduled to launch in twelve hours. Let Tango do it, Pontowski kept telling himself. Don't interfere. It's his baby now. Let go.

Van der Roos cornered him in the hall. "The first Puma is here," he said.

"I saw it."

Jake Madison came in with his crew. The pilot's face was drawn and tired. "How did it go?" Pontowski asked him.

"It's a fiasco out there," Madison told him. "We've lost contact with Skid and Blue Force gets the livin' bejesus mortared out of them any time they move. We've managed to sterilize the area around the ravine where they're trapped, but—"

"You did good out there," Pontowski interrupted. He sent Madison into Intel and searched for Leonard. He found him in the command post.

"This is turning into a piece of shit," Leonard told him. He handed Pontowski a chart.

"So I've heard."

"But we're getting our sierra together," Leonard added. "It's gonna be a max effort in the morning when we launch the SAR for Skid. It's out of the Puma's range so we set up a refueling site here." He pointed to the small town of Hanover on Pontowski's chart, eighty miles south of the Blue Train.

"I'm worried about that bomb no one can account for," Pontowski said. "Someone had to drop it. But who? Some vigilante from the South African Air Force?"

Leonard got up and paced the floor. "Don't count out the ever-present militia from the Iron Guard. One thing's for sure, Boss. Someone's out there lying in the weeds and they're gonna bite our ass."

Tuesday, March 10
The Karoo, South Africa

The pilot lay motionless on the ground as the dark on the eastern horizon yielded to the rising sun. Below him he could still hear a gentle snoring. How far did sound travel at night on the Karoo? He didn't know. He was wrapped in his parachute and warm enough, but soon the heat would start to build and with it, the wind. Could he evade his pursuers another day? Again, he didn't know. Now he could hear rustling below: The men were waking up. He felt for his nine-millimeter Beretta.

Slowly, the land took on definition as the horizon turned a bright orange. He loved sunrises, the best part of the day. Especially when there was going to be a Hash. He could make out movement below him. No Hash today, he thought.

Captain David "Skid" Malone had three great loves in his life: his wife, flying A-10s, and Hashing—not necessarily in that order. The first two, most people understood. But he had long given up trying to explain the joys of being a Hash House Harrier. The Hash was an organization devoted to running, drinking beer, and singing rude drinking songs—the cruder the better. It did have a loose, very loose, international organization with worthy goals, but the knowledgeable described it as "a drinking club with a running problem." But the Hash had one redeeming feature—its ten-kilometer hare-and-hound races. Skid Malone was in excellent condition and used to being chased across rough terrain.

How did they get so close? Malone wondered. And where did the dog come from? Below him, less than fifty meters away, he counted six men and a dog. The last time he had had a good count, there were only three and no dog. Things change, he thought. The dog was straining at its leash, pulling in his direction. Did the dog have his scent? Malone calculated the probability of the men moving on without seeing him or his chances of sneaking unnoticed out of his hide. He came out with a sum roughly equivalent to the proverbial snowball's chance in hell. And unless things changed, he was about to be a deceased sinner.

He unwrapped himself from the parachute. How long did he have? He took a long drink out of one of his water bottles, draining it. Slowly, he munched the last of the power bars he always carried in a leg pocket while he checked his remaining water bottle. It was full and the cap was screwed on tight. The growing light revealed just how close his pursuers were. Now Malone was certain he would have to run for it. There is going to be one hell of a Hash today after all, he decided.

He emptied his pockets, deciding what to take with him. It wasn't much. He cut off his pants legs above the knee followed by the sleeves of his flight suit at the shoulders. He wished he had his running shoes, but luckily he was wearing relatively lightweight flying boots. He retied his shoelaces, zipped his survival radio into his chest pocket, laid out the extra clip for the Beretta next to his water bottle, and rolled into position. Slowly, he sighted the Beretta down the hill. He was ready.

Malone didn't have to wait long. One of the men stroked the dog and looked up, toward his hiding place. He's a white guy! Malone thought. The men all laughed and looked in his direction. Malone fought his panic and concentrated. Do they have a good fix on me? There's another white guy. That makes two. Where did they come from?

The men spread out, three on each side of the dog, and started to move—straight toward him. Malone waited as they scrambled up the steep face of the hill. When they were less than fifteen meters away, he squeezed the trigger and emptied the Beretta's fifteen-round clip into the dog and the white men on each side. He ejected the clip, jammed in the fresh one, grabbed the water bottle, and ran.

The two Warthogs came in at two thousand feet and circled the area where Skid had last been seen. Twice, Gorilla Moreno keyed his radio, trying to raise Malone on Guard, the emergency frequency. "It doesn't look good," he told his wingman, Bag Talbot. Gorilla transmitted again.

"Too bad the jets aren't LARS-capable," Bag said. Gorilla grunted an obscene answer to himself. If the Warthogs had been equipped with LARS, lightweight recovery system, they could have interrogated Malone's PRC-103 survival radio with a coded radio transmission. Malone's radio would have automatically responded with a discrete beacon that allowed the Warthogs to home on his position. The LARS was accurate to within a few feet, but budget cuts had delayed the installation of the system.

The pilots set up an expanding square search pattern. They would have to find Malone the old-fashioned way with a visual search. Since they were carrying two external fuel tanks and loitering, gas wasn't a problem—yet. They both knew the odds of survival and desperately wanted to find their friend. He had been too long on the ground and the chances of finding him alive were plummeting off the scale of probability.

The morning air was clear down to five hundred feet, but below that, a gusting wind kicked up dust and reduced visibility. They kept at it, fighting a growing sense of failure and refusing to concede defeat. "No joy," Gorilla radioed. "Let's split the area. You go south, I'll go north." Bag answered with two clicks on his transmit button.

"Hold on," Gorilla transmitted. "I got movement on the ground at three o'clock. A mile out." Gorilla's eyeballs were sharper than most and he had seen movement in a brief eddy. He banked sharply to the right and headed for the spot.

Bag followed, slightly in trail and two thousand feet to the left. "Dog shit vis down here," he radioed. Both pilots shouted "Tallyho" at the same instant. Ahead of them they could see Skid Malone running for all he was worth. Less than a hundred yards behind him were four men, strung out in line, running hard. Gorilla dropped to two hundred feet and flew over the runners. Malone kept right on running while the four men fell to the ground and scrambled for cover. "That'll give him a little breathing room," Gorilla said.

"I'm in," Bag radioed as he rolled in for a strafing run. Malone had opened up enough distance for the Warthog to make a pass. "Off dry," he told Gorilla. "Poor vis. It gets worse closer to the ground." He hadn't fired a round, worried that he might hit Malone.

"Yeah," Gorilla replied, "I lost sight of Skid."

A breathless "Skid on Guard" came over their UHF radios. The downed pilot was up and talking to them on the emergency frequency. He had turned off his survival radio during the night to conserve its batteries and had forgotten to turn it on.

"Read you loud and clear, good buddy," Gorilla answered. "We got a helicopter inbound. Should be overhead in twenty minutes. Can you keep on trucking that long?"

"Can you . . . discourage 'em . . . that long?" Malone answered, breathing hard. "I've been booking . . . for over . . . an hour. Need some shiggy." Shiggy was Hasher talk for any unpleasant terrain, a swamp or jungle. The more unpleasant the better.

Bag understood. "You got some rocks and heavy brush at your two o'clock. About a quarter mile away." There was no answer as Malone conserved his breath and headed for the shiggy.

As flight lead, Gorilla started talking to Lifter, the C-130 orbiting near the Blue Train. "Lifter," he transmitted, "Sandy has radio contact." Sandy was the call sign the Warthogs used when they flew a combat SAR mission as fighter escort. "Skid's in the open, running. We need extraction—now."

Lydia Kowalski answered. "Vixen has refueled and is inbound." Vixen was the call sign for the Puma helicopter.

"If it's comin'," Gorilla replied, "I hope it's panting hard, because Skid is. He's been running for over an hour."

"Vixen copies all," van der Roos radioed. He had pushed the Puma to the red line and the indicated airspeed needle was bouncing off 150 knots.

"Sandy," Kowalski asked, "can you discourage the opposition until Vixen is on station?"

"We will if we can see 'em," Gorilla promised. Now it became a waiting game. Twice, Gorilla and Bag flew low passes hoping for a shot at Malone's pursuers. Both times they lost sight of their target because of blowing dust and dirt. "The vis is getting worse," Gorilla radioed.

"I have the Sandies in sight," van der Roos transmitted.

"No tally on Skid," Gorilla said.

Malone's voice came over the radio. "I'm in . . . a gully." He was tiring but still running.

Gorilla rocked his Warthog up on its right wing and flew a tight circle at two hundred feet above the ground. Below him the wind was worse. On his second orbit, he saw a wide gully. Momentarily, he caught sight of two of the pursuers.

One paused long enough to squeeze off a short burst of submachine gun fire at the A-10 before he started to run again. "I've got two of the bad guys in sight," Gorilla radioed. "I think they're closing in."

"Where's Skid?" Bag asked.

"No clue," Gorilla replied. "My best guess is that he's a little ways in front."

Van der Roos took over. "Sandy," he radioed, "you lead, I'll follow. Run in from behind the bad guys and call when you're overhead their position. I'll be right behind you."

Gorilla acknowledged and rolled in. He dropped his flaps and slowed so he wouldn't outrun the helicopter. This time, he saw all four of Skid's pursuers. He passed over and made the radio call. "Overhead now." At the same instant, he saw the pilot. "Skid's less than fifty yards in front!" he yelled.

"Roger," van der Roos answered. His voice was calm, sounding a touch bored. He dropped his helicopter down to fifty feet and overflew the four men. He rolled into a tight right turn and told the American sergeant standing in the door to fire. The 7.62mm machine gun hammered away, deafening the men in the rear of the Puma.

"I can't see squat all," the gunner reported. "But nobody's movin' around down there."

"Cease fire, cease fire," van der Roos ordered. "I've got him in sight. We're passing overhead . . . now." The Puma passed over Malone and settled to the ground, less than twenty yards in front of him. The gunner swung the machine gun aside and pulled Malone on board.

"Go!" the gunner shouted into his boom mike. "We got him!" Then, "We're taking ground fire!"

"Return the favor," van der Roos grunted as he lifted the Puma into the air. The machine guns on both sides of the Puma erupted, firing blind. "How's our passenger?"

"He's a mess from running through thornbushes," the gunner answered. "He's cut up pretty bad." A short pause. "I've got him on a headset. You can talk while I clean him up."

"Where's the beer?" Malone asked. He had a raging thirst and felt he had earned it.

"Sorry," van der Roos answered, "all our flight attendants are on strike demanding safer working conditions.

What happened on the ground?" Malone told them about his escape and the long run through the bush. "You sure you got the two white men?" van der Roos asked.

"They sure as hell looked dead," Malone answered. "I didn't hang around to find out. The other four were after me in a flash. Those bastards can run." There was a grudging respect in his voice.

"Can you can find the place again?" the pilot asked.

"In this blowin' crap?" Malone answered. "Who knows?"

The Puma banked to the left. "Let's give it a try," van der Roos said.

"Why?"

"To get the bodies," van der Roos replied. "I want to know who was shooting at us."

Tuesday, March 10
Near Colesberg, South Africa

"Basher flight," Kowalski radioed. "I have trade for you."

"Go ahead, Lifter," Bull Menke answered.

"Sterilize the open areas to the east and behind the train," Kowalski ordered.

"Can do," Bull answered. The two Warthogs split apart to gain separation and sequence their attack. It looked easy as they rolled in one after another, pickling off their CBUs and repositioning for another run. The CBU, cluster bomb unit, was a bomblike canister the A-10s used for area denial and soft targets. When one was released, it split open like a clamshell and spread 650 baseball-sized bomblets over a wide area. Each bomblet exploded into 260 fragments, like a grenade, and was guaranteed to discourage trespassing.

Bouchard's voice came over the radio. "Blue Force is in radio contact with a commando," he told Kowalski. "Do you have an FM radio?"

"Negative FM capability," Kowalski replied. "You will have to relay."

"The commando requests you stop bombing the area," Bouchard said.

"What the hell is a commando?" Bull asked.

"The cavalry," Kowalski answered.

Sam's ears were still ringing from the last of the CBUs when she saw Gordon running her way. The reporter darted from boulder to boulder, making use of whatever cover was available on the side of the ravine. She skidded to the ground next to Sam. "Any water?" she asked. Sam handed her the last of the water they had taken from the train. Gordon took a small swallow and passed it back. "Give the rest to Marcus," she said. "Get your Betacam and let's go."

"What's happening?" Sam asked.

"According to Bouchard, we're about to be rescued. He's really angry."

"Whatever for?" Sam asked.

"It's the Iron Guard doing the rescuing," Gordon told her.

Before they could move, gunfire erupted on their right. "It sounds different," Sam said. They heard the dull whump of mortars firing from behind them. Sam chanced a look and bobbed her head above the edge of the ravine. The hill on the far side of the train was laced with puffs of smoke as the mortars found their targets. She looked again. Two pickup trucks with machine guns mounted in the back were racing toward the hill. The gunners were firing and clearing a path for the trucks behind them. Sam stood up and recorded the action.

When the lead pickup truck reached the base of the hill, Sergeant Michael Shivuto radioed for his men to cease fire, abandon their weapons, and disappear. Shivuto focused his binoculars on Beckmann as he got out of the lead pickup and motioned his men to sweep the area, firing into the underbrush and lobbing grenades as they advanced up the hill away from Shivuto's position. All was going as planned, and Beckmann walked toward the spot where Shivuto was hidden.

When Beckmann was less than ten meters away, Shivuto stood up. He could see a pleasant smile on Beckmann's face. "Koevoet did well," Beckmann called.

Shivuto nodded, basking in the general's praise. All had

gone exactly to plan and Koevoet had stopped the Blue Train. Beckmann motioned to him and Shivuto scrambled down the steep slope. Beckmann was still smiling pleasantly when he raised his submachine gun and fired, stitching Shivuto's chest with six rounds.

"Stupid kaffir," he muttered. "He should have surrendered as instructed."

"They put up almost no resistance, abandoned their weapons and fled into the bush," Beckmann told Bouchard. Sam zoomed in as the two men talked and framed Beckmann. Behind them, exhausted passengers were being loaded onto trucks for the journey to Bloemfontein.

"I want to examine the bodies and weapons," Bouchard said.

Sam followed the men as they walked to a remote spot on the far side of the train. "As I expected," Beckmann said, "it was a typical mix of AK-47s, RPGs, and stolen weapons. Kaffirs make good terrorists, not soldiers, and we only found one body." Beckmann nudged Shivuto's body with his toe. "He had a radio and map and was probably the leader, but who knows?"

Sam panned the pile of weapons and for a reason she did not understand, briefly zoomed in on Shivuto. That's the man that wanted to kill us, she thought. She lowered the Betacam and walked back to the trucks and Gordon. They still had to interview the survivors.

Wednesday, March 11
UN Headquarters, Constantia,
Cape Town

Pontowski walked into de Royer's offices at exactly 6:00 A.M. Van der Roos was right behind him carrying a briefing board with flip charts. Both men were showered and shaved and dressed in service uniforms as demanded by de Royer. Neither had slept and their fatigue was obvious, but they were ready. "Time to beard the lion in his den," Pontowski told his aide.

"Mais oui," van der Roos agreed.

De Royer sat at his desk and listened without comment as Pontowski recapped the attack on the Blue Train, the successful SAR for Skid Malone, and how the Iron Guard had finally rescued the passengers and Blue Force. None of the anger Pontowski had seen Monday afternoon was there and the general was his normal, impassive self. But Pontowski sensed something different. Or, he thought, am I finally learning how to read the man?

When Pontowski had finished, the general stood and looked out the window, focusing on the sky. A bearded wisp of cloud was rolling off the top of Table Mountain and trailing out to the south.

"There are many unanswered questions," de Royer said. "I am convinced the Iron Guard is behind the attack. But we have no proof other than a few captured weapons, and I cannot act on suspicions. There is still the matter of the bomb that was dropped on the Blue Train that killed six people. Where did it come from? The Ministry of Defense is adamant that none of their aircraft were flying."

"The Iron Guard has a few planes," Pontowski said.

"Unfortunately, no one saw the aircraft," de Royer said. "At least, we know it wasn't ours."

Now it's "ours," and not "my" aircraft, Pontowski thought. Well, that was some progress.

"Also," de Royer continued, "there are the two men who Captain Malone killed and Captain van der Roos recovered. They were white, not wearing uniforms, and were well armed." De Royer sat down and fixed Pontowski with the old stare. "Finally, there has been a most unfortunate newscast by your Elizabeth Gordon, who was on the train."

Things are back to normal, Pontowski decided. "She's not mine, General," Pontowski assured him. "I haven't seen it."

"She is more aggressive than the other reporters covering our operation, and her stories have caused severe criticism in your country," de Royer said. "She described my command as 'amateurish' and the Iron Guard as a militia of volunteers protecting their country."

"Did she accuse us of dropping that bomb?" Pontowski asked.

"No," de Royer answered. "She was very clear on that. The situation is very confused, your government is reacting badly, and I have been summoned to the UN in New York. Until I return, I have stopped all operations." He fell silent and thought for a moment. "Perhaps, this is an opportunity to present our case to the public."

He walked over to the flip charts and turned the pages until he found the details on the death of Staff Sergeant Patricia Owens. He turned to van der Roos. "Arrange transportation for me, General Pontowski, and Sergeant Owens to Washington, D.C. We must all travel on the same plane. Military honors on arrival for Sergeant Owens with the press in attendance." He walked to the window. Pontowski assumed the meeting was over and started to leave.

"General Pontowski, tell your people that I am very pleased with their performance."

Back in his office, Pontowski telephoned Leonard at the air base. He quickly explained that he and de Royer were taking the body of Sergeant Owens back to the States and told Leonard to pass on the general's compliments to the working troops. "Tango, while I'm gone, I don't want you flying. I need you on the ground to run the show."

"You're doing a de Royer on me," Leonard protested. "I'm running a wing, not flying a desk at some headquarters."

Pontowski remembered the bitterness he had felt when de Royer had grounded him. "Yeah, you're right. Make Kowalski your deputy commander . . ."

"Kowalski!" Leonard protested. "Give me a break. My God, the woman was passed over—"

"She can hack it," Pontowski shot back. "You want to fly? One of you is always on the ground."

"Will do, Boss."

Pontowski hung up and spent the next hour clearing his desk. Finally, he stood up and looked out the window. I need some exercise, he told himself. Now what in the hell is bothering you? A vague itch at the back of his mind was tormenting him—something that he had forgotten or overlooked. But he couldn't find it to give it a hard scratch.

Forget it, he told himself.

Thursday, March 12
Bloemfontein, South Africa

Sam climbed the scaffold that had been erected in King's Park for the TV crews filming the rally. The CBS director was arguing with the media coordinator that "Dan is not going to like this type of treatment," while the CNN crew fought with the BBC crew for the best position. Rather than fight with the heavyweights, she shouldered her Betacam, climbed down the stairs, and searched for Gordon.

She jostled her way through the crowd that was filling King's Park as the sun set. Twice, she stopped to shoot families dressed in voortrekker costumes. Her press card gained her access to the area behind the wooden stage and she found Gordon sipping champagne under a marquee with the other distinguished guests. Sam hit the record button and panned the group before focusing on Gordon. Sam gave her high marks for her recovery from the ordeal on the Blue Train. Her long skirt and matching safari shirt were perfect for the occasion. A silk scarf held her hair in a loose bundle over one shoulder and not a strand was out of place.

Sam was all too aware that her own cheek was still badly bruised from the blow by Pendulo's goon. But she wasn't the one in front of the camera. She tried to catch Gordon's attention but too many dignitaries were surrounding her. Nice to be a guest of honor, Sam thought as she made her way back through the park filming the crowd.

It was dark when she saw the torches coming through the city and up the boulevard. Little girls in voortrekker costumes ran past her, their faces flushed with excitement. "Sam," Gordon said from behind her, "give me the microphone." Sam turned and smiled. Gordon was still being the reporter and not giving in to the celebrity status Beckmann had heaped on her as the "heroine of the train." Well, at least not totally.

A huge bonfire had been lit and cast eerie shadows across the crowd as an ox-drawn wagon groaned past with a family

242

in voortrekker costumes. A young giant of a man led the ox, his beard full grown, a long-stemmed pipe clenched between his teeth. Sam recorded the scene, focusing on the beautiful young woman sitting on the seat. Her blond hair caught the torchlight and her dress was carefully arranged. A little boy, a miniature of his father, sat beside her, also in costume.

Gordon was talking as the procession wound past, ". . . a scene from the past as the citizens of Bloemfontein honor the Iron Guard." Now the marchers paraded by, each carrying a torch. Then came the battered pickups and trucks carrying the commandos who had rescued the Blue Train. "The excitement is electric," Gordon said, "moving and delighting the crowd." As if by magic, the crowd parted, forming a corridor leading to the stage. A lone man walked forward followed by a small group of the militia who had answered the call to rescue the train.

It was Beckmann, wearing the battle dress uniform that had become his trademark, with a beret stuffed under an epaulet. He took the stage as cheer after cheer roared over him, a tidal wave of emotion and triumph. He started to speak in Afrikaans, his voice low and husky, compelling the two Americans to listen even though they didn't understand a word. "What's he saying?" Gordon asked.

The man standing next to her partially translated. "An island of peace in a sea of chaos . . . with our black brothers who are with us, we can march into the future. . . . Are we afraid of the future? . . . We alone can hold the laager of freedom against the forces of violence . . . this is our land . . . do not forget your heritage . . . your covenant with the land. . . . .Think with your blood!"

The crowd surged forward, chanting *"Blut und Boden! Blut und Boden!"*

Gordon turned to face the lens. "Hans Beckmann has electrified this crowd with his vision of a future. Perhaps we are witnessing a rebirth of this nation."

Sam lowered her Betacam, staring at Gordon. The reporter was glowing with excitement. Sam turned and walked back to their hotel, sick with what she had seen. It was pure Nuremberg.

Friday, March 13
The Capitol, Washington, D.C.

Carroll sat at the witness table of the closed committee hearing while Mazie fanned out a stack of documents and reports on the table. Arrayed in front of them was a tier of senators and representatives, the Joint Senate-House Select Committee on Intelligence. As usual, a large group of aides milled around behind the seated legislators, ready to be of instant service.

The cantankerous chairman puffed a cigar to life and sent a bilious wave of smoke cascading over his fellow committee members. He smiled when he heard Ann Nevers politely choking. He was certain she would not complain and risk his displeasure. He gaveled the session to order. "Mr. Carroll," he began, "let me personally thank you for appearing before this committee. Hopefully, we will not take too much of your valuable time."

Carroll spoke into his microphone, carefully choosing his words. "Thank you, Senator. Please let me introduce my special assistant, Mrs. Mazie Hazelton. While I will answer every question, in some cases, I would prefer to let Mrs. Hazelton fill in the details."

The chairman looked up and down the row for objections. There were none, and he let Nevers start the questioning. The civilities were over.

"Mr. Carroll," Nevers began, "this committee has been tasked by Congress to examine our participation in the United Nations peacekeeping force in South Africa that is in contravention of the National Security Revitalization Act. How does the administration justify what it has done?"

"Mrs. Nevers," Carroll answered, "the Emergency War Powers Act of 1965 specifically gives the president the authority to commit our forces for up to ninety days. Congress has wisely never taken that authority away. To do so could put our country at risk. Congress still retains its oversight power—"

"Which is why we are here today," Nevers interrupted. "The rescue of UN soldiers by the so-called Iron Guard and our current intelligent estimates paint a rather gloomy picture of the situation."

"There are encouraging developments," Carroll said. He motioned at Mazie, who picked up his words without a break.

"First," she said, "we are seeing a realignment of the population into more compatible groupings. Second, the UN safe zones are working and are creating areas of stability. Finally—"

Nevers's time for questions had almost expired and she interrupted. "It is becoming increasingly clear that there is no justification for the president sending our men and women to South Africa."

Carroll nodded at Mazie, who stood and passed out a thin folder labeled *Zenith Prime* and stamped TOP SECRET to each member of the committee. A hushed silence fell over the room when they realized what they were reading. "Is this the reason for our involvement?" Nevers asked, looking over her reading glasses at Carroll. "Do you believe this?"

"I personally doubt it," he managed to say, "but . . ."

Mazie picked it up. "We are still investigating and until we are sure, the implications are too great to ignore."

Nevers caught the growing hubbub of whispered instructions to aides going around the table. They hurried out of the room to place phone calls to stockbrokers and make changes in the investment portfolios of the committee members. Nevers stared at Carroll. He had outmaneuvered her. "Mr. Chairman," she said, "I recommend we summon Colonel Pontowski to appear before this committee for a more detailed examination of our involvement. Until then, I suggest we recess to fully digest this revelation."

Before Carroll could point out that Pontowski was a general and not a colonel, the chairman agreed to Pontowski's summons, placed the committee in recess, and hurried from the room, anxious to place a phone call to the banker who managed his blind trust. If Prime was a fact, he didn't want to be holding any shares of oil stock, and the political deals he had cut with the oil companies be damned.

Mazie gathered up their notes and papers. "Mr. Carroll," she said, not looking at him, "that report is misleading. We really don't know if Prime works or not."

RICHARD HERMAN, JR.

"I never claimed it worked."

"Then why the concern over South Africa?"

"Because it is a powder keg being fed by too many weapons and too much hate. I'm not ready to totally discount the possibility of someone throwing nukes around down there. Even chemical weapons are part of the equation now. What's next? Biological warfare? Mazie, it's not just South Africa. What happens in the rest of the world, sooner or later, to some degree, affects us. We are not an island. There are times we have to get involved. It's the one lesson of the twentieth century we must not forget."

Mazie placed her hand on his shoulder. "You're a fraud, Mr. Carroll. Deep down inside, you're an idealist."

He shook his head. "If I do this wrong, Matt will be the scapegoat."

"You're willing to put him at risk for an ideal?"

"And a lot of other good people," he told her.

246

CHAPTER
16

Sunday, March 15
Andrews Air Force Base, Maryland

The. dark gray C-141 Starlifter taxied slowly into the blocks, its speed matching the solemnity of the occasion. The pilot cut the engines as the ramp at the rear of the huge cargo plane lowered. With measured pace, the honor guard marched into position, forming a corridor under the tail. The click of drumsticks marked the cadence. Six pallbearers, including two French Army sergeants, marched down the corridor formed by the honor guard and climbed the ramp into the C-141.

A *"Pre . . . sent arms"* echoed across the ramp as the pallbearers reappeared, carrying the flag-draped coffin down the ramp. The gathered crowd came to attention and the military among them saluted as the standard-bearers lowered their flags in tribute. An unfamiliar silence ruled the noisy air base as the TV cameras registered the moment against a cloud-marked sky.

Staff Sergeant Patricia Owens had come home.

A reporter spoke quietly into his microphone. "The tall figure following the coffin," he said, "is General Charles de Royer, the commander of all United Nations forces in South Africa. He is being escorted by Brigadier General Matthew Pontowski, the grandson of the former president, Matthew Zachary Pontowski." The cameras zoomed in on de Royer as he approached the waiting dignitaries. He stopped in front of a lone couple, Sergeant Owens's parents, and ignored the waiting generals. He drew himself to attention and saluted the couple with the open-hand, palm-forward salute of the French Army. He spoke a few words and listened to their reply before moving on.

The protocol was faultless as the coffin was loaded into a waiting hearse. Then it was over, the dignitaries exited, and the crowd dispersed.

Another TV reporter maneuvered into position for the wrapup and closing shot with the C-141 capped by a majestic cloudscape in the background. "The growing controversy surrounding the UN role in South Africa took a backseat today when General de Royer arrived with the remains of Staff Sergeant Patricia Owens, the first American killed in South Africa. We have yet to learn what the general said to Sergeant Owens's parents, but from the vantage point of this reporter, his words seemed to offer much-needed consolation. But the unanswered question still haunts all who were here today: How many more coffins will we see like this one?"

Piet van der Roos caught up with Pontowski outside the passenger terminal. "This is another side to our general," he said, loading their bags into a waiting staff car.

"The general is a showman," Pontowski conceded. "The United Nations will love him."

Monday, March 16
Ysterplaat Air Base, Cape Town

The crew chief marshaling the Warthog into the chocks crossed his wrists above his head signaling Leonard to stop. The crew chief made a slashing motion across his throat to cut engines. Leonard's hands flew over the switches, shutting the Hog down as the crew chief dropped the boarding ladder. Leonard threw his helmet and the two canvas bags carrying his charts and flight publications to the waiting sergeant.

"They want you in the COIC, big time," the crew chief said. "It sounds like something big has hit the fan."

"Can't go away for an hour without some bastard screwing things up," Leonard grumbled.

Lydia Kowalski was waiting for him when he entered the COIC. "The UN command center is on the secure phone," she said.

"I'd like to take a piss first," he muttered as he headed for the command post, handing his flying gear to a sergeant. He motioned for Lydia to stay with him. "What the hell's going on?" She shrugged an answer as he picked up the receiver to the STU-III secure phone.

Leonard listened for a few moments, hung up, and turned to Kowalski. "There's a food riot at Douglas," he told her. The fifth safe zone the UN had created was centered on the small town of Douglas, seventy miles west of Kimberley. "The command center is talking to de Royer in New York. We're tasked to airlift in Bouchard's legionnaires and supplies until a relief convoy can get through."

Lori Williams stuck her head in the door. "Colonel, Captain Van der Roos is on the phone," she announced. "He wants to know today's flying schedule."

"How many sorties can the C-130s generate today?" he asked Kowalski.

She pulled a face and ran the numbers. "Twelve in the next twelve hours."

Leonard relayed the number and takeoff times to van der Roos and broke the connection. "Who's flying the first C-130?" he asked Kowalski.

"Brenda Conklin."

"What the hell," he said, making a snap decision. "Waldo and me will tag along. It's a good chance to work out escort tactics. You hold the fort here."

Monday, March 16
Near Douglas, South Africa

The Great Karoo stretched out below the Hercules as it descended through ten thousand feet. "Douglas is on the nose at twenty miles," the navigator told the aircraft commander, Brenda Conklin.

Conklin keyed her intercom. "Landing in ten minutes," she told her crew. "I want hustle on the ground . . . we're moving cargo today." She was often described by those who did not know her as "glamorous," but "professional" was more fitting. And when the occasion demanded, "tyrannical" was totally appropriate.

Leonard's voice crackled over the UHF radio with an urgency that shocked her. "Lifter, we've got two bogies at your eight o'clock. Come left forty degrees for a visual." Conklin flicked the autopilot off and rolled the Hercules onto the new heading.

"Tallyho!" the copilot shouted. "What the hell are they?"

"Lifter, they're on you! Break!" Leonard shouted in a rapid staccato. Conklin rolled the big cargo plane into a forty-five-degree bank and turned hard into the bandits. A small jet flashed in front of the Hercules as Conklin reversed the turn and dove for the ground.

Leonard pulled the nose of his Warthog onto the bandits and hit the UHF transmit button to call his wingman. "Waldo, jettison now," he ordered. The two A-10 pilots reacted simultaneously by punching at the PUSH TO JETT button on the armament control panel and twisting the wafer switch beside it to AIM-9, even though they were not carrying the deadly missile or any bombs.

The two simple actions took less than a second and their external fuel tanks tumbled away, freeing them from weight and drag that hindered their maneuverability. At the same time, their head-up displays flashed, giving them the symbology for an air-to-air engagement. They were ready to engage the bandits and do what every fighter pilot dreams of—shoot down an enemy aircraft. But they only had their cannons to do it.

"Waldo," Leonard transmitted, "come back left. Bandits at your six o'clock."

"Comin' back left," Waldo answered as he dropped the nose of his Hog and turned hard to the left. "Tallyho," he called when he saw one bandit a mile in front of him. Leonard reversed course by climbing and turning hard to the right. He rolled out above and behind his wingman in a chase position. He could see the bandit Waldo was chasing but had lost sight of the other one. "I got smash on him,"

Waldo shouted when he realized he had a positive overtake speed on the bandit.

"Press," Leonard answered, clearing Waldo in for a tail chase while he rolled from side to side, looking for the other bandit. "I'm at your six but no joy on the other bandit," he told Waldo. There was no answer. Now Leonard jerked his Hog twenty degrees to the right so he could get a better look behind him. He came back forty degrees to the left, took a good look behind him, and rolled inverted to look down. He couldn't find the other bandit. "Still no joy," he radioed.

"Ten seconds," Waldo answered. He was almost inside the firing parameters for the Warthog's thirty-millimeter Avenger cannon.

"You're clear," Leonard replied, telling Waldo that his six-o'clock position was clear.

"He's pulling away!" Waldo shouted. "He's going for the deck."

A sickening feeling hit Leonard when his brain finally kicked in. They had been lured away from the C-130, leaving it exposed. He buried the nose of his jet and sliced back toward the C-130. "Waldo!" he roared, "come off right! They're on Lifter."

Waldo never questioned the call and immediately reversed course, ignoring the bandit. Like Leonard, he realized they had been suckered, victims of buck fever and the desire for an air-to-air kill. Now they had to find the C-130 before it was gunned out of the sky.

"Everybody," Brenda Conklin shouted over the intercom, "heads up. We've got two bandits out there." She spoke to the loadmaster, "Perk, strap in. It's gonna get wild."

"Strapped in," Tanya Perko answered. "Cargo secure."

Leonard's voice came over the radio. "Lifter, say position."

"Approaching the big bend in the river to the north of you," Conklin answered. "Heading oh-two-zero."

"Jink and head for the deck," Leonard said. "Suspect multi bandits in the area are looking for you."

"Outa two thousand for five hundred," Conklin answered as she started the short, random, jerky heading changes called jinking.

"Bandits!" the copilot shouted. "Five, six . . . *Oh my God!* Eight bandits on us!"

Conklin wracked the Hercules up onto its right wing, nosed over, and firewalled the throttles, diving for the deck. A fighter flashed by in an overshoot and pulled up. "Hold on!" Conklin shouted as she came back to the left, loading the plane with two *G*s.

"We're too heavy!" the flight engineer shouted. "We can't maneuver at this weight."

"Open the cargo door and lower the ramp," Conklin told her copilot. "Perk, can you get to the jettison handle? We got to get rid of this cargo."

"Almost there," Perko answered. "Ready," she said.

Conklin rolled the Hercules out straight and level. *"Now!"* she ordered. Perko pulled the release lever that retracted the locks holding the five cargo pallets in place as Conklin raised the aircraft's nose a few degrees. The pallets moved a few feet toward the rear ramp and came to a sudden stop. The first pallet in line out had twisted in the side rails and jammed, blocking the load. "The end pallet's jammed!" Perko shouted over the intercom as she made her way to the rear.

The loadmaster kicked at the edge of the pallet and it started to move. Encouraged, she kicked harder. But this time her foot caught in the webbing holding the cargo to the pallet. Before she could pull free, the pallet was moving, dragging her with it.

A bandit skidded into the C-130's slipstream, its machine gun firing.

"Lifter in sight," Leonard shouted over the UHF. Ahead of him, he saw a cargo pallet tumble out the rear of the C-130 as a bandit converted into a firing position. Automatically, Leonard depressed the trigger on his stick to the first detent, activating the Warthog's video camera. There was nothing else he could do as the small jet closed on the C-130. He watched in disbelief as the bandit collided with the last pallet of cargo to fall free of the Hercules.

"Splash one," he transmitted. "Oh, no!" A body was falling with the pallets and a coppery taste flooded his mouth. "One's joining on Lifter," he radioed, his words quick and angry as a white-hot killing rage swept through him.

"Waldo, go high. I'm low," he transmitted, sealing the contract the two pilots would hold for the next few minutes. Leonard would enter the engagement from below the bandits and Waldo from above. Neither would cross through the C-130's altitude unless he had the other Warthog in sight.

Leonard dove for the deck and leveled out at two hundred feet above the ground. Ahead of him, he could see the Hercules's belly a few hundred feet above him. "Lifter, can you take it lower?" he radioed. Flying low was a way of life for the Warthog drivers and Leonard was going to use the ground as an ally.

"Come on down, you muthas," he muttered. "What the hell are you?" By identifying the type of aircraft, he could anticipate their tactics and weapons.

A flaming wreckage tumbled out of the sky and Waldo answered the question for him. "Splash one Czech Aero. They're guns only, negative markings."

Leonard turned hard underneath the C-130 as a bandit cut in front of him and flew right into the funnel. The funnel, or low aspect gunsight, was projected on his HUD and marked the area in space where he could gun a bandit out of the sky. His finger flicked on the trigger and the Avenger gave off a brief buzz, sending a mix of fifty-four depleted uranium and high-explosive bullets into the funnel. Only one high-explosive slug hit the Aero, but it was enough. The small aircraft broke in two.

He was vaguely aware of a rattling sound on his left. He turned his head and saw the snout of another bandit pointed at him. The rattling was the sound of bullets striking the titanium tub that surrounded the cockpit. He wrenched his Warthog around, right into the Aero. Above him, the wingtip of the C-130 flashed by as Conklin maneuvered to shake off another bandit. A flaming wreckage missing a wing corkscrewed to the ground. Waldo was having a very good day.

The Aero and Leonard passed canopy to canopy and he felt a slight jar. He twisted around to see what had hap-

pened as he pulled up. The bandit's tail had struck his left
vertical stabilizer, ripping the upper third away. But he had
lost sight of the bandit.

The engagement turned into a close-in knife fight as the
two A-10s flew around the C-130, swatting at the Aeros
whenever they came too close. "Lifter," Leonard ordered,
"head south." Now he was thinking of fuel. They got fuel
problems, too, he thought, so how much longer can they
keep the furball going? On cue, the bandits broke off. "Ops
check," Leonard radioed, taking advantage of the break.
The bandits would be back.

"Four point one," Waldo answered. Leonard automatically translated that into forty-one hundred pounds of fuel
left. He was a little better. He checked his nav computer.
Ysterplaat was four hundred nautical miles away and at ten
pounds of fuel per mile, they were pushing flameout on
final.

Waldo was running the same numbers. "We can recover
at Beaufort West," he said. "But it's gonna be tight, especially if we engage again."

"I've called for help on the SatCom," Conklin added.
"Bull's on his way with two. Rendezvous in thirty minutes."

Good thinking, Leonard thought, clicking his mike button twice in acknowledgment. "They're like leeches," he
said.

"And they're good," Waldo acknowledged. Both pilots
had the measure of their adversaries. The Aeros were faster
and more agile, but what the Warthog gave away in speed
and maneuverability, it gained in greater firepower and
heavier armament. And the two Americans were more
aggressive, willing to engage a superior number of bandits.

"Who the hell are they?" Leonard said.

"They're white guys," Conklin answered. "I got a look on
one pass, he was that close."

"Two o'clock, high," Waldo called. "Very high." Four
bandits were dropping out of the sky for another attack.

Leonard squinted as he brought his nose onto the bandits.
This attack felt different, and a shiver shot down his spine.
"It's one pass, haul ass," he radioed.

"I hope so," Waldo answered. He pulled his Warthog into
the vertical and rolled, a ballet dancer pirouetting in the sky

as Waldo brought his jet's nose onto the first bandit. Reddish-brown smoke belched from the Warthog's cannon.

Sweat poured down Leonard's face, stinging his eyes, as he turned into the second bandit. He grunted hard, fighting the *G*s. Automatically, he let off the turn, worried about his damaged left rudder. He rolled for a belly check. Two more bandits were coming at him from below and behind. His mouth was dry and he ached with fatigue.

"Waldo!" he shouted, his voice machine-gun quick. "Two on me! Six o'clock low." He turned his Hog hard, bleeding off airspeed as he brought the big jet around. There was no chance of a shot, but he mashed the trigger anyway. "Honor the threat!" he shouted. It worked and his two attackers broke off, afraid of the Avenger cannon. Leonard turned back toward the C-130, looking for the first bandit he had engaged.

"On us!" Conklin shouted. "Twelve o'clock!" Leonard looked for the C-130 and saw a bandit on a head-on collision course with the C-130. It wasn't a suicide pass but a shoot-'em-in-the-face tactic. Conklin headed straight for the Aero, jinking hard.

Then Leonard saw another bandit swooping into Conklin's six o'clock. It was a well-coordinated attack with one objective—kill the C-130. Leonard didn't hesitate and cut behind the Hercules, rolling so he could see the attacker, trying to position for a gunshot. A missile leaped off the Aero. The speed of the air-to-air missile defied the imagination as it accelerated to over fifteen hundred miles an hour. But Leonard had time to mash the flare button on his right throttle. Three flares popped out behind his Hog and captured the infrared seeker head of the missile.

But the missile's flare reject mode functioned as designed and the seeker head ignored the flares and used them as steppingstones leading to Leonard. The missile hit the exhaust of the right engine and exploded.

Suddenly, the sky was empty of Aeros and Waldo joined on the C-130, looking for Leonard. "Tango, say position," Waldo radioed.

"He won't answer," Conklin answered. "He cut behind us in the last engagement to draw off a bandit at our six. I saw a fireball . . . it was a Hog . . . no chute."

"What did they come from?" Waldo asked. There was no answer.

Monday, March 16
The White House, Washington, D.C.

Mazie Hazelton paced back and forth as she talked, at ease in the cluttered mess of her office. Pontowski sat quietly, his eyes moving from the petite woman to Cyrus Piccard and back again to Mazie. "Your arrival yesterday at Andrews generated a lot of favorable coverage by the press," Mazie told him. "De Royer is a showman."

Piccard listened while Mazie prepped Pontowski for his appearance before the Joint Select Committee on Intelligence. The hearing was scheduled for later that day, and they believed a few members would be more sympathetic—thanks to de Royer. "Expect the hard questions from Nevers," Mazie told Pontowski. "Take your time answering, and it's much better to say too little than too much. Cyrus will be with us and don't be afraid to confer before answering."

"We're seeing a new side of Nevers lately," Piccard said. "Much more rational but still hard-driving."

"She has a new handler," Mazie said. "Jeff Bissell."

"Senator Lucknow's advisor?" Piccard said, not really asking a question. "He's one of the shrewdest intelligence experts on the Hill."

"He's also an image consultant," Mazie added. "I think Nevers is going for something much bigger . . . maybe a vice-presidential nomination." She turned to Pontowski. "The best strategy when testifying is to answer their questions, make it simple and keep it brief."

He stared at his hands. "Does the committee understand low-intensity conflict in the Third World?"

"Don't sell them short, Matt," Mazie said. "They may be politicians, but they're not dumb. They won't be playing politics, since this is a closed committee hearing."

"That's encouraging," Pontowski replied.

Mazie's computer beeped at her, and she keyed her

message board. She shot a worried look at Pontowski and then looked back to the screen. "Matt, you need to see this."

He pulled himself to his feet, still weary from jet lag, and read over her shoulder. Suddenly, he was old, aged by responsibility and burdened by caring. The images came flooding back, demanding to be remembered: The first time he had met John Leonard . . . when he had given Leonard his call sign, Tango . . . when Tango and Sara Waters had fallen in love . . . the time in China . . . Tango and Sara's wedding . . . Sara bidding him good-bye at Whiteman.

"Goddamn it to hell," he growled. "The itch." Now he knew what his subconscious had been trying to tell him. That lone bomb no one could account for was the clue. There was a new threat out there—someone had fighters and was willing to use them. He had been warned and had disregarded it. He hadn't thought it out, taken the time to analyze the threat, and he had thrown his Warthogs into an unknown situation they couldn't handle. He had been too wrapped up in the problems of command and had overlooked the threat.

Perhaps if Maggot had been there. Maggot . . . the best weapons and tactics officer in the Air Force . . . the man he had fired. Still, he couldn't pass the buck. He hadn't done his job.

"I'll have to tell Sara," he said, walking to the door. "And Sergeant Perko's family."

"The committee meeting," Mazie protested.

"This is more important," Pontowski replied.

"They'll hold you in contempt of Congress," Piccard told him. But he was talking to an empty doorway.

Monday, March 16
Knob Noster, Missouri

It was late afternoon when Sara Leonard saw the dark blue staff car drive up and park in her driveway. She froze when Matt Pontowski got out and she knew. It had happened before. "Melissa," she called, "please come here." The teenager responded to the sound of her voice and hurried to her mother's side. "The next few moments are going to be terrible," Sara said. "We must do this together because I can't do it alone."

"Mom, what's wrong?"

Sara did not reply and walked to the door, opening it before Pontowski could ring the bell. For a moment, neither said a word: They only looked at each other. "It's John," she said, a simple statement of fact.

Pontowski nodded dumbly, searching for the right words.

Melissa clenched at Sara's hand. "Oh, Mother," she whispered.

"Please come in," Sara said, leading the way into the family room. She was seven months pregnant and moved with a clumsy grace. "I was working on a layette," she told him as she shifted the baby clothes piled on the couch to one side and sat down.

"Sara, I'm sorry. It happened last night . . . I couldn't let anyone else tell you."

"What happened?"

"We don't have all the details yet, but he was escorting a C-130."

"Was the C-130 okay?" she asked.

He nodded, not knowing what to say. If they had been carrying Sidewinders, he thought. If we had been training for air-to-air. If . . . so many ifs.

Melissa watched her mother gather her emotions, taming them despite the tears flowing down her cheeks. "Mom," Melissa whispered, "I love you." It was a moment that marked her life, and she would never forget the lesson being played out in front of her.

Sara stood and walked into the kitchen. "Tango knew the risks. He did it willingly." She paused. "Does Little Matt know you're here?" A shake of his head. "Melissa, please go find him. He needs to see his father." Melissa hurried from the room while Sara methodically made coffee.

She stopped and stared at the ceiling, fresh tears flowing. "What am I? A black widow who conceives life and condemns her mate to death? Damn it, Muddy, I don't deserve this . . ." She stopped in midsentence, aware that she had called Pontowski by her first husband's name. The truth was on her face.

"Damn you to hell. All of you. You're all alike, there isn't one bit of difference between you. You are willing to risk your lives for people who don't even deserve to polish your boots. Why? Because you love humanity? You do it because of some crazy idea you carry around about duty . . . obligation . . . you can't even talk about it. But it's there, driving you. And damn you, you leave us behind to pick up the pieces."

Little Matt ran through the door, shouting with delight. He threw himself into his father's arms and held on. Then he realized something was wrong, and in his seven-year-old mind, it had to be something he did. "Daddy . . ."

Matt held him tight. "It's okay, good buddy."

"Come here and give me a hug, too," Sara said. "I've got something very sad to tell you and you must be brave. Can you do that? It's okay to cry if you want. Brave people aren't afraid to cry."

Melissa watched from the door as her mother gathered Little Matt into her arms and told him about death. She looked over at Pontowski, surprised by his tears. When Sara was finished explaining to Little Matt why John Leonard would never return, she sent him back to his father. "Matthew Zachary," she said, recalling another time in China when she had told him about Shoshana's death, "we have to quit doing this to each other."

A dark sadness edged Pontowski's voice. "Sara, I would give anything not to be here."

Sara Leonard shook her head. He didn't understand. "I don't mean just you and me . . . I mean all of us. We've got to quit doing this to each other."

Wednesday, March 18
The Capitol, Washington, D.C.

I was wrong, Cyrus Piccard thought. It's just not in Matt. He doesn't have that controlled, highly focused need to drive events, to lead, to impose his will on others. It was in his grandfather, carefully concealed and hidden from view. Perhaps he is still in shock from yesterday. It totally escapes me why the Senate would do that.

The old man looked up at the Joint Senate-House Select

Committee on Intelligence that had been grilling Pontowski and Mazie for over an hour on South Africa. He resigned himself to the inevitability of it all. The worst was yet to come when Nevers started her questioning.

Nevers took a sip of water. "Colonel Pontowski, I hope you are fully cognizant of why the Senate refused to confirm your promotion to brigadier general yesterday. Perhaps next time, after you have had time to mature in your present rank. But until then, we must all abide by the will of Congress." She referred to her notes, certain she had at last destroyed the man. It had been a simple matter to exercise the "old boy" network and use "congressional privilege" to have the Senate disapprove his promotion to brigadier general.

"I understand," Pontowski replied, wanting to get it over with.

"I, for one," Nevers continued, "am not satisfied with your excuse for not promptly answering this committee's summons."

Pontowski went rigid, lost for a reply. What is the matter with you? he thought, cursing himself. So the bastards took your star away. So what? Nevers peered at him over her reading glasses, a satisfied look on her face. Her look opened a floodgate and all his doubts and reservations washed away. He studied the committee for a moment, seeing them for what they were: a mixture of good and bad tainted with more than their fair share of ego and venality. Without exception, they were power freaks, more than willing to tell him how to do his job, even though only the crusty old chairman had ever seen combat. And he was neutral.

"Colonel Pontowski," Nevers said, "did you understand my question?"

"Are you okay?" Mazie asked him. "Can you go on?"

"Please excuse me, Mrs. Nevers. I had a bad moment." He reached under the table and squeezed Mazie's hand.

"Apparently, you've been having many bad moments lately," the congresswoman retorted.

"I wasn't aware you asked a question, Mrs. Nevers."

Piccard heard the tone in his voice and stiffened. It was a voice from out of the past. He sounds like his grandfather, Piccard thought. So much like Zack . . .

"The summons read," Pontowski continued, "to appear at the earliest possible time. This is that time."

"You were in Washington two days ago," Nevers replied, looking at him over her glasses.

"I was notified that two of my people had been killed in combat. One was my second in command and the other a heroic loadmaster. Both had served their country honorably, and it was my responsibility to—"

Nevers cut him off. "Normal channels, Colonel. Ever hear of them?"

"Yes, ma'am, I have. But these were my people and I had to tell Colonel Leonard's wife. I had to tell Sergeant Perko's parents that their daughter had been killed in the line of duty."

"That hardly answers why you failed to appear before this committee," Nevers interrupted.

Pontowski wouldn't cave in. "These were my friends, the men and women I have been entrusted to lead. I don't abandon my people." His last words carried a force that stunned the committee into silence.

Nevers was an astute politician and knew the committee chairman would gladly leak any display of insensitivity or arrogance on her part to the press. She tried a new approach. "Colonel, you spoke earlier of responsibility."

Where is she headed now? Piccard thought.

"It appears," Nevers continued, "that the South Africans act more responsibly than you."

Pontowski's tone was calm and measured as he answered. "What is responsible, or for that matter moral, about ethnic cleansing . . . the senseless murder of innocent men, women, and children because they are of a different tribe . . . stealing food and medical supplies to sell on the black market . . . the wanton destruction of a country in the name of greed and stupidity?"

Well, Piccard told himself, I was wrong about Matt. He does have the will to power, and like his grandfather, he keeps it hidden. He settled back into his chair and enjoyed the next hour.

Piccard led the way into Bill Carroll's office for the wrapup on the committee hearing. He almost twirled his

261

cane like a baton as he marched through the door. "Well?" Carroll asked from his chair.

"It was magnificent," Piccard said.

"At least, it ended well," Mazie told him. She quickly recapped the hearing for Carroll.

"The committee found the concept of duty and responsibility very disconcerting," Piccard mused. "Because of our young friend's performance, and in spite of the sound and fury emanating from Ms. Nevers, I don't see any precipitous change in our South Africa policy."

"Matt, I talked to the secretary of defense," Carroll said. "He'll get your star back . . . right after you get out of Africa and clear of the UN. Any assignment you want, you can have."

"I'll stay right where I am," Pontowski replied. "I want to know who nailed Tango. Where did those Aeros come from?"

Piccard stared at him. There was no doubt that he was Zack's grandson . . . the same quiet determination, the unshakable resolve, the hard look in his eyes . . . it was all there.

Mazie finally answered Pontowski's question. "It was probably the Iron Guard."

Pontowski gritted his teeth, and his eyes drew into a narrow squint. "You're not certain?" he asked.

"Not absolutely," Carroll said. "There is enough doubt to preclude a retaliatory strike. The South African minister of defense—"

"Pendulo is a little shit," Pontowski said, interrupting him.

Carroll disregarded the remark and pressed ahead. "—claims the attack on the C-130 and the A-10s took place in South African airspace and therefore is an internal matter. Obviously, the political situation is confused and we haven't got all the players sorted out."

"Give me the rest of my wing and I'll sort them out."

"We can't do that," Carroll replied. "At least for now, our policy locks us into supporting the UN, the safe zones, and humanitarian relief efforts."

"Then tell me what the Iron Guard has to throw at us. I'm tired of operating in the dark. Also, we've walked into one too many ambushes. We got a leak the size of Niagara Falls over there and we got to plug it."

"Do you have any idea where it might be?" Mazie asked.

"I haven't got a clue."

"Mazie," Carroll said, "show Matt the latest we have on the Iron Guard's order of battle." She nodded and escorted Pontowski out of the office, leaving Piccard and Carroll alone.

"Well?" Piccard asked. Carroll didn't answer and leaned back in his chair, closing his eyes. "You left Matt hanging," Piccard said. Still no answer from Carroll. "I refuse to believe that you are going to let the Iron Guard get away with shooting down one of our aircraft."

"I'm not," Carroll replied. "But our first priority is still Prime."

"Ah, the great enigma," Piccard said.

Carroll smiled. "Fortunately, science is in the brain and not in a laboratory or a book. The key is the scientist, Itzig Slavin."

"Who is working for a madman who has the resolve, not to mention the weapons, to fight."

"That does complicate the situation," Carroll allowed. "I believe the director of central intelligence is about to receive some very firm marching orders."

"When are you returning to Cape Town?" Mazie asked as she opened a safe in her office.

"The first flight I can get on is Saturday. I'm flying out of New York with de Royer. At least it's a chance to spend time with my son and show him the UN."

"Have you seen our profile on de Royer?" Mazie asked. Without waiting for an answer, she handed him a thin dossier. "And here is the file on the Iron Guard and Beckmann. I think you'll find this interesting reading."

He thumbed through the Iron Guard's order of battle. The list of weapons was impressive. "This is a surprise I didn't need. Why haven't we seen this before?"

"The CIA released it yesterday. The spooks are caught up in a big internal reorganization and it's been chaos at Langley . . . all kinds of turf squabbles . . . work slow-downs . . . people afraid to take responsibility."

"What's the matter with those idiots? They're playing bureaucratic games while my people are in harm's way. Look at what the Iron Guard has got. I don't want to tangle with these guys." He sat down and started to read. He read the dossier on de Royer next, and as Mazie had promised, it was interesting reading. De Royer was described as intellectual, politically astute, decorated for heroism eleven times, and wounded twice in combat. One paragraph pounded at him. De Royer's wife and two sons had been killed in a terrorist bomb blast meant for him. On the negative side, de Royer was described as "an extremely aggressive battlefield commander prone to take high risks."

"This isn't the de Royer I've seen," Pontowski muttered to himself.

Then he turned to the files on Beckmann and the Iron Guard. When he was finished, he reached for the phone and punched in a number, calling his wing at Whiteman Air Force Base in Missouri. A familiar voice from Operations answered on the first ring. "Find Maggot," he ordered.

CHAPTER
17

Thursday, March 19
Bloemfontein, South Africa

MacKay was tired when he returned to his apartment after a long day at Security Systems, Inc., the cover business the Boys had set up for him. They had done a good job and the business was flourishing. He bent and checked the telltales that sealed the bottom of his front door. They hadn't been disturbed and he went inside, not bothering to go through the drill of clearing the door, scanning the apartment, and searching for bugs or cameras.

"Not smart," a voice said from the bedroom.

He gave a mental sigh. It was one of the Boys. A tall, very slender, middle-aged woman came out of the bedroom. Her hair was cut short like a man's and she wore big glasses. She smiled at MacKay, more like a friendly family counselor or teacher than a CIA agent. "I scanned the apartment," she told him. "It's clean. How's your cover working?"

"Too good," he answered. "I'm actually making money."

"That's nice. Spend it."

"So why are you here?" he asked.

"The boss wants to meet Doctor Slavin," she replied.

"That's dumb," MacKay said. "I can't make that happen. Tell Standard to quit pushing so hard or it will blow the whole operation apart."

"Set it up for next week," she said, smiling as if she hadn't heard him.

"Now how am I supposed to do that?"

"Use the girl."

"I won't see her until next month," he lied.

"Oh, I didn't know that." She reached into her purse and handed him a set of photos. Each photo was imprinted with the date and time and showed Ziba entering his apartment almost every night since he had been at Bloemfontein. "I assume she'll be here tonight."

"You took these?"

The smile never left her face. "Of course."

"I'll need leverage to get Slavin here."

She reached into her purse again, produced another photo, and handed it to him. The smile vanished and her face filled with hurt. He froze. Ziba was in bed with Slavin. "Where did you get this?"

"From our contact in Inkatha," the woman replied.

"She told me she had left Inkatha."

"She had. But she got caught up again when she met you. This isn't a game you play at on weekends and Inkatha won't let her go." She pointed at the photo. "That's the way women are used in this business."

"I know," he muttered, still staring at the photo. Why couldn't he look away? Why couldn't he let it go? He felt the woman touch his arm.

"We need to talk to Slavin soon, before . . ." Her voice trailed off.

"Before what?" he demanded.

"The Company's shrinks think Beckmann has gone over the edge. We're not sure what he'll do. And he's got nerve gas."

"Sweet Jesus," MacKay whispered. "You think the crazy mutha will use it?" She nodded. "I'll set it up," he said.

MacKay answered the door at the first knock. As expected, Ziba was standing there, and without a word, he held the door for her to enter. Once inside, he sat down and watched her as she moved around the room, making herself at home. The hurt was back and with it a rage that kept building, taking him with it. "What is wrong?" she asked.

"This," he said, tossing the photo at her. It spun across the room and landed at her feet. She glanced down at it and raised her head. Her face was calm and her eyes fixed on him. "Well?" he demanded. Her answer was silence. "I thought Zulu girls took their virginity seriously," he growled.

No emotion crossed her face. "We do. You were the first."

The truth of it destroyed what little self-control he had left and he came out of his chair. She didn't move as he grabbed her arms. "You fuckin' bitch . . ." He slapped her, hard, still holding on to her arm with his left hand.

She broke free of his grasp, surprising him with her strength, and slapped him back. It was a controlled reaction, fast and decisive, struck without hesitation. The force of the blow stunned him and he stepped back, ready to come at her again, but her look stopped him. She was no match for him but she was still the image of a queen, proud and defiant, regal until the end. "There are things here you do not understand," she said.

"I understand you're fuckin' Slavin."

She stared him into silence. "What do you want?"

"To meet Slavin, here, Saturday."

"No," she said. "I won't do that." Her face softened and she shook her head. "I'm sorry that it came to this, John Author." She turned and left, leaving the door open behind her.

MacKay picked the photo up and sat down. For a few moments he stared at the open door, hoping she would come back. He fumbled for a match on the end table beside him and burned the photo. He held it until the flames seared his fingertips.

Saturday, March 21
Cape Town, South Africa

Richard Davis Standard was angry, intensely and furiously enraged. He stalked his office like a caged tiger, unleashed violence rippling under his skin. Fortunately, the focus of his fury was eight thousand miles away and, thanks to the time difference, not yet at work. Otherwise, it would have been the first recorded murder by long-distance electronic evisceration, a telephonic disemboweling.

He paused long enough to smooth out the latest dispatch from his boss, the division chief for Sub-Saharan Africa at Langley. "Gengha Dung is an idiot," he muttered under his breath. But Standard was a professional and knew there was little he could do but give his superiors the blood sacrifice they were demanding. He had developed every contact, every line of investigation possible trying to crack Prime. But since only MacKay had been successful, he must be sent inside. He reread the latest epistle written in Gengha's stained-glass prose, those models of grammatical composition that earned her promotion.

But the message was unequivocal and clear: Get results fast or you're history. Standard had never received such strongly worded marching orders. Damn! he raged to himself. Do they think Prime is the only case I'm working on? I've got the Azanians wired for sound and found Erik Beckmann, thanks to the fiasco at Vanwyksvlei when the UN tried to set up its first safe zone and relief center. Doesn't that count?

He reread the last paragraph, detailing an additional problem: An informant in Cape Town was passing on information about UN operations to the Iron Guard. He picked up the phone and called the Boys. This was an easy problem to fix.

He checked his watch. MacKay was an hour overdue for the meeting.

"The plane was late," MacKay said when he finally arrived, two hours late for the meeting. The delay had not helped Standard's blood pressure. "Am I finished at Bloemfontein?"

Standard shook his head. "Not hardly. The company still wants action on Prime. You're all I got in position and we've got to turn up the rheostat a few hundred degrees."

"How? You saw the report. I lost Chembo." Now MacKay was pacing the floor, another caged carnivore. "I screwed up and totally blew it."

"The clock's ticking," Standard said.

"Tell me. Any suggestions?"

The emotion behind MacKay's words surprised Standard. He's totally involved in this, Standard thought. Why? Standard was silent, evaluating the man. What was motivating MacKay? Was it race? But that didn't track. MacKay was too complex and intelligent to be motivated by that narrow issue alone. No doubt the racial issue was there, but it was not enough. What was in MacKay's background to drive him to the edge? Again, he didn't know. Standard was angry at himself for not understanding blacks better. So, lacking understanding, he fell back on the only reference he had—himself.

It has got to be the woman, Ziba Chembo, Standard decided. He's fallen for her. That's the key to the poor bastard. "I want to send you inside," Standard said, breaking the long silence.

"When?" MacKay asked.

Standard worked the problem. MacKay was what the CIA called a NOC, an agent posing as a businessman with nonofficial cover. His chances of successfully penetrating Iron Gate as a spy were too low to even calculate. Unless . . . The pieces all came together. "First," Standard said, "we've got to give you the background and motivation to become a mercenary for the Iron Guard. Second, you need an entrée."

He buzzed for the Boys. "The gunman you terminated in Joburg . . . you're going to use his ID . . ."

"That's dumber than a can of rocks," MacKay muttered.

Standard allowed a tight smile. "But not in the way you think." The door opened and the Boys entered. "Good morning, ladies," he said. "Make yourselves comfortable." Two sat down on a couch while the tall one sank to the floor yoga-style. Their leader leaned against a wall and folded her arms across her chest, waiting to be surprised.

He paced his office, wearing a path in the rug. "I want the Iron Guard to recruit MacKay as a security expert. He needs credentials that will make them wet their pants and overcome any objections they might have about hiring a black American."

The woman sitting on the floor perked up. "Sicherheits Dienste, A.G., is still in business in Germany. They did the security systems for the Bruderbund. The Bruderbund is the Iron Guard's biggest supporter in Europe." She looked at Standard expectantly. "Perhaps Mr. MacKay worked for Sicherheits Dienste at one time."

Sicherheits Dienste, A.G., Security Service, Inc., was a front company started by former Nazis working for the CIA in the 1960s. They had deliberately named the company after Hitler's security service to attract a certain clientele. Because of its connections to the past and supposed political orientation, the company had installed an elaborate security system for the Bruderbund, a new fascist political party in Germany.

"Of course MacKay worked for them," Standard said. "Set the connection up. When the Iron Guard asks for a reference through the Bruderbund, our good friend here will look like a money-hungry, unprincipled, computer genius freelancing security systems. While you're doing that, teach Mr. MacKay how to make those ID cards." He paused, thinking. "Ruin his business at Bloemfontein . . . something about government corruption and bribes. We've got to move fast on this one."

The woman leaning against the wall was not surprised. "We can do that," she said.

Saturday, March 21
JFK International Airport, New York

The large number of people waiting to board the South African Airways flight to Cape Town swirled around Pontowski. Little Matt held on to his hand tightly, afraid of the crowd. Martha Marshall held back to give them space to be alone before the flight was called.

Little Matt was still bursting with questions about their tour of the United Nations. "Was there a real person talking to us on the earphones?" he asked. "Or was it a recording?" Pontowski explained that they had been listening to a real person translate the speech being given to the General Assembly. "I'm sure glad they translated," his son told him. "I didn't understand a single word. Do you really work for the man who was talking? He speaks a funny language. How tall is he?"

Pontowski smiled "Yep. That's the general I work for. His name is General Charles de Royer and he sounds funny because he was speaking French. But he can also speak English. I'm not real sure how tall he is, but I'd guess about six feet ten inches. You know, good buddy, it might be a good idea if you learned to speak a foreign language."

"What language did my mom speak?"

"She spoke Hebrew," Pontowski told him, recalling how Shoshana could make that harsh, guttural language sound soft and tender.

"I'll learn Hebrew," Little Matt announced.

Pontowski tousled his hair and smiled. "She would like that." They talked until the speaker blared the last call for boarding. They went through the departing ritual that had become an ingrained part of their lives. "I'll do good in school," Little Matt promised. Pontowski headed for the jetway leading to the Boeing 747-400. He turned and waved. Little Matt waved back, holding on to Martha's hand. He could see the tears in her eyes but Little Matt was smiling. I've got one great kid, Pontowski decided. I've got to stop running out on him.

The flight attendant directed him to the top lounge of the first-class section directly behind the flight deck. He climbed the circular stairs and was surprised to find the small lounge empty of passengers and only a flight attendant waiting for him. "Please make yourself comfortable," he told Pontowski. "It's eighteen hours to Cape Town with a brief stop in the Cape Verde Islands for fuel. We'll depart as soon as our last passenger arrives." He turned at the sound of a commotion on the stairs. "Here she is now. We'll push back and be on our way in a few minutes."

Elena Martine stepped onto the lounge deck and sat down next to him. She was wearing a dark, conservative business suit and her hair was carefully arranged in an old-fashioned bun. Her image was totally different than in Cape Town. Her UN persona, Pontowski decided. "I didn't know you were here," he said.

"I was recalled after the attack at Douglas," she told him. "Some of my colleagues are losing their nerve, and my mission to South Africa is under review. I am being criticized for not having maintained the proper neutrality and objectivity as required by UN charter."

"Where is de Royer?" he asked.

"He may be relieved of command and was called to Paris at the last moment."

"Who in the hell is running the show in Cape Town?"

She gave him a studied look and looked around the empty lounge. "This should be very nice, don't you think? Excuse me while I change into something more comfortable for traveling." She disappeared into the lavatory.

She rejoined him wearing a floor-length, very simple, loose-cut black gown. Her dark hair was combed out and hung in a heavy mass down her back. He watched her move, seriously doubting that she was wearing anything underneath the gown. She curled up in the seat opposite him, smiled, pulled a thick report out of her briefcase, and started to read, a pair of reading glasses perched becomingly on her nose.

Pontowski fell into his own thoughts, mulling over the situation in Cape Town. With de Royer gone, who was in command? It certainly wouldn't be him, not since he had lost his star. There was no doubt in his mind that Nevers had used congressional privilege to lobby the Senate into disapproving his promotion to brigadier. Normally, that was the kiss of death to any officer's career, and regardless of what Secretary of Defense Elkins had promised, he seriously doubted that the Senate would ever approve his promotion. But was he going to let Nevers drive his future? True, he wanted to make a life for Little Matt, and he could do that outside the Air Force. But what kind of father would he be if he ran from the hardest challenge in his life?

Nevers had not directly attacked him but had knifed him in the back. How many times had his grandfather complained, always in private, about the total lack of integrity among so many of his colleagues. Political integrity, Pontowski thought, is the ultimate contradiction in terms.

Then he considered the smear job Gordon had done on de Royer and himself. Why did she do that? Was she seeking retribution because of that press briefing when he had called her on the mistakes she had made? Or was she pushing a hidden agenda? Perhaps journalistic integrity rated right up there with the political variety. Are you done feeling sorry for yourself? he asked himself. Get on with the job.

They were silent until the 747 leveled off at altitude over the Atlantic. Elena dropped the report and studied his face until she had his attention. "Matt, why did they do that?"

"Disapprove my promotion to BG? Who knows." He gave her his best grin. "It happens."

The flight attendant served dinner and after clearing the remnants of the meal away, discreetly withdrew and turned the cabin lights down, leaving them alone in an island of soft light. "Matt," she said, "please forgive me for asking, but was that your wife and son with you at the airport?"

"That was Martha Marshall, Little Matt's nanny. She flew out to take Little Matt back home. I never remarried after I lost my wife, Shoshana."

"Oh, I'm sorry." She leaned back in her seat and gave him a bewitching look. "Your Martha is a very handsome woman. For a moment, I thought you were a man who preferred older women." They laughed together. Then she leaned forward, the low neckline of her dress falling open as her hand touched his knee, letting him see her body. He had guessed right about what was underneath the gown.

"Matt"—the way she called his name sent shivers down his back—"I am very fond of you."

The grin was back. "All things considered, I hope so."

She moved onto the seat beside him, her movements fluid and graceful as she touched his arm. Her hand was warm and she seemed to glow. Up close, she was even more beautiful, and her lustrous brown eyes carried an unspoken promise. Her scent embraced him like a warm summer night's breeze, making him think of his first love. Suddenly, his defenses were up and he pulled into a mental defensive crouch. Why?

She sensed his reaction and spoke in a low voice, almost a whisper. "Matt, we have had our disagreements, but don't be afraid of me." She came into his arms.

It was going to be a long flight to Cape Town.

Sunday, March 22
Ysterplaat Air Base, Cape Town

The sun was setting when Pontowski walked into the COIC and found Waldo at his normal job as duty officer. The pudgy captain stood up and his mouth fell open when he saw the eagles on his shoulders. "Sir, I . . . ah . . . oh, shit."

"You got that right, Waldo," Pontowski told him. "It happens. Congress refused to confirm my promotion to brigadier."

"That's not fair, sir. It's just not fair."

"Life has never been fair," Pontowski said. "Where is everybody?"

"The UN isn't doing a thing, so Colonel Kowalski stood us down." A worried look shot across his face. "Probably a smart thing . . . things are pretty bad around here."

"Okay, Waldo. Spill it. What's going on?"

"Sir, you better talk to Colonel Kowalski. She's still in her office."

"Is it that bad, Waldo?"

"Yes, sir."

Pontowski sat quietly while Kowalski paced back and forth in her office. "It all started when I submitted Colonel Leonard and Sergeant Perko for the Air Force Cross. Perko's came back immediately—disapproved. After that, everyone split apart and pulled into their separate caves." She gave him a hard look as if he had been personally responsible. "It's the trash-hauler thing. We're taking most of the casualties here and we're getting dumped on, no promotion, no medals."

"Lydia," he said, his voice matter-of-fact, "we all get dumped on. I'll sort the medals out. Now let's get morale turned around."

She looked at the eagles on his shoulders. "I don't know how to turn it around," she admitted.

"Just like last time," he said. "Step number one, do

274

something. Even if it's wrong. We start by flying, that's our job."

"But there's no tasking."

"Then we train until we get tasking from the UN." He grinned at her. "Hell, they're just like us, floundering in the dark. Get the schedulers in here. First training sorties launch at oh seven hundred."

"Sir, that's only twelve hours away."

"Oh seven hundred, Lydia," he interrupted. "By the way, why is Waldo always duty officer?"

"That's an A-10 thing and he volunteers for it."

"Change that."

"He's an A-10 driver. I can't tell them what to do."

"The hell you can't. You've got the wing." He smiled at the look on her face. "Supposedly, I'm still the vice-commander and running air operations for the UN. Your orders come from me, right?"

"But a wing commander . . . that calls for a full bull or a BG. I'm still a . . ." Her voice trailed off and she stared out the window.

"Lieutenant colonel," he finished for her. "And my slot calls for a brigadier general. I'll tell the Air Force and the UN to sort it out. While they fumble, we do it by the book—the highest-ranking qualified officer gets the job. That's you." He gave her an encouraging smile and left.

Colonel Bouchard, de Royer's aide-de-camp, was waiting for him outside Kowalski's office. "Sir, I heard you had returned"—he gaped at the eagles on Pontowski's shoulders—"ah . . . ah . . . there is a message from the UN. Until General de Royer returns, you are in command."

"Doesn't that beat all," Pontowski said.

Tuesday, March 24
UN Headquarters, Constantia,
Cape Town

The intercom on Pontowski's desk buzzed. "Colonel," Piet van der Roos said, "there's a Captain Stuart here to see you."

"Send him in," Pontowski told him. "And please ask Colonel Bouchard to step in." He stood up as Maggot came through the door. "Thanks for coming," he said, extending his hand. They shook hands.

"Have a seat," Pontowski said, waving him to a couch. Maggot sat and listened as Pontowski described the problems he was facing. "Basically, I need a concept of tactical operations that ties everything we're doing together. All I've got right now are pieces." Van der Roos interrupted, saying Bouchard was waiting outside. "Bouchard is one of the pieces I was talking about," Pontowski said. He introduced Maggot to Bouchard and Piet and motioned the three men to sit down.

"Colonel Bouchard," Pontowski began, "I'm an old fighter jock who hasn't got a clue about the way ground forces are employed. So until General de Royer comes back, I want you to be in command of the UN ground forces." His announcement was greeted with silence.

"Sir," Bouchard finally replied, "of course I will do as you ask. But this is most unusual."

"The nice thing about being in charge," Pontowski said, "is that I can do unusual things." He turned to Maggot. "For example, I want a full-up ACT program." ACT was air combat tactics—dogfighting to civilians. But the slow and ungainly Warthog had not been designed to engage other aircraft in air-to-air combat.

"You got it," Maggot assured him.

"What happened to Tango isn't going to happen again to anyone," Pontowski told them. "I'm tired of getting our asses kicked around every time we do something. From now on, we're the kickers and not the kickees. The problem is, we're doing this operation on the cheap because no one really wants to get behind us with the support we need. So how do we do the job?" For the next two hours, the men held a council of war.

When they left, Pontowski sank back in his chair and thought about Maggot. Dwight Stuart was a changed man and had finally grown up. Has he lost his edge in the process? Pontowski wondered. Is he still the Maggot I need;

the go-for-broke, fangs-out, shoot-'em-in-the-face, aerial assassin who knows how to fly and fight?

Only time would tell.

Bouchard was waiting for Pontowski when he returned from lunch. "We have a problem," the Frenchman told him. "Pendulo is demanding to see General de Royer at the Defense Ministry. But as the general has not returned . . ."

"The ball is in my court," Pontowski said.

"Madame Martine is with him," Bouchard said.

"She knows de Royer isn't here and I'm in command until he gets back . . . or replaced." Pontowski grabbed his hat. "I'd appreciate it if you'd come with me."

The two men were kept waiting for over an hour before being escorted into the minister's office. Pontowski masked his irritation at the delay and said nothing as he waited for Pendulo to finish talking on the telephone. Elena Martine was sitting in a comfortable chair, drinking tea. Pendulo finally hung up and looked at the two men.

"Perhaps you remember," he began, "the unfortunate incident with the Afrikaner inspectors you ordered to leave the supply tents? As you know, they were authorized by the UN Observer Mission to inspect all relief supplies before shipment. Further, Ysterplaat is a South African air base and falls under my jurisdiction. You exceeded your authority when you ordered them to leave the base and embarrassed my government."

"They will be allowed to return," Elena said, "and you must apologize to them. It has all been decided at the UN."

Pontowski clamped an iron control over what he wanted to say. Instead, he said, "No way. They threatened to shoot down my aircraft and I always honor the threat."

"Nevertheless"—Elena smiled—"you must apologize and assist them in every way. As I said, it was been decided."

"We have a problem," Bouchard said. "The inspectors are from the AWB. They are an armed group and have threatened the Americans with violence. Therefore, the UN in its peacekeeping role must separate the two factions. Since I am the ground commander in General de Royer's absence, I will not allow anyone from the AWB to approach the American tents."

"You do not have that authority," Elena said, glaring at Bouchard.

Bouchard's face was frozen into a waxen mask. "Ah, but I do. If they disobey me, I will shoot them."

"Since I have made Colonel Bouchard my ground commander," Pontowski said, "I must support him. Is there anything else?"

A deep frown cut across Elena's face as Pendulo shook his head. Bouchard held the door for Pontowski to leave. *"Au revoir,"* he said, following Pontowski outside.

"Whose side is she on?" Pontowski asked in French.

Bouchard gave a very Gallic shrug. "The UN must remain neutral at all times. But for the bureaucrats like Martine it becomes a game, keeping their impressive titles, enjoying their privileges, antagonizing no one, and accomplishing little."

"Anyway," Pontowski said, "thanks for saving my backside in there. I didn't know a ground commander had that authority."

"I made it up," Bouchard told him.

Pontowski shook his head. "I'll be damned."

"Colonel, may I offer you advice?"

"Certainly," Pontowski replied.

"Stop sleeping with Martine."

"Is it that obvious?" Pontowski asked.

"She expected your support in there," Bouchard answered. "When you opposed her, she was very angry. Martine is very calculating and all is for a reason. It is one of their games."

"I'm not sure I understand," Pontowski told him, still speaking in French.

Bouchard looked at him with his one good eye. "She sleeps with you to gain control. You must look for connections."

Pontowski thought about it. They had made love on the 747 coming back from New York, three days ago. She had mentioned her mission to South Africa was being criticized for not being neutral. But if she knew about allowing the inspectors back on base, why didn't she tell him then? Was she softening him up in advance? Were there other connections he had missed? Maybe there was something to the French way of thinking. "Is Elena French?" he asked.

"She is German."

Thursday, March 26
Bloemfontein, South Africa

Sam was awake early, researching a story lead, when Gordon returned to their suite in the Landdrost Hotel. She gave Sam a quick look and flopped into a chair near the big window. "I can smell him on you," Sam said. "Did you have to sleep with him?"

Gordon gave her a mind-your-own-business look. "Is there any coffee?" she asked. Sam moved over to the sideboard and poured her a cup. "He is the most unique man I've ever met," Gordon said.

"He's Hans Beckmann," Sam reminded her.

"He's not what you think," Gordon protested. "He's so innocent—"

"Right," Sam interrupted.

"—in some ways," Gordon finished. "He's . . . well . . . he's different."

"It sounds like you're confused," Sam said, handing her the coffee.

"Sam, this is good for my career. I can feel it in my bones."

"That's not the only place you can feel it," Sam said. "Liz, you've got to quit sleeping around."

"Oh, Sam. How many men have I slept with?"

"You don't know?"

"Sam, counting Hans, there's only been four in the past ten years."

"That doesn't match your reputation."

"I was pretty wild before AIDS came along," Gordon admitted. "It got me what I wanted."

"Well, I hope you're practicing safe sex now."

Gordon sighed. "I'm not stupid. Besides, he did." She looked at Sam, feeling the need to explain. "When we were in bed . . . I couldn't think . . . I was caught up . . . I trusted him."

Sam sat down and propped her feet up on an ottoman. "How can you be so stupid." She immediately regretted saying it when she saw the hurt look on Gordon's face. "I'm sorry, I didn't mean that."

"Sam, this time it's different. He's so tender. The way he touched me and talked . . . all I could do was close my eyes and listen." She closed her eyes, remembering. "I climaxed twice before he came. He knows me, Sam."

"It certainly sounds like it."

Gordon smiled. "Hans says there's a story in Kimberley and we can scoop the other reporters. We're booked on a flight this evening." She walked into her bedroom, shedding her clothes.

After a few moments, Sam heard the shower start to run. She walked over to the window and looked out over the garden. "Oh, Liz," she murmured. "He's using you."

Thursday, March 26
Durban, South Africa

MacKay was sitting alone on the veranda of the George Hotel overlooking Marine Parade. Clustered around him were tight little knots of white mercenaries, all searching for employment. Occasionally, one would shoot a curious or hostile glance his way, wondering what a black was doing in the midst of a group of men who wanted to kill Africans for money. But better judgment prevailed and he was left alone.

MacKay folded his newspaper and studied the people walking by. He stifled the impatience that was eating at him. I've only been here thirty-six hours, he told himself. I've put out the bait like the Boys said. Now wait for the nibbles.

He didn't see the newcomer enter the veranda. The man searched the crowd until he found a mercenary who was bigger and taller than MacKay. Satisfied with his choice, he spoke to the mercenary who, like MacKay, wore a beard. The mercenary got up and walked over to MacKay.

"Hey, nigger," he said, "time to get the fuck outa here. You can tell time, right? Or you movin' on fuckin' African time?"

MacKay looked up and motioned for a waiter. "Please sit down," he said. He pushed a chair back for the mercenary.

The man kicked it over. "You stupid, nigger? I said it was time to leave. Maybe you're hard of hearing." He reached over and flicked MacKay's right ear with a snap of his forefinger and thumb. "That knock any wax out?"

MacKay's voice was controlled and polite. "No. Please sit down and let me buy you a beer. I'd like to ask you a few questions."

"Whatcha gonna 'axed' me?" the man said, snarling the inner-city pronunciation of "asked."

MacKay saw the newcomer standing at the bar, watching him. The local recruiter, he decided, and this is press-to-test time. He leaned into the mercenary as if to share a confidence. "I was going to 'axed' you to quit acting like a flaming asshole." The man blinked. "And ask why your fly is open." The man blinked again. A very bad mistake. MacKay grabbed his beard and jerked hard, slamming his chin down onto the table. He grabbed the mercenary's hair with his other hand and lifted, only to jerk down again. MacKay set up a piledriver motion, repeatedly smashing the man's chin onto the table.

Another mercenary was coming at him to rescue his buddy. MacKay's right foot shot out and dislocated his kneecap. A third was moving, a switchblade in his hand. MacKay smiled at him. "You're not that good."

"Enough," a voice from the bar said. It was the newcomer. He walked over and sat down. "Get these fools out of here," he said in a loud voice, pointing at the two men lying on the floor. "May we have some privacy?" The bar quickly emptied and the two men were dragged out. "Clean up the blood," he ordered. A waiter scurried over with a wet towel to mop the floor.

"I'm impressed," MacKay said.

"They know me," the newcomer said, extending his hand and introducing himself. "Marius Kreiner."

MacKay shook his hand. "John Mills," he said, using his cover name from Bloemfontein.

"Well, Mr. Mills, I heard your speciality was security systems. But this is not what we had in mind."

You're talking to me, MacKay thought, so it must be

pretty damn close to what you had in mind. "I specialize in computer-based security systems. I use to work for Sicherheits Dienste in Germany and developed their system. It's the best in the world."

"So I've heard," Kreiner said, working to contain his excitement at finding someone with those credentials. "I assume Sicherheits Dienste will vouch for you."

"Ask them," MacKay said.

"I will, Mr. Mills. I will." Kreiner stood up to leave.

"Show them this," MacKay said. He threw an ID card on the table. It was like the card he had taken off the killer's body in Johannesburg, but it had his picture on it.

"Where did you get this?" Kreiner asked.

"I made it."

"But how?"

MacKay threw the original ID card on the table. "From this one. I had a disagreement with its owner just before Christmas."

"He's one of ours," Kreiner told him.

"Was one of yours," MacKay corrected. "Was. He was celebrating in Soweto . . . something about finishing an assignment . . . and wanted some action with my lady. He said he could afford the price."

"And," Kreiner urged, very interested.

"He couldn't afford the price," MacKay told him.

"We'll be in contact, Mr. Mills."

The knock on MacKay's hotel door came just before midnight. It was Kreiner. "May I come in?" he asked. MacKay motioned him in and closed the door. "Your credentials are most impressive, Mr. Mills, and we have need of someone with your skills. Obviously, we hire blacks. But they must be willing to support us against other Africans."

"I'm not an African," MacKay said. "I had a good business going in Bloemfontein until some 'Africans'—the black bastards—got their hands on my stock in a warehouse. When I couldn't come up with the 'commissions' to bribe them, my business licenses were revoked and my bank accounts impounded. They ruined me. They even took my passport away." He threw a new passport onto the table. "So I made this one."

"Why don't you leave the country?" Kreiner asked.

"I will . . . when the time is right. I need to tie up some loose ends. Where would I be working?"

"Does it matter?"

"The loose ends I mentioned are in Bloemfontein."

"Ah, I see," Kreiner said. "Revenge. It can be arranged."

CHAPTER
18

Friday, March 27
Kimberley, South Africa

Elizabeth Gordon was standing on the observation platform overlooking the Big Hole while Sam Darnell shot the background. "Done," Sam said. She focused on Gordon and cued her to start talking.

"The ancient hunters and gatherers who lived here centuries ago," Gordon began, looking into the lens, "called this part of South Africa 'Karoo,' the thirsty land. It is ironic that the world's largest diamond strike occurred here, in such a desolate place. Behind me is the Big Hole, once the world's richest diamond mine. It is over a half-mile deep and almost a mile across. Over fourteen and a half million carats of diamonds, that's three tons, were mined before the Big Hole played out. Today, all that remains is this huge, man-made pit, partially filled with water."

A loud noise momentarily distracted her. She paused, then continued. "In many respects, the Big Hole is a prime example of the impact of the modern world on this ancient land and its people. The more I know of this strangely beautiful land . . ." Gunshots echoed over the two women, and they looked toward the parking lot. "What's going on?" Gordon gasped.

The sounds of a full-fledged demonstration were coming their way. "Head for the car," Sam said. They ran for the car and piled in. Sam drove and headed for the entrance, past a large crowd that was moving toward the observation platform where they had been moments before.

"Hold on," Gordon said. "I've seen lots of demonstrations, and this is not a hostile crowd. I want to get it."

Sam looked at her in amazement. "You crazy?" She had covered too many demonstrations that had become ugly, and every time, the mob had turned on the female photographers first.

"This is our job," Gordon told her. "Stop the car." Sam did as she ordered and pulled over.

Gordon held the remote microphone as they hurried toward the crowd. She held the microphone up to a group of chanting boys who were waving a gold and black flag. The sight of two foreign white women conducting TV interviews did the trick, and they smiled, saying they were the Azanian National Liberation Front fighting for black freedom. "What are you chanting?" Gordon shouted over the noise.

"The future is ours! The land is ours! We are the people!" came the reply in English. The boys crowded around, pleased with the attention, and escorted them through the mass of people as they made their way back to the observation platform.

Sam saw it first. "Not the observation platform," she warned Gordon. They angled away from the crowd, telling the boys they needed a panoramic shot of the crowd. The boys let them go their own way and rejoined the crowd.

"What's wrong?" Gordon asked.

"They've got someone tied up." Gordon followed Sam's direction and saw two men dragging a body. Sam ran along the low wall that ringed the Big Hole until she had a clear shot of the observation platform. "Start talking," she commanded, zooming in on the crowd.

"What started as a peaceful demonstration in support of the Azanian National Liberation Front has turned ugly," Gordon said. "A few agitators are whipping the mob into a frenzy and demanding revenge for past injustices. From my vantage point, it appears that the leaders are going to give it to them. You may not be able to hear it, but the shouting is now a roar . . . Oh, my God! They're dragging a man to the edge . . ." She couldn't speak as the mob roared its approval.

"Talk!" Sam demanded. "I'm getting this."

Gordon held the microphone up to her mouth. "This is a ritual sacrifice—" she hesitated and forced a calm into her voice she did not feel,"—in effigy. They are throwing a white male mannequin from a store window off the platform. The Azanian National Liberation Front has found a new use for the Big Hole."

Sam lowered her Betacam, relief on her face. "Let's get out of here before they decide to go for the real thing." They returned to their car, skirting the crowd.

The three boys Gordon had interviewed ran up to the car waving an Azanian flag. "Take us to town," one called. Sam had no choice and waited while they piled into the back. More teenagers sat on the front and climbed on the rear bumper. The car was a human float as they drove slowly into Kimberley, where the streets were filled with people. Many in the crowd shouted and waved at them and the boys waved back.

"It's like a holiday," Gordon said.

"Let's get back to the hotel," Sam told her. They dropped the boys off and headed into the center of town. In the distance, they could hear the distinct wail of a fire truck. "The holiday is over," Sam said. "Now comes the looting."

They passed a phalanx of guards posted outside their hotel and went inside. The assistant manager, a University of London–educated Indian from Calcutta, was calming a flock of nervous guests. "Do not have the worry," he said, reverting to the singsong English of his childhood. "There is much goodwill here. We will be safe."

"Do you believe that?" Sam asked incredulously. The sound of shouting echoed from outside.

Gordon looked perplexed. Hans Beckmann had told her there might be a little trouble, but nothing on this scale. "I don't understand," Gordon said. "Hans said there would only be a demonstration."

"Maybe this is what he had in mind by a demonstration," Sam answered. "Let's cover this from the roof. I'm not going outside until help gets here."

Saturday, March 28
Ysterplaat Air Base, Cape Town

Maggot Stuart waited patiently on the stage of the wing's main briefing room as the crews filed in. Most of them were still clutching cups of coffee, trying to shake the last vestiges of sleep and be fully awake for the mission briefing that was scheduled to start at 3:00 A.M. A few were showing the distinct ravages of a hangover.

Typical, Maggot thought, watching the crews find seats. The C-130 crews huddled in a tight cluster surrounding Kowalski while the Warthog pilots found seats as far back as they could. Get together, folks, he thought, you're going to need each other.

The muffled sound of Vibram-soled boots echoed in the hallway, and Maggot smiled as the crews twisted their heads to identify the source of the sound. Four officers and six NCOs in dark-green battle dress uniforms marched down the aisle and claimed the front row, leaving the end seat vacant. They remained standing.

Lydia Kowalski barked, "Room! Ten-hut." The Americans stood as one and came to attention as Pontowski strode down the aisle.

Pontowski called out "Seats, please" and sat down next to the newcomers.

Maggot started the mission brief. "Good morning. I'm Captain Stuart and this is the mission brief for Operation Dragon Blue, the third employment of the United Nations Quick Reaction Force—the QRF. First, let me introduce the Blue Force ground commander, Colonel Valery Bouchard of the French Foreign Legion." Bouchard stood and nodded. Maggot caught the traces of a grin on Pontowski's face as Bouchard sat down. He knows something about that man that we don't, Maggot decided.

The first overhead slide flashed on the screen behind Maggot. "Yesterday afternoon, widespread rioting broke out at Kimberley. Sticking to their long-standing tradition of nonviolence and noninvolvement, the South African government has asked for our help." A titter of laughter worked its way around the room. The government's refusal to use its own forces was a subject of much derision and laughter. "Our objective is to insert the QRF at Kimberley Airport at first light this morning. Once on the ground, Colonel Bouchard's legionnaires will move into town, establish the UN presence in force, and restore order. Reports indicate this is a civil disturbance and we do not expect any organized resistance."

The second slide flashed on the screen. "Here are the Rules of Engagement," Maggot said. "Please note and remember number one. You cannot initiate fire and can only return hostile fire when directly fired upon. There are no exceptions to this rule so I'd suggest you tattoo it on your butt for handy reference." He paused to let it sink in before continuing.

De Royer is going to have a fit when he hears I went along, Pontowski thought as he climbed onto the flight deck of Kowalski's Hercules. But he's not here to tell me no.

On the cargo deck behind him, Bouchard and a ground control team of eighteen legionnaires were sitting on the parachute jump seats dressed out in full equipment for a combat drop. "Welcome aboard, Colonel," Kowalski said. "Hopefully, we'll be able to land at Kimberley and not have to do an air drop. Colonel Bouchard wants to go out at five hundred feet, which is not something I'd want to do." Pontowski agreed with her. Bailing out of a C-130 at five hundred feet above the ground at 130 knots was not conducive to a long life if your main canopy malfunctioned. But it did get the jumpers on the ground fast—one way or the other.

Kowalski went through the start-engines routine and all four turboprops were on line when two Warthogs taxied past. Maggot was in the lead A-10 and gave them a thumbs-up. Kowalski taxied out behind the Warthogs and waited while Maggot and his wingman, Gorilla Moreno, went through a quick check at the end of the runway. Crew chiefs darted under the two A-10s, pulling safety pins off the ordnance and checking for any leaks or loose panels. More thumbs-up from the ground crew and the two Warthogs taxied onto the active runway and took off with twenty-second spacing.

Operation Dragon Blue was under way.

Saturday, March 28
Kimberley, South Africa

The sun had broken the eastern horizon and most of the airfield was still in heavy shadows as the two Warthogs flew down final approach. Twice, Maggot's voice came over the radio. "Kimberley Tower, how read this frequency?" Twice, there was no answer. Maggot leveled off, displaced to the right of the main runway and overflew the field at two hundred feet. He glanced at the control tower to see if he could get a visual signal from an Aldis lamp. Broken windows and black smoke scars warned him that the tower was not going to answer his radio calls. "Gorilla, go tactical," he transmitted.

Gorilla broke off and flew over the main terminal and parking lot as Maggot talked to the C-130 that was five minutes behind them. "Lifter, we got two trucks parked on the runway and no signs of life in the control tower."

"How do the taxiways look?" Kowalski asked.

"Vehicles are parked all over the place," Maggot answered. "No signs of activity but you ain't gonna land here."

"I've got people stirring out in the parking lot," Gorilla transmitted. "We woke somebody up."

On board the C-130, Kowalski turned to Pontowski. "Decision time," she said. "We can't land and if we're going to drop the control team, we need to do it fast, before the welcoming committee wakes up. The jumpers are hooked up and ready to go." She gave the jumpmaster the three-minute warning while Pontowski made a decision.

"Do it," was all he said.

"Roger that," Kowalski replied. She leveled off at five hundred feet and riveted the airspeed at exactly 130 knots indicated. The navigator started the countdown to the green light. "Looking good," Kowalski said.

"Green light," the navigator said. The copilot hit the

switch for the green light by the rear jump doors and the legionnaires shuffled rapidly out both sides of the C-130.

"All clear," the loadmaster said over the intercom.

"That was quick," the copilot said.

"You should see the colonel move," the loadmaster replied. "The jump light started to flicker green and he went. Almost no reaction time at all. The team went out right behind him back-to-belly like an express train."

Pontowski rotated the wafer switch on his intercom to UHF Transmit. "Maggot, fly cover," he radioed.

"They're already doing it," Kowalski told him. "It's part of the plan Maggot laid out. Until Colonel Bouchard gets set up on the ground, we're an airborne command post."

I'm getting in the way, Pontowski thought. Let them do their job. I should have stayed on the ground at Ysterplaat.

Kowalski flew one orbit over the field, allowing Pontowski to see what was happening. Below, the legionnaires were out of their parachutes and pushing one of the trucks off the runway. The UHF radio crackled with Bouchard's heavy accent. "Lifter, this is Blue Force. We are on the ground and taking ground fire from the roof of the terminal building. The approach end of the runway will be clear in two minutes."

Pontowski was amazed at how cool and collected Bouchard sounded. Suddenly, he envied Bouchard, who was in the thick of the action while he played spectator.

"Colonel, are we cleared to use the Hogs for fire suppression?" Kowalski asked.

"Affirmative," Pontowski answered, feeling at last a little useful.

Kowalski cleared Maggot and Gorilla for a strafing run on the terminal building. Pontowski wrote on his clipboard, noting the time and circumstances leading to his decision to employ the Hogs. He watched as Maggot rolled into a low-angle strafing pass, expecting to see reddish-brown smoke billow back from the Warthog's nose when Maggot triggered the A-10's thirty-millimeter cannon. No smoke.

"Off dry," Maggot transmitted. "The roof is jammed with people. Lots of women and children. It looks like they were sleeping there. I can't sort the bad guys." The Warthog's slow speed and Maggot's super-sharp vision had saved them from a massacre. "Gorilla, buzz 'em. One pass only. Maybe that will keep their heads down."

"Just like Vanwyksvlei," Gorilla replied. "Heck of a way to fight a war." He firewalled his throttles and buzzed the roof of the terminal, clearing it by ten feet. Maggot crossed behind him at a ninety-degree angle while Gorilla repositioned for a second run. "How much longer do you think this will work?" Gorilla asked.

"Blue Force," Kowalski radioed, "are you still taking ground fire?"

"A little," Bouchard answered. "The runway is clear. I want to start landing the C-130s."

Kowalski cleared the three Hercules carrying the main force of the QRF over to Bouchard's frequency. "Maggot, Gorilla," Kowalski transmitted, "we need to discourage any shooters still in the terminal. Can you hose down the ramp in front of the terminal and kick up a lot of smoke and debris?"

"Can do," Maggot replied.

Pontowski said nothing. He found some consolation as Kowalski maneuvered the C-130, giving them a grandstand seat to the action. The first C-130, piloted by Jake Madison, touched down as Maggot strafed the ramp and set a truck on fire. It created a smoke screen of sorts between the terminal and the landing C-130. The next C-130 was on short final as Madison taxied clear of the runway. The ramp of his Hercules came down and legionnaires streamed off. They fanned out and ran for the terminal as Gorilla positioned for a second strafing run.

Kowalski radioed Bouchard, asking if they were still taking ground fire. Bouchard responded with a brisk "Negative ground fire." Kowalski called Gorilla off and sent him into a nearby orbit as the second C-130, piloted by Brenda Conklin, landed. The third C-130 was one mile behind.

"Those Legion guys don't mess around," Kowalski told Pontowski. "Bouchard just declared the airport secure. We're cleared to land." She maneuvered her Hercules to fall into trail behind the third C-130, which was on short final. It was a routine approach and landing.

The loadmaster from Madison's Hercules marshaled the C-130 into a parking spot. The props were still spinning down when Pontowski climbed off, looking for Bouchard. But the ramp was amazingly quiet and only the burning truck remained as evidence of the battle. "Where are the legionnaires?" he asked.

"There're a few still in the terminal and a couple in the control tower," the loadmaster answered. "The rest are headed for downtown. They commandeered a bunch of vehicles and were gone. Colonel, I got to tell you, those Frogs do move."

"No can say 'Frogs,'" Pontowski grumbled as Kowalski joined them.

"Sir, the terminal is secure," Kowalski said. "You can go in if you wish." Pontowski grumped an answer. "Colonel," Kowalski continued, "we were briefed to return to Ysterplaat as soon as possible."

Pontowski cleared her to take the four C-130s back to Cape Town and headed for the terminal. He passed the burning truck and had to jump over the three-foot-deep trench Maggot's cannon shells had dug in the cement when he had walked a long burst up to the truck. Inside the terminal, janitors were already cleaning up the mess and four bodies were lying in a corner, covered by a blue tarp. Two legionnaires patrolling the lobby approached and saluted. "Good morning, Colonel Pontowski," the oldest said. "Can I help?" He spoke with an American accent.

"American?" Pontowski asked.

"Corporal Rogers," the legionnaire replied, introducing himself. The bewildered look on Pontowski's face made him smile. "There are a few of us. In the Legion, only the officers are French. Everyone else supposedly is a foreigner because of a law that prohibits Frenchmen from fighting outside France. That's why they have the Foreign Legion."

"But the officers?"

"They are allowed to volunteer under a special exemption. It's the fast track to promotion for them."

"Why did you join?" Pontowski asked.

"I was in the U.S. Army for a while, sir. But I wanted in on the action and to get away from all the bullshit." He grinned. "The Legion is all business. Like when we hit this place, we did it running and sorted out the players real quick."

Pontowski looked around the lobby. "I can believe that," he said. "Any casualties?"

"Not on our side," Rogers told him.

"Liz," Sam said, "listen." The two women strained to make sense out of the sounds echoing in the street below. "Soldiers!" Sam shouted. They ran to the edge of the roof. Sam breathed more easily, shedding the tension that had been building during the night. "The blue helmets . . . they're United Nations."

"It's about time," Gordon said. "We need to get into the street for some coverage."

Sam hesitated. "I don't know . . ."

"Sam, it never got that bad. Look how they waved at us yesterday. I don't think the situation is as bad as you thought." Sam gave in. As always, her camera was ready to go and within moments, they were outside in the street.

"Get this," Gordon said when she saw a squad of eight blue-helmeted soldiers coming down the street. Sam framed the shot and used the shotgun microphone for natural sound as the legionnaires moved past, their riot shields at their sides. A looter came out of a store, her arms full of clothes, and almost bumped into the soldiers. The sergeant yelled at her and pointed to the store with his baton. The woman threw the clothes back into the store and ran, a big smile on her face.

Sam used her zoom lens to record the chaos in front of the soldiers. "Pan behind them," Gordon said. Sam swung her Betacam in the direction Gordon was pointing. The street behind the legionnaires was quiet. Gordon spoke into her microphone. "The United Nations peacekeeping force has arrived and is patrolling the streets of Kimberley. The ease of restoring order indicates this was not a major civil disturbance but an isolated demonstration at the Big Hole followed by random looting." She switched off the microphone. "Let's follow them. We'll be okay." They ran after the soldiers.

"Can you talk to us?" Gordon asked one of the legionnaires, jamming the microphone in front of his face. The man grunted an answer in French. "I'm sorry," she said, "but I don't speak French. What country are you from?"

"Country?" The man was puzzled. "My country . . . La Légion Étrangère."

"What?" Gordon replied.

"He's from the French Foreign Legion," Sam told her.

"That's not a country," Gordon said, still keeping pace with the soldiers as they swept the street and turned onto a main boulevard leading to the town's center. "Where are you going?" she asked the NCO leading the squad.

"L'hôtel de ville," the sergeant answered.

"City hall," Sam translated.

"I didn't know you spoke French," Gordon said.

"Strictly high school," Sam told her.

The sergeant slowed at the sound of sporadic gunfire and motioned his squad to take cover. They fell into a well-practiced routine, leapfrogging and covering each other as they advanced down the street. They moved quickly and silently, using hand signs to communicate. "This is good stuff," Sam said, pointing and shooting as they moved. The gunfire tapered off and the sergeant sent two men forward to reconnoiter while the rest of his squad took refuge in a building. Within minutes the two men were back, talking to the sergeant.

"What are they saying?" Gordon whispered.

"Be quiet," Sam told her. She listened as the sergeant established radio contact with Bouchard's command element at the city hall. She pulled Gordon aside. "The sergeant says we're cut off and surrounded," she whispered.

"They're overreacting for our benefit," Gordon told her.

Pontowski was in the control tower when the first reports filtered in. Corporal Rogers, the American legionnaire, handed him a map of the city. "Bouchard has been forced into this building," Rogers told him. "He tried to arrange a cease-fire but the man he sent out under a white flag was gunned down." He circled the building where Gordon and Sam were trapped. "Another eight men and two civilian reporters are hiding here."

"Are you in contact with Cape Town?" Pontowski asked. He felt like a fool when Rogers handed him a telephone. He dialed the UN's command center at Constantia to update them on the situation. He was surprised when Elena Martine came on the line. What was she doing there? he wondered. Keeping an eye on me? Then he reconsidered. Dragon Blue was a UN operation, and she was the head of the UN Observer Mission to South Africa. Filling in for de Royer required more political networking than he had imagined.

"Matt, you should be here," she told him.

He knew she was right. "Elena, we've been set up." He quickly described the situation.

"Do you have a recommendation?" she asked.

She's passing the buck, he thought. "If we don't break them out, it will be a massacre."

"I don't believe it's that bad," she said. "Be patient and see what develops." She broke the connection.

And get rescued by the Iron Guard again, he thought. "No way," he muttered aloud.

"Beg your pardon, sir," Rogers asked.

"Nothing," he said, dialing the command post in the COIC. Within seconds, he was talking to a controller. "Get me a STU-III up here so we can talk." The STU-III was a portable, plug-in-anywhere telephone scrambler smaller than a fax machine. "We got problems." He didn't want to say any more on an insecure line.

Now he had to wait. He used the time to think and ran the numbers in his head, blending time and geography. They were 450 nautical miles from Cape Town; an hour and fifteen minutes flying time for the Warthogs, fifteen minutes more for the C-130s, and over three hours for the Puma helicopters. He checked the time: four hours to sunset. He paced the floor, thinking and planning.

By the time the next C-130 had landed with the last of the legionnaires and the STU-III, Pontowski knew what he was going to do. He plugged the secure phone into the telephone jack, dialed the command post at Ysterplaat, and talked to Kowalski. "Lydia, we were bushwhacked again. I'm pulling back to the airport. But two groups are cut off at the city hall. We're going to get them out at first light tomorrow morning. I want two Puma helicopters and one Herk up here as soon as it's dark. Configure the Herk for MedEvac.

Have the other three on alert. Starting at oh five-thirty local time, I want a steady stream of Hogs on station. Sequence them in flights of four, thirty minutes apart."

"How do you want them configured?" Kowalski asked.

"For antipersonnel and soft-skinned vehicles," Pontowski answered. "I need to talk to Maggot about tactics."

At last, he was doing something useful.

Kimberley's electrical power and water failed shortly after three in the morning and the buildings around Gordon and Sam became shadowy, vaguely defined masses in the early morning dark. An occasional flare would light up the street below them and freeze the scene in stark relief for a few moments before darkness recaptured the city. "I hate the waiting," Gordon said, moving back from the edge of the roof where they had stationed themselves. "I need to find a toilet that works."

"You can use any toilet," Sam told her. "You just can't flush it."

"Oh," Gordon said, wandering off. "I hadn't thought of that."

Sam looked through her camera's viewfinder. She was starting to get images as the dark yielded to the rising sun. Encouraged, she angled the camera toward the city center. "What the . . ." she muttered, trying to make sense out of the shadowy movements she was recording. A short burst of gunfire erupted, startling her. Then it was quiet again. Men were separating from the shadows, moving down the street.

"Sam!" Gordon's voice caught her attention. "They want us downstairs." The two women pounded down the stairs and found the squad of legionnaires crouched by the front entrance, ready to leave. "Who's doing all the shooting?" Gordon asked. There was no answer.

"Follow us," the sergeant said. He spoke into his radio and looked down the street.

"Where are we going?" Sam asked.

"*L'hôtel de ville*," the sergeant answered. "From there we will go to Queen's Park where helicopters will pick us up. The park is very close but the streets are blocked and we will have to fight our way through."

296

"The poor bastards," another legionnaire added.

"Why don't we go now, while it's still dark?" Sam asked.

"Ah," the sergeant said, "it has been decided to let the American Warthogs open a corridor for us. It has all been coordinated and we must move fast."

"They're playing cowboys and Indians again," Gordon said in a low voice.

The sun broke the horizon and Sam keyed her camera as more men ran down the street toward the city hall. From their vantage point, they were little more than a ragtag mob. "Sam, this doesn't make sense," Gordon said. "The legionnaires can stop this with a snap of their fingers. We saw them do it yesterday."

They tensed at the sound of approaching jets. The sergeant spoke into his radio and held out his other hand, palm open facing down. The sound of the jets grew louder. With a suddenness that made Sam jump, a Warthog passed directly overhead, just above the rooftops, flying down the street toward the city center. A loud buzz echoed over them as smoke billowed from its nose. The street erupted in a rushing wave of dust, debris, and explosions as the pilot walked his cannon fire down the street.

The sergeant's hand flashed in a forward motion, his forefinger pointing to the city hall. Without a word, the men ran from the building with Sam and Gordon right behind them. Silence ruled the street, broken only by the sound of their running feet. Gordon stumbled. She looked down and gasped. She had tripped over the remains of a man, his arms and legs blown away. Little was recognizable as human life. Sam saved her from falling and they ran on. The sergeant pushed them through a door into the city hall and Sam collapsed to her knees, gasping for breath. She looked up and saw Gordon retching in a corner.

"Oh, my God," she rasped, struggling for breath. "It was horrible." It was her first encounter with the receiving end of modern firepower, and nothing she had seen during the attack on the Blue Train had prepared her for this.

Another A-10 flew overhead, blasting a path down the street that led to Queen's Park. Sam stood up and recorded the pass. The cars and trucks blocking the street seemed to explode in a madcap rhythm. Another Warthog sliced in from the left, stabilized and pickled off two canisters. Sam went for a distance shot and caught the canisters as they split open like clamshells. A hail of baseball-sized bomblets peppered the street. Some exploded as they hit the ground while others bounced into the air and burst, sending a cloud of killing shrapnel into the attackers.

The action held the women spellbound as another A-10 rolled in, this time closer to Queen's Park. Again, the deadly ballet repeated itself, but this time, distance made death more impersonal. Sam kept her camera going as Gordon talked into her microphone. But her words were meaningless to Sam.

A fourth A-10 attacked, dropping its load of canisters. Later, Sam would learn they were CBU-58s. But for the present, she was learning firsthand what the innocuous-sounding name CBU meant. She zoomed in as an incendiary pellet buried itself in a man's back. He ran screaming down the street until a single shot ended his agony.

"A legionnaire shot him," Gordon said.

"We must go now," a sergeant said. They followed him and ran into the street, falling in with the men evacuating the city hall.

"Is this everyone?" Gordon asked, shocked by the small number of soldiers.

"Only a few officers and NCOs are left," the sergeant said. "They will follow shortly. The Legion does not abandon its men."

"I want to get this," Gordon said. The two women stopped in the middle of the street and turned toward the city center. Sam shouldered her camera. "A mob," Gordon said into her microphone, "trapped a small number of legionnaires in the city hall last night. No attempt was made by the United Nations to free them through negotiations. Instead, American A-10s blasted open a corridor, cutting a street of death and destruction through this city. Words fail to describe the carnage around me."

Sam panned the area and zoomed in on Gordon's face. The reporter's hair was tangled and dirty, pulled back into a loose knot on the nape of her neck. Fatigue lines etched with sweat and dirt added years to her face—sure professional death for a woman reporter—yet she would never be better. "When I look around," she concluded, "I can only ask, Why? Why this senseless butchery of civilians who have every right to be angry at their government?"

The sound of a helicopter reached them and they ran toward Queen's Park. Ahead of them, a Puma was settling behind a line of trees. Sam paused long enough to pan the street and record for one last time the slaughter behind them. A legionnaire yelled at them to hurry, but a sniper's bullet slammed into him, cutting off his words. Gordon ran to help. "He's still alive," she yelled. "Help me!" Sam helped her pick the man up and they hobbled toward the trees, driven by a hail of bullets. Bouchard and three men caught up with them, firing as they retreated. They were the rear guard.

"Oh, no!" Sam yelled as the helicopter lifted clear of the trees. "They're leaving us behind!"

Bouchard grabbed the wounded man. "Run!" he yelled, pushing Sam toward the trees and safety. Bullets kicked up the grass around her as she ran. She reached the trees and again, she turned her camera on the action, this time recording Bouchard and Gordon carrying the wounded man as they ran the gauntlet of fire. Above her, she could hear the distinctive sound of turboshaft engines blending with the beat of a helicopter's rotor. She looked up in time to see the silhouette of another Puma fly over. She had a momentary impression of the door gunner firing his machine gun and smoke trailing from an engine.

The small group broke from the trees and ran for the helicopter that was now on the ground. The legionnaires who had been holding the perimeter were pulling in and climbing on board when Bouchard and Gordon reached the Puma. One of the crew relieved them of their load: "He's dead," the sergeant said.

"Carry him on board," Bouchard said, his voice amazingly controlled. "I must count." Methodically, he counted his men, not bothering to explain that no one, not even their dead, would be left behind.

Gordon climbed on board and went forward to get the pilot's name. Piet van der Roos was sitting in the right seat of the cockpit and turned so he could check the loading in the cargo compartment. He recognized her immediately. "Welcome aboard, Miss Gordon. Are you signed up for the United Nations' frequent flier program?"

"That's not funny," she snapped. "Have you seen the hell you made out there?"

Van der Roos ignored her and spoke into his microphone. "Strap in," he told her. "Everyone is on board." Action transformed the easygoing captain into a human dynamo. "Coming up. Clear left? Clear right. Overhead?" The crew answered his questions and the Puma took on a new life as he jammed the two throttles on the overhead console full forward. Van der Roos lifted the helicopter, still trailing smoke, clear of the park while the rattling bark of the helicopter's two door-mounted machine guns deafened the passengers.

Pontowski was standing in the control tower at Kimberley airport as the last helicopter approached from the north. Van der Roos had shut down the left engine and it was no longer trailing smoke. The Afrikaner's voice came over the radio. "Evacuation complete. I have one KIA and several wounded. Elizabeth Gordon and her photographer are on board."

"Just what we need," Pontowski grumbled. "Why does she always show up at the wrong time?" He keyed his personal radio and alerted the crews on the ramp to transfer Gordon to the MedEvac C-130. He trained his binoculars on the landing helicopter. It had taken extensive battle damage. "How in the hell did Piet keep it flying?" he wondered aloud, not expecting an answer. He left the control tower to talk to the pilot and Bouchard.

Pontowski waited outside the terminal as Bouchard climbed off the helicopter. Behind him, van der Roos was ushering Gordon onto the C-130 with the last of the wounded. Pontowski walked toward the Frenchman as the C-130 taxied out for takeoff. I'm glad they're gone, he thought.

Bouchard was haggard and drawn, his battle dress uniform torn and bloodied. "I recalled all the other ground teams last night," Pontowski told him. "You were the only ones cut off."

"Casualties?" Bouchard asked.

"So far, two dead, four wounded."

"It is two too many," Bouchard said, relieved that more of his Quick Reaction Force hadn't been killed. "If all our people are accounted for, I suggest we withdraw."

"I'm not sure we should abandon the airport," Pontowski told him. "We have a secure perimeter and need to repair the helicopter."

"Destroy it," Bouchard said. "We need to withdraw now."

"Why now?"

Bouchard's voice was hard. "We were fighting the Azanians again. At Vanwyksvlei . . . when they trapped the C-130 and the relief team on the ground . . . they were nothing but a mob. Now they have heavy machine guns and recoilless rifles mounted on trucks and they outnumbered us by at least twenty to one."

"Who outnumbered you, Colonel?" a woman's voice said.

Pontowski turned and saw Sam standing a few feet away. She was dirty, blood-spattered, and on the edge of collapse. Damn, he raged to himself, why wasn't she on that C-130?

"Are you okay?" he asked.

"Did you see what your fighters did out there?" She waved a hand at the city and lost her balance. Instinctively, he reached out to steady her. "Don't," she said. "Don't touch me, you bloody bastard." She crumpled to her knees, gasping and crying.

Bouchard ignored her. "We need a decision, Colonel," he said.

"Destroy the helicopter and withdraw."

"And the woman?" Bouchard asked.

Without answering, Pontowski helped Sam to her feet and led her inside, ready to catch her if she collapsed. "Leave me alone," she muttered.

"Gladly," Pontowski said, "as soon as I get you on an airplane."

CHAPTER
19

Tuesday, March 31
Iron Gate, near Bloemfontein

MacKay stood up when Beckmann entered the security control room. "Generaal," Kreiner said, "this is the new man I told you about, John Mills. He has been here only three days and—"

"Yes, yes," Beckmann interrupted, smiling at MacKay. "You have certainly impressed Kreiner. He says we can now track the whereabouts of everyone on base using ID cards and card scanners at the entry control points."

"It was fairly simple," MacKay said. "All the hardware was in place and the computer programs were easily modified. It was simply a matter of using what you had."

When the Boys had built MacKay's cover story as a security systems specialist, they had back-doored the Iron Guard's computer system by analyzing the magnetic strip on the original ID card MacKay had given them. The encoded data was better than DNA and led them to the American contractor who had installed the security system for the Iron Guard. The right leverage had been applied—the mention of an IRS audit in conjunction with a sexual harassment lawsuit—and they had the complete system. Then, at Standard's urging, the Boys had come up with a way to make the system more efficient. Their work was MacKay's entry ticket.

"There are still a few problems," MacKay told him. "I

still haven't sorted out the bugs in the housing area . . . too many people with random access . . . give me a few more days."

"Still, I am most impressed," Beckmann said.

You should be, MacKay thought. It isn't often the CIA shares its technical expertise with the opposition.

Beckmann grew serious. The cover story the Boys had planted with Sicherheits Dienste had been dutifully relayed to him through the Bruderbund. According to Sicherheits Dienste, MacKay was a computer genius and totally loyal to whoever was paying him. But he had a dark side to his personality—he had a talent for violence. Because he was black, MacKay was the perfect front man for the Iron Guard's security service. He could terrorize the black population in the Boerstaat. And once MacKay had served his purpose, he could be disposed of like Sergeant Shivuto. "May I ask why you did not return to the States after leaving Sicherheits Dienste and came to South Africa?" Beckmann asked.

So they've already checked me out, MacKay thought. He hoped the Boys had done their job right. "There's a hostile reception waiting for me in the States," he answered, "and I'm here because of the money."

It was the answer Beckmann wanted to hear. MacKay was the man he needed. "I have other projects for you," Beckmann said. "I want you to create a system in Kreiner's security compound that totally integrates communications and information systems from all sources—banks, taxes, phone calls, credit cards. I want to track a large population over a large area."

"Like a national identification system?" MacKay asked.

"Exactly," Beckmann said. "Also, I want you to run our network of black informants in Bloemfontein. Kreiner tells me you have unfinished business with a few of our local citizens."

MacKay forced what he hoped was a vicious smile. "A minor matter quickly solved."

"Can you handle all of this at once?" Kreiner asked.

"Let's find out," MacKay said.

"Good," Beckmann said. "Kreiner will show you the security compound later today."

MacKay kept telling himself the security compound wasn't real and that he was caught on the set of a very bad B movie. But the evidence was too strong, too compelling, and no matter how he sliced it, he was working for the Gestapo and Marius Kreiner was a modern version of Heinrich Himmler.

"Does the gallows bother you?" he asked.

"No," MacKay answered. Kreiner looked at him, expecting more. "As long as the paycheck is on time," MacKay continued, "I don't care what you do."

Kreiner led him down the stairs and into the basement. "This is Interrogation," he explained.

MacKay was stunned. He had reached a lower ring of hell.

Late that afternoon, MacKay walked through the housing area checking the card scanners at the various entry control points everyone had to pass through to enter or leave. Satisfied his cover was established, he wandered through the houses. He stopped short of a playground. Ziba was sitting on a bench while the Slavin children played on the swings. For a moment, he watched, not letting her see him. Then he walked over and sat down.

"Good afternoon, John," she said, not looking at him. "Why are you here?"

"To say I'm sorry. Ziba, I couldn't handle it at first. The idea of sharing you with another man tore me apart. But you said something at the time . . . there were things here I didn't understand. I'm learning."

"What have you learned?"

"Beckmann must be stopped."

"There is more than that," she said, getting up to leave. "Itzig"—MacKay caught her use of Slavin's first name— "can help my people. That is why I was told to seduce him."

She turned to look at him and the old feelings swept over MacKay, but they were tinged with sadness and a deeper understanding. "Beckmann is crazy. Tell Slavin to get out. Now."

"Itzig won't leave his work," she said, walking away.

Wednesday, April 1
The Executive Office Building,
Washington, D.C.

Cyrus Piccard and John Weaver Elkins, the secretary of defense, were waiting backstage of the small auditorium when Carroll slipped in unnoticed from the White House. He parked his electric scooter in the back hall and walked slowly, the two Secret Service agents who were now his constant companions at each elbow, ready to catch him if he stumbled. "You've got a full house," Elkins told him. "It looks like every reporter in D.C. is out there." He waited while Carroll sat down to catch his breath.

"That's why we're doing the press conference here," Carroll said. "The idea is to put some physical distance between the conference and the White House." He grinned. "Besides, there's more room here and I'm expendable."

"I don't like this," Piccard said. He studied Carroll, worried about his emaciated look. "There must be a better way to defuse the issue. The media has gone into a feeding frenzy over the fiasco in Kimberley."

"No reporter over there is stirring the pot like Liz Gordon," Elkins replied.

Carroll stood up and laughed. "You're mixing your metaphors. Let's do it." He handed Piccard his cane and walked onstage. It was only ten short steps to the podium, but it was an effort. Slowly, he pulled himself onto the stool that had been placed behind the podium and grabbed the edge of the lectern. He leaned into the microphone as the TV cameras came on.

"Thank you for coming on such short notice," Carroll began. "Needless to say, the White House has received more than a few questions after Elizabeth Gordon's broadcast from South Africa Sunday night. Hopefully, we can provide a few answers." A titter of disbelief grew into a loud grumble. A few of the reporters shouted questions. Carroll said nothing and waited for the noise to subside.

"They're gearing up for a human sacrifice," Piccard said, watching from the wings.

"Can you blame them?" Elkins replied. "Gordon's coverage of the mess at Kimberley will get her an Emmy. She made us look like a bunch of mindless butchers . . . and very heavy on the racism."

"It was spectacular reporting," Piccard admitted. "And she was right in the thick of it."

"But the network edited the hell out of it," Elkins said. He fell silent as the crowd quieted.

"Elizabeth Gordon," Carroll continued, "was right when she looked around, saw the carnage in the streets of Kimberley, and asked 'Why?' I would like to show you why, not with our information, but by taking a careful look at what Elizabeth saw." The big screen behind Carroll came to life.

"Because of time constraints, the network did not show the first part of her telecast." Gordon's face filled the screen. Behind her was the Big Hole.

"Apparently," Carroll said, "the news director felt that blacks sacrificing a white in effigy is not news the American public needs. I'd like to replay what the public did see and—"

"You're wasting our time," a reporter called from the audience. "We've all seen it." He got up and left. As far as he was concerned, anything more than forty-eight hours old was ancient history.

Carroll smiled. "Please bear with me." He fast forwarded the tape and froze a frame of the eight blue-helmeted legionnaires Gordon and Sam had linked up with. "Please note their weapons." He used an electronic pointer to highlight the riot gear they were wearing. "These soldiers were prepared for riot control and were only lightly armed."

He restarted the tape and waited for the action in front of the building where the reporters had been trapped with the legionnaires. Carroll froze another frame. The crowd in the street had changed. They were all men, carrying weapons. "These men were not looting or rioting," he said. He leapfrogged quickly ahead, briefly pausing at five preselected frames. "Although they were not wearing uniforms, they were armed with new assault rifles of the same make and model." He paused at another frame. "This man is carrying a sixty-millimeter mortar manufactured in Italy. These two men are his ammunition bearers." Two more frames were frozen for the reporters, all showing different mortar teams with the same equipment.

Again, Carroll fast-forwarded Gordon's telecast. Images of the damage at the city hall were briefly highlighted before he got to the A-10's attack and the breakout by the legionnaires. The grisly images of what Gordon had called "the street of death" had not lost their shock value. "Our analysts," Carroll said, "counted seventeen crew-served weapons in this street alone. And these are the bodies"—he framed the destroyed hulk of an armored car—"of white mercenaries."

A voice from the audience yelled, "How do we know this tape hasn't been doctored by the CIA?"

"You can verify what I've shown you here by replaying your own copies of Gordon's broadcast."

Backstage, Elkins muttered, "Gotcha, asshole." Three more reporters left the auditorium.

Now the tape ran at its normal speed and Gordon's face filled the screen. ". . . no attempt was made by the United Nations to free them through negotiations. Instead, American A-10s blasted open a corridor . . ."

Carroll stopped the tape. "Liz Gordon did not know," he said, "that a UN soldier had been gunned down in cold blood trying to negotiate a cease-fire. However, the network did, yet they made no attempt to set the record straight." Another reporter left, not willing to listen to any criticism of the media.

Carroll started the tape. "When I look around," Gordon was saying, "I can only ask one question. Why?" The screen froze on her face.

"I believe," Carroll said, "that Miss Gordon had the answer to her question in front of her. The United Nations peacekeeping team had been trapped by a large, well-armed, and well-trained group of irregulars led by mercenaries. It was either fight their way out or be killed. By relying on surprise and overwhelming firepower, and confining the fighting to the area around the city hall, civilian and United Nations casualties were kept to a minimum."

The screen went blank and he looked at the audience expectantly. It was time for questions. "Why didn't Gordon see what you've shown us?" a reporter asked, his voice hard with contempt.

Backstage, Piccard looked at the reporter. "Please, Bill," he said, "don't ask him if he's ever been in combat."

"That reporter?" Elkins scoffed. "Only at happy hour."

Carroll lowered his head for a moment and then looked steadily at the reporter. "Elizabeth Gordon," he answered, "had been in combat for over twenty-four hours. She was tired, hungry, and thirsty. She reported what she saw. But it took hours of combat analysis by trained professionals to discover what was actually going on around her. They were not aching with fatigue, they were not in fear of their lives, they were not in the midst of an ongoing battle. In short, they had time to carefully analyze the situation and make sense out of it. Time is the one commodity that is not available when the bullets are flying."

The tenor of the questions changed, and they were less hostile. Finally, Carroll turned the podium over to Elkins, who came out onstage. The secretary of defense keyed the remote control and the screen came to life.

"This is what we call the order of battle," Elkins said. "We know the United Nations airlifted 206 legionnaires in an anti-riot configuration to restore order in Kimberley. We estimate they were attacked by over three thousand armed irregulars."

"Are you saying," a reporter asked, "that the United Nations walked into an ambush?"

"It's very possible," Elkins replied. He fielded more questions and a few more reporters quietly left the auditorium. "One more question," he said.

A woman stood up. "I have a question for Mr. Carroll," she said. "Is there any truth to the rumor that you are ill and considering resigning as the national security advisor?"

Carroll's face was calm as he answered. "I have been diagnosed with ALS, Lou Gehrig's disease, and yes, I am offering my resignation to the president." Sorry, Liz, he thought. I know I promised you the story . . . if I could. Silence ruled for a few seconds before a flurry of questions erupted from the reporters. Elkins retreated into the wings to let all attention focus on Carroll.

"That," Elkins said to Piccard, "was the mother of all press conferences."

Thursday, April 2
The White House, Washington, D.C.

The president looked up from his desk when Carroll entered the Oval Office. He tossed the budget proposal he was reading to his chief of staff with a sharp "This is pure bullshit. Tell Agriculture to rework it and get back to me. Twelve percent, that's the bottom line. They decide where the cuts are going to be or I will." He kicked back in his chair, and motioned his other two advisors out of the office. "How's it going, Bill?"

"Not bad," Carroll answered. "All things considered."

The president picked up a letter. "I'm not going to accept your resignation, not after the press conference yesterday."

"I'm becoming a liability, sir."

"Not hardly." A satisfied look spread across his face. "We're getting all sorts of positive fallout. This morning the Lords of the Hill called. They're calling off all committee hearings for now." He chuckled, picturing the discomfort of certain congressmen. "Think how it would look on national TV . . . you sitting alone at a table . . . your cane propped beside your chair . . . a panel of hostile congressmen grilling you."

He lit a cigar and puffed contentedly. The president was having a good day. "Rumor has it the Honorable Ann Nevers is furious." He paused. "No, you are definitely not a liability. I want you to stay on. The only question is, Do you want to resign and spend more time with your family?"

Carroll considered the question. Yes, he did want to be with his family, but that was happening now. What would be the best example he could set for his two children? Should he let them see him wither away at home and become a vegetable? Or should he remain a useful, productive individual as long as possible? What would Mary want?

He knew the answer. "Please tear it up. But when I'm not hacking it, tell me. I will not be a burden."

"Don't worry," the president replied. "I will." It was an easy decision for the president and he wanted to keep Carroll as an advisor as long as possible. Not only was Carroll at the peak of his abilities, but the president knew good press when he saw it. The image of a dying, wheelchair-bound advisor in the halls of the White House had all the makings of high drama and tragedy.

"Bill, have you seen today's PDB?" Carroll nodded in answer. The PDB, President's Daily Brief, was a summary of the best intelligence available to the United States. The slickly produced document was highly classified and read only by the highest-ranking policymakers. "The UN was ambushed at Kimberley by the Azanians. What do we know about them?"

"The Azanian Liberation Army," Carroll answered, "is a black liberation movement trying to carve a big piece of territory out of South Africa for themselves. They get support from a lot of sources, including OPEC."

"Is OPEC the main problem here?" the president asked.

Carroll shook his head. "They're a minor problem. They also back the ANC and Inkatha. Then no matter who wins, they have an entrée. The real problem is still the Iron Guard."

"Wait a minute," the president said. "The Iron Guard is part of the white resistance movement. What do they have to do with the Azanians?"

"The CIA has evidence that the Iron Guard is encouraging the Azanians to cause trouble. That weakens the legitimate government and keeps the UN busy while the Iron Guard consolidates its position."

"Given what I know about the Iron Guard," the president said, "you'll need some damn good evidence to convince me there's a connection between them."

"Erik Beckmann, the brother of the Iron Guard commander, is with the Azanians. We've monitored phone calls between them."

The president came alert. "Erik Beckmann . . . isn't he a terrorist?"

"One of the most notorious," Carroll replied. "Just about everyone wants him. Including us."

"So the Iron Guard is using the Azanians as a shield. Getting to the Iron Guard is like peeling an onion to get at the heart." The president drummed his fingers on his desk. "Bill, I want to take the Azanians off the table."

"The question," Carroll replied, "is 'How?'"

"I want to expand the rules of engagement—surprise retaliatory strikes strictly in self-defense. Talk to the French and let's put some teeth into UN peacekeeping operations and start peeling that onion."

"That may cross the line into peace enforcement," Carroll said.

"But not quite," the president replied. "I want to test the idea, free of public attention. It's time to find out what the UN can really do."

"We can do that," Carroll said. "I'll get Mazie working it." He paused. "We're going to scramble a lot of eggs."

"Just don't get any on our face."

Sunday, April 5
Ysterplaat Air Base, Cape Town

It was just after midnight, early Sunday morning, when Pontowski glanced at his watch; he had been talking to his son for over fifteen minutes. Their phone calls had become a ritual, four to five times a week. Fortunately, the time difference worked in his favor and he called before he went to bed. But the phone bills were astronomical. Hell of a way to be a father, he thought. "Let me speak to Martha," he said, "and I'll call you Monday afternoon about this time."

Martha Marshall came on the line. "How's Sara doing?" he asked.

"Considering she just lost a husband," Martha answered, "and is due in six weeks, amazingly well. Little Matt is doing fine." She hesitated, trying to find the right words. "Sara is going to stay here until after the baby is born and things settle down. But she wants to move back to Kansas City. Matt, I'll have to go with her."

Pontowski understood what Martha was telling him. He had to make a home for his son and quit relying on others. "Thanks for the heads-up," he told her. "I should be back in a month or so." He hung up and lay back in his chair. Soon he was going to have to leave the Air Force, no doubt about it.

Almost immediately the phone rang. "Colonel Pontowski," a man's voice said, "this is Stan Pauley, Techtronics International." Pontowski immediately made the connection. It was the CIA station chief, Richard Standard, using one of his covers. "Can we meet at my office as soon as possible?" Standard asked.

"See you in fifteen minutes," Pontowski replied.

Mazie Hazelton was waiting when Pontowski arrived at Standard's office. "Mazie tells me you know each other," Standard said.

"We go back a ways," Pontowski told him.

"To China," Mazie added.

Pontowski knew the protocols used for handling supersensitive information, directives, and orders. Mazie was a messenger carrying something too critical to be entrusted to electronic transmission. "I'm almost afraid to ask what brings you here," he said.

Mazie gave him a little nod. "Mr. Carroll sent me to be sure there was no confusion over this." She paused, carefully selecting her next words. "The president wants to expand your role so you can carry out delayed strikes, without warning, against any group that has attacked UN forces."

"Like the Azanians?" Standard asked. Mazie nodded in agreement.

"Are we talking covert operations?" Pontowski asked.

"Not exactly," Mazie answered. "We carry out the planning in secret to maximize the element of surprise. I've just come from Paris, where I talked to the French. They have agreed to the concept and are willing to let de Royer's legionnaires participate."

"Speaking of which," Pontowski said, "what has happened to de Royer? He's been gone almost three weeks.

That's a hell of a long time. Is he coming back or am I the permanent commander here?"

"He's coming back as soon as he assembles a backbone for the French politicians," Mazie said.

"So he's having political problems, too," Standard said.

"Much worse than ours," Mazie told him.

"My problem is operational security and execution," Pontowski said. "I need tight control at this end. The UN Observer Mission, the South African government, everyone you can think of, has got to be cut out of the picture. I've got to have total control at this end and not have to coordinate with anyone. And once the decision is made, we move fast."

Mazie nodded in agreement. "The Azanians are your first target."

"Payback time for Kimberley?" Standard asked.

Mazie ignored him and handed Pontowski a thick folder with photographs and maps. "The best window of opportunity is Tuesday morning. We have information that the Azanian leadership will be at their main headquarters. It's a golden opportunity."

"That's less than forty-eight hours," Pontowski said. "I'll talk to Bouchard and see what his Quick Reaction Force can do."

"Colonel," Standard said, "we can help."

Tuesday, April 7
Near Kimberley, South Africa

The radar antenna rotated above the large farmstead the Azanian Liberation Army had plundered and then taken for its headquarters. A cold wind whipping down off the Karoo had driven the guards into the barns to await the first light of dawn, and they were asleep, certain that no officer would be making the rounds at one o'clock in the morning to check on them.

The young Azanian surveillance operator in the radar shack studied the only target on the radar scope in front of him. The first beads of sweat rolled down his dark face and he wiped at his forehead with a dirty rag. The German who had trained him had been very insistent about not spilling any liquids onto the keyboard. It was cool in the radar shack and he was sweating because this was his first night shift and the first time he had been confronted with an unusual situation without the German to help him. He glanced over at the sleeping Syrian and decided not to ask him for help. The Syrians were as worthless as the brothers, he decided. Still, he did have to deal with the problem.

He played with the computer's track ball and rolled the cursor over the target. His forefinger pressed the middle button above the track ball, commanding the radar to interrogate the IFF transponder on the unidentified aircraft. Nothing. His fingers danced on the keyboard and an overlay of the nearby airway appeared on the scope. The return was definitely not on the airway. His fingers flashed again and numbers appeared on the scope next to the return. The Azanian easily interpreted them: altitude thirty-two thousand feet, speed three hundred knots, heading 210 degrees.

Afraid that he was doing something wrong, he called to the Syrian. The Arab grumbled, got up, and came over to the scope. He pushed the African out of the seat and glanced at the monitor. "Stupid," he growled. "It will miss us by twenty-five miles. See how it will intercept the airway here?" He jabbed at a point fifteen miles in front of the offending aircraft. "It's an airliner off course." He muttered the Arabic equivalent of "Stupid black bastard" and went back to his bed.

The surveillance operator continued to stare at the target, certain that something was wrong. But he didn't know what and was afraid to wake the German who was asleep in the back room.

Only the red glow of the instrument lights cut the darkness on the C-130's flight deck. "Depressurization checklist complete," the flight engineer said. Speaking into an oxygen mask gave his words a strained, baffled sound.

"Rog," Jake Madison said, his voice sounding much the same. "Everyone keep an eye on your buddy. We don't need anyone going hypoxic up here and passing out. Depressurize the aircraft." The flight engineer reached up to the overhead control panel and turned the pressurization switch to vent. A light whooshing sound filled the flight deck as the cabin pressure equalized to the outside altitude.

"Cockpit at thirty-two thousand feet," the flight engineer said. "We're depressurized."

"Oxygen check," Madison said. They had never dropped parachutists this high and he was worried about oxygen starvation. The crew checked in by position and the pilot relaxed.

"Three minutes out," the navigator called. "Slow down."

Madison pulled the throttles back, slowing the Hercules to 130 knots indicated airspeed. The noise on the cargo deck was deafening as the jump doors at the rear of the aircraft were opened, the air deflectors extended, and the jump platforms locked into place. The jumpmaster turned the red lights down a notch, dimming the light in the cargo compartment even more. But the jumpers could still clearly see him as he took his position between the jump doors. He keyed his personal radio that linked the men together. "Prepare to stand!" he ordered in French.

The heads of the forty men sitting in the parachute seats, twenty to each side of the aircraft, turned as one to face the jumpmaster, proof that all had heard him and their radios were working. The drill had started and Bouchard felt the inevitable adrenaline rush. He was alive as the commands came in quick succession.

Then he stepped out the door, into the starlit night sky. He fell free of the C-130, feeling his body decelerate, losing the forward speed of the aircraft. The sound of the Hercules receded into the night and only the howling wind cut the silence. His team had been briefed to keep radio transmissions to a minimum during the drop and silence carried the message that all was well. He waited for his parachute to deploy automatically when he descended through thirty thousand feet.

The canopy rustled open and broke his free fall with a jerk. Instinctively, he checked his oxygen connection. It was secure and he was not showing any signs of hypoxia. Next, he checked the rectangular, mattresslike canopy above him. He could see the position lights on each side, green on the right and red on the left, which would burn out before he descended through ten thousand feet. He looked down at the GPS, global positioning system, receiver strapped to the top of his emergency parachute.

The GPS was so precise that he could navigate to within thirty feet of his objective. The glowing LED readout told him he was left of course. He reached for the riser extensions that allowed him to steer the parachute and still keep his arms below his heart, pulled, and turned to the right. Slowly, the course bar on the GPS centered as the miles-to-go counter decreased to twenty.

Bouchard was hanging under a highly modified version of the FXC Guardian parachute. It was not a parachute in the conventional sense, but a steerable, nonrigid airfoil that had a five-to-one forward glide ratio. By combining the Guardian parachute and GPS, a jumper could glide almost twenty-five miles and land on a pinpoint target. For the jumpers, their main problem was to avoid running into each other on landing. Their night-vision goggles would help prevent that. If all went as planned, Bouchard was going to land his thirty-nine men inside the Azanian Liberation Army's headquarters compound in exactly fifty minutes.

The young Azanian had quit worrying about the airliner when it entered a holding pattern south of Kimberley, eighty miles south of the farmstead. Instead, he tried to make sense of the flickering returns that ghosted across his radar scope. Birds, he decided. But did birds large enough to reflect radar energy fly at night? He didn't know. He turned the moving target indicator down, trying to get a speed on the slow-moving targets. At first, the radar could not determine their speed. Finally, he got a readout of twenty-eight miles an hour. Now he was alarmed and remembered to check the altitude: twelve thousand feet. That was definitely too fast and too high for birds. Or was it? He was going to wake the German in the back room when the radar broke lock and with it, his resolve.

He checked his new wristwatch: fifteen minutes before two o'clock. Frustrated, he walked outside and looked up, hoping he would see birds flying. Instead, he saw five very faint lights moving across the star-pocked sky. One by one, they disappeared. They are too slow for shooting stars, he reasoned. Was that another one, coming down toward him? It winked out. They had to be shooting stars, he decided.

What he had mistaken for a meteor shower were the position lights on the parachute canopies burning out as the raiders descended toward the compound. Only his young, and very keen, eyesight had allowed him to pick the lights out against the starlit sky. The Azanian thought for a moment. This was a very strange night. His emotions took over and he started to shake.

There was no guard to stop him as he ran from the compound.

Tuesday, April 7
Ysterplaat Air Base, Cape Town

Pontowski sat at the commander's position in the command post. The two controllers on duty had established a no-go zone around him and he was cocooned in a circle of silence. He hated being out of the stream of activity flowing past him, but he sensed the wisdom of it. A commander needed time to think and concentrate on the big picture. Accepting it was the problem.

The master clock on the wall in front of him clicked to 0150 hours local time while the elapsed-time clock below it announced they were two hours and twenty minutes into the operation.

He breathed easier when the radio squawked. It was Madison with a status report. His copilot passed the information in short blocks while the controllers copied it down, filling in the formatted message form. The senior controller handed Pontowski the completed message form: The airdrop had gone off on schedule. The three helicopters led by van der Roos had landed eighty miles south of the target area, refueled, and taken off. Again, all was proceeding as planned.

What can go wrong now? Pontowski thought. He considered the possibilities. "This sucks," he grumbled to himself, standing up. He paced back and forth, feeling the need for action. Don't second-guess them now, he warned himself. Trust your people. Why the doubts? he asked himself. Will it always be like this? the loneliness? the worrying? He knew the answer to the last question as he paced back and forth, alone and safe while his people were in harm's way.

Tuesday, April 7
Near Kimberley, South Africa

Bouchard spiraled above the compound, his hands working the parachute's riser extensions as he steered toward the large open area behind the two main barns. He kept the spiral going as he descended and visually swept the large farmstead with his night-vision goggles, looking for any signs of activity. No movement. His timing was perfect and at a hundred feet above the landing zone, he rolled out of the spiral onto his final approach. He braked the parachute and landed in a standing position. His feet were cold from the long descent and protested in pain.

Before Bouchard could collapse his parachute, two more raiders were on the ground beside him. By the time he had freed the submachine gun strapped to his side like an overlarge side arm, two more men were down. He kept counting the shadows as they dropped to the ground, never losing the tally. No commands were given, no signals exchanged, as the shooters formed up into squads of four and moved silently into position.

At forty-five seconds, Bouchard's count stood at nineteen. His group was one man short. He waited, counting the seconds. A shadow passed overhead and the last man touched down. It had to be Rogers, the American, he reasoned. He was always getting lost.

He checked his watch: thirty-five seconds to go. The last arrival moved into position and Alpha Group was ready. He glanced at his watch, did a mental countdown for the last five seconds, and at exactly two minutes past the hour, keyed his radio with three short clicks. Two clicks answered, telling him the second team of twenty shooters, Bravo Group, was in place and ready to go. Bouchard waited while the second hand swept toward 02:03. He spoke in a low voice, "On my count: three, two, one, mark." The clock had started.

IRON GATE

The tension that had coiled inside Bouchard like a tightly wound spring found its release in action and he erupted from cover, leading three squads of Alpha Group into the farmstead. The remaining eight men had to secure the landing zone, act as a reserve, and establish radio contact with the helicopters that were inbound. Bouchard slowed and allowed the point man of his squad, Corporal Rogers, to take the lead as the two other squads fanned out. It was an intricate ballet with each step planned to deconflict their movement and fire. And it was all on a strict time schedule.

The point man for each squad led the way to a preselected target while the backup man brought up the rear, more concerned with what was behind them than where they were going. The low and high men in each squad were sandwiched between and concentrated on clearing their flanks. Rogers reached their objective, the radar shack, and paused, mentally counting down. He tested the door handle, surprised to find it unlocked. He signaled his team, carefully opened the door, threw a flash-bang grenade into the room, and closed the door. "Cosmic little suckers," he mumbled as the grenade exploded, filling the room with a deafening concussion and blinding light.

Around them, the farmstead erupted in a deafening blast as grenades and gunfire shattered the silence. Rogers threw the door open and fired into the room at an angle, sweeping the half of the room opposite him. Bouchard was crouched on the other side of the door and fired from his angle, clearing the other half of the room. The high man in his team was through the door, firing as he went. He raked the door of the back room with a short burst before kicking it in and clearing that room. "All clear," he called. Bouchard stepped into the main room. It was a shambles. The radar console was chewed to pieces and smoking, filling the room with the acrid stench of burning insulation. A lone body lay half out of one of the bunks on the back wall. "Arab," the high man guessed.

Bouchard walked into the back room and looked around. The bed showed signs of recent occupancy and he wanted to see a body with at least two bullets in its head. Bouchard's reaction was instinctive, born out of long experience. "Out," he barked. The urgency in his voice drove the men out of the building and into the dark. Bouchard was the last man out of the radar shack, running for all he was worth. Behind him, the building erupted in a fiery blast that knocked him to the ground.

"Alpha Group," he radioed, "status." His men checked in—all okay. "Attention," he transmitted, "the radar shack was rigged for destruct. Check your areas for demolitions."

The men swept their areas and reported finding the communications shack, the motor pool, and the ammunition dump wired for destruction. The attack had been so swift that only the demolitions in the radar shack had been activated. "Main house secure," the leader of Bravo Group radioed.

"LZ secure," another voice said. The eight shooters Bouchard had left behind had cleared the landing zone for the three helicopters.

"LZ, call in the helicopters," Bouchard ordered.

"Every high-value item in the place was wired for destruction," Rogers said. "Why did they do that?"

"It's a good preparation when you have low confidence in your people," Bouchard said. "It also stops theft. Fortunately, they were poorly trained. Unfortunately, there's at least one bastard wandering around out there who is well trained."

"Only one?" Rogers asked.

"There was only one bunk in the back room and it had been slept in," Bouchard answered. "There should have been a body to go with it."

"Whoever it is, he's pissed," Rogers said.

"Obviously," Bouchard said. He spoke into his whisper mike. "Alpha Group has one hostile unaccounted for. Hold your position." Throughout the compound, the raiders froze and watched for any signs of movement. Bouchard turned into a frozen gargoyle in the night, a demon from hell shaped by his night-vision goggles and rucksack, waiting patiently for a victim. It was a flushing tactic that often worked in the strange time warp following a firefight. Time dragged and each passing second expanded into minutes.

Rogers's voice came over the radio. "Movement outside the vehicle shed."

"I want him alive," Bouchard replied.

"Can do," Rogers replied. Bouchard counted the seconds. At the count of four, a single shot rang out. "He's down," Rogers radioed. "Left knee."

"Bring him in," Bouchard transmitted. "Bravo Group, I'm joining on you."

"Come on in," Bravo Group leader replied.

Bouchard moved quickly and reached the main farmhouse in forty-five seconds. He was cleared inside and ripped off his night-vision goggles. "Damn," he muttered, "I hate these."

"Well done," Bravo Group leader said. "We're ahead of schedule. It was easy."

"For you," Bouchard replied. "We almost had pieces of the radar shack blown up our asses. We may be in for a repeat." He blinked his eyes, adjusting to the light. His second in command was standing by a table, holding a water bottle. The room was a makeshift command center with files and communications equipment lining the walls. Six bodies lay crumpled on the floor. "Search them," Bouchard ordered.

Rogers and another shooter entered the room carrying a wounded European. Bouchard's head jerked in recognition and he sprang at the prisoner, grabbed him by the hair, and spun him around. At the same time, Bouchard kicked at the back of his good knee and shoved him to the floor. "Chair," he growled, holding the man down. Before a kitchen chair could be passed, he started banging the man's head against the floor. Finally, he lifted the man into the chair.

"Tape," Bouchard demanded. One of his shooters handed him a roll of heavy tape and the Frenchman bound him to the chair, cutting deep into his skin. Not once did the man utter a sound as Bouchard tied a wire noose around his neck and strung him to the ceiling. "If he moves," Bouchard said, "kick the chair over."

"An old friend, perhaps?" Rogers murmured.

Bouchard leaned against the table, still coiled tight. "Not likely." He looked at the two men who had brought the prisoner in. "You are lucky to be alive."

"Who is this guy?" Rogers asked.

"Erik Beckmann," Bouchard replied, fixing him with a cold stare. "We were wondering what had happened to you,

Erik." Beckmann spat at him. The sound of approaching helicopters demanded Bouchard's attention. He checked his watch and radioed the LZ team. "Bring them in. Quick. They've got thirty-one minutes." Now they waited.

The radio crackled as the helicopters landed and four figures jumped off. They ran through the compound, led by a legionnaire. They reached the farmhouse and were cleared inside. Bouchard shook his head as the Boys came through the door. It wasn't his idea of how to fight a war, but Pontowski had insisted this team of four women inspect the headquarters before it was destroyed. Bouchard suspected they were CIA. He watched as they went to work.

"They are very good," Blue Group leader told Bouchard in French.

One of the Boys handed Bouchard a map. "The Azanians' training and supply area is here," she said, pointing to a small village thirty miles away.

"How much longer do you need?" Bouchard asked, pleased with the results they were producing.

"Days," the woman answered. "We'll take what we can. Can you help?" Bouchard nodded and ordered six men to help them. Again, he waited while the women worked furiously. Grudgingly, he had to agree with Bravo Group Leader: They knew their business. He checked his watch. "It is time for us to go, Erik."

"Du kannst mir mal an den sack fassen!"

"Sticking to your German cover, Erik?" Bouchard asked. He turned to the other men. "Herr Beckmann wants us to perform self-intercourse. Not a pleasant sight." He looked at Beckmann in resignation. "He won't help. Besides, I don't want him on the same helicopter with us."

"Who is he?" Rogers asked.

"A very dangerous man." Bouchard's gloved left hand stroked the left side of his scarred face. "He did this to me."

"I never heard of him," Rogers admitted.

"That is what makes him so good," Bouchard said. Again, he checked his watch. He keyed his radio. "All units, withdraw to the LZ on my count: three, two, one, mark." The clock was running again. Rogers led the four women out of the house. Each was carrying two or three boxes. Bouchard deliberately folded the map, taking his time.

"What about Beckmann here?" Bravo Group leader asked.

Bouchard's face was a blank mask and his voice was strangely gentle. He shook his head slowly. "I'll have a little chat with Monsieur Beckmann . . . after you leave."

"The demolitions are set to blow in six minutes," Bravo Group leader told Bouchard. He darted out the door, leaving the two men alone.

Five rapid shots echoed from the main farmhouse as the first helicopter took off.

CHAPTER

20

Tuesday, April 7
Ysterplaat Air Base, Cape Town

Pontowski scratched the time on his notepad when the second radio transmission from the raiders was received. He knew the command post controllers would note the time, but he had to do something. He glanced at the master clock on the wall. It still read 02:48. Time was slowing, creeping along and losing the race to fast-moving snails.

"Sir," the senior controller called, "Colonel Bouchard wants to speak to you."

Pontowski picked up his mike and toggled the transmission/encryption switch on, relieved that he had something to do. "Go ahead," he transmitted.

"It went by the clock," Bouchard said, "no casualties." The combination of satellite and frequency-hopping radios gave his words a tinny, staccato ring. "But no joy on the second objective."

Pontowski wanted to ask what went wrong. Why hadn't they destroyed the arms and ammunition the CIA claimed the Azanians were stockpiling? But long experience had taught him that the answers to those questions could wait. His first priority was to get his people safely home.

Bouchard studied the map the Boys had found in the Azanians' headquarters. "But we know where it is. We can take it out."

"What do you have in mind?" It wasn't a question Pontowski wanted to ask.

Bouchard quickly outlined the follow-up operation he had in mind. Pontowski hesitated before answering, calculating their chances of success. Bouchard was proposing a very simple operation, but could they do it? Too much was spur of the moment, not planned out. Did he want to play this one by ear? What factors were in their favor?

"Colonel," Bouchard said, "van der Roos says he can insert us with no trouble. We only need his helicopter and four A-10s."

Pontowski knew Bouchard was nudging him to a decision. "You're winging it," he finally said.

"True," Bouchard answered. "But look who we're going against. Very low grade."

He's right, Pontowski thought. He made his decision. "Do it. When and where do you want the A-10s?"

Bouchard read off a set of coordinates. "Have them on station at oh six-thirty local time. I'll update when we're in position."

"They'll be there," Pontowski promised. He toggled the transmission/encryption switch to the off position. "Sergeant Gonzalez," he called to the senior controller, "I need to speak to Colonel Kowalski." He checked the mission status board to see who was sitting alert and would fly the sorties requested by Bouchard. "Maggot's going to like this," he muttered to himself.

He checked the master clock on the wall: 02:51. It had taken him three minutes to put his people back in danger. He sank into his comfortable chair and tried to relax. But the clock refused to let him escape as each second dragged, making him wait.

Tuesday, April 7
Over the Great Karoo, near Kimberley

The Puma helicopter skimmed low over the Karoo, twisting and turning with the terrain, hiding in canyons and ravines. Once, van der Roos descended too low and the rotor kicked up dust, momentarily marking its position. The gunner stationed at the 7.62-mm machine gun at the right door called "rooster tail" over the intercom and van der Roos's muscles contracted, making the minute control inputs on the collective and cyclic that commanded the Puma to climb yet still hydroplane the earth's surface.

The copilot sitting in the left seat monitored the moving map display slaved to the GPS and constantly updated van der Roos. "Almost there . . . come left three degrees . . . almost there. Slow . . . slow . . . we're there." This time, van der Roos's movements were obvious as he made the Puma respond to his will. The long-extinct Khoikhoi who named the land would have known the machine for what it was—a giant bird of death and destruction descending onto their world.

The men on the cargo deck were out the moment the wheels touched down. Bouchard came forward and stood between the pilots, listening to the radio that linked him to his men. Vague shadows were starting to form in the early morning dawn and he could see two of his men sweep the area in front of the helicopter. One by one, the ground team checked in. "The area is secure," he told the pilots.

"Shut 'em down," van der Roos said. The copilot killed the engines as the rotor spun down. Outside, van der Roos's two gunners were unrolling camouflage netting to hide the helicopter. He turned to Bouchard. "Good hunting, sir."

Bouchard lay in a shallow depression below the crown of a low hill, his eyes fixed on the valley below him. The long shadows of morning twilight slowly lifted, revealing a jumble of parked trucks, tents, half-strung camouflage netting, and piles of crates. He was downwind from the base and the wind carried the pungent odor of poorly dug latrines. Cars were parked haphazardly around a clump of whitewashed huts, the original village.

His face was impassive as he scanned the valley with binoculars and searched for the guard posts. His stomach churned when he saw three children run through the village. He knew what was coming their way. Rogers skidded into the depression and flopped down beside him, gasping for breath. The beads of sweat coursing down his face traced dirty lines over the camouflage he was wearing, giving him an unearthly look. "You might have waited for me," he finally managed.

Bouchard ignored him and pulled out his GPS. He switched it on and within ten seconds, a latitude and longitude flashed on the small screen. He knew their position to within thirty feet. He double-checked his radio to make sure the battery was still good and waited, watching the village.

"Talk about luck," Rogers muttered. He pulled out his binoculars. "Look at that. They were too lazy to disperse. These clowns haven't got a clue."

Bouchard did not respond and his eyes were drawn into a tight squint. He was thinking of his own two small children safe in their home near Aubagne, France, the headquarters of the French Foreign Legion, ten miles east of Marseilles. "We must flush the village first," he told Rogers.

"Good idea. How?"

Again, Bouchard did not respond. He was thinking, wrestling with the dilemma of modern warfare. He was on the side with modern technology and all that went with it. He had the ability to destroy a target, using whatever violence and destruction was necessary to do the job. His men were educated, well trained, at home with technology, and could make it work in combat. They blended the simple and complex, the old-fashioned and the new into patterns that were always changing. They were highly disciplined and they never forgot the basics, like the dispersal and camouflage of supplies and the protection of noncombatants. Below him was the side with modern weapons and little knowledge about their use.

"We need to educate them," Bouchard said.

"Isn't that why we're here?" Rogers replied.

The two A-10s swooped in low over the Karoo. The lead aircraft pulled up to twelve hundred feet and entered a racetrack holding pattern to the left while his wingman stayed low and behind him. "Alpha Group," Maggot called over the UHF radio. "How copy this frequency?"

"Read you loud and clear," Bouchard answered. "How me?"

"You're coming through broken but readable," Maggot replied. "Say target, threat, and friendlies."

Bouchard read off his position coordinates. "We only have one—I repeat, only one—target for you. The target is in the valley southwest of my position. It is a military compound next to a village. No threat observed. But expect small arms and Grails." Grail was the NATO name for the Russian-built, shoulder-held surface-to-air missile that had become the generic description for the threat. "Friendlies are in the village."

"Not good," Maggot replied.

"Can you strafe first?" Bouchard transmitted. "Hit the far side and work toward the village."

Maggot paused before answering. Bouchard wanted to warn the villagers by walking the attack toward the huts, giving the occupants time to escape. And like Bouchard, he did not want to kill innocent people. But he knew the odds. The best tactic to maximize his own survival was to bomb first and strafe later. Was he willing to take the risk?

He made his choice. "We'll strafe first." The decision felt good. Automatically, he scanned his HUD Control panel and selected the air-to-ground gunsight. He rolled to the left and quickly scanned the area before rolling out. He repeated the maneuver to the right. He was not joyriding but creating a mental picture of the terrain that made sense to him. He had never flown in the area before and he needed visual clues to help him maintain situational awareness in the heat of a strafing or bomb run.

"You're cleared in," Bouchard radioed.

"Rog," Maggot answered. Now he had to sort out the attack with his wingman, Buns Cox, and the second element of two inbound A-10s. "Buns, go tactical. Ninety cross, separate, reverse to reattack behind me." Maggot was using a verbal shorthand to describe their tactics. Next, Maggot radioed the inbound aircraft. "Skid, copy all?"

"Copied all," Skid Malone replied.

"If we can't clear the village," Maggot said, "we're taking our bombs home."

"Roger that," Skid answered.

"I'm in," Maggot radioed, firewalling his throttles and heading for the valley. His wingman, Buns, angled off until

he was four thousand feet to the right and slightly in trail.
Maggot dropped to three hundred feet above the deck to use
terrain masking for concealment. Instinctively, he double-
checked his weapons panel again, ensuring the master arm
switch was up and he was in WD-1, the mode that gave him
a gunsight display in his HUD. A ridgeline loomed in front
of him. He pulled back on the stick and rolled 135 degrees
as he came over the top and the valley spread out before
him. He pulled the Hog's nose toward the ground and rolled
out. "Holy shit," he breathed. Ahead of him was the most
target-rich environment a Warthog pilot could dream of.

"Unbelievable," Buns radioed. "Unfuckin' believable."

Instinctively, Maggot fixed the village's relative position
to the target and hills. It wasn't something he thought
about, it just happened. The picture he carried in his mind
became more complete.

Maggot was aware of running figures as he rolled in on the
outer edge of the supply dump. The sight picture in the
HUD was good: dive angle seven degrees, airspeed 315
knots, and the analog range bar inside the gun reticle circle
at the top of the HUD was unwinding past six thousand
feet. He made it look easy, but it wasn't. When the pipper
dot inside the gun reticle circle was on a target, he depressed
the trigger to the first detent and held it, engaging the
PAC—precision attitude control.

The autopilot stiffened the stick and held the gun aim
steady with the pipper centered on the target he was going
to destroy. He was a mechanic going about the business of
death and destruction, deciding who would live and die.

But the defenders on the ground had other ideas. At first,
a single stream of tracers reached out for him. Maggot
overrode the PAC and jinked a little before restabilizing.
His finger started to tighten on the trigger. The ground in
front of him erupted in a mass of tracers and sticks of
flames—Grails—converged on him. Maggot jinked hard,
breaking off the attack.

Bouchard watched as Maggot flew through the wall of flak
and missiles. Flares popped out behind the A-10 as Maggot
slammed his big fighter down to thirty feet above the deck.
The second A-10 crossed behind Maggot at ninety degrees,

its cannon firing. Bouchard was absolutely certain both Warthogs were hit. Suddenly, Maggot's Hog pulled up in a steep climb and Bouchard was certain Maggot was going to crash. But he was wrong, and Maggot ruddered his aircraft around and brought its nose back onto the defenders. *"Merde,"* Bouchard breathed.

Maggot rolled back in, jinking hard, challenging the men on the ground shooting at him. Sweat poured off his face and he disregarded the sharp pings as small-arms fire bounced off the cockpit's armor plating. Two rounds punctured the canopy above his head. He pressed the attack. "Buns!" he radioed.

"Reversing now," his wingman replied. Buns had held to his contract and after crossing Maggot's run in at ninety degrees, had pulled off straight ahead to clear the area for Maggot to reattack. Once he had separation, Buns pitched back into the attack, holding to the original tactic Maggot had called for.

Maggot walked a burst of cannon fire into the heart of the Triple A shooting at him. He stood the Warthog on its right wing and turned ninety degrees. Now he was heading in the same directions as Buns, who was right behind him, two miles in trail. An explosion lit the ground between them and smoke pillared into the sky. Buns flew through the smoke and found his target. His cannon fired and he rolled left ninety degrees to pull away from Maggot, who was in the pop again, reversing course to reattack.

In the hands of an aggressive pilot like Maggot, the Warthog was in its element, and it was too much for the defenders. Shooting at the A-10s only seemed to make them more angry and more determined to reattack. It was a type of personal attention they did not want. As suddenly as it had begun, the defenders stopped firing, abandoned their weapons, and ran for safety.

"We got 'em running," Maggot said over the UHF. He kicked the rudders and lined up on another target. The sight picture was perfect and he sent eighty rounds into a line of trucks. He mashed the trigger again before pulling off to the target.

"Two's in," Buns replied. "Gotcha in sight."

Maggot circled over the huts. The villagers were also

running away. He wondered why so many of them were falling to the ground. He tightened up his circle and dropped to a hundred feet. A loud "Sumbitch!" exploded when he saw two men shooting at the fleeing men and women. He horsed the A-10 around and climbed, never taking his eyes off the two shooters. He was flying on pure instinct. The sight picture in the HUD was perfect when he brought his Hog's nose to bear on the shooters. He was about to perform lethal surgery, this time with malice.

His right forefinger flicked on the trigger and he fired seven rounds. The two men simply disappeared, torn apart by the high-explosive cannon shells. Again, he circled the huts, relieved to see more people running away. He radioed Bouchard. "It looks like everybody is out of the village. Who was shooting at them?"

"Nice work," Bouchard answered. "From here it looked like the soldiers were shooting."

"At their own people?" Maggot was incredulous.

"Trucks are moving," Buns interrupted.

"CBU time," Maggot replied. "You in position?"

"Rog," Buns answered.

"Cleared in. I'll cover."

Buns popped to three thousand feet, rolled, and came down the wire at a twenty-degree dive angle. His airspeed was riveted on 350 knots when he hit the pickle button at two thousand feet. Four canisters of CBU-58 separated cleanly from under the wings and split open, spewing a deadly hail of baseball-sized bomblets. The exploding bomblets cut a wide path through the trucks.

"This is too good to be true," Maggot radioed. "I'm in." It was a repeat of Buns's delivery, except this time his path was at a ninety-degree angle to his wingman's. "I'm clear." Maggot called the second flight. "Skid, you're cleared in hot. We're off to the south."

"Copy all," Skid answered.

Another voice came over the radio. "I hope you left some for us." It was Gorilla, Skid's wingman.

"Plenty to go around," Maggot assured him. "And the welcoming committee done left the party." Buns joined on his right wing and they headed for Ysterplaat.

* * *

Bouchard watched the second flight of two A-10s work the Azanians over. It's turned into a turkey shoot, he thought. He focused his binoculars on a car and truck racing for safety at the far end of the valley. A lone A-10 chased them down and pulled off as a huge fireball engulfed the vehicles. The A-10 banked hard to the left and disappeared behind the dark cloud. "That's some secondary," Rogers said. "I wonder what that truck was carrying?"

Bouchard shrugged an answer. The two men were silent as they watched the A-10s go about their work. There was little left that was recognizable when Gorilla mopped up. He rolled in, squeezed off a short burst of cannon fire, and pulled off. He kept close in and brought the Warthog around, a study in precision as he repeated the performance, leaving a trail of explosions and fires. All that remained in the valley was a burning desert littered with charred hulks. The small village had disappeared, blown away by the blast of two five-hundred-pound Mark-82 AIRs that had impacted four hundred feet away.

The sharp crack of unexploded ordnance cooking off echoed over them. "No one's going down there for a long time," Bouchard said. "Head for the LZ." He scanned the trucks with his binoculars. He stood and walked away, his face a blank mask.

Rogers followed him, holding back. He had been with Bouchard long enough to know when he was angry—very angry.

"Roll up the netting," van der Roos told his crew when Bouchard checked in on the radio. "It's time to go."

"Captain," a guard said, pointing to the far side of the clearing.

Bouchard appeared out of the bush and climbed on board the helicopter without saying a word. "What's the problem?" van der Roos asked Rogers. "I thought it went well."

"It did," Rogers answered. "A walk in the park. A real bad day for the bad guys."

"Then why is he so angry?"

"I guess the colonel didn't like some of the losing spirit he saw," Rogers answered. "They were killing the villagers, their own people."

Van der Roos shook his head. "The villagers were probably Vendas. Most of the Azanians are from different tribes and think Vendas are worthless cow dung. Those are their words, not mine."

"So it was tribalism," Rogers ventured.

"It's the African form of racism," van der Roos told him.

Thursday, April 9
Iron Gate, near Bloemfontein

Kreiner's piglike eyes darted back and forth between MacKay and the Azanian. Sweat trickled down his back as he considered his next move. He desperately wanted MacKay to be on the receiving end of Beckmann's wrath. *Can I trick the black bastard into it?* he thought. *He may be an American, but he's still a kaffir, as dumb as all the rest.*

"You brought him here," Kreiner said, "and you talked to him first. Since you know all the details, it would be more efficient for you to brief the Generaal."

Much to Kreiner's relief, MacKay agreed. "I can do that. Set it up." Kreiner jerked his head yes and made the phone call. *What's the sleazeball up to?* MacKay thought.

"The Generaal will see you now," Kreiner told him.

MacKay motioned to the young Azanian and walked into Beckmann's office. *"Goeimôre,* Generaal," MacKay said. A stray thought came to him: *In ancient Egypt, slaves carried bad messages to the pharaohs because the bearer of bad tidings was put to death.*

"Kreiner said you had important news," Beckmann said.

MacKay did a quick evaluation of the man. His voice was calm and matter-of-fact and his body language neutral. "There is very bad news, Generaal," MacKay began. "I wish I could change it." He plunged ahead. "This man was at the Azanian headquarters when it was attacked. My informants found him and turned him over to me. He claims a German mercenary was killed who matches the description of your brother."

Beckmann stared at MacKay, not saying a word. "My brother was there," Beckmann finally said. "But he has been reported killed many times before."

MacKay told the Azanian to repeat all that he had told

him and Kreiner. The story was a long one, embellished with a hundred reasons why he had run from his post in the radar shack. "I went back after the helicopters had left," he told Beckmann, "and waited for the fire to go out in the main house." He described how he had found the corpse of the German tied to a chair and shot many times.

"Why wasn't the body burned beyond recognition?" MacKay asked.

"It was burned very badly," the Azanian answered.

"But you are sure it was the German," MacKay said.

"Oh, yes," the Azanian replied. "He had a ring . . . I took it off his body . . . I gave it to you."

MacKay handed the ring over to Beckmann, who turned it over and over, carefully examining it. "It is Erik's ring. Our father gave one to each of us when we first saw the Voortrekker Monument. It was December sixteenth, the day of the Covenant and our sixteenth birthday. You see the connection? A kaffir stole mine years ago." He slipped the ring on his finger.

Relief flowed through MacKay and he relaxed. His worries about Beckmann were unfounded. The man was filled with remorse and sadness, not vengeance. Beckmann picked up the phone and punched a button. "Kreiner, please come in. You will need assistance." He continued to look at MacKay. "It is a shame," he murmured.

"Please accept my regrets," MacKay told him.

The door burst open and Kreiner marched in with two armed guards; one had his pistol drawn and the other carried two pairs of handcuffs. Beckmann waved a hand at MacKay and the Azanian. "Hang them," he ordered.

MacKay walked briskly over to the guards, not believing they were making so many mistakes. His hands flashed and his body twisted in one continuous motion as he slapped the guard's pistol away and jammed the rigid fingertips of his right hand into the man's throat. He came around and kicked the other guard's hand and his half-drawn pistol. It clattered to the floor as he kicked again, high and hard, breaking his jaw and knocking him to the ground. MacKay scooped up the pistol and fired, killing the first guard. Then he kicked the second guard in the temple.

Kreiner was moving for the door when MacKay swung the pistol at his head and knocked him to the floor. He kicked Kreiner in the stomach, doubling him up in pain. He marched back to Beckmann's desk and slammed the pistol down, flat and hard.

"Train your guards better," he said, his voice tightly controlled. "I meant it when I offered my regrets. But hanging me because I brought you the bad news changes nothing. Or do you only want stupid cowards around you?"

Beckmann calmly picked up the phone as if nothing had happened. "Please send in a medic to help Kreiner. And clean up the mess." He stood up. "Come." He pointed to the Azanian. "Bring him."

Beckmann led the way to the security compound next to the headquarters building and spoke quietly to the lieutenant on duty. The execution played out with a speed and precision that stunned MacKay. The Azanian was stripped naked, his wrists handcuffed behind his back, and led into the interior courtyard. His legs gave out when he saw the gallows and two burly guards dragged him up the steps. A wire noose was slipped over his head and the trap door fell open. But the wire was already tight and the Azanian did not fall. Instead, he swung there, twisting in the wind as he strangled.

But nothing could quench Beckmann's anger. An inner voice demanded revenge for his brother's death while another chastised him for inaction. The voice that had always urged caution grew weaker and weaker. Finally, he turned to MacKay. "Do not disobey me again. Come with me." MacKay followed him back to the headquarters building.

The crazy mutha has totally lost it, MacKay warned himself for at least the sixth time. He listened while Beckmann talked to his staff as if nothing had happened and they were discussing the normal business that each day brought. But there was nothing normal about what Beckmann was planning.

"The so-called UN peacekeepers have finally shown their true colors," Beckmann said, letting emotion flow into his words. "Their attack on the Azanians was a warning that we must not ignore. We must send them a message in the only terms they understand." He was in full flow, his words carrying his audience. "But we must not forget the traitors among us. Too many of our brothers who dare to call themselves voortrekkers are deserting the Boerstaat and seeking refuge in Cape Town. We must expel the United Nations foreigners from our land and punish these traitors! It is time for action! Action!"

How do I warn them of what's coming? MacKay thought. The room echoed with shouts of *"Blut und Boden!"* What have I gotten into?

Friday, April 10
UN Headquarters, Constantia,
Cape Town

De Royer had returned from Paris the day after the attack on the Azanians and promptly disappeared. Pontowski caught a brief glimpse of the general on Thursday morning, but other than that, de Royer was a ghost in his own headquarters. The summons finally came Friday morning when Bouchard asked Pontowski to join the general in the gardens. "Does he know the details of the attack?" Pontowski asked.

"Both of our after-action reports are on his desk," Bouchard said.

Pontowski found the general walking slowly down a path, his head bent. "Sir," Pontowski said, catching his attention.

De Royer did not look up and continued to pace in silence. Pontowski fell in beside him. "I do not understand the actions of your government," de Royer said.

"Most of the time, I can't figure out what they're doing either."

De Royer glanced at him. "Why did they refuse your promotion?"

"Politics," Pontowski allowed. "I was only frocked, breveted, allowed to wear my new rank until the Senate approved the promotion list. They disapproved my promotion and I was returned to my former rank."

"In my country," de Royer said, "only priests are un-frocked. Generals are shot. I like your system better."

Pontowski chuckled. The general had actually made a joke. "You need someone with higher rank for your vice-commander. The Air Force has lots of brigadiers who can do my job."

"I was in contact with your secretary of defense," de Royer said. "Doctor Elkins says you will be promoted. I want you to remain as my second in command."

Pontowski was shocked. "Thank you, sir. I appreciate your confidence. But personally, I think Doctor Elkins is blowing a lot of smoke. There is no way the Senate will ever confirm my promotion now."

De Royer shook his head. "You are just like Bouchard. You don't know your own worth."

"General," Pontowski said, "I want to start flying again."

"D'accord," de Royer said. "There are times when we must be with our men, when we must share their danger. It is the price of leadership." The general fell silent and slowly paced the garden, his steps measured and rhythmic. "I was almost relieved of my command," he said. "That is why I was delayed in returning. They don't understand what we are doing here."

"Exactly what are we doing?" Pontowski asked.

"At first, I was allowed to do nothing different and there was no larger strategy for keeping the peace. Now, thanks to your president, we are developing a new concept of opera-tions for United Nations peacekeeping efforts. But it is a trial-and-error experience while we learn. The way you used South African helicopters is an example of what can be done."

"We proved that we could do it at Kimberley," Pontowski told him. "Then we decided to integrate them on the raid against the Azanians. But both times we were improvising from the word 'go' and were damn lucky."

"But you had the resolve to carry it through to a success-ful conclusion. It worked because the politicians were not involved and you had the freedom to act. Now the politi-cians must deal with success."

"Being successful, or right, is not always the politically astute course in my country," Pontowski said.

"It is the same in my country," de Royer replied.

"One question, sir. What would you have done if we had failed?"

For the first time, de Royer smiled. "Recommended you for a court-martial, of course."

"But of course," Pontowski muttered. "So what now?"

De Royer's head came up. "We will continue."

Elena Martine was waiting for them in de Royer's office. As always, she was elegantly cool and composed, with a hint of sexuality lurking below the surface. "Charles," she chimed when they entered, "you have been avoiding me." De Royer did not respond and handed his kepi to Bouchard. He walked over and stood looking out the window.

"I have tried to discuss the Azanian affair with Minister Pendulo," she told them. "But he refuses to discuss it until his investigation is complete."

"What has he discovered?" Pontowski asked.

"Nothing," Elena answered. "He has sealed off the area and refused access to my inspectors, the press, everyone. He claims it is an internal matter."

"Pendulo knows what happened," de Royer told her.

"How does he know?" Elena asked, her voice much lower than normal.

"I told him we bombed the Azanians," de Royer said.

"What was the justification?" Elena asked angrily.

"It was in response to Kimberley," de Royer replied. "Think of it as retroactive self-defense."

Elena shook her head. "Retroactive self-defense? There is no such thing."

"An idea whose time has come," Pontowski mumbled under his breath.

"The operation against the Azanians was outside the scope of our operations," Elena protested. "And I was not consulted."

De Royer turned and fixed her with his dead-fish stare. "Of course not." He turned back to the window. The meeting was over and Pontowski escorted her to the parking lot and her BMW.

She hesitated before opening the door. "Matt, dinner Saturday night? My place?" Before he could answer, her fingers brushed lightly against his hand and lingered for a moment. "Eight o'clock?" she murmured.

Pontowski watched her drive away. Is Bouchard right about her? he wondered. Is she using sex to control me? Maybe it was time to find out. "I can't believe I'm doing this," he muttered to himself. Then, "Duty is a terrible burden."

He laughed and headed for his car. He was going to go fly.

Friday, April 10
Ysterplaat Air Base, Cape Town

Lydia Kowalski cornered Pontowski the moment she saw him in the COIC. "Have you seen this?" she said, handing him a message. "Those dickheads have disapproved your request for more C-130s and Warthogs. We only get replacements."

He read the message and handed it back. "Are you surprised? We've been unwanted stepchildren from the word 'go.' We've got to do this one on the cheap." He changed the subject. "How are the helicopter jocks working out?"

"Great," she told him. "They're a fine bunch of guys."

"Most people are," he said. "Especially after you get to know them. Even de Royer." She gave him a look of pure disbelief. "He's cleared me to fly again."

"All right!"

"But I'm not current," Pontowski said. "Schedule me with an instructor pilot."

"Waldo's free."

"Waldo?" he asked.

"Waldo. He's a great IP."

Pontowski scrambled up the boarding ladder and over the canopy rail of the waiting A-10. He settled into the cockpit and savored the moment as he pressed his back against the hard seat cushion. This is where I belong, he thought. Not in some office pushing paper.

He went through the routine, strapping himself into the A-10 before he donned his helmet and gloves. He hesitated.

His hands should have been flying around the cockpit automatically, setting switches and punching in numbers, as he brought the Hog to life. He glanced over at Waldo. His head was bent over as he went through his routine. Get out the checklist, Pontowski thought.

"Damn," he muttered. It wasn't right. He had never referred to a checklist before. It was part of him, committed to memory and as much a part of his flying skills as the unconscious use of the rudders. He had been out of the cockpit too long. "Waldo!" he shouted, getting the captain's attention. Pontowski made a slashing motion across his throat and motioned for them to get out.

"What's the matter?" Waldo asked when he reached Pontowski's Warthog. "I was ready to go do it."

"But I wasn't," Pontowski admitted. "You need to run me through some cockpit training before I kill myself. We're going to be here for a while." They pushed a maintenance stand up against the cockpit for Waldo to stand on while he drilled his commander.

Kowalski and Maggot were waiting when Pontowski walked in from the flight line with Waldo. "Boss, what happened?" Maggot asked.

"I got a lesson in humility," Pontowski answered. "I was too eager to fly and had gotten rusty."

"It happens to all of us," Kowalski said.

CHAPTER
21

Sunday, April 12
Bantry Bay, Cape Town

The morning came hard for Pontowski, as it always did, and he fought off the shadows of sleep as he tried to focus. Sunday morning, he thought. Elena's. She murmured and turned into him, shedding the blanket. Her naked body glowed in the half-light as she stretched, arching her back, pressing her stomach against his. Then she collapsed against him, murmuring as a leg twisted around his. She went back to sleep. He sucked in his breath as he felt the stirrings of a fresh erection.

Hesitantly, he stroked her back. He wanted to look at her and caress every part of her body. She was breathtaking, perfectly proportioned and smooth. Her breasts pressed against his chest and he could feel her heart beat. The memory of last night was still warm and fresh: the way she had whispered and loved him with tenderness and then wild abandon, always holding him.

He had not been so alive since . . . since Shoshana, he told himself. He reached down and pulled the blanket up.

She rolled over and up on an elbow. She looked at him dreamily, her hair hanging down, caressing him. "Matt," she murmured. Then she collapsed against him and cuddled her face against his chest. He slept.

The phone jarred him awake, and he was vaguely aware of

Elena reaching over him to answer it. She handed him the phone. It was Waldo Walderman, the ever-present duty officer. "Colonel, we got a problem and need you in the COIC."

"Be right there," Pontowski told him. He hung up. "I've got to go to work," he told her.

Elena leaned against him. "I had plans for today," she said. "You and me, alone." She nuzzled his ear. "Can't it wait?"

"I wish it could," he said, rolling out of bed. She sat on the edge of the bed and watched him get dressed. Then she walked with him to the door, still naked.

"Come back if you can," she murmured.

"I will," he promised. Outside he ran for his car.

Sunday, April 12
Ysterplaat Air Base, Cape Town

People were streaming into the COIC when Pontowski arrived. "What's going down?" he asked Waldo.

"The UN command center called twenty minutes ago," Waldo told him. "They've lost all contact with the safe zone at Vanwyksvlei. So I called you and Colonel Kowalski. She ordered a recall and a loadout." He pointed toward the command post. "She's in there."

"Good work," Pontowski told him.

Waldo watched as Pontowski went through the door into the command post. "Talk about a well-laid look," Waldo muttered to himself. He had heard the rumors about Martine, and Pontowski had left her telephone number in case he needed to be contacted. Well, rank did have its privileges.

Pontowski sat beside Kowalski at the commander's console and watched the big board, marking time as aircraft and crews came on status. Bouchard's wrong about Elena, he thought. She's not using sex to influence me.

The last A-10 radioed in as manned and ready to launch. "We're ready to go," she told him. "What now?"

He reached for the hot line to de Royer's command

center. "Time to find out," he said. In short order, he had his marching orders from de Royer and hung up. "They've also lost contact with a convoy," he told Kowalski. "The general wants us to do a road recce and fly a QRF team into Vanwyksvlei. The team should be here in twenty minutes. Launch one C-130 and two Hogs for a CAP."

Sunday, April 12
Near Vanwyksvlei, South Africa

Maggot flew a lazy eight pattern along the road leading north to the safe zone at Vanwyksvlei. His wingman, Bag Talbot, was on the opposite side and always crossed behind him on the crossover, clearing Maggot's six o'clock position. Three miles ahead, Maggot saw six white trucks strung out along the deserted road. "Convoy in sight," he transmitted over the UHF radio. Brenda Conklin acknowledged the call from her C-130, five miles in trail. Her copilot relayed the information to Groundhog, the command post in the COIC.

Maggot flew a tight orbit overhead the convoy at two thousand feet before dropping to a lower altitude. "Negative movement," he told his wingman. "Checking it out." Maggot nosed his Warthog over and dropped to five hundred feet. "I don't see any damage," he radioed, "no signs of life." There was a long pause as Maggot slowed and descended to one hundred feet above the trucks. "Oh, shit!" he roared over the radio as he ballooned his jet, trading every bit of airspeed and power he had for altitude.

"Bag, standoff," Maggot said, his words fast and clipped over the radio.

"What's the matter?" Bag asked. "I didn't see any reaction from the ground."

"They're all dead," Maggot said. "Most are still in the trucks. I saw two bodies on the shoulder."

Bag made the connection. "NBC?" NBC was nuclear, biological, and chemical warfare.

"Like in China," Maggot answered. Both pilots had seen

mustard gas used on civilians when they had been in China.

"Do you have any symptoms?" Bag asked him.

"Negative," Maggot answered, his breathing slowing.

Conklin interrupted them. "Say all again."

Maggot quickly repeated what he had seen. "Tell Groundhog we are negative NBC gear and proceeding to Vanwyksvlei." The two A-10s climbed to ten thousand feet and headed north.

Conklin came back over the radio. "Groundhog says to stand clear at Vanwyksvlei," she told them.

"I don't need any convincing," Maggot grumbled. "Air-patch in sight." Ahead of him, he could see the small town of Vanwyksvlei and the airstrip to the west. The two Warthogs circled high above the runway. "I can't see too much from up here," Maggot told Conklin.

"We'll check it out with binocs," Conklin told them. "We're at eight thou, ingressing from the south." Conklin overflew the runway at eight thousand feet and set up a tight orbit. "Negative movement on the ground," she reported. "The field scans clean for damage. RTB." Return to base.

"Roger on the RTB," Maggot said. "Call for decontamination on landing. I'll see if I can find a cloud to fly through on the way back."

Sunday, April 12
Ysterplaat Air Base, Cape Town

Elena was standing next to Pontowski in the control tower gasping for breath after the long run up the steps. She had been at the UN command center with de Royer when the wing had called reporting a suspected chemical attack. She had hurried to the base while de Royer called the UN secretary general. "Are you sure it was gas?" she finally managed.

"We won't know for sure until we get an NBC team on the scene," Pontowski told her. "Have you ever seen a decontamination?" She shook her head, still short of breath. "Maggot's going to need one when he lands. He's probably okay since he hasn't reported any symptoms. But a hundred feet above the convoy got him right into the envelope. He flew through a few clouds on his way back but we can't take a chance."

He pointed to an area on the far side of the base. "They'll test for chemicals before and after scrubbing Maggot's Hog down. Then he can get out." He handed her a pair of binoculars.

They watched as four dark-suited figures surrounded Maggot's A-10 and scrubbed the jet down with long-handled brushes. Then the aircraft was hosed down. "The decon crew," Pontowski told her, "are wearing MOPP suits. MOPP stands for mission operative protection posture." It took over twenty minutes before Maggot's canopy opened and he crawled out.

The tower controller caught their attention. "General de Royer is on the secure line in the command post," he told them. Pontowski thanked him and headed down the stairs with Elena right behind.

The conversation with de Royer was very short and to the point. "A group of voortrekkers are being attacked near Beaufort West," the general told him. "They are in a laager and can't hold out much longer. Pendulo doesn't trust his own generals to respond and has asked for our help. I'm sending in four Pumas and the Quick Reaction Force."

Pontowski recalled the time he had passed by Trektown, the voortrekker camp, when he and Sam Darnell were returning from the van der Roos winery in Paarl. It seemed as if a century had passed since then. "You'll need A-10s for close air support," he said.

"D'accord," de Royer replied. He broke the connection.

This is turning into Black Sunday, Pontowski thought. How much more can go wrong? He found out when Maggot came into the command post. "Was it chemical?" Pontowski asked.

"Fuckin' A right it was," Maggot answered. "The decon team found traces of Sarin."

"It's a whole new ball game," Pontowski said grimly.

"What's Sarin?" Elena asked.

"A nerve gas developed by the Germans in World War II," Pontowski told her.

Sunday, April 12
Near Beaufort West, South Africa

The A-10 overflew the smoking wreckage on the ground and pulled up. "Looks quiet," Skid Malone radioed.

The second A-10 crossed at a thirty-degree angle, much slower and lower. "Somebody is moving down there," Gorilla Moreno transmitted. "They didn't use nerve gas here."

Skid radioed for the Pumas to come in as the two Warthogs set up a CAP over the circle of destroyed vehicles. "Lots of smoke and fires," Skid said. "Not much left down there."

"Only hot fingernails, hemorrhoids, and eyeballs," Gorilla told him. It was a try at black humor, anything to gloss over what they were seeing on the ground.

The first two Puma helicopters descended into the area and landed on the nearby highway. Sixteen legionnaires jumped out of each Puma and set up a defensive perimeter. A third helicopter circled the smoldering wreckage before landing. Twelve more legionnaires quickly jumped out. Then a tall figure emerged from the passenger compartment. It was de Royer. He was dressed in the same BDUs as the legionnaires, but instead of wearing a blue helmet, he wore a blue beret.

Piet van der Roos climbed out of the cockpit. "The area is not secure," van der Roos told de Royer. The general gave him a cold look and walked toward what had been a defensive laager of vehicles thrown up by the voortrekkers. "I cannot believe this," van der Roos kept repeating as he followed the general. Over a hundred Afrikaners, men, women, and children, had been butchered. A lone woman, the survivor Gorilla had seen, was on her knees beside a dead child, rocking back and forth.

De Royer poked through the wreckage, his eyes drawn into narrow slits. "It was a massacre," he told van der Roos.

The shrill incoming shriek of mortar rounds drove van der Roos to the ground. But de Royer only stood there, a tall target in the afternoon sun. Calmly, he keyed his hand-held radio and directed Skid onto the mortars. Gunfire kicked up the ground around him as he called in Gorilla.

From flat on the ground, van der Roos watched fascinated as the general orchestrated the attack and directed his legionnaires to sweep the area. Shamed, van der Roos stood up as bullets whistled around him. Slowly, the gunfire died away. A lone Warthog flew over and rocked its wings. De Royer threw the departing aircraft a sharp salute and continued to walk through the burnt-out vehicles. He nudged a doll aside with his toe.

"The attack on the voortrekkers was the bait to draw us here for an ambush," he told van der Roos. "They miscalculated." They walked back to the highway where the legionnaires had stacked captured assault rifles, two heavy machine guns, and a mortar tube. De Royer spoke into his radio. "You may join us now, Mr. Pendulo."

A fourth Puma hovered into view and landed. The side door slid back and the South African minister of defense appeared. He looked around as Elena Martine climbed down and extended a hand to help him out. They walked over to the pile of captured arms. "Is this all?" Pendulo asked.

De Royer speared him with a drop-dead look. "We are still searching," he said. Two legionnaires appeared carrying the body of a Caucasian and dumped it next to the arms. "We found him with six Africans," one legionnaire said.

"A mercenary," Pendulo announced.

De Royer examined the body. "Search him." He walked over to the weapons and knelt on one knee. "All are German or Italian," he said.

Van der Roos bent over and carefully examined them. "They are all new," he said. Then, more forcefully, "Who would do such a thing?"

"We shall find out," de Royer told him.

"We must leave, we must leave," Pendulo whined in the background. Panic was caught in his voice. "I should have never come here."

De Royer ignored him. "Show me the other bodies," he ordered.

"Where was our army?" van der Roos asked. "Why did my country let this happen?"

"Ask him," de Royer said, jerking his head in the direction of Pendulo.

Monday, April 13
UN Headquarters, Constantia,
Cape Town

The TV screen flickered with a life of its own, mesmerizing the small audience in de Royer's office. Pontowski stood beside the TV set, explaining the action. "According to Maggot, this is exactly the way Vanwyksvlei looked when he overflew it yesterday."

But this time, the scene on the TV was from the flight deck of a C-130 and not from the cockpit of a Warthog. The crew were wearing MOPP suits, which gave them an alien appearance. The photographer had plugged the video camera's audio into the intercom and the voices sounded hollow and strained. Lydia Kowalski's voice sounded the truest as she landed the Hercules.

The minicam video camera continued to record the action as the C-130 rolled out, turned onto the narrow taxiway, and stopped. Two NBC specialists got off with their detection kits and automatic sensors. They moved quickly out in front of the aircraft and ran their tests. Satisfied that it was safe, they gave the crew the all-clear by removing their headgear and masks.

"All clear," Kowalski told her crew. "But stay suited up and keep your masks handy."

The minicam took on a weird angle as the photographer stripped off his gas mask. "That's better," a voice said.

"Here's where it gets grisly," Pontowski warned the viewers. He turned up the audio so they could hear the comments coming from the other members of the team who moved with the photographer.

"My God! Look at that!" a voice said. The minicam swung onto a scene of four bodies contorted in an agony that ended in death.

"That's a mother trying to protect her baby," another

voice said. The sound of retching came from behind the photographer. More scenes played out for the audience as the photographer moved into a building. A man had held a towel over his face in an attempt to save himself.

"Here are the survivors," Pontowski said. The scene shifted to a small room where two legionnaires had packed in a dozen children, black and white, and sealed off the room. Pontowski shut the videotape off. "We counted over four hundred casualties. Thirty-one of them were white relief workers and missionaries. We lost eight UN personnel. We estimate that over one hundred mortar rounds with nerve gas hit the airfield. Fortunately, the wind was away from the town or it would have been a disaster."

Elena looked sick. "That's terrible, terrible."

Pontowski put in another tape. "Here's the convoy." Again, the screen came to life and the same photographer walked around the six trucks. But they had all been looted and only the bodies remained. "We lost eleven people here," Pontowski told them. "The cause of death is the same, but we couldn't find a single trace of a mortar round."

"So where did the nerve gas come from?" Elena asked.

The men did not answer, although they all knew the answer.

"Well?" she demanded.

"An aircraft," Pontowski said.

"Whose?" Elena demanded.

"I think we know," Pontowski said as he turned off the TV.

Tuesday, April 14
Iron Gate, near Bloemfontein

The note was lying on the floor of MacKay's quarters when he got up in the morning. Someone had passed it under the door during the night. He unfolded it. "Meet me." It was unsigned but he knew it was from Ziba.

"Damn, woman," he muttered, knowing he would do it.

He delayed until after lunch before driving to the housing area. He took a leisurely stroll and sat on the bench by the playground where he had last met her. Much to his surprise, it wasn't Ziba who brought the children to the playground, but Slavin. He sat down beside MacKay. "Ziba saw you and told me to come talk to you. She said you are a righteous man and can be trusted."

"Did she tell you anything about me?" MacKay asked.

"She said you are interested in Prime," Slavin replied.

"Are you willing to help us?" MacKay asked. Slavin nodded. "Why?"

"Last Saturday, I went to work early. My laboratory is in an old weapons storage bunker, and men were moving canisters out of the next bunker. They were dressed in protective suits with gas masks. I asked one man what they were doing. He laughed and said they were 'exterminating kaffirs and other vermin.' I recognized the markings on the canisters. It was Sarin."

"Nerve gas," MacKay said.

"I will not give my work to a man who uses nerve gas, and I tried to leave the base with my family. But the guards stopped us at the gate. We're prisoners here." Slavin looked at his two children playing on the swing set. "When do we lose our innocence?" he asked, not expecting an answer.

MacKay gave him one. "When we become responsible for others."

Kreiner was waiting for MacKay in his office, an angry look on his face. "Why were you talking to Slavin?" he demanded.

"The Jewish guy?" MacKay asked. "I want to get it off with his maid."

Kreiner shook his head. Kaffirs, he thought. Always thinking with their gonads. "You have business in Bloemfontein. We have more informants for you to contact." He spun around and left, satisfied that he had the key to MacKay and could settle the score.

Wednesday, April 15
Bloemfontein, South Africa

MacKay used the rear entrance to the hotel and took the service elevator to the roof. He walked along the southern side and turned into the heat and air-conditioning machinery room. Standard was waiting for him. "You're late," he said.

MacKay didn't reply and sat down. The man is agitated, MacKay thought. Someone is biting at his ass. Hard.

"Washington wants to know who used nerve gas on the UN," Standard told him. "I've never seen message traffic like this before. The heavies are crying for blood and want answers two days ago. I told them that the UN thinks it was the Iron Guard but they want independent confirmation."

"It was definitely the Iron Guard," MacKay replied. "It was Sarin, a nerve gas. They used mortars and Czech-built Aeros for delivery. Slavin saw them moving it Saturday morning. You know why Beckmann did it?" A head shake from Standard. "Vengeance. For killing his brother. He wanted to hurt the UN and send them a message at the same time—'Stay away from the Boerstaat and Prime.' I told you he was crazy."

"But why did he attack those voortrekkers, his own people?"

"He considers them traitors for leaving the Boerstaat. But he won't use nerve gas on whites. He was hoping to sucker the South African police into an ambush. He got the UN instead, which surprised the hell out of him."

"Beckmann stirred up a hornet's nest on this one," Standard said. He thought for a moment. "When do they expect you back?"

MacKay shrugged. "I'm free to come and go pretty much as I choose. But they'd get suspicious if I stayed away too long."

"Good. You're coming with me to Cape Town."

"Why?"

"You need to talk to the Boys."

Wednesday, April 15
Iron Gate, near Bloemfontein

Beckmann was waiting on the steps of the main entrance when the helicopter landed. The smile came easy when Liz

Gordon and her photographer climbed out of the Gazelle he used for his personal transportation. "Hans," Gordon said, "this is my photographer, Samantha Darnell." The officers surrounding them winced at her use of his first name.

"Welcome to Iron Gate, Miss Darnell," he said. He shook Sam's hand and escorted them in to lunch. "Whatever we can do, please ask."

"We do have some ideas," Gordon said. "We can talk about them over lunch."

As she had promised Sam, the lunch was simple but superb and Beckmann a charming host. "I thought your coverage of the riots in Kimberley was brilliant," he told them. "I hope you win an award . . . not the Pulitzer but . . . ah . . ."

Gordon smiled at him. "An Emmy."

"Yes, that's it. Magnificent reporting."

"I was telling Sam," Gordon said, "that the Iron Guard is not a racist organization and that you have many Africans in your ranks."

"More and more are joining us all the time," Beckmann said.

"I want to do a feature on the black angle," Gordon told him, "and focus on the Africans in the Boerstaat. They are so much better off here than anywhere else."

Beckmann leaned on his elbows and clasped his hands in front of his mouth, holding his chin with his thumbs—the pose of a thinker. "What you see here is misleading. Up north, around Johannesburg, there is chaos. We haven't made a difference there."

Sam wanted to dislike the man, but his honesty was disarming. "Do you have blacks in positions of authority?" she asked.

"Only one. He is an American we hired to manage our security systems and computers."

"But no Africans."

Beckmann gave Sam his best smile. "Before you rush to a judgment, I wish you would visit our schools."

"Can I shoot what I want?" Sam asked.

"Within reason," Beckmann told her. "After all, this is a

military base. I'll introduce you to your escort. By the way, she is Xhosa."

"I'll get my camera," Sam said.

Gordon leaned across the table while they waited for Sam to return. "Will I see you tonight?" she asked.

"Go ahead, Sam," Gordon challenged, "tell me you are not impressed." They were standing on a playground in the housing area.

"It's too good to be true," Sam replied.

"Hans made it this way. He wants to show the world his vision of the future."

A showplace, Sam thought, like a movie set. She looked around her with new eyes. The base was a complete community, with neat houses arranged in tidy rows with playgrounds, schools, and a shopping center. The military side of the base was clustered around the runway like an industrial park and it was all bounded by high ridges to the east and west, the big gate to the north with its massive stone and iron work, and the tall rock outcropping to the south. "Showplaces aren't for real," Sam said.

"Let me show you the home of a black sergeant," Gordon said. She spoke to the young woman who was escorting them and they drove to the home of Sergeant Michael Shivuto. "I had lunch here with Hans," Gordon explained. She walked up to the door and knocked. Shivuto's wife answered, but she was a changed woman. Instead of smiling and happy, she was drawn and tired, burdened with worry. "We came at a bad time," Gordon said, sensing that something was wrong. "Please forgive me."

The woman forced a smile. "You're most welcome, Miss Gordon. Please come in." She stepped aside and welcomed the three women into her home. A prominent photograph of her husband, draped in black, was hanging on the wall.

"You're in mourning," Sam said. "I'm so sorry."

"My husband was killed in a training accident," she told them. "It happened five weeks ago."

"The Boerstaat will take care of her and the family," their guide announced. "But she will have to move into town in a few weeks."

"We need to get this," Gordon said. "It's good human interest and makes my point."

Sam used the black-draped photograph as the lead-in to the sound bite with Shivuto's widow. When they were finished, Sam went outside and recorded the children at play.

It was late afternoon when they finished touring the base. Their guide dropped them off at the guest residence opposite the headquarters building and said she would pick them up at nine o'clock the next morning. Inside, a large bouquet of flowers was waiting for them with an invitation to dinner. The card was signed by Beckmann. "Liz, why don't you go," Sam said. "I'm tired and want to edit what we got today." Gordon agreed and disappeared into her bedroom to get ready.

It was past midnight and Sam was still at work. She glanced at her watch. "Looks like Liz is doing an all-nighter," she muttered. She turned off the lights and crawled into bed, determined to get a good night's sleep. But it didn't happen. She kept twisting and turning. "Okay, what's wrong?" she grumbled to herself. She switched on the light and went back to work.

Reluctantly, she admitted they had a good story. But if it's so good, she thought, what's wrong? She fast-forwarded to the sequence with Sergeant Shivuto's widow. She concentrated on the house: a TV set, refrigerator, spacious and well-furnished. By African standards, the family was rich. Sam hit the pause button and framed the photograph on the wall. Her eyes opened wide and she was fully awake. "Oh, my God," she whispered.

Sam was still awake and pacing the floor when Gordon returned to the guest residence just after sunrise. "I thought you were going to get a good night's rest," she said.

"Look at this," Sam said, sitting her down in front of the camera she was using as an editor. She hit the play button.

"Sergeant Shivuto. So?"

"Think back to the Blue Train. Do you remember the shot I got of the dead terrorist?"

"It was too grisly for the network," Gordon said. "They didn't use it."

"Think, Liz. Doesn't he look familiar?"

Gordon studied the image of the photograph. "It's not," she finally said.

"It most certainly is," Sam told her. "The tapes from the Blue Train are still at Cape Town. I'll prove it once we're back there."

"Sam, you're obsessing."

Sam shook her head. "Shivuto's widow said he was killed five weeks ago. The Blue Train, Liz. Five weeks ago. What was the Iron Guard doing five weeks ago? They weren't on a training exercise. They were rescuing us."

Elizabeth Gordon was many things, but at heart she was a reporter. "It's worth following up," she allowed. "Get packed. We're getting out of here—now."

The security technician in the building behind the guest residence noted the time and turned up the volume on the tape recorder. The bugs monitoring the bedrooms were not as well-placed as those in the living room and he didn't want to miss any conversation between the women. He picked up the phone and made a call. "They are talking about Sergeant Shivuto and the Blue Train."

As promised, their escort knocked on their door at exactly nine o'clock. She was surprised to see their bags packed and the two women ready to go. "But this was not arranged," she protested.

"Sorry," Gordon said. "Something came up. We've got to go."

"But it's not possible," the young woman told them.

"Honey," Gordon said, "anything is possible. Let's go." She helped Sam carry their equipment to the car. Like all well-equipped foreign correspondents, they had a portable satellite communications transceiver, an extra camera, blank videotapes, and spare batteries. Their escort stood at the door to the guest residence, reluctant to move.

"I know the way," Sam said. "I'll drive." She got behind the wheel and started the engine. They drove slowly down the road leading to the main gate, neither saying a word. The drive was longer than they remembered, and it seemed to take forever to cover the three miles. There were few cars on the road as they drove through the gate.

But the barrier was down. The guard, a white corporal, stepped out and asked to see their papers. "We're General Beckmann's guests," Sam protested.

The guard shook his head. "I'm sorry," he said, "but without an exit permit, I cannot allow you to leave."

"Call the general's office," Gordon ordered.

"It's not possible," the guard told them. It was the second time they had heard those words that morning. "Please return to your quarters." He waved the snout of his assault rifle toward the base. The hard look on his face warned Sam to do as he ordered. She reversed the car and drove back.

Their escort was gone when they arrived at the guest residence. Sam dropped their bags inside the door and flopped into a chair while Gordon telephoned Beckmann's office. She was put on hold. "Damn, Sam," she moaned, hanging up. "What's going on?"

Sam held a finger to her lips and shook her head. She scribbled a note and handed it to Gordon. *Bugs. They know. They won't let us go.*

Thursday, April 16
The White House, Washington, D.C.

Carroll stared at his right hand. His fingers were curled into a hook and he knew what it was—*main en griffe.* His mind scrolled like a computer and he called up the details: a fasciculation of muscles, spasticity. Call it what it is, he raged to himself. It's the claw.

Slowly, he made it pull the computer keyboard toward him. Then he pecked at a key and the computer screen in his desk came alive. He tapped in his code, one number at a time. The claw was doing his bidding. He consoled himself with the temporary victory and held up his hand to examine it.

The disease was spreading with its own terrible momentum through his body, picking up speed. How much longer do I have? My speech is starting to slur, especially when I'm tired. How soon before it picks up momentum, like my hand. *Not yet!* he shouted to himself. There are things I can do. I can still make a difference.

It's the march of the disease, he thought, picking up speed, building to a climax. Like life, he reasoned. Events often took on a momentum and a will of their own, building to a fiery climax. How many times had he seen it before? The first time had been in the Persian Gulf with Muddy Waters. It had happened again during the rescue of Mary, his wife, and the POWs out of captivity in Iran. Then Matt Pontowski had led twelve F-15 Strike Eagles into Iraq. But that was nothing compared to China, where events had run wildly out of control. Now it was happening again, only this time in South Africa. And to him.

His secretary's voice brought him back to the moment. "Time for the meeting," she said.

"Thanks, Midge." Slowly, he pulled himself to his feet and hobbled down the hall on his two canes, taking the few short steps to the small office next to the Oval Office where the president preferred to work. Wayne and Chuck were ready to catch him if he stumbled. They waited outside when he entered and would be there when he came out.

The president waved Carroll to a seat between Secretary of Defense Elkins and the DCI, the director of central intelligence. The president jammed a cigar in his mouth and chewed, not bothering to light it. "Are our scientists making any progress on cold fusion?"

"None to speak of," the DCI answered.

The president frowned. "And the Iron Guard is?"

"Apparently so," the DCI replied.

"This Hans Beckmann who leads the Iron Guard, is he considered a rational actor?"

Elkins answered the president's question. "Not after using nerve gas on the UN. We know the Iron Guard used mortars and aircraft, Czech-made Aeros. We also have a high degree of confidence they were the same aircraft that jumped the C-130 and shot down the A-10."

"How strong is the Iron Guard?" the president asked.

Carroll knew the answer. "It is a very credible militia-type organization that is still growing in strength. In total size and resources, it is four or five times larger than the UN peacekeeping force."

The president lit the cigar. "The South Africans have

their own military . . . a damn good one as I recall . . . why don't they use it to stomp the Iron Guard?"

"Internal instability," Carroll answered. "The minister of defense, Joe Pendulo, is black. The generals and the command structure are predominantly white."

"I thought they had some black generals and colonels," the president said, interrupting him.

"They do," Carroll answered. "But they're political appointees and worthless. Pendulo is afraid that if he orders the whites to fight the Iron Guard, they will mutiny. If he orders the black generals and colonels to do it, they will conspire to overthrow him and the government rather than take on the Iron Guard."

The president chomped hard on his cigar. "So we are facing a well-armed militia led by a madman who is running amok and may control the discovery of the millennium, cold fusion."

The DCI nodded. "That's a fair summation of the problem."

"Then," the president said, "we either deal with the Iron Guard now or it will deal us a worse hand later." He liked poker analogies. "We're calling them. No more raises."

"Are you considering military action?" Elkins asked.

"It's the only thing those bastards understand. The sooner the better."

"Are you overreacting?" the DCI asked.

The president's answer was a simple "No." He puffed on the cigar. "What's the best way to do it?"

Now it was Elkins's turn. "Given the current climate in Congress, we don't want to act unilaterally."

"We will act alone if we have to," the president said.

"The Honorable Ann Nevers," Elkins continued, "is waiting for the right opportunity to raise the war cry of 'neo-intervention.' If we make a mistake, we'll give her the next election."

"Not a pleasant thought," the president said.

Carroll leaned back in his chair. "There is a way to avoid direct involvement. The UN set a precedent by taking out the Azanians for what they did at Kimberley. The South Africans did not protest because it solved a problem for them. By doing the same thing to the Iron Guard, the score card is balanced—the Azanians were black, the Iron Guard is white—and another problem is solved for the South Africans."

The president thought for a few moments. "You said the Iron Guard was much bigger than the UN forces in South Africa."

"True," Carroll replied. "But they are organized like a militia and it takes time to get them all together. We beef up the peacekeepers for this one operation and use the element of surprise to get in and get out fast."

Elkins nodded. "That's a viable option. I'll draft a shopping list for Pontowski so he knows exactly what additional forces he can ask for. Now all we have to do is convince the UN secretary general and the French to do it."

"Appeal to their best and worst sides," the president said. "Moral outrage over the Iron Guard's use of nerve gas and venial economic self-interest in regard to Prime. Personally, I think cold fusion is bullshit."

"But what if Doctor Slavin has discovered cold fusion?" the DCI asked.

The president allowed a tight smile. "Then rescue Slavin."

"We've considered it," the DCI said. "But the Iron Guard's stronghold, Iron Gate, is one tough nut to crack."

"Rescues are very tricky and hard to pull off," Elkins explained. "It's easy to go in, but hard to get out alive."

The president stubbed out his half-smoked cigar. His decision was made and the discussion was over. "Make it all happen. Those bastards will not use nerve gas again. I want the world to get that message loud and clear."

"I'll get Cyrus Piccard and Mazie Hazelton on it," Carroll told him.

The president nodded his approval. "Bill, I need to speak to you in private." His voice was soft and gentle. Both Elkins and the DCI suspected the subject was Lou Gehrig's disease and they quickly left. "How much longer?" the president asked.

Carroll shook his head. "I don't know."

"Any recommendations for your replacement?"

"Cyrus Piccard."

"He's too old."

Carroll thought for a moment. "Mazie."

"With a name like that?"

"Mazie's a nickname," Carroll answered. "Her real name is Mazana."

CHAPTER
22

Friday, April 17
UN Headquarters, Constantia,
Cape Town

The letter was on Pontowski's desk when he came to work. At first, he ignored it in the rush to clear his desk. He was on the schedule to fly with Waldo and was pressed for time. Fortunately, most of the message traffic was from divisions in the Pentagon looking for ways to justify their existence, and he fed those messages directly into a shredder. Working for the UN did have its advantages. Finally, he picked up the letter. He wished he hadn't.

> Dear Colonel Pontowski,
>   I am resigning my commission in the SADF and therefore can no longer serve as your aide-de-camp.
>
> Very respectfully,
> Piet van der Roos

Well, Piet, Pontowski thought, you always were a man of few words. But why? You're one of the best helicopter pilots I've ever met and an outstanding officer. Why kick it all over now? "Oh, no," he moaned, answering his own question. Piet was going over to the Iron Guard.

Friday, April 17
Near Paarl, South Africa

The white BMW wheeled into the van der Roos winery and crunched to a halt on the gravel outside the wine-tasting cellars. It was a cold day and the cellars were closed. "Thanks, Elena," Pontowski said. "I'd have never found it on my own." He grinned at her. "Or gotten here so fast."

"You owe me, Matt Pontowski," she murmured. "I expect to collect tonight."

"I don't go this cheap," he told her. She gave him a smile and got out of the car. They walked up to the main house and Pontowski knocked on the door.

Aly van der Roos, Piet's sister, opened the door. "He's in the kitchen," she told them. She held Elena back. "Let them talk alone."

Piet was sitting at the table in the big kitchen drinking coffee with his father. Without a word, he poured Pontowski a cup and motioned him to a chair. The elder van der Roos drained his mug, stood, and left the room. "Why?" Pontowski asked.

Piet stared into his cup. "You once asked what I would do if you ordered me to fly against Afrikaners. I didn't know the answer."

"And now you know?" Pontowski asked. Piet nodded. There it was. Piet was an honorable man who had made the hardest decision of his life. He wasn't the first soldier who had had to choose sides when his country was coming apart, and he wouldn't be the last. "Thanks for being honest," Pontowski told him.

"I have watched you lead your men," Piet said. "Then I flew for you at Kimberley and on the raid against the Azanians." He stared into his coffee cup. "Then I talked to Maggot." A little smile played at his lips. "He's an ancient warrior."

"He's all of thirty-two years old."

"He will follow you into the gates of hell. Like Bouchard will follow de Royer. I didn't understand the general until I saw him at Beaufort West. Mortars, bullets, and death were all around him. He stood there, never flinching, and fought back. Do you know what I did?" He didn't wait for an answer. "I crawled in the dirt with the worms. With the worms. I was ashamed. Why do all of you do this? Why did Sergeant Owens and Perko, two women, and Tango come here to die?"

It was a fair question, but Pontowski didn't have an answer. "Hell, Piet, I don't know. Perhaps it's because you're worth it. And maybe, just maybe, I'll have to ask you to do the same for me someday."

Piet took a sip of coffee. "Why did you come here? Today, to my home."

Another fair question. But this one he could answer. "I was afraid you were going over to the Iron Guard."

"Am I?"

"No, Piet, you're not. Like most Afrikaners, you're caught up in your past and can only wait for the future to happen. Thanks for the coffee." He stood and walked to the door.

"Colonel," Piet said, "I was afraid you would ask."

"Ask what?"

"To follow you into hell."

"Against your own people?"

"I would have. But I don't know if I could have lived with myself afterward."

Pontowski smiled at his friend. "You don't have to worry about that now. Good luck, Piet." He walked from the kitchen.

Friday, April 17
Bantry Bay, Cape Town

The wind roared off the South Atlantic and rattled the big window overlooking Bantry Bay. Elena lay curled up in a blanket in front of the fire, snug against the cold outside. "I like a man who pays his debts promptly," she said.

Pontowski reached down and stroked her hair. "I didn't know it got this cold here."

"It can get much colder inland, on the Karoo." She waited for him to talk. Silence. "Are you going to talk about it?" she asked.

"Talk about what?"

"Piet."

"There's nothing to talk about. I was worried he was going over to the Iron Guard. He's not."

"And that would have been terrible."

"Yeah, it would have." He stood up. "Elena, I've got to go. I want to call my son."

"You can call him from here."

"Thanks, but I'll do it from my quarters. Besides, I've got a briefcase full of work."

Saturday, April 18
Iron Gate, near Bloemfontein

The stakeout was drifting in and out of sleep. He jerked awake and looked around, relieved that he was still alone. He checked the time: two-thirty in the morning. He fiddled with the volume control knob, turning it up to be sure no one was prowling around inside the guest residence while he scanned the video monitors. Nothing. Satisfied the two women were asleep, he took off his headset and went to make a fresh pot of coffee.

Sam was looking out the bathroom window and saw the kitchen light in the next building come on. Gotcha, she thought. While Gordon had tried to contact Beckmann and bargain for their release, Sam had scouted the opposition and discovered the stakeout team in the building behind the guest residence. They had been too obvious, standing at the window and talking. Then she had searched the residence until she had found the bugs. The miniature cameras had been easier to locate and she had almost smashed the one in the bathroom. But common sense warned her off. Better to show the bastards a little skin and know where the camera was. She became very good at making steam.

She moved away from the bathroom window, sacrificing speed for silence. She did not want to wake Gordon and explain what she was doing. Silently, she opened the French doors that faced the stakeout's building. She didn't have a choice, for only the French doors opened to the north. Then she stepped back into the room and pulled out the collapsible satellite antenna dish from behind the couch. This was the tricky part, opening the umbrellalike antenna in the dark and aiming it in the general direction of the geosynchronous relay satellite in orbit over the equator. She had to get it as close to the door as possible but still stay in the shadows.

The light in the kitchen was still on. Stay there, you bastard, she thought.

She covered the transmitter with a blanket to hide the glowing lights and muffle the sound. The tape she had made after Beckmann's thugs had confiscated all of her videocassettes was already inserted in the machine. The Iron Guard had reasoned that without cassettes, all of Sam's equipment was worthless. They were right. Fortunately, the goons had overlooked the spare cassettes in the bottom of Gordon's makeup case.

Sam hit the on and trans button. She waited for a receive signal. Come on! Nothing. Reposition the antenna. She inched her way back to the doors, moved the antenna closer, and raised the tilt. She heard a clicking sound as a relay closed. Too loud! But they had an uplink. It took her an eternity to move back to the transmitter. Carefully, she raised the blanket to see if the tape had played. Damn! she moaned to herself. The hold light was on. They were caught in a queue, waiting for a channel to open for a downlink, or the network wasn't receiving.

Back to the bathroom window to wait. Damn! The light in the kitchen across the way was out. The stakeout had to be back at his position, probably with a fresh cup of hot coffee to keep him awake and alert. Were the bugs sensitive enough to pick up the transmission sounds when they downlinked? She didn't know. She needed a cover, anything to distract the bastard. She gave a little sigh and turned on the light.

Slowly, she started to undress. Do this right, she told herself. Men are so damn stupid. Get the bastard twanging at E above high C. But she wasn't very good at it. She was down to her panties and bra when she turned on the water in the shower. Then she walked out and came back with a portable radio. Music helped. Sam promised herself she would laugh about this someday. But not now.

She posed in front of the mirror and ruffled her hair. Then she stepped into the shower. She made it last as long as she could before getting out. Drying off was a big production and at last, she discovered the art of exotic dancing—tease with everything but reveal nothing. Who exactly is exploiting who in a situation like this? she thought.

She reached over and turned out the light. Quickly, she moved to the window. The bathroom light in the stakeout's building was on. I hope you're in there beating off or having a heart attack, she raged to herself. She checked on the transmitter. The transmission had gone through! She pulled the antenna back and shut the French doors. Now it was simply a matter of erasing the tape and putting everything back in order. And she had the rest of the night to do it.

Friday, April 17
New York, New York

One of the many assistant news editors at the network was at the console when the satellite signaled a transmission was waiting for them. "Liz isn't scheduled for a broadcast," she said to the technician sitting in front of her. With the time difference, it was early the next day in South Africa. "It must be a hot one."

The technician accepted the transmission, hit the record button, and sent the signal out to various monitors in the building. "Hey, it's Sam. Why is she doing a comm check?" They watched the short transmission play out.

The assistant editor picked up the phone and called the news editor. "You had better get down here, sir. We got a satellite feed from Liz Gordon and Sam Darnell you need to see."

The news editor had also seen it on his monitor bank and made a few disparaging comments about assistant editors who didn't know news when it chased them down the street and bit them in the ass. "You are absolutely right," the assistant editor said matter-of-factly. "This isn't news. But Sam flashed every distress signal in the book at us." She slammed the phone down. "Did that bite *you* in the ass?" She gave him five minutes to get there or she was giving the tape to CNN. He made it in three.

Sunday, April 19
Ysterplaat Air Base, Cape Town

Pontowski came awake with a jerk. He was fully conscious and alert, a first for five-thirty in the morning. He didn't need a caffeine jolt and quickly showered and shaved. Why? he asked himself. What was bothering him? Was his subconscious sending him a warning? He was getting dressed when the phone rang. It was Standard. "My office. Now." The line went dead.

"Well, I'll be . . ." Pontowski muttered as he went out the door.

The elevator at the Broadway Industries Centre was slow in coming and Pontowski trotted up the stairs to the fourth floor. The same signal that had jolted him awake was still pushing him on. The moment he entered Standard's office and saw Mazie Hazelton, he knew. "Is it the Iron Guard this time?" he asked. She nodded.

"We can't do it," Pontowski said.

"The White House wants the UN to do it," Mazie replied.

"Then someone had better tell the White House the UN is going to get its ass kicked."

"The UN is one hundred percent behind this," Mazie told him, "and de Royer is probably talking to his superiors right now."

"De Royer is not going to buy it," Pontowski told her. "He knows what the Iron Guard has got. It may not be big, but it's bigger than us."

"Can you use surprise?" Standard asked.

"I can't rely on it," Pontowski answered. "There's a leak somewhere in the UN."

"We're working that problem," Standard said.

"Solve it," Pontowski growled. "It's my people who are on the line."

"What will it take to do the job?" Mazie asked.

"A complete force package," Pontowski told her. "Air defense suppression, CAP, EW, you name it."

She handed him a list. "We can give you this." It was the "shopping list" Elkins had promised the president.

Pontowski scanned the list of forces the United States was willing to make available to support the operation. He shook his head. "It's not enough."

"You take your orders from de Royer," Mazie reminded him.

Pontowski exploded, giving full vent to his anger. "Get real! We're a small peacekeeping operation. If you're serious about this, think carrier task force. Let the webfoots do it."

"We can't do that," Mazie said. "The political situation—"

"Screw the political situation," Pontowski interrupted.

"You know the resources we're willing to commit," Mazie said. "We also want you to rescue an Israeli scientist."

"A Doctor Slavin," Standard added. "The man working on cold fusion."

"Fuck me in the heart!" Pontowski shouted at them. Silence. "You don't want much," he muttered.

"Talk to de Royer," Mazie told him.

"He's not going to buy it, Mazie."

"So you've said."

Pontowski stormed out of the room, talking to himself. "Nothing is impossible for the bastard who doesn't have to do it himself."

Standard took a deep breath. "There goes one angry man."

"That's one of the reasons I'm here," Mazie said. "He'll calm down."

"The other reason you're here?"

"Getting Slavin out is of prime importance."

"Pun intended?" Standard asked.

"Do what it takes," she told him.

"The man we need to talk to is here. MacKay."

Mazie's head came up. "John Author MacKay?" A nod

answered her. "Was he Zenith?" Another nod. "Oh," she whispered.

Standard punched at his intercom and asked for MacKay to come in. She didn't recognize him when he came through the door. "The last time I saw you," he said, "you were a little butterball. What happened?"

"I got married," she told him. She reached up and touched his face. "You look better."

"I take it you know each other," Standard said.

"We were on Operation Jericho together," Mazie told him.

"I'll be damned," Standard muttered, recalling the rescue of three Americans out of Burma.

"Believe me, we all are," MacKay said.

MacKay listened as Mazie and Standard outlined his part in the operation. Since he was in the field, he was only told what he needed to know, but his mind filled in the blanks. "I've got to catch the afternoon flight to Bloemfontein," he told them. "I'd like to talk to the Boys before I go. I want to throw some grit into the system." Standard made the phone call and sent him on his way.

"What next?" he asked Mazie when they were alone.

"Any progress on the leak in the UN?"

"Leaks are like rats," Standard replied. "Find one and you know there's more in the woodwork. One big rat was Pontowski's aide, a Captain Piet van der Roos. We monitored him making phone calls asking about sorties and launch times, including the day Leonard was shot down and Perko killed. But he's out of the picture now."

"Have you found other leaks?"

Standard smiled at her.

Sunday, April 19
Iron Gate, near Bloemfontein

MacKay presented his identification card to the guard at the main gate and tried to act bored. Going through the massive stone entrance always bothered him. The young soldier took his card and ran it through the scanner. The video monitor flashed and a message scrolled up on the screen. "A message for you," the guard said. "Report immediately to the security compound."

"When was the message posted?" MacKay asked.

The guard glanced at the screen. "Twenty minutes ago."

MacKay thanked him and drove onto the base with every inner alarm in overdrive. What's going down? he thought. An NCO was waiting for him at the entrance to the compound and escorted him to Kreiner's office. "Wait here," the sergeant commanded. MacKay sat down and cooled his heels for the next half-hour.

Kreiner burst into the room, all hustle and activity. Two armed guards were right behind him. MacKay adopted his most bored look. "Kreiner, what dumb thing are you doing now?"

"The Generaal wants to see you." MacKay gave a shrug and followed him down the stairs to Interrogation. "Wait," Kreiner said, pointing to a chair. MacKay sat down and leaned back against the wall. Beckmann's hard leather heels echoed over their heads as he came down the stairs.

"There you are," Beckmann said amiably. "Why were you at Cape Town?"

"Is that what this is all about?" No answer. "I was checking out a breach in security."

"Security is always a primary concern," Beckmann said. "Kreiner."

Kreiner stepped up to the curtain that covered the one-way window into the interrogation room. He glanced at MacKay in triumph and pulled the cord. The curtains swooshed back.

Ziba was sitting on the table. She was naked.

"Your woman," Kreiner chortled. It was payback time.

MacKay joined Beckmann by the window, a firm grip on his emotions. "Getting your jollies off, Kreiner?" he asked. One wrong move and you're dead, he thought. He looked at Ziba. She was unhurt and alert. They hadn't begun the interrogation yet. "Why did you bring her in?" he asked.

"We became worried when you went to Cape Town without telling us. So we took the normal precautions," Kreiner said.

MacKay couldn't take his eyes off Ziba. The memory of the first time they had met came rushing back. Like then, she was regal. A queen. They could strip her, shackle her, imprison her, even kill her. But nothing they could do would ever degrade her. "Hostages, Kreiner?" MacKay scoffed. "You're suffering from a massive case of brain farts. I was chasing pussy, not looking for a long-term commitment."

Beckmann smiled at MacKay, his eyes bright and unblinking. "Slavin tried to escape with his family and she was with him. I want to know if she is part of the security problems you have discovered. This is your interrogation."

MacKay glanced at him and then fixed his eyes on Ziba. In that split second, he almost killed Beckmann. But the guards weren't making any mistakes, not after the Azanian incident, and the attempt would have been suicide. "After you, Generaal." He opened the door into the interrogation room.

Kreiner entered first and placed a straight-back chair directly in front of Ziba. Beckmann sat down on it backward, his arms resting on top of the back. "Proceed," he said. His eyes had stopped blinking.

Kreiner stood beside Ziba and lifted one of her breasts. "Generaal, please. This is my duty."

"Not this time, Kreiner. I want MacKay to solve this problem for us."

"Solve the problem?" MacKay asked. "No sweat, Generaal." His hands flashed and he spun Kreiner around. Kreiner tried to resist but MacKay stunned him with a rabbit punch, kicked at the back of his knees, and snatched the pistol out of his holster. Kreiner was going down as MacKay chambered a cartridge. He reached over Kreiner's head with his left hand and hooked two fingers in his eye sockets. He held Kreiner's head up, jammed the pistol's muzzle against his temple and fired.

The guards were coming through the door. MacKay let the body fall to the ground and threw the pistol to the first guard, stopping him. MacKay held up his hands. "Problem solved."

The violence had satisfied whatever need Beckmann felt, and his face was normal. "Clean up this mess," he ordered. He looked at MacKay. "We need to talk."

* * *

Four guards with drawn automatics surrounded MacKay as he sat in Beckmann's office. "Kreiner and I go back years," Beckmann said. "He was a trusted lieutenant."

MacKay threw a small booklet on the desk. "I was in Cape Town checking up on your 'trusted lieutenant.' That's his bank balance." The savings account passbook in Kreiner's name was part of the "grit" the Boys had given MacKay to throw into the system. "I found it in a safe deposit box in Cape Town. You'll notice there's a rather large recent deposit."

"This is a large amount of money," Beckmann said.

"Thrifty little bugger, wasn't he?"

"Do you think he sold out?"

MacKay paused. "Where did he get all that money? It does answer a lot of questions, Generaal."

Beckmann gave an audible sigh. "There is still the question of the girl. She did try to escape with Slavin and may have been working for Kreiner."

"Perhaps," MacKay said. "Release her but don't let her leave the base. We can watch her for a few days, use her as bait, and see if anyone tries to contact her. Or she might lead us to someone else."

"An excellent suggestion," Beckmann said. "There is still one more problem. I told you never to disobey me again. You did. You also killed one of my best men."

"I killed a traitor, Generaal. And I did not disobey you. You said to solve the problem. I did."

"Based on suspicions," Beckmann said. "Only suspicions."

"You need to see what's in my briefcase," MacKay told him. "It's in my car." A heavy silence came down as one of the guards ran to get the briefcase. The guard was back in moments, not wanting to miss anything that might happen. "Let me open it," MacKay said. "It's booby-trapped." He smiled at Beckmann. "I told Kreiner I was good at my job. He didn't know how good." He flipped the top open and stepped back. The briefcase was full of blank ID cards—thanks to the Boys. "These were in his safe deposit box."

Beckmann was shaken. "But why?"

MacKay forced a sadness he did not feel into his voice. "I don't know, sir. Money? Sex? Who knows?"

Beckmann rummaged through the cards. "These cards have caused more trouble than they are worth."

"That's because the system was rigged to be compromised," MacKay told him. "I can fix that."

"I need a replacement for Kreiner. Are you interested, Mr. Mills?"

"I was going to suggest it if you didn't," MacKay told him.

"Is Mills your real name?"

MacKay shook his head. "John Author MacKay. I deserted from the U.S. Army years ago. You can check it out." He rattled off his Social Security number. It was as deep as MacKay's cover went.

"We will, Mr. MacKay, we will."

Monday, April 20
Ysterplaat Air Base, Cape Town

"It's called mission creep," Pontowski told Bouchard, "and I can't think of a better way to get your ass in a crack. We should have never gone after the Azanians. We showed the politicians what we can do, now they want us to do more with less." Bouchard let him talk, aware that the American was blowing off steam. "I was certain de Royer would tell them to go piss up a rope."

"Piss up a rope?" Bouchard asked. The mechanics of doing that specific act eluded him.

"Get lost, no way José," Pontowski answered.

Bouchard nodded, finally understanding. Although he spoke English, American slang eluded him. "The general never rejects anything out of hand."

"So I found out," Pontowski said. He had been certain de Royer would reject the idea to attack the Iron Guard without a second thought. But the general had only said, "Study it." No direction, no comment, just, "Study it." Then de Royer had disappeared. Lacking direction, Pontowski gave Maggot the so-called shopping list and set him to work. Then early Monday morning, Standard had called from the Consulate. A package had arrived in the diplomatic pouch he needed to see. It was the latest satellite imagery of the Iron Gate, courtesy of the National Reconnaissance Office via the CIA. The resolution and quality of the photographs indicated that someone in Washington was getting very serious.

Pontowski gave the photographs to Maggot and went back to pacing the floor. Now, he and Bouchard were at the base ready to see the results of Maggot's "study." Waldo came out of the Intel vault and asked them to come in. "We had to clean the place up," he said. Inside, Kowalski and Maggot were standing beside a papier-mâché model of Iron Gate. "I studied architecture in college for two years," Waldo said. "The only thing I liked about it was the modeling."

Bouchard walked around the table, looking at the model from every angle. His one good eye darted from feature to feature, taking in every detail. *"C'est bon,"* he allowed.

"What does this prove?" Pontowski asked.

"We can do it," Maggot announced.

"I didn't want to hear that," Pontowski said.

"I will tell the general," Bouchard said. Half of his face was smiling.

Monday, April 20
The White House, Washington, D.C.

The claw held the telephone to Carroll's ear. The encryption/decryption cycle gave Mazie's voice a tinny ring and he listened without comment. It wasn't a long call, a follow-up message with details was on the wires, but she thought he should know in advance that de Royer had okayed the operation. He had named it *Dragon Rouge,* Red Dragon.

Carroll dropped the phone into its cradle when they were finished and tried to calm the emotions that tore at him. He started to shake. Slowly, he regained control. It's the price we pay, he told himself. How do the others do it? How can they play fast and loose with people's lives? It's distance, he told himself. If you can't match a face or a personality to the name, then you can do it. Then you can send people to their deaths and still live with yourself. Call off this operation, he warned himself. But he didn't have a choice. He understood the equations of power only too well: Sacrifice a few now to save thousands later. Running from the problem would only make it worse.

Two hours later, Midge came in with a message. "From Mazie," she said. It was the "shopping list" coming back to haunt him. He scanned the additional force elements Pontowski and de Royer needed to carry out the operation. The list was much shorter than he had imagined. "They'll need to know how soon we can have everything in place," he said, reaching for the phone to call Secretary of Defense Elkins.

After talking to Elkins, Carroll held up the claw and looked at it. He felt an overpowering urge to wash it. He made the claw respond to his will and hit the intercom button. "Midge, please call Cyrus Piccard. I need to see him." There were times when even the national security advisor needed his hand held. Even if it was the claw.

Tuesday, April 21
Cape Town, South Africa

Richard Davis Standard drummed his fingers on the desk. The Boys were in their usual configuration, two sitting, the tall slender one on the floor yoga-style and their boss leaning against the wall with her arms folded across her chest, challenging him to surprise her. "We've got less than ninety-six hours to plug the leak at the UN," he told them. "Otherwise, Dragon Rouge will lose the element of surprise." The women tuned him out and held a brief discussion. The one on the floor smiled sweetly at him, her way of saying they had the problem well in hand. He hated it when they did that to him.

"Second," Standard said. "Pontowski wants to set up a forward operation location within range of the helicopters and where they can launch unobserved. I want to open up Desert One."

Deception was part of Standard's personality and he misnamed everything. Desert One had little to do with the desert. It was a base with a nine-thousand-foot runway hidden in a semiarid mountain valley in Lesotho, ninety-three miles from the Iron Gate. The CIA had spent millions of dollars creating the facility in the late 1970s as part of the effort to counter a very real communist threat to destabilize South Africa.

The woman leaning against the wall was surprised. "Gengha Dung won't authorize that," she said.

"Screw Gengha," Standard muttered.

"She won't like that either," the woman replied. "Well, we were all looking for jobs when we found this one."

"Go to work," Standard told them. He motioned for their boss to wait. "I need you to go to Bloemfontein and contact MacKay."

"I'm not a courier," she told him.

"You are now."

"Make one little compromise and everyone thinks you're easy," she mumbled to herself.

Tuesday, April 21
Ysterplaat Air Base, Cape Town

Maggot was bent over a planning table, measuring distances off a chart. "Perfect, absolutely perfect," he murmured. "Thirty-five minutes flying time for the Pumas."

Kowalski and Waldo examined the chart. "It should do the trick, Boss," Kowalski told Pontowski. "If it's secure."

"The CIA says it is," Pontowski assured her. "You can check it out this afternoon when you start prepositioning men and equipment. There's a safe corridor here." He sketched a route leading from Desert One southeast to the Indian Ocean. The corridor crossed through Lesotho and the Transkei, two of the homelands, or Bantustans, created under apartheid and then ignored by the government.

Kowalski measured a route from Cape Town that looped out over the ocean, around the southern coast of South Africa, before coasting in at the safe corridor. "Nine hundred nautical miles," she announced. "Let's go do it."

"Boss," Maggot said, "I want to go along and see what we got." Pontowski told him to get going.

Waldo kept studying the chart. "What's bothering you?" Pontowski asked.

"Just an itch, sir."

"Then scratch it," Pontowski said.

"After I jettisoned architecture," Waldo said, "I majored in geography."

Pontowski couldn't believe it. "Geography?"

"My specialty was climatology," Waldo said. "Boss, we need to talk to a weatherman who knows the area."

Tuesday, April 21
Desert One, Lesotho

The woman dressed in civilian clothes had not said a word during the three-hour-twenty-minute flight and had been content to sit on the crew bunk at the rear of the flight deck and read a book. Now she was standing beside Maggot and asking for a headset.

"You won't see the runway until you are on short final," she told Kowalski.

"So how do I find it?" Kowalski asked.

The woman pointed out the visual landmarks for the landing pattern. But no runway was visible in the sparse vegetation below them. "Fly a standard downwind leg," she directed. Kowalski did as she said and called for the before-landing checklist. "Okay, turn base here." Again, Kowalski followed her instructions. The pilot looked out her left window. But where there should have been a runway was only low scrub and a barren mountain valley. "Turn final here and keep your descent going."

"What the hell do I line up on?" Kowalski growled.

"Click your transmit button seven times," the woman said. Again, Kowalski did as commanded, and a two-bar VASI came on. The VASI, or visual approach glide slope indicator, was a set of lights on each side of a runway that gave a pilot a visual glide path reference to the touchdown zone of a runway. "Click your transmit button five more times," the woman ordered. Five clicks and a bright line of lights appeared, cutting through the landscape. "Those are the runway center lights," the woman explained. "You'll see the runway when you descend through two hundred feet."

As promised, the runway materialized when the C-130

was two hundred feet above the ground. The runway was painted to blend with the surrounding terrain and vegetation. It became visible at low level when the perspective changed and a pilot could separate the form of the landscape from the color.

The C-130 touched down. "Welcome to Desert One," the woman said. "The fuel pits are over there and you can offload next to those revetments."

"Son of a bitch," Maggot mumbled. "You got a crash wagon here?" The woman shook her head and asked if it was important. "We can launch the Warthogs from here," he said. "But we want to land where we got emergency crews available—just in case we get the shit shot out of us and need help."

"Does that happen often?" she asked.

"It only has to happen once."

CHAPTER
23

Wednesday, April 22
Ysterplaat Air Base, Cape Town

It was a nonevent. Four men, two South African pilots temporarily assigned to the UN peacekeepers from the South African Defense Forces and two U.S. Air Force sergeants, climbed on board a Puma helicopter, started engines, called for clearance, and took off. Colonel Valery Bouchard was inside a hangar going through a final inspection with the Quick Reaction Force. Equipment was spread out on the floor, and NCOs were examining each weapon and radio with infinite care. In one corner, two parachute riggers were packing six FXC Guardian parachutes under the watchful eyes of five men. The parachutes were for them and Bouchard.

General Charles de Royer was sitting quietly in the UN command center at his headquarters, his kepi on the table beside him. An NCO grease-penciled the takeoff time on the status board and de Royer left without a word.

Matthew Zachary Pontowski came out of a briefing room in the COIC with Waldo. They headed for personal equipment to pick up their flying gear for a routine training mission. Lydia Kowalski watched them walk past and went back to work, scheduling Thursday's airlift missions.

Captain Dwight "Maggot" Stuart was in the Intel vault. He stared at the papier-mâché model of Iron Gate. "What have I missed?" he wondered aloud. But no one heard him.

From all outward appearances, it was business as usual. Except that the Puma helicopter would not return to Ysterplaat. When it had lifted off, the countdown for Operation Dragon Rouge had begun.

It was dark when Pontowski came out of the mess hall after eating dinner. He got into his staff car and drove slowly around the ramp. All four of the helicopters were gone now and half the revetments for the A-10s were empty. They would cycle the six missing Warthogs back in on Thursday and they would fly normal training missions. But when the sun set, only two Warthogs would be left in the revetments. The other ten would be at Desert One with the four Puma helicopters.

A dark-gray Hercules taxied in and was parked between two revetments, hiding the trapeze antenna hanging under the tail. Only a highly skilled observer with powerful binoculars would notice the many antennas and extra pylons hanging under the wings. Standard had assured Pontowski that no one was watching who would note that a Compass Call EC-130H Hercules from the 43rd Electronic Combat Squadron out of Sembach Air Base, Germany, had landed.

Thursday, April 23
Mozambique Channel,
USS Oklahoma City (SSN-723)

The control room was quiet when the skipper stepped through the hatch. "Captain's in the control room," the quartermaster of the watch announced. The skipper automatically checked their position on the automated plotting board, which wasn't really automated. They were in the Mozambique Channel splitting the island of Madagascar and Mozambique and were 150 nautical miles abeam the city of Mozambique. They had been at flank speed for sixty hours at three hundred feet, and except for a periodic slowing to turn and check their baffles, it had been a straight run down the eastern coast of Africa.

But the message that had broken them out of their patrol

off the Persian Gulf and sent them on the long dash southward had been anything but routine. "I have the conn," the skipper said. This time, the four simple words sent a little shock of adrenaline through his body, making him come alive. He turned to the diving officer. "Make your speed twenty knots."

The watch tensed. It was angles and dangles as they turned to check their baffles, the area of disturbed water in their wake that a pursuer could hide in. "Make your depth sixty feet. Speed ten knots." Again, they slowed, and when the keel was at sixty feet, the periscope was raised. Sonar had cleared the area and the skipper did not expect to see anything. The scene was projected onto a number of screens around the boat, reassuring the crew that the surface and a sky were still up there. At the same time, the antenna for the GPS receiver locked on two satellites and updated the boat's position. Another antenna was raised and a detailed coded message transmitting a wealth of targeting data in digital form was downlinked to the *Ok City*.

"Periscope down. Make your depth three hundred feet." The *Ok City* dove. Again, the skipper checked their position on the plotting board. "Make your speed thirty-five knots." A very faint hum filled the boat as the *Ok City* pushed aside tons of water and the hull set up a high-frequency vibration.

The skipper left the control room and went aft into the reactor compartment to check on steam and heat. Not that he was worried—the machinery was meant to be run until it smoked. But the nuke officers did like to see a friendly face from time to time.

Thursday, April 23
Iron Gate, near Bloemfontein

The major in charge of security came out of Beckmann's office after going through the morning ABCs. He motioned for MacKay to join him and they walked back to the security compound. "Kreiner's duties," the major explained, "were very specific. He provided a safety valve for the Generaal."

"A valve for what?" MacKay asked.

"To relieve the terrible stresses imposed on him. Kreiner recognized the symptoms and knew what to do. The symptoms are present today and you must be prepared to act." Among the staff, Hans Beckmann was a well-studied commodity.

"Act? In what way?"

The major looked at MacKay. "Interrogation. Anything you do there will relieve the pressure. It doesn't matter who or what."

The telephone call from the U.S. Embassy came in at two o'clock that afternoon; the ambassador wanted to speak to Beckmann. Since they were considered to be friends, the call was put through. The ambassador was calling about Elizabeth Gordon. Her network was putting pressure on the State Department . . . some nonsense that she was being held against her will. Could Beckmann help with the problem, considering all the favorable coverage Gordon and the network had given the Iron Guard?

Beckmann assured the ambassador he would look into it. They exchanged the customary courtesies before breaking the connection. Beckmann immediately telephoned for his chief of security. "Come to my office and bring MacKay," he said.

MacKay listened without a word as the two Afrikaners discussed the ambassador's call. "Let them go," he finally said.

"He doesn't know they made the connection to Shivuto," the chief of security said in Afrikaans.

Beckmann answered in the same language. "We found the videotape with the evidence and erased it. They have nothing else, so let them make their charges." He looked at MacKay and spoke in English. "How can I justify detaining these reporters for a week?"

MacKay thought for a moment. "Claim we found drugs in their possession and we were conducting an investigation. Produce the evidence and turn them over to the American ambassador as a goodwill gesture, provided they immediately leave the country."

"But they will still be ... ah ... very hostile and cause trouble," the chief of security said.

Beckmann smiled, satisfied he had a solution. "Not if I keep the photographer here," he said. "To insure Gordon's goodwill."

"How can we let Gordon go and not release the other one?" MacKay asked. He regretted giving them the idea. Quit winging it, he warned himself.

"We have strict laws against selling drugs," Beckmann said. "A search of her luggage will find a large amount of heroin or cocaine." His eyes did not blink. "Perhaps a kilo of heroin."

"Possession of that amount is very serious," the chief of security said.

"I am aware of our laws," Beckmann replied, his voice matter-of-fact. "It is my duty to enforce them."

"What's the delay?" Gordon said, pacing back and forth beside the waiting car. Only her bags had been brought out and loaded. Sam, her equipment, and her luggage were still inside. A major she did not recognize came out of the guest residence and strutted up to her. "You may leave, Miss Gordon, but there is a problem with Miss Darnell. Heroin has been found in her suitcase."

"Sam!" Gordon protested. "Don't be stupid. She doesn't use drugs."

Another car drove up and a tall, bearded African got out. He walked up to her and handed her the videocassettes the Iron Guard had confiscated from Sam and edited. He spoke in a low voice. "My name is MacKay, Miss Gordon. General Beckmann returns these with his compliments. I suggest you leave immediately."

"I'm not leaving without Sam," she said, taking the cassettes.

"You can do more to help her in Cape Town than here. I suggest you contact the American Consulate."

"You're an American?" Gordon asked. MacKay nodded. "What are you going to do with her?"

"For now," MacKay said, "she is under house arrest pending an investigation." He fixed her with a hard look. "Good behavior is a factor."

"What's the charge?" she demanded.

He gave a mental sigh. Gordon wasn't listening. "Possession of an illegal substance."

"What's the fine?" she spat at him. She was certain this was a setup and a big enough bribe would make it all go away. It was the first principle of doing business in Africa. "Can I pay the fine to you so we can leave?"

"They found over a kilo of heroin. There is no fine for dealing in drugs in the Boerstaat."

"Sam is not a pusher." Her eyes grew wide and she caught her breath. "What's the penalty for pushing?"

"Hanging," MacKay told her. "But I'm sure General Beckmann will take good behavior, your good behavior, into account. I have to go." I hope you're listening, he thought. He walked back to his car, climbed in, and headed for the main gate. He had to meet with the Boys and do some listening himself.

It was sunset when MacKay returned from the meeting with two of the Boys, and he was still sorting out all he had to do in the next twelve hours. The guard at the gate ran his ID card through the scanner. "A message, sir. You're wanted in the security compound." MacKay thanked him and drove under the raised barrier. What now? he thought. I've got things to do. He could feel his pulse race. Don't blow your cool, he thought. You've got plenty of time. Besides, as Kreiner's replacement I can go to Slavin's house any time I want. He breathed a little easier since everyone was where they had to be. Well, everyone except him.

A sergeant was waiting for him at the entrance to the security compound. "Generaal Beckmann is waiting for you in Interrogation," he told MacKay.

MacKay hurried down the long hall leading to the basement steps. Beckmann was at the foot of the steps, waiting with two armed guards. MacKay's reputation had spread and these guards held back, not making any mistakes.

Without a word, Beckmann led him into the examination room. MacKay froze.

"Why don't we have dinner before I interrogate her," MacKay said, trying to recover and gain time.

Much to his surprise, Beckmann smiled. "What an excellent idea. Kreiner would never have thought of that."

Thursday, April 23
Ysterplaat Air Base, Cape Town

The Intel vault was packed with bodies as Maggot went through the mission briefing. The pilots had expected Pontowski to be there but were surprised when de Royer and Bouchard entered and sat down. As the briefing unfolded, the reason for Bouchard's presence became obvious. Pontowski slumped in his chair and listened, probing for flaws in the operations. But Maggot had covered every base. It would work. Maggot ended the briefing with the traditional, "That's all I got. Any questions?"

Waldo held his hand up and asked the weatherman if he had done a detailed climatological study of the area. The weatherman gave him a drop-dead look and said that he had. But Waldo was like a bulldog and kept worrying the problem. The weatherman shook his head. "The weather is forecast to be absolutely clear. There's nothing to worry about."

Pontowski nodded to Maggot, who called the room to attention. De Royer stood and marched out.

Kowalski wandered over to the papier-mâché model with a few of the A-10 pilots. "It's a mop-up operation," she told Pontowski. "A piece of cake." The Warthog drivers agreed with her.

Waldo was in a corner flipping through a loose-leaf binder with the weatherman. "You're blowing smoke," the weatherman told him and slammed the book closed.

"Give it a rest," Maggot said to Waldo. "Time to hit the bunk. Tomorrow's a big day."

Good advice, Pontowski thought. He left the COIC and returned to his quarters for crew rest. Before he went to sleep he called his son and they talked for a few minutes.

The last of the cargo had been loaded on the C-130 and the ramp was raised when the six passengers dressed in tan uniforms got off the bus. The loadmaster gave them a passenger's briefing while Lydia Kowalski climbed into the left seat on the flight deck. No one seemed to be in a hurry, and it was just another routine cargo mission launching in the late evening. The passengers climbed on board and the number-three prop started to turn.

Bouchard led the way back to the first cargo pallet and opened a big box, pulling out equipment. The other five men joined him and did the same. They stripped off their uniforms and quickly dressed in BDUs.

Thursday, April 23
Iron Gate, near Bloemfontein

The ADSO, air defense surveillance officer, was sitting in the command bunker buried at the foot of the rock outcropping that rose five hundred feet above the valley floor at the southern end of the Iron Gate. High above him, on the roof of the Eagle's Nest, the observation bunker on top of the rock pillar, a radar antenna swept the horizon every twelve seconds. But only one return was on the radar screen in front of the ADSO. He rolled the track ball under his right hand and positioned the cursor over the return. A finger flicked and pressed a button. Digital numbers flashed on the radar screen and identified the target. It was a United Nations C-130 on a routine flight from Cape Town to Johannesburg. It was on the airway and had filed a flight plan.

He keyed his intercom and called the tactical commander, explaining the situation. "Didn't the attack on the Azanians start in a similar manner?"

"I'll notify the Generaal," the tactical commander said.

Beckmann was in a jovial mood when he entered the bunker seven minutes later with MacKay. "Well," Beckmann said, "you interrupted a most pleasant dinner." He slapped the tactical commander on the shoulder. The ADSO explained the situation and pointed out the radar return. MacKay studied the radar scope for a few moments and said nothing. "What do you make of this?" Beckmann asked.

"It's a routine cargo flight going into Johannesburg," MacKay replied.

"But there was an aircraft in the vicinity when the Azanians were attacked," the tactical officer protested.

"I was the one who questioned the Azanian and discovered what had happened," MacKay said. "That aircraft was acting suspiciously and was probably a command ship. This is a C-130 on a routine mission. It will land at Johannesburg, offload its cargo, and return in approximately two hours; same airway, headed for Cape Town." His explanation seemed to satisfy everyone. I've got to keep Beckmann busy, MacKay thought. Otherwise, he'll want to go to Interrogation. How long can I stall?

MacKay glanced at a clock on the wall and ran the timetable the Boys had given him through his own mental calculator. He played off what he knew about the Iron Guard against what was coming. The pieces all came together in a rush. "Generaal, this is an excellent opportunity to exercise the system. I recommend you order an alert, convene your battle staff, and bring the base to a full defense posture."

"How long?" Beckmann asked, thinking of the pleasures he had to postpone.

"At least until the C-130 returns." Then, sotto voce, "What's two hours? This is an opportunity for me to evaluate how your people respond and learn where your problems are. Besides, why take chances?" In a very low voice he added, "The girl isn't going anywhere. Enjoy the anticipation."

Beckmann's eyes were bright. "Order the alert," he said. MacKay had introduced him to the pleasures of forced anticipation, gratification postponed with the certain knowledge that it was waiting for him in the end. He savored the waiting. And MacKay was right: Why take chances?

Friday, April 24
Near Bloemfontein, South Africa

It was after two in the morning when the C-130 finally returned from Johannesburg, headed south for Cape Town.

"Oxygen check," Kowalski ordered, her voice muffled and flat. The crew checked in. "Depressurize." The flight engineer reached up to the overhead panel and turned a wafer switch. A swooshing sound filled the flight deck. "Lower the ramp," Kowalski said.

"It's cold back here," the loadmaster said.

"It won't last long," Kowalski said as she slowed the Hercules.

"One minute," the navigator said.

"Red light is on." This from the copilot.

"Jumpers are on the ramp," the loadmaster said. They waited.

The navigator began the countdown. "Ready, ready, ready. Green light."

Bouchard stepped off the ramp and disappeared under the empennage into the night. Five more jumpers followed him.

"Clear," the loadmaster said.

Kowalski firewalled the throttles. "Button her up and repressurize," she ordered.

The loadmaster climbed onto the flight deck, pounding his hands together. "I almost froze."

"Let's go home," Kowalski said.

Behind them, six parachutes descended toward Iron Gate, twenty miles away.

Friday, April 24
Iron Gate, near Bloemfontein

"Where is MacKay?" Beckmann asked.

His battle staff looked around the command bunker,

searching for the American. A sergeant answered. "He is roaming the base, checking on the response to the alert."

Beckmann stood up. "Cancel the alert and return to normal readiness." The sound of his hard leather heels echoed over the hushed bunker as he left.

Audible sighs of relief were heard as men slumped in their chairs, exhausted after the exercise. "Over six hours," a kommandant grumbled. The alert had lasted until the C-130 had flown past on the return flight to Cape Town, much longer than the two hours promised by MacKay.

MacKay was standing under a tree next to the playground in the housing area. His hand-held radio crackled with commands as the base stood down from the alert, the time when security would be the most lax. Lights in the houses started to come on as life returned to normal and men returned home. He keyed the radio. "Generaal, how read?" Beckmann answered that the transmission was loud and clear. "It was a shambles out here, Generaal."

A long pause. "Really? Report to me in Interrogation."

MacKay clenched the radio . . . hard. "ETA twenty minutes," he said.

He waited. Twice, his radio squawked with orders for him to meet Beckmann in Interrogation. He answered with a "Roger," and ignored requests for his location. Beckmann was getting impatient. The major in charge of security was calling for him when the first shadow dropped out of the sky onto the playground.

Bouchard pulled on the risers and flared the chute, breaking his forward momentum. He took three quick steps and the chute collapsed. "Over here," MacKay said as the second jumper touched down. Bouchard gathered his chute and waddled toward the tree, encumbered by 150 pounds of equipment.

Again, the major called for MacKay to answer his call. MacKay switched the radio off. Now all six parachutists were on the ground. MacKay led them around the edge of the playground and to the Slavins' house.

Itzig Slavin was waiting at the door of the darkened house and motioned the men inside. Without a word, his wife led them to the dining room and pointed to a very small surveillance microphone. Bouchard placed a small black box over the bug. Now the surveillance technician monitoring the house would only hear the sounds of a sleeping family until the battery went dead. A legionnaire followed Slavin around the house, placing the shielding devices over five more bugs. Then they swept the house with a wand, searching for magnetic abnormalities. They found two more bugs and neutralized them. Now they could talk.

"Where's Ziba?" Slavin asked.

"Beckmann's got her," MacKay answered, his voice low and hard. He glanced at his watch. "I got to go. Bouchard, hold the fort here. Another woman may show up, Samantha Darnell."

"I know her," Bouchard answered.

MacKay ran into the night. How much longer could he stall?

The two guards waiting with Beckmann split apart to cover each other when MacKay entered Interrogation. "Now," Beckmann said.

"Generaal, you got problems that won't wait," MacKay said. He was improvising wildly, anything to buy time.

Beckmann was silent for a full ten seconds. "Really?" he replied.

"Generaal, you pay me to tell you the truth. Sometimes the truth is only a hunch and my gut is telling me that something is going down. I can't figure out what it is, but there are people here who can. Use them. Now."

Beckmann considered what MacKay was saying. He prided himself on being a disciplined man—always doing first things first. "Who do you suggest?"

"Talk to your intel officer," MacKay said. Beckmann nodded and called his chief of Intel on the telephone and handed the receiver to MacKay. What now? he thought. A cold feeling swept over him. He had run out of time and would have to take Beckmann out. But the two guards against the wall would get him. And Ziba.

He held the phone, aware of the warmth from Beckmann's touch. It was a wild hunch, a guess born out of desperation. "What's the current status at Ysterplaat?" MacKay asked.

Beckmann stared at him. "How did you know the base was watched?"

"It's rather obvious that someone would be monitoring activity at the base," MacKay answered.

Friday, April 24
Ysterplaat Air Base, Cape Town

The crew bus stopped in front of the Hercules parked between two revetments. Fifteen men and women climbed off the bus and walked the short distance to the waiting aircraft. They lined up and dutifully presented their security badges to the guard standing at the crew entrance. Only when he was sure of each person's identity and had checked his or her name off a list did he permit them to climb on board.

Once inside, they turned right and passed through an aluminum door that sealed the cargo compartment off from the flight deck. After the door was shut and locked, the two pilots, navigator, and flight engineer climbed up the ladder onto the flight deck.

Pontowski was doing his walk-around inspection when the Compass Call EC-130H taxied past. He glanced up, noted the time, and continued the preflight. Besides two bags of gas, his Warthog was only carrying two Sidewinder missiles on station one, the extreme right outboard pylon, and an AN/ALQ-131 ECM pod on station eleven, the extreme left outboard pylon. He hoped he wasn't going to have to use either of them.

He was standing outside the revetment relieving himself on the ground when the EC-130H took off. It would have been a perfect time to take a smoke, if he smoked. Instead, he followed the EC-130H's anticollision light until it disappeared into the night.

I don't know any of them, he thought.

Waldo joined him and relieved himself on the ground. He

zipped up and checked his watch. "Time to do it, Boss."
Pontowski climbed the boarding ladder to his jet and settled
into the hard cold seat. The strapping in and before-start-
engines routine came easy this time. He checked his watch:
eleven minutes to engine start.

He waited.

Friday, April 24
The Indian Ocean,
USS Oklahoma City (SSN-723)

"I have the conn," the skipper said. He took the mental
equivalent of a gulp as the adrenaline hit him. Few men,
very few, had the raw power that he was vested with, and in
the next few minutes, all that he had trained for, spent years
of his life working to attain, would reach a climax. But it
wasn't what he had envisioned or wanted. Given a choice,
he would have taken his boat into action against a Russian
Akula-class attack submarine, pitting every ounce of his
skill and that of his men against the best any enemy had to
offer. But that wasn't going to happen.

"Make your depth sixty feet." The submarine rose out of
the depths of the Indian Ocean, a dark specter of death and
destruction. "Make your speed six knots." The *Ok City*
slowed as the last commands from the Command and
Control System were fed into the twelve Tomahawk missiles
in the Vertical Launch System, VLS, tubes in the bow. "Up
periscope." The head of the Mark 18 search periscope broke
the surface and raised twelve feet into the air. The skipper
swept the area. Nothing, surface calm. "Down periscope."

"Make the VLS ready in all respects." The low murmur
of voices reached him, confirming the system was fully
operational and ready. A tension held the control room as
the men waited.

Again, "Up periscope." A last sweep of the surface.
"Down periscope." He checked the chronometer on the
bulkhead.

"Commence firing sequence."

The *Ok City* nosed through the water, reaching the launch
coordinates that had been programmed into the Toma-

hawks moments before. The loud metallic clanging of the first VLS hatch opening, followed by the explosive charge propelling the twenty-foot missile out of the tube, echoed through the boat. More noise as water rushed into the empty tube and the hatch clanged shut. Eleven more times the sequence repeated itself as the *Ok City* salvoed its twelve Tomahawks.

Like all submarines, the *Ok City* was a quiet boat, for noise was the enemy that could lead to their detection and destruction. But the silence that held the boat for a few seconds was different—a hunter at rest, a beast of prey pausing to catch its breath. The skipper looked at his executive officer. "You have the conn."

Suddenly, he was tired, and an empty feeling drained him of strength. He stood there, numb, and wondered how many people he was going to kill in two hours.

Friday, April 24
Lesotho, South Africa

To the east of Bloemfontein, the terrain starts to rise, and with the change in elevation, the semiarid climate gives way to a temperate plateau regime. When the conditions are right, normally in the fall and spring, a gentle western breeze will push an air mass into the hills of Lesotho. If the air is humid enough and its temperature right, the change in elevation will cool the air mass until its dew point matches the ground temperature. And if the breeze is gentle enough, not more than five miles per hour, an upslope fog will form in the valleys.

But if the wind increases to no more than eight miles an hour, it will push the fog out of the valleys and over the hills, forming a band of fog along the entire western slope.

On April 24, at 4:05 in the morning, the conditions were perfect and fog spilled out of the valleys and formed a wall a hundred miles long, thirty miles wide, and eight hundred feet high, blanketing all below it in near-zero visibility. But this fog was different. The temperature hovered at exactly zero degrees Celsius, thirty-two degrees Fahrenheit, and freezing crystals of ice formed, hanging in the air.

Six hundred miles to the southwest, an A-10 rolled down the runway at Ysterplaat Air Base. The second one followed it twenty seconds later.

Friday, April 24
Desert One, Lesotho

Maggot was standing on the ramp smoking a cigar when the four Puma helicopters lifted into the early morning dark. Damn, it's cold, he thought, stubbing out the half-smoked cigar. The weatherman hadn't said a thing about low temperatures. He walked the short distance to his waiting Hog and patted the three Mark-82 AIRs hanging on station three before he climbed the ladder.

From his vantage point, he looked down the line of ten A-10s. Each one was loaded with Mark-82 five-hundred-pound bombs and CBUs. Their job was to go in after the Tomahawks and mop up. At the same time, they had to seal off the housing area while three Pumas landed part of the QRF outside the main gate. The QRF's job was to lob a few mortar shells into the main gate, blow up any traffic on the road, and act as a decoy before withdrawing. While they created confusion, Bouchard had to secure a landing zone, call in the fourth Puma, and get Slavin and his family on board.

Pontowski was escorting the Compass Call EC-130 and acting as airborne mission commander, controlling the attack. He and Waldo would have to handle any Aeros that might find the EC-130. But if the Tomahawks performed as advertised, the Aeros wouldn't be a problem.

Surprise is a wonderful thing, Maggot thought as he climbed into the cockpit.

Twelve minutes after taking off, the lead Puma hit the fog bank. The pilot immediately transitioned to instrument flying while his copilot navigated using the new GPS the Americans had installed. Ice started to form on the windscreen and the pilot nudged the collective and climbed a hundred feet. But his radar warning gear, another gift from the Americans, warned him that he was in the beam of a search radar. He descended back to low level. "This is very bad," he warned his copilot. He was sweating in the cold.

Friday, April 24
Iron Gate, near Bloemfontein

"The status report from Cape Town is eight hours overdue," MacKay told Beckmann.

"That is not unusual," Beckmann said. "It means there is no change from the last report."

MacKay spoke into the telephone. "What was the last reported status for Ysterplaat?" Again, he listened to the reply. "Generaal, all the helicopters were gone, at least half of the A-10 revetments were empty, and a fifth C-130 was reported at the base."

"I am aware of that," Beckmann said. "Our information indicates the Americans are conducting some type of training exercise. Their commander is a fanatic on training."

MacKay paced the floor, trying not to think about Ziba still sitting on the table in Interrogation. He checked his watch and the timetable he carried in his head. Almost, he thought. Just a little longer. "Sir, do you have any other sources you can check?"

Beckmann paused. MacKay is not stupid, he reasoned, and he thinks like an American. "I will make a phone call. Wait here." He spoke to the two guards and left.

Be cool, MacKay thought, keep stalling. He checked his watch and sat down beside the two Afrikaners. "You dudes play poker?" The two men shook their heads in unison. They were tired of guarding the woman but weren't going to let up. MacKay dealt himself a hand of solitaire.

He was dealing a second game when the phone call came ordering him to the command bunker. He dropped his cards and ran up the stairs. Outside, he could hear the sound of jet engines starting.

He found Beckmann in the command bunker talking to his chief of Intelligence and air operations officer. "You were right," Beckmann told MacKay. "There are strange things going on at the air base. A C-130 and two A-10s took off an hour ago."

"Not enough to worry about," the Intel officer said.

"But where are the other aircraft?" the operations officer asked.

"Americans like to target high-value resources," Beckmann said. "That's why I'm scrambling my Aeros, so they won't be caught on the ground."

"And they can shoot down any intruders," the air operations officer added.

A sour taste flooded MacKay's mouth. He hadn't considered Beckmann scrambling the Aeros. The carefully constructed timetable the Boys had given him was coming apart because he was improvising. He had to get to Slavin's house and get a message out.

"Generaal!" a voice shouted from behind them, "the tactical commander reports many radar targets!" Beckmann ran over to the radar monitor. MacKay headed for the entrance, hoping he could leave unobserved. A loud clang echoed down the corridors as the heavy blast doors at the entrance were closed and sealed. He was locked inside.

Friday, April 24
Cape Town, South Africa

Richard Davis Standard was shaving when he heard the knock at the front door. Being a cautious man, he picked up the Glock nine-millimeter automatic he carried around the house and checked the surveillance monitor. He relaxed. It was two of the Boys, the ones he had on stakeout, monitoring a wiretap. He opened the door and the two rushed in.

"Listen to this," one said. She hit the play button on the cassette recorder she was carrying.

Standard listened, wiping off the last of the shaving cream. "I'll be damned," he said.

CHAPTER
24

Friday, April 24
Near Bloemfontein, South Africa

The first Tomahawk flew down a fogbound valley, oblivious to the near-zero visibility, and headed straight for a ridge. Since the *Ok City* did not have the database onboard to program the missile's guidance computer for contour matching, its Terrain Contour Matching system was in standby. But the GPS was working as designed and it updated the midcourse guidance unit. The missile altered course slightly to the right and climbed, skimming the top of the ridge. A computer signal armed the thousand-pound warhead when the Tomahawk came out of the valley and dropped to two hundred feet above the ground.

The Digital Scene Matching camera in the nose cone came on and matched the image it recorded with the target scene stored in its guidance computer. The Tomahawk turned sharply, overflew the main gate leading into the base, flew between the two long ridges that flanked the base to the east and west, and headed straight for the Eagle's Nest. Four batteries of twenty-millimeter Twin Guns situated on the ridge tops were quiet. But the fifth and sixth batteries were still manned, held on status by their very irate commander for responding too slowly to the alert. Both batteries opened fire on the Tomahawk. Possessing infinite courage, the Tomahawk flew through the barrage and lined up on the Eagle's Nest. The scenes matched perfectly.

The radar antenna on top was facing the Tomahawk full on when the missile exploded, decapitating the Eagle's Nest and blinding the Iron Guard's radar warning system.

The pilot in the lead Puma helicopter was on the edge of panic. He had never flown so low to the ground on instruments for so long. He glanced out the ice-encrusted windscreen. He was caught in an ice cloud and could feel the weight of the ice buildup through his controls. Sweat poured down his face. "It's too much!"

"Climb!" his copilot shouted. Slowly, the ice-laden helicopter climbed. This time their radar warning gear was silent. Both men breathed easier when they popped out of the fog bank. Two more Pumas followed them. Then the fourth appeared, barely skimming the top of the ice cloud. The ice on the windscreen peeled away and the tension that had bound the pilot since takeoff eased. Ahead, he saw the edge of the fog bank. It was bright and clear beyond.

"Dive!" the copilot shouted. Coming at them head-on was a Czech Aero. The four Pumas dropped into the protective cover of the fog.

It was too much for the pilot and he broke radio silence. "Abort, abort, abort," he radioed.

The blast from the first Tomahawk shattered the bedroom windows of the guest residence. Only the drapes Sam had pulled saved her from glass splinters that shredded the heavy cloth. She rolled out of bed and lay on the floor, panting hard, and pulled on her shoes, thankful she was fully dressed. She grabbed her camera, slapped in a fresh battery, and stuffed an extra battery and two cassettes into her fanny pack. She was buckling the fanny pack on when the room shook with a second explosion.

Sam ran out the door in time to see a Tomahawk fly by, headed for the runway. She shouldered her camera and hit the record button. The Tomahawk flew down the runway as shaped-charge cratering munitions fired out its belly. Then it crash-dived into a maintenance hangar and exploded. Sam ran, the camera still on her shoulder. Twice, she stopped to shoot the action as trucks sped past. Her shotgun microphone above the lens caught the sound, adding to the realism of the scene.

She panned the western ridge line with the sun at her back as a Tomahawk flew along the ridge, using the same cratering munitions to sweep the ridge clear of AAA and SAM sites. For a moment, she panicked, not knowing which way to run. Another Tomahawk smashed into the eastern hillside. They're targeting the munitions storage bunkers, she told herself. The headquarters building behind her disappeared in a fiery blast. She added Beckmann to her target list.

Then it came to her. It was a well-executed surgical strike, and the housing area was totally untouched. A truck was cutting across the open grass areas and headed her way. She dove into a clump of bushes.

Maggot was skimming along the top of the fog bank when he heard Puma lead call "Abort, abort, abort." At the same time, he saw the first Aero.

"Bandits, bandits," Gorilla shouted over the radios. He had seen them first.

Maggot didn't hesitate. The Warthogs had to shed their ordnance or they would be sitting ducks for the Aeros. "Jettison, jettison," he radioed. The ordnance from the ten Warthogs rippled off and disappeared into the fog. Maggot called up the air-to-air gunsight and turned into the first Aero he saw. He wanted to take the fight down to the deck, but the fog had taken that option away. Much to his surprise, the Aero overshot, as if it had never seen him. The compass-gray paint of Maggot's Warthog had blended in with the fog.

But Gorilla wasn't so fortunate. The lead Aero was on him. "Gorilla!" Maggot shouted over the radio. "Break left!"

The Compass Call EC-130H cut a lazy orbit twenty miles west of the Iron Gate. Pontowski and Waldo were stacked above it in a CAP and followed it around the sky. Normally, F-15s or F-16s escorted a Compass Call because there was too much talent and high-priced top-secret technology onboard the EC-130H to put it at risk. Since no F-15s or F-16s were available, the Warthogs were given the job instead.

Pontowski's headset exploded with shouts as Maggot's Warthogs engaged. Instinctively, he sorted the threat. Maggot and his Warthogs were fifteen miles east of the base, thirty-five miles from his position, and had been jumped by a dozen or more Aeros. Damn! he thought, how did the Aeros get airborne?

"Do we go help 'em?" Waldo asked over the radio.

Pontowski made a hard decision. "We stay with Sparky," he replied. Sparky was the call sign of the EC-130H they were escorting.

An unfamiliar voice came over the radio. "We appreciate that." Among other things, Sparky monitored communications, friend and foe, and could play havoc with radio transmissions.

"Can you help them out?" Pontowski asked.

"We are," the voice answered. "They ain't talking to each other." The "they" were the Aeros, and Sparky was jamming their radio frequencies with an ear-splitting, deafening noise.

The Aeros were sequencing onto the A-10s in pairs when they were hit with the high-pitched, shrill shriek of comm jamming. It was a painful, major distraction that could not be ignored. The two pilots in the lead barely had time to turn their radios off before they merged with the Warthogs. The pilots behind them automatically cycled to a backup frequency only to be met by the same screech. Then they turned off their radios.

Sparky had taken away the Aeros' communications and made it an even fight.

Maggot had reacted instinctively when he saw the Aero going for Gorilla, and his "break left" call was in the time-honored tradition that when in doubt, you put your nose on the bandit. Gorilla had not seen the Aero and had reacted instinctively.

Now both A-10s had their noses on the Aero, their throttles firewalled. Gorilla was head-on to the Aero and Maggot was at the Aero's low four-o'clock position. But

Gorilla had bled off his airspeed in the hard turn and put his nose over to regain his cornering speed. All fighters have a speed range in which they maneuver best in a knife fight. The Warthog's happens to be very narrow.

An aerial engagement is fought largely on instincts, because the pilot does not have time to rationally consider his next move. The pilot must have the ability to sort the mass of information flooding into the cockpit, instantly focus on what is critical, and then react instinctively. Those instincts are the product of hours of flight training and years of experience. A green or low-time pilot dies because of poor instincts or instincts that have not been developed. Contrary to popular imagination, time does not stand still nor is it compressed in an engagement. A pilot must be aware of the time factor as well as his position in space, for disorientation can kill as quickly as inexperience. All together, it is called situational awareness.

This fight lasted another forty-five seconds.

Gorilla squeezed off a short burst of cannon fire to distract his adversary. Then he bunted his nose over and disappeared into the fog deck below him. Immediately, he was on instruments and pulling, breaking out of the fog. The ground was somewhere down there and his radar altimeter was useless in the rapidly changing mountainous terrain.

Maggot was at the Aero's four-o'clock position when Gorilla took his shot. Maggot automatically turned right, anticipating the Aero's reaction. The Aero also turned to the right, coming into Maggot's gunsight. If either A-10 had been carrying a Sidewinder, the Aero would have been dog meat. But the A-10s escorting the Compass Call EC-130H had the only Sidewinders. The Aero pilot solved Maggot's problem and kept his turn coming, right into Maggot's gunsight.

Before he could gun the Aero out of the sky, Gorilla bounced out of the fog and into the Aero. It looked like a minor midair, the wings of the two aircraft barely brushing. But the forces were horrendous and both aircraft went out of control. Maggot honked back on his stick and ballooned over the two fighters. He rolled violently to the left and pulled his nose to the ground as another Aero shot past, canopy to canopy, its gun firing. Maggot had not seen it until the very last moment. The Aero pilot nosed over and ran for safety, disengaging as another pair of Aeros sequenced in for a hit and run.

Maggot caught sight of a parachute disappearing into the fog bank. Whose?

More shouted commands as the two Aeros blew on through, never slowing down. "Circle the Hogs!" Maggot shouted. He fell in behind two other A-10s as they came around to take on another element of Aeros coming into the fight. An A-10 fell in behind Maggot. Jumping into a chain of Warthogs was not a recommended tactic for increasing one's longevity, because at least one Hog would always be in a position to bring its cannon to bear.

But this time, one of the Aeros had the time, position, and range to launch a Kukri, the South African version of the Sidewinder. The lead Warthog flared. The fight turned into a true furball as two more Aeros swooped into the fight. Of these four, only one made any attempt to turn with the Hogs. For the others, it was one pass, haul ass. Maggot was almost in position to fire on the turning Aero when another Warthog cut in front of him and gunned the Aero out of the sky. The radio traffic was deafening.

"Chief, come back right!" Chief Twombly was in trouble.

"Say position!" Someone was confused and lost.

"Goat! Bandit seven o'clock!" A good call that saved Goat Gross.

"Where they go?" The fight was over and the Aeros were gone. The radios were eerily silent.

Maggot forced his breathing to slow, another instinctive reaction learned from experience. Hyperventilation in combat was a real danger. "Join up," he ordered. "Ops check." Now fuel was a concern. Maggot remembered checking his once during the engagement but he couldn't be sure if the others had.

One by one, the Warthogs checked in with their call sign and fuel remaining. Goat Gross was last. He had taken battle damage and was flying on one engine.

Because they had launched from Desert One, they were good on fuel. But there were other problems—three A-10s had not checked in. "Chief," Maggot called, "say state." No answer. "Bull, how copy?" Silence. "Gorilla, you copy?" The radios were silent.

Pontowski's voice came over the UHF. "Recover at homeplate," he ordered.

The attack on the Iron Gate had been a bloody fiasco.

Friday, April 24
Near Paarl, South Africa

Piet van der Roos was working with his father in a vineyard when he heard the sound of approaching jets. Like all aviators, he looked up. A flight of four Warthogs in route formation passed overhead. His eyes followed them. "They are returning from an early-morning training mission," he told his father. "Pontowski is a devil when it comes to training."

Then he heard more. He followed the sound until he saw a formation of three A-10s flying line abreast. He glanced at his watch: ten minutes to eight in the morning. It was too early and too many aircraft for a training mission. His eyes squinted, trying to see if they were carrying ordnance. But they were too high to tell without binoculars.

He counted the minutes, waiting. Two more Warthogs came into view, flying much slower. One was trailing smoke, and even from his distance, van der Roos could see the left vertical stabilizer was missing. "They've been in combat," he said in a low voice.

"Who with?" his father asked.

"There's only the Iron Guard." Piet van der Roos looked up again. "They lost either one or three aircraft."

"How can you tell?"

"The Americans fight in twos or fours," he told his father.

"Is three bad?" the elder van der Roos asked.

"One is bad enough. But three out of twelve is a twenty-five percent loss rate."

"You like the Americans," his father said. It wasn't a question, only a simple statement of fact. "Were your Pumas part of it?"

"Probably," Piet answered. "They're good lads and would want part of the action."

"Why do they do this?" the old man asked.

"I don't know, Papa."

The old man looked at his only son. He was glad Piet was back at home and out of harm's way. But he also knew his son. "Do what you have to do," he grumbled.

Piet walked out of the field, past the small group of workers trimming the vines back, and climbed into the waiting Range Rover.

Friday, April 24
Iron Gate, near Bloemfontein

Sam was shaking, partly from the cold but also from the aftershock of the attack. She had counted twelve explosions before the shelling stopped, but smoke still billowed into the sky, surrounding her with dark pillars. She poked the lens of her camera out of the bushes where she was hiding and panned the eastern ridge line, which was capped by a line of fires. She saw people running toward the main base and pulled back into the foliage. How long before they would start searching for her?

Sam turned the camera in her lap and ejected the cassette. It was almost played out. She unzipped her fanny bag and fished out a fresh cassette. God, I'm thirsty, she thought. Behind her, the wail of sirens echoed down the valley.

Move now, she told herself, while there is still confusion, before they start to search. She grabbed her camera and ran for the housing area, pointing and shooting as she ran. She skidded under the low branches of a tree next to a playground. Again, she focused on a house, documenting damage from the attack. Her camera only recorded broken windows. But she knew what flying glass could do. She panned to the next house and froze.

A man was walking directly toward her.

Itzig Slavin stopped short of the tree Sam was hiding under. He motioned for her to follow him and they walked quickly back to his house. He held a finger to his lips, signaling her to be silent. She followed him into the kitchen and collapsed into a chair. His wife handed her a glass of water and went back to cooking breakfast. "We can talk here," he told her, pointing to one of the bugs that had been masked. "But no loud noises and stay away from the windows."

"Thank you," she said, handing the glass back. "More, please." He refilled it and handed it back. "How did you know I was out there?"

"MacKay told us and we were watching for you. Where is he?"

Sam shook her head. "Who's MacKay?"

"The black American who works for Beckmann. Are you alone?"

Sam nodded. "I was trying to escape." Slavin set a large breakfast in front of her and Sam ate, surprised she was so hungry. When she was finished, she was shown to the bathroom and then taken into the dining room. Six legionnaires were lying on the floor. Three of them were asleep.

Bouchard raised his gloved left hand in recognition. "Miss Darnell," he said, "please join us."

Beckmann was standing at a center console in the command bunker asking questions and issuing orders. Not once did he hesitate as he drove his staff, recovering from the attack. He knew exactly what he wanted and how to make it happen. MacKay's view of the man had been conditioned by a narrow association, mostly through Kreiner, and this was an entirely new side. The bastard is good, MacKay thought. One part of him may be crazy, but not this part. And he has his priorities absolutely right.

A critical key to any military unit is how fast it can reconstitute after an attack and get ready to fight again. The first clue came when the Aeros landed. The runway had been cratered and made unusable by a Tomahawk's runway denial munitions. Yet it took Beckmann's engineers only eighteen minutes to fill in enough holes for the Aeros to land. The Tomahawk had been wasted on the wrong target. The Tomahawk that had swept the ridge line with the same munitions had been more effective.

MacKay made a mental note to pass that information on to the weaponeers and mission planners. If he ever got out of there.

The more MacKay watched Beckmann, the more he understood. The man was a genius who hovered on the edge of sanity. MacKay listened as the major in charge of security, MacKay's immediate superior, blustered his way into trouble. The American photographer was missing and the major kept repeating, "She cannot escape."

Beckmann stared at the major and said nothing. Then, "Really?" It was the same word, spoken in the same way, that MacKay had heard twice earlier. MacKay had no illusions about his own capabilities, and at that moment, he knew he was no match for Beckmann. And he had told Beckmann that the response to the alert had been a shambles. Beckmann knew it was a lie. Or did he? The cold fear of uncertainty captured him.

Two facts emerged in the aftermath of the attack. First, the Iron Guard was a very small organization, much smaller than MacKay had been led to believe. For most of its manpower, it relied on a reserve-type militia made up of "commando" units. Second, and equally important, all command flowed from Beckmann. There was no downward shift of authority. None. It was a product of his paranoia.

At one point, Beckmann turned his attention to MacKay and ran a mental scorecard. Why had the American lied about the response to the alert? Yet MacKay had been the one to push him into action that had ultimately saved his Aeros and spoiled the attack. His feverish mind arranged the pieces in a pattern that made sense to him. He understood the black American. "Return to Interrogation," he told MacKay. He watched MacKay go and turned to more pressing matters. First things first.

"When will the telephones be on line?" Beckmann demanded.

"Twenty-four to thirty-six hours," came the answer. Beckmann's silence demanded an explanation. "There was extensive damage to the headquarters building where the main relays were housed. We still have the base radio system."

"Estimated time in commission for the radar?" Beckmann asked.

The tactical commander made a radio call and asked the same question. "In approximately nine to ten hours," he told Beckmann. "By eighteen hundred hours at the latest."

Sparky, the EC-130H, had monitored the radio call.

Friday, April 24
Ysterplaat Air Base, Cape Town

The base was organized chaos as the A-10s taxied in. The aircraft were marshaled into the revetments and maintenance crews swarmed over them, checking them for battle damage, refueling, and uploading ordnance. At the same time, Intelligence debriefed the pilots for the first reports that had to go out while Lydia Kowalski and Lori Williams, Pontowski's executive officer, demanded his attention.

"How'd it go?" Kowalski asked.

"It was a shambles, a fuckin' massacre," he told her. "The Aeros were up and we lost three Hogs." The look on his face matched the bitterness in his voice. "And another one ain't gonna be flyin' for a long time."

"De Royer is in the command post," Kowalski said.

"Why am I not surprised?" Pontowski growled.

Now it was Lori's turn. "Colonel, the guard at the main gate called. Elizabeth Gordon is there and is demanding to see you."

"Tell the guard to arrest her if she even looks this way." He handed his flying gear to Lori and asked her to take it to personal equipment. "I've signed for the survival vest," he told her. "Make sure the Beretta gets turned in." He barged through the door into the command post. "Are you in contact with Sparky?" he asked the on-duty controller. The captain nodded. "Are they in radio contact with any of the pilots?"

"Yes, sir," the captain answered. "Gorilla, ah . . . Captain Moreno, is talking on his survival radio. A Puma is going in after him."

The load that had been bearing down eased a notch.

"Anything on Bull or Chief?" A shake of the head. "Who called the Puma in?" Pontowski asked.

"General de Royer," the captain replied.

De Royer was sitting in front of a bank of telephones and radios, his back ramrod straight. Four of his staff from the UN command center were with him. "Thank you, sir," Pontowski said. What do we do now, he thought.

De Royer answered his unspoken question. "We have a small element of surprise on our side and we must attack again, before the Iron Guard recovers. I need to speak to your planning staff, the Compass Call aircraft"—de Royer fixed Pontowski with the old dead-fish look—"and your CIA chief of station."

Pontowski turned to the controller. "Recall Sparky and get Maggot and Kowalski in here." He glanced back at de Royer. The general was pacing the floor, ticking off commands to his own staff. Pontowski shook his head as he remembered the dossier Mazie had shown him on de Royer: "an extremely aggressive battlefield commander prone to take high risks."

Pontowski retreated to the privacy of Kowalski's office. He used her secure phone to call Standard at the Consulate and explain the situation. "You got to be crazy!" Standard shouted. Silence. "I'll be right there," he said, breaking the connection.

Pontowski leaned back in the chair and used the time to gather his thoughts. De Royer was right, they had to react quickly. Lori Williams knocked at the door. "Sir, you have visitors, Madame Martine, Captain van der Roos, and—"

"Piet!" Pontowski interrupted. "Show them in." Lori held the door open and it all went sour. Elizabeth Gordon was with them. "What the hell," he growled at Lori.

"You never gave me a chance to finish," Lori said with indignation, closing the door as she left. From the look on Pontowski's face, she was glad she had turned the Beretta in with his survival vest.

Elena touched his arm. "Matt, she stopped me at the main gate . . ."

Pontowski turned on her, ignoring Gordon and van der Roos. "Get her out of here."

Elena wouldn't let it go. "You need to listen."

But he refused even to acknowledge Gordon's presence. "She's the enemy. Get her out of here."

"I can help," Gordon said.

"Sure you can."

Tears streaked her face and she fumbled in her bag. "Damn," she muttered. In her frustration, she dumped her bag on the desk. Five videocassettes tumbled out. "These are from Iron Gate . . . maybe they can help . . . I've seen things."

"I doubt that you saw or filmed anything important," he told her. "They would have confiscated your tapes." He opened the door. "We've got all the imagery we need."

"They've got Sam!" she cried.

It was enough to stop him. "And you want me to help?" She nodded an answer. He unloaded on Gordon, letting go of all the anger and frustration bottled up inside. "Hey, don't you remember? I'm an 'irresponsible cowboy.' We throw bombs around like 'moral Neanderthals.' We're 'bumbling incompetents.' Those are your words lady, not mine. So why do you need us now?"

Gordon pushed the videocassettes toward him. "Please," she begged. "Please help. They've threatened to hang her."

Van der Roos interrupted. "Beckmann will do it. He's crazy."

Pontowski hesitated. An image of Samantha Darnell standing at the Afrikaanse Taal with him and van der Roos flashed in his mind's eye. The wind was whipping at her hair . . . then her voice when she left his room that morning . . .""You and me, Matt." He looked at the cassettes and shook his head. They were a pitiful peace offering, the only thing Gordon had to offer.

His anger was spent and he relented. "I'll do what I can. You might be able to help." He picked up the cassettes, walked to the door, and called for Lori. "Please take Madame Martine and Miss Gordon to Intel for a debrief." He handed Lori the cassettes.

Pontowski turned to van der Roos. "It's good to see you," he said. "What brings you back?"

"I saw the Hogs recover . . . I want to help."

"We need every bit of help we can get," Pontowski told him. They shook hands.

Outside, Gordon tried to repair the damage to her face. "Thank you," she said to Elena.

"I knew he would help. Did you see the look on his face when you said they might hang Sam?"

Lieutenant Colonel Lee Bradford didn't know what to do. As the mission crew commander on board the Compass Call EC-130H, he had to maintain security at all costs and keep his mission and equipment safe from compromise. Access to their mission statement alone required a confidential clearance, and everything they did was classified *Secret Noforn*. The *Noforn* meant no foreign dissemination, and de Royer certainly fell in that category. Now that same foreigner was asking him for very specific information.

"Just answer the questions," Pontowski said. "You don't ave to say how you got the information."

"I can't do that," Bradford replied. "It's the no foreign dissemination requirement."

Pontowski pressed the issue. "Then tell me the answers, not the general. I'll take the heat for any breach of security."

"I'm sorry, sir," Bradford said. "I can't do that either."

Pontowski was running out of time and seriously considered beating the man senseless. "Look, I lost two pilots on that raid and we're going back—with or without your help." He turned and started to storm out of the command post.

Bradford took a deep breath. "Colonel Pontowski," he said, stopping him, "what do you need to know?"

The command post was packed when Richard Davis Standard arrived. Pontowski turned the meeting over to him and he quickly summarized what the CIA knew about Beckmann and the Iron Guard. Gengha Dung is going to have my balls for breakfast when she hears about this, he kept telling himself. What the hell? he rationalized. I'm not revealing my sources, only information. And they've got to rescue the Israeli scientist if we're going to get at Prime. I've got to help them bring it off.

Now de Royer stood and paced the floor, revealing his intentions in a flat monotone. The men and women in the command post listened in shocked silence. The speed of the operation was dazzling, and there was no doubt they were in the presence of a tactical genius. They were in for the ride of their lives. Even Maggot was impressed. "As you can see," de Royer said, "the success of the entire operation depends on the opening phase. We will only have a very narrow window to determine whether to continue or abort the mission. The timing of that decision is critical and cannot be made here. It must be made on the spot. Colonel Pontowski, you will be on scene as the airborne commander. You will evaluate and make the decision to continue or abort."

"What if something happens to me and I can't make the decision?" Pontowski asked.

"Then it will fall to your deputy, Captain Stuart," de Royer answered. "If he is not in a position to make it . . ." he paused, considering the implications, "then the opening phase will have failed and I will abort the mission from here. Once you have made the decision, proceed to Desert One and assume operational control. If you lose contact with me at any time when you are at Desert One, you will assume overall command of the mission." He paused and looked around the room. "Are there problems?"

Maggot scratched his chin and looked at the clock. "Today is too soon. We need more time to get our act together."

"How long will the Iron Guard have been in a state of readiness by six o'clock this evening?" de Royer asked.

"Twenty-two hours," Bradford answered.

"They are at a physical and psychological low point," de Royer said. "We must exploit it and keep them that way."

Maggot shook his head. "We can do it from our end. But the helicopter jocks are at Desert One. We haven't heard from them."

Piet van der Roos stood up. "They are good boys," he said. "I know them. They will jump at another chance."

"Do you have enough time to get them ready?" Pontowski asked.

"If I lead them, yes."

De Royer swept the command post with a slow, impassive

411

stare. "H-hour is seventeen-thirty this evening." H-hour, the time an operation started. The meeting was over and the command post emptied.

Pontowski checked his watch: a little over six hours to go. He called Kowalski and van der Roos over to him. "Fly Piet to Desert One as soon as you're loaded." He looked at them. "Lydia, we're leaning pretty far forward on this one. If you have any doubts, I can still shut it off."

"I got lots of doubts, Boss," she said. "But this is what we get paid for. You get paid to do the worrying. Come on, Piet. Time to earn your combat pay."

"Combat pay?" van der Roos asked. "What's that?"

Pontowski watched them leave. He stood there, thinking. There was one more hole to plug. He cornered Standard and they spoke quietly.

Elena Martine came out of the COIC and unlocked the door to her BMW. She slipped in behind the wheel and fumbled with her keys. She looked up in surprise when Richard Standard opened the passenger door and got in. "We need to talk," he said.

"What about?" she asked.

"Phone calls."

"I make many phone calls."

"Did you ever talk to Piet van der Roos?" he asked.

"My office did," she told him. "Every day when there was flying at the air base. We coordinated the flying schedule."

"Why?"

"It is part of our agreement with the government," she answered.

That explains all the phone calls van der Roos made to the base, Standard thought. But how did that information get relayed to the Iron Guard? "What did you do with the information?" he asked.

"We passed it on to an office in the Ministry of Defense."

"Was it always to the same person?"

"No," she replied. "Just to whoever answered the phone."

"I need the phone number."

She wrote the number down and handed it to him. It was the number the Boys had wiretapped and monitored earlier that morning. He had the chain that led from the wing, to van der Roos, to Martine, to the Ministry of Defense, to the Iron Guard. More important, he had his rat.

Martine's fingers lingered on his wrist for a moment. "Richard, why don't you ever call?"

"I don't need another heart attack," he told her.

"We can be careful," she promised.

Friday, April 24
Iron Gate, near Bloemfontein

Beckmann had not slept in over thirty-six hours and the mental fog swirling around him held the promise of rest, but he couldn't give in to it, not yet. He gulped the two pills and waited. The powerful stimulants hammered at him, and he felt his heart quiver as the fog cleared.

The command bunker came into sharp relief and as he scanned the status boards, an inner voice warned him that he had a serious problem. What was it? The base was recovering as quickly as could be expected. He checked the time: another five hours before the radar would be operational. The same voice told him that was not the problem. Something was out of balance.

"Sir," a jubilant technician shouted. "We have some telephones!"

Automatically, Beckmann punched at the buttons to test the line. He heard the ring. "Interrogation," a guard answered. Why had he called that number? An inner voice told him what to do.

MacKay stopped playing solitaire when the guard answered the phone. He watched as the guard hung up. Without a word, the guard drew his pistol and aimed at MacKay. MacKay tensed, waiting for the slight contraction of the trigger finger that would launch him into action. "Handcuff the kaffir," the guard said. Before MacKay could move, the other guard sprayed him with Mace and beat him with a truncheon. MacKay fell to the floor as the first guard filled a syringe.

CHAPTER
25

Friday, April 24
Friday, April 24
Ysterplaat Air Base, Cape Town

Pontowski was sitting in the command post with de Royer when Kowalski radioed Ground Control for clearance to start engines. They listened to the small loudspeaker above their heads as the start-engines, taxi, and takeoff sequence played out. Nothing in Kowalski's voice indicated it was other than routine.

From the tower: "Lifter One, cleared for takeoff."

Kowalski: "Rolling."

"Are they overweight?" de Royer asked in French.

The waiting must be getting to him, Pontowski decided. It wasn't like de Royer to engage in small talk. "They're not overweight," he answered in the same language. "But they are jam packed with bodies."

"What is bothering you?" de Royer asked.

I can't hide anything from him, Pontowski thought. Well, out with it. "We had four days to plan the first attack and we failed. We planned this one in less than four hours. And we're outnumbered, both men and aircraft."

"You must read more Napoleon," de Royer said. Now they were speaking English. "We have a window of opportunity to attack because they are exhausted and have degraded communications. That window will not stay open for long."

"How can you be so sure?" Pontowski asked.

"Mr. Standard supplied the clues. The Iron Guard has little depth and must call on its commandos for support. It is also very centralized . . . a weakness we can exploit. It was a shame I didn't know this sooner."

"The CIA doesn't like sharing information," Pontowski replied, recalling when he had seen the Iron Guard's order of battle in Mazie's office. "This just doesn't feel good," he muttered.

"It is the uncertainty that disturbs you," de Royer said. "You must learn to live with it."

"Why the rush? Is it because Bouchard is trapped?" De Royer stared straight ahead, not moving. He is one cold-blooded bastard, Pontowski decided.

"That is part of it," de Royer finally replied.

"Is it because of Prime?" When had they switched back to French?

"That is also part of it," the general answered as he looked at Pontowski. The American did not understand, so why tell him? Then he relented. "Beckmann is an obscenity who must be destroyed."

Pontowski pushed his chair back and stood. "I've got to brief for the mission."

"Good hunting," de Royer said.

Maggot, Waldo, and Lee Bradford from the EC-130H were waiting for Pontowski in a briefing room. Waldo had already filled out the mission data card for him and all the times were listed. Pontowski checked the sequence off as Maggot ran the coming scenario. All too soon, they were finished, and Maggot asked if there were any questions.

Pontowski looked at Bradford. "Can you do all this?"

"In a heartbeat," Bradford told him.

Pontowski pushed himself to his feet. "Maggot, I think we're crazy."

"It certainly helps, Colonel."

Outside, another C-130 radioed for engine start.

Friday, April 24
Cape Town, South Africa

A late-afternoon quiet settled over Joe Pendulo's mansion when he returned from the Ministry of Defense. While his staff slept, Pendulo retreated to his private office and told his two bodyguards to wait outside. He locked the door before settling down behind his computer. He used the modem and was soon talking to his bank in Geneva, Switzerland. His fingers flew over the keyboard, punching in his secret bank account number. He smiled when he saw the deposit that had been made that afternoon.

The early-morning phone call from the Iron Guard had been most unusual but very profitable. He liked dealing with people who were so prompt in meeting their obligations. And so generous. A strange, muffled sound came from the outer office. It sounded like *phuut-phuut*. His guards knew better than to disturb him. He would speak to them about it. Then he heard it again. Now he was angry. He was coming out of his chair when the door lock exploded with a much louder *phuut*. The door swung open and he saw the bodies of his two bodyguards lying on the floor in pools of blood. "What do you want?" Pendulo asked, not seeing anyone.

Two men, both black, stepped into the office. Pendulo's knees gave out and he sank back into his chair. He knew who they were. "Why are you here?" he blustered. "If the director of national intelligence wishes to speak to me, he should do it in person, in my office."

One of the men pulled out a mini tape cassette and hit the start button. Pendulo's voice was clear and distinct as the recording of the morning's telephone conversation played out. "Who gave this to you?" Pendulo demanded, trying to regain control.

"Some friends," the man replied. "Very good friends."

Pendulo's eyes jumped from one man to the other. "I can make you wealthy," he said. "Very wealthy."

The men stared at him, not accepting the bribe. "We're

not going to kill you," the one with the minicassette said. "We only need some answers for the president."

The other man smiled. "You are going to live a very long time," he promised. Pendulo lost control and felt a spreading warmth in his crotch. It was the one promise he did not want to hear.

Friday, April 24
Iron Gate, near Bloemfontein

At sixteen thirty-three the mobile radar antenna started to rotate. It was anchored in the rubble that had been the Eagle's Nest and its beam swept the horizon. The team of workers breathed a sigh of relief. They were over an hour ahead of schedule.

Forty-five miles to the southwest, the EC-130H was entering its first racetrack pattern while Maggot, Pontowski, and Waldo lagged five miles in trail, conserving fuel.

In the rear of the EC-130H, Bradford was hovering behind the radar ECMT, electronic countermeasures technician, waiting for the search radar to come on line. They had monitored a test burst five minutes before when the system first powered up. The spectrum analyzer flashed when the EC-130H's sensitive antennas captured the first energy pulse. They had thoroughly analyzed the radar signature from the previous mission and the microprocessors were ready. The transponder sent a flurry of similar signals down the waveguide to an antenna. But these signals had been delayed and distorted.

The radar ECMT on board the EC-130H smiled and looked up at Bradford. "I've captured their radar's range gate," she told him.

"They'll never figure out what we're doing to them."

"Colonel Bradford," one of the communications specialists called over the intercom, "they put two Aeros on cockpit alert."

"That's not what we want," Bradford said. "Show 'em a bigger threat."

The radar ECMT's fingers danced on the computer keyboard.

In the Iron Gate's command bunker, the radar processor unit interpreted these signals as multiple returns, all going away from Iron Gate at a high rate of speed. The tactical commander pointed out the problem to Beckmann and called for the technicians. "A minor startup problem," he assured Beckmann.

Beckmann studied the scope. "Is it jamming?" he asked.

"I have never seen anything like this," the tactical commander replied.

"But it is all in the southwest quadrant," Beckmann said. His fingers beat a rapid tattoo on the table. Suddenly, the scope cleared and four bright returns flashed on the scope for one sweep. But these were to the north. Then the multiple returns were back. This time they were converging on the base at a high rate of speed from all quadrants.

Beckmann's voices woke up.

"Generaal!" the ADSO, air defense surveillance officer, shouted. "We're tracking multiple targets to the north, inbound." Before Beckmann could reach his position, heavy strobes spoked out from the center of the scope. "That is brute jamming," the ADSO said. "But we are burning through." He hit the antijam switch. Now the multiple targets were back for a few sweeps only to be replaced by more brute jamming. "They are getting closer," he told Beckman. "The speed indicates they are A-10s."

"Scramble all the Aeros," Beckmann ordered.

"But, Generaal," the tactical commander protested, "it would be better to only scramble four." Beckmann shot him a hard look, shutting him up.

It turned into a game of hide and seek as the Aeros searched the evening sky for the intruders. Twice, a flight of two came within fifteen miles of the EC-130H and the three Warthogs, but each time the EC-130H sent out a new flurry of false radar signals drawing the Aeros off. Not once did the EC-130H jam the Iron Guard's radios. That was for later. For now, they were only listening.

"Sparky, how much longer?" Pontowski asked the EC-130H over the Have Quick radio.

"The first Aeros are returning to base now," Bradford told them. "All are low on fuel."

Pontowski ran the numbers through his head. It was time. "Sparky, scramble the helicopters. Maggot, Waldo, join on me." The sun was low on the horizon as the three Warthogs dropped to the deck and turned toward the Iron Gate.

Ninety miles to the east of the Iron Gate, four Puma helicopters lifted off from Desert One and headed to the west. This time there was no icy fog waiting for them. Behind them, four C-130s taxied slowly out to the runway, their cargo decks jammed with paratroops.

One hundred nautical miles to the southwest, five A-10s led by Skid Malone jettisoned their empty wing tanks, helping to reduce the drag generated by the ordnance hanging from every station.

"Fence check," Pontowski transmitted, reminding Maggot and Waldo to arm their cannons and turn on their ECM pods. They were four minutes out.

The three Warthogs were on the deck in a loose V formation with a thousand feet separation as they approached the western ridge of the valley. The sun was at their backs as they climbed to crest the ridge line by two hundred feet, rolled 135 degrees, and pulled their noses to the ground. They swooped into the valley. Ahead of them was the runway. Two Aeros were on landing rollout and still on the runway. Another two were taxiing in, and the landing pattern was full of Aeros, all low on fuel.

"Tallyho!" Pontowski shouted.

The control tower operator saw the Warthogs first and managed to shout a warning over the radio before the jamming started. It was like nothing he had experienced and pierced his eardrums with pain. He ripped off his headset. It was worse for the Aero pilots because the landing pattern was full of Warthogs. In desperation, they broke out of the pattern, turned off their radios, and armed their weapons while trying to avoid each other.

No one had ever told them the Americans were this aggressive.

An Aero was turning base to final with gear and flaps down when the pilot got confused. He cross-controlled the aircraft, left rudder and right aileron, at low airspeed. The Aero did as he commanded and snap rolled to the right. The Aero stalled and pancaked into the ground inverted.

"Fox Two, Fox Two," Maggot radioed over his Have Quick. The frequency-hopping radio saved them from their own jamming. He hit the pickle button and a Sidewinder missile leaped off the left inboard rail and homed on an Aero turning into him. The cooled infrared seeker head flew up the Aero's right intake. The warhead malfunctioned and did not explode. But the missile's kinetic energy tore the engine apart.

The pilot in the Aero touching down did the only thing he could. He firewalled the throttles, snapped the gear and flaps up, and accelerated straight ahead. He ignored the screeching in his headset and concentrated on flying the aircraft. He flipped the master arm switch up, arming the fire-control circuits. He had two Kukri air-to-air missiles and 150 rounds for his twenty-three-millimeter twin-barreled cannon.

His airspeed was touching 120 knots when he saw a Warthog coming at him head-on. The closure speed was 480 knots or 810 feet a second. The pilot had never been in a situation like this or even thought about it. But Pontowski had done both. Smoke streamed back from the Warthog's nose as Pontowski literally shot him in the face with a thirty-millimeter depleted uranium slug.

A ground defender ran out of his bunker with a U.S.-built Stinger missile. He shouldered the weapon and tracked a Warthog—Waldo. He mashed the trigger and the missile leaped out of its launcher tube. A mistake. There were too many targets in the area for the seeker/tracker head to sort. Waldo mashed the flare button on his throttle quadrant and three flares popped out behind him. An Aero at Waldo's six o'clock sucked a flare up its intake. The Stinger's seeker head stepped over the two flares and looked for a target compatible with its programming. It homed on the Aero that had just swallowed the flare. Now the Stinger had a clear target signature that matched its programming and it functioned as designed.

Waldo stood his Warthog on its right wing in time to see the Aero tumble into the ramp. He rolled out at seventy-five feet above the ground and walked a burst of cannon fire across the two Aeros racing for the safety of a shelter. The worst nightmare of every fighter pilot is a cockpit fire. The second worst is to be caught on the ground, in the open, during an attack. Nightmare number two killed the two pilots.

The crew of a twenty-millimeter Twin Gun battery on the eastern ridge were inside a bunker eating their first hot meal in twenty-four hours. They were tired, dirty, and mentally exhausted. They had been raked by the munitions from a low-flying Tomahawk and harassed by a captain who lived in mortal fear and admiration of Beckmann, which was not a good mix for leading men in combat. The crew's first reaction had been to hunker down, but their NCO was made of sterner stuff and had driven them into the gun pits.

As soon as the auxiliary power units were on line, the gunners traversed their cannons toward the west to acquire the attacking aircraft in their open sights. But they were looking directly into the sun that was just above the ridge line on the other side of the valley. They were only partially blinded and could see a Warthog, Skid Malone, pull off from a bomb run along the western ridge. They watched in horror as canisters of CBU-58s split open and peppered the ridge line. Another Warthog was rolling in behind Skid.

Their NCO was shouting at them over the fixed-wire communications net to traverse their guns to the south. A pair of Warthogs were on them. Both guns traversed, acquired the Warthog, and transitioned to their optical sights. The two gunners were well-trained and easily placed the reticle on the nose of the A-10. Each pushed his joystick down to slave the gun to the computer. The farthest gun reached a firing solution milliseconds first and sent a long burst of HEI into the A-10. The second gun joined in.

The leading edge of the A-10's right wing peeled back and the nose shredded under the pounding. The right rudder simply disappeared as large chunks of the fuselage fell away. The right engine exploded and blew away from the fuselage. But the Warthog was still flying!

The ammo boxes on both guns were empty and the

loaders worked feverishly to reload as the Warthog pickled its load and pulled off target. Nothing the Tomahawks had done could rival the damage caused by six Mark-82 AIRs walked with precision across a target. The gun crews never had time to appreciate that fact.

Goat Gross did not check for BDA, bomb damage assessment, as he pulled off the target. His Warthog was dying. No one could have been more surprised than Gross when he realized he had control of the Hog. His hands flew around the cockpit as he transitioned to manual reversion. He made a Mayday call and headed for Desert One. If I can make the base, he figured, I can punch out. He pulled the first-aid kit out of his survival vest and dumped the contents in his lap. He had to stop the bleeding.

One of the Russian pilots hired by the Iron Guard found safety at full throttle and fifty feet above the ground. He crossed under Pontowski and turned away, scampering for safety across base housing. For a brief instant, he was on the wing of his countryman. The two were used to communicating without radios and exchanged hand signals. One tapped the side of his helmet, made a fist, held up two fingers, and pointed to the north. His wingman understood and they turned to the north. They split the stone and iron mass of the main gate.

Piet van der Roos was soaked in sweat as he neared the eastern ridge. He was flying at 140 knots, fifteen feet off the ground. His copilot told him they were coming up on power lines and he pulled up to clear them. Then he slammed the helicopter back down to the deck. "Ridge in sight," the copilot said. The eastern ridge of the valley loomed in front of him. He made no attempt to climb and flew directly toward the hillside. At the last moment, he turned and paralleled the hill while climbing. He popped over the top and settled to the ground. The sixteen legionnaires in the back piled out and spread along the ridge line. Van der Roos lifted off just as the second Puma came in with its load of legionnaires. The same scene repeated itself on the western ridge opposite them. The four helicopters headed back to Desert One to refuel and pick up their second load. As scheduled, Sparky stopped communications jamming long enough for van der Roos to make a single transmission.

Pontowski circled the runway at one hundred feet. The sun was down below the ridge now and much of the base was in dark shadows. Maggot came around on the opposite heading, circling above him. Waldo was five hundred feet above Maggot. "Negative bandits," Waldo radioed.

Bradford's voice came over the Have Quick radio. "The ridge lines are secure." The Legion had taken the high ground and the window of opportunity de Royer had planned for was open.

Pontowski circled one more time checking for movement on the ground. This was the reason de Royer had sent him on the mission—he had to make the decision to continue or abort. He took a deep breath and committed them. "Lifter One, you are cleared to drop. Repeat, cleared to drop." His voice sounded tinny and hollow over the Have Quick radio.

An unbelievably cool "Lifter One copies 'cleared to drop'" answered him.

The first C-130 flew down the valley at five hundred feet and lined up on the runway. Jumpers streamed out the back. The American legionnaire, Corporal Rogers, was the last man out. He went out the jump door in a perfect position: facing backward, right hand on the emergency chute D-ring, bent at the waist, knees slightly bent, feet together. He reached the end of the twenty-foot static line and felt the familiar tug. He immediately looked up to check the canopy for deployment. He had a streamer! His right hand jerked, pulling the D-ring to the emergency chute. The chute streamed out above his head and was snapping open when he hit the ground in a sitting position.

The second C-130 crossed the field. Two more were right behind.

"It was a good drop," Kowalski told her copilot as they flew past the main gate. "Let's go get the flare ramp." The C-130 climbed into the darkening sky and headed for Cape Town. The other three Hercules fell into trail.

"What's happening!" Beckmann screamed, filling the command bunker with his frustration. Most of his telephones were still inoperative, the radios unusable because of jamming, and his radar still spooking. He was blind and deaf. He paused, clamping an iron will over his emotions. Then, very calmly, "Send runners and set up a relay." He fought the urge to go and find out for himself—a commander had to stay in his command post, no matter what. He sat down and waited.

Slowly, the reports filtered in, whipsawing at his emotions. It was an unmitigated disaster. Three A-10s were circling the base, challenging anyone to shoot at them, paratroopers had landed on the runway and set up a defensive perimeter, and worst of all, the ridges overlooking the base were in enemy hands.

Nothing on Beckmann's face hinted at the battle going on inside. He gained control by focusing his hate on his adversaries. A face appeared. It was Pontowski, still vivid from the time they had met in Cape Town.

The major in charge of security was on the edge of panic. "Sir, we should abandon the base now, before it is too late. We can withdraw to the south and regroup at Bloemfontein."

"Really," Beckmann said. He drew his pistol and shot the major in the head. The echo died away and a heavy silence hung in the bunker. "Get this traitor out of here," he told the hushed staff. "We have a battle to fight." He actually smiled at the stunned faces. "Which we are going to win." There would be no more talk of abandoning Iron Gate.

Friday, April 24
Near Bloemfontein, South Africa

The two Aeros flew parallel to the highway leading north out of Bloemfontein. When the pilots saw the bridge, they slowed and configured their aircraft for landing. Landing on a highway presented no problems, not after the training they had received in the old Soviet Union landing on sod airstrips in dispersal exercises. They taxied off the main highway onto an asphalt access road and stopped. The engines were shut down and the canopies popped open.

The two men climbed out and walked over to a large

garage. One of the pilots examined the locks on the main door. He muttered a few words in Russian, drew his pistol, and shot the locks off. They raised the door. Inside were steel drums with jet fuel, a long hose, and a manual pump. It was all very familiar, and they went about the process of refueling the jets, taking turns at the pump. While one of them checked the oil and hydraulic fluid, the other found a canister of compressed air and checked the tires. That was all they could do.

The senior ranking pilot found the phone in the rear of the garage and called the command bunker at Iron Gate. He was surprised when the tactical commander answered on the first ring. He listened. Yes, the planes were fully operational. Yes, they each had two air-to-air missiles and a full load of ammunition. Yes, they had the modified Aeros. More instructions. He hung up.

"They want us to wait here. A truck is coming." The other pilot shrugged and rummaged around until he found the emergency food supplies and a sleeping bag.

Friday, April 24
Iron Gate, near Bloemfontein

Sam was crouched at a window in the Slavins' dining room with her camera, waiting for more action. But the attack was over. Bouchard motioned for her to move away from the window and handed her a flask of water. "What now?" she asked.

"We wait."

Sam tried to relax but her nerves wouldn't let her. She envied Bouchard, who had been sleeping most of the day. "What are you doing here?" she asked.

"Rescuing the Slavins," he replied. "There are problems. The helicopter never arrived."

"What are you going to do now?"

He turned his radio on only to be greeted by a loud screeching sound. It sent Sam's nerves up an octave. "Jamming," he said, turning the radio off. "We wait."

Sam wanted to scream. Waiting wasn't what she had in mind. She managed a fairly calm "Waiting for what?"

"For someone to come and get us. They know where we are but I don't know where they are. Otherwise, we would go to them once it's dark."

Friday, April 24
Ysterplaat Air Base, Cape Town

De Royer sat in the command post as the reports filtered in. When Desert One reported that Pontowski had landed and was taxiing into the fuel pits, he stood up. "Please tell Colonel Pontowski that he has operational control." He walked out to the flightline where his equipment had been stacked and waited for the inbound C-130s.

Kowalski's C-130 was the first to land. The ground crews were waiting and there was no delay as refueling began and the flare dispenser was strapped to the end of the ramp. When the fuel truck pulled away, the waiting paratroopers climbed on board. De Royer was the last in line and took the seat next to the rear right paratroop door. He would be the first man out.

Friday, April 24
Iron Gate, near Bloemfontein

Beckmann's face was drawn and haggard and a tic played at his right eyelid. He swallowed another two pills. "What is the source of the jamming?" he asked his tactical commander.

"Twice, they have stopped jamming and we have detected a single target here." He touched the radar scope where the Compass Call EC-130H was orbiting.

Part of Beckmann's genius was to sense an opportunity and act on it. He followed his instincts. "Why did they stop the jamming?"

"Probably because it interfered with their own communications," the tactical commander replied.

"So they only have one jamming platform. Excellent." Beckmann paced the floor, tasting victory. "It will have to land to refuel. That will give us a window to attack. How many commandos are responding?"

"Twenty-three," the tactical commander answered. "They are coming from all over the Boerstaat."

Beckmann ran the numbers. A commando averaged approximately fifty men each; that gave him 1,150 in troops addition to his 1,800—almost 3,000 men. It was enough. Now he had to contain the bridgehead at the airfield and get his men in place. With his degraded communications and the distance some of the commandos had to travel, that would take time. He studied the map of the base on the wall. Red circles had been drawn around the enemy positions. It infuriated him that they had penetrated the Iron Gate—his lair, his keep, his hope for the future. He felt violated.

They want you, an inner voice told him. Then it was quiet. A thrill shot through him: He had never been so close to his own death. "Have the trucks reached the Aeros?" he asked.

"They should be there in another hour," the tactical commander told him.

"We will counterattack when the jamming stops," he announced.

Friday, April 24
Desert One, Lesotho

Pontowski taxied into the fuel pit and kept his engines running for a hot refueling. Waldo and Maggot lined up behind him to wait their turn. When the refueling crew gave him a thumbs-up, he taxied out of the pits and into a revetment where Munitions was waiting to upload. This time, he shut the engines down while ammunition was cranked into the Avenger's ammo drum and twelve five-hundred-pound bombs were hung under the wings. But these were the old Mark-82 Snakeyes, a weapon he hadn't seen in years.

As planned, Bag Talbot was waiting to replace him. A fresh pilot replaced Waldo, and the two men walked past

Maggot, who was just pulling into an open revetment. He gave them a thumbs-up signal. They made their way down the unfamiliar ramp, looking for the command and communications van. It was parked on the dirt, well back from the parking area. Standard was waiting inside. "What the hell are you doing here?" Pontowski asked.

"Who do you think is going to have to account for all this?" he replied. "Besides, there is no way I'd miss it."

The controller on duty handed Pontowski the message that he had operational control until de Royer joined him. Waldo sat down at the mission director's position and Pontowski at the commander's console. This was where they would fight the battle. Pontowski checked the mission board: two Hogs were on station over the Iron Gate, Kowalski was inbound for her second drop before going on station as a flare ship, the EC-130H had another two hours on station before landing for fuel, and Goat Gross was safe on the ground with only minor wounds. "Are we in contact with Blue Force?" he asked.

"Affirmative," the communications specialist told him. "The airfield is secure and they are reporting light sniper fire."

Frequency-hopping radios are wonderful things, Pontowski thought. Maggot checked in on the radio: He was refueled and rearmed. Five Warthogs were sitting on the ramp, armed and ready to launch, fifteen minutes flying time from the Iron Gate.

Piet van der Roos stuck his head inside the door. "The Pumas are refueled and ready to go," he told Pontowski. "We took heavy ground fire on the last sorties but are okay."

Resistance is stiffening, Pontowski thought. "Try to get some rest, Piet. We'll have more business for you when the next C-130 lands."

Standard waited until van der Roos had left. "Is de Royer going for the whole enchilada?"

"Yep," Pontowski replied. "He wants to rescue Slavin and take Beckmann out."

"Why Beckmann?"

"He crossed the line when he used nerve gas and de Royer considers him 'an obscenity.'"

"The general has got that right," Standard told him.

Friday, April 24
Iron Gate, near Bloemfontein

Skid Malone buzzed the airfield and pulled off to the right, challenging anyone to shoot at him. There were no takers, and Kowalski's C-130 flew down the runway as jumpers streamed out the back. Two lines of tracers reached out from the hillside and converged on the C-130. They missed. "I'm in," Malone's wingman called. The hill exploded in flashes as he walked a stick of CBUs across the slope. The tracers stopped. Malone sequenced in behind him in case someone made a foolish decision and started shooting again. No one did.

A stick of flame, a Stinger, came out of the housing area and reached toward the C-130. But the range was too great and the missile arced downward. The self-destruct mechanism activated and it flashed in the night. Malone had to call off his wingman. "Housing is off-limits," he radioed.

"How would you like some light on the situation?" Kowalski said over the Have Quick radio.

"Hold above twelve thou," Malone said. "That will keep you clear of small-arms fire."

"Any SAM activity?" she asked. The C-130 could survive only in a very low-threat arena and was no match for surface-to-air missiles.

"Only what you saw."

"We'll stick around," she told the Warthog pilots. A string of twelve flares blossomed in the night, casting an eerie glow over the valley. "Vehicles are moving through the main gate," she told them. The first of the commandos had arrived.

"That's not off-limits," Malone said.

De Royer walked into the hangar and dropped his bundled-up parachute with all the others. His radioman and weapons bearer did the same and followed him over to the dark form lying on the ground. It was a body bag. De Royer paused and looked down. Another legionnaire was dead. "Corporal Rogers," he said in French. "An American." He saluted the body and walked into the bunker serving as a makeshift command post.

The men came to attention and fell silent. He was the last person they had expected to see. "General . . ." the colonel in command of Blue Force stammered.

De Royer glanced at the situation map tacked to the wall. "I want to see the perimeter."

"Certainly," the colonel said. He called for a lieutenant to act as a guide. "Your orders, sir."

De Royer paused before leaving. "Continue as before," he said.

Brenda Conklin lowered the flaps and gear and lined up on the grassy area beside the runway. She wired the airspeed at 120 knots and a drogue chute streamed out the back of the C-130. Ahead, she could see flashes near the main gate. She inched the big cargo plane down with the main gear almost touching the grass as the runway flashed by on the left. "Green light," she barked. The loadmaster released the locks holding the cargo pallets in the side rails. The drogue chute was anchored to the end pallet, not the Hercules, and pulled the four cargo pallets out the back.

Conklin firewalled the throttles and shouted for the gear and flaps to be raised. But it never happened. A hail of small-arms fire erupted in front of her, tearing into the cockpit and shredding the wings. Conklin pulled back on the yoke as pain exploded through her body. She was still trying to fly the aircraft when it hit the ground.

Legionnaires ran for the pallets and ripped the webbing away as smoke from the C-130 washed over them. They had nine tons of ammunition.

The cost of delivery: two pilots, a navigator, flight engineer, loadmaster, and a C-130.

Beckmann could feel his base come alive as more telephones came on line and the network of runners expanded. But the report that the main gate had been bombed and two commandos destroyed pushed him to the edge as a shiver of pure rage shot through him. The gate, that massive structure of stone and iron, had been the symbol that gave meaning to his cause, more so than the war cry of *"Blut und Boden!"* And he needed those commandos.

The report that a C-130 had been shot down sent shouts of triumph through the command bunker, carrying him with it, lifting him. The tactical commander was also shouting. At first the words did not make sense. Then he understood. The jamming had stopped! Beckmann bent his head in prayer, his faith restored. The enemy would be delivered into his hands! The covenant was not broken.

As suddenly as it had begun, the high crashed. His legs gave out and he had to sit down. For a moment, he thought he was going to vomit. He reached for the bottle and gulped two pills. He watched the minute hand of the wall clock move. Three minutes passed and nothing happened. He gulped two more pills. Now he could feel it. He stood up, his face alive with anticipation. "It is time," he announced. "We attack."

CHAPTER
26

Saturday, April 25
Desert One, Lesotho

The news that de Royer was on the ground with Blue Force inside Iron Gate reached Pontowski two minutes past midnight. "What is he doing there?" Pontowski muttered, trying to make sense out of it. Then he got busy.

Skid Malone reported in, saying he was returning to base with his wingman, ordnance expended, and that a C-130 had crashed at the airfield. Before Waldo could scramble two Warthogs to replace Skid, the EC-130H called for landing clearance. Pontowski made the decision. "Scramble the Hogs," he told Waldo, "but hold them short of the runway if Sparky is on final. Get Sparky turned and launched ASAP."

While Waldo made it happen, Pontowski considered his next move. He glanced at the wall clock when the EC-130H landed. How long before it could refuel and get airborne? Bradford had promised they would keep the jamming going as they headed for Desert One, but would lose effectiveness with increasing distance. The sound of the two A-10s taking off filled the communications van.

"Put two Hogs on cockpit alert," he said. Again, Waldo made it happen.

Standard leaned over Pontowski's shoulder. "Ask Malone what he was bombing." Pontowski relayed the question.

They listened to the answer. "Not good," Standard said. "It sounds like commandos are answering the call."

Saturday, April 25
Iron Gate, near Bloemfontein

De Royer walked into the bunker and studied the situation map. "Has the jamming stopped?" he asked.

"Three minutes ago," the colonel told him.

"It is time. Commence firing."

The order went out and a barrage of mortar fire erupted as the legionnaires sent round after round arcing over the base. But it was not indiscriminate fire. Most of the rounds were impacting a few hundred yards in front of the legionnaires. The gunners depressed the elevation and rolled the barrage toward the main base as the legionnaires moved forward, running, taking cover where they could, but always moving.

The units of the Iron Guard encircling the airfield were in a state of confusion. For the first time, they were talking on the radios and were saturated by orders and demands for information from Beckmann's command bunker. At the same time, commando units were arriving and needed directions to move into position. Then Beckmann ordered an attack to retake the airfield. Since the Iron Guard outnumbered the Legion by five to one, he was confident it would be a short fight.

But de Royer and the Legion were of a different opinion, and the mortar barrage was their opening argument. The legionnaires quickly overran the forward positions facing them and spoiled the pending attack. What happened next was determined at the platoon level, not in de Royer's bunker. When the legionnaires ran into stiff opposition, some would dig in as a covering force and radio their position to de Royer's bunker, while the others would work their way past. Where the opposition was light or nonexistent, they pushed ahead.

One squad overran a howitzer battery that had been moved into position to shell the eastern ridge line held by the Legion. The sergeant in command of the squad promptly obeyed the Legion's unofficial standing order of the day, *Démerdez-vous,* an obscene version of "Make do." They turned the gun around and shelled the base until they ran out of shells.

Bouchard listened to the gunfire, separating the sounds. "The Legion is attacking," he told his team. He issued orders and they sorted their kit, getting ready to leave. Bouchard told the Slavins to dress the children in dark clothes.

"What's happening?" Sam asked.

"The Legion is attacking the Iron Guard," he told her.

"Are they coming for us?" she asked.

Bouchard shook his head slowly. "Perhaps later."

"What are they doing?"

Bouchard hadn't made himself clear. "Destroying Beckmann." He picked up his radio and turned it on. The jamming had stopped, and he contacted de Royer's bunker on the assigned frequency. He spoke rapidly in the half-French, half-idiomatic jargon the Legion had developed over the years that was a code in itself. He shoved the antenna in, turning the radio off. "They will send a helicopter when the jamming starts again. We will wait here. It won't be long."

Beckmann had never been on the receiving end of a mortar barrage and it unnerved him. He steeled himself as round after round slammed into the roof. The forty feet of dirt and concrete above his head saved him from the mortars but not the information flowing into the bunker. Before, he had not had enough information, but once the jamming stopped, he had too much. He forced himself to concentrate, winnowing the important facts from the chaff. In one terrible moment, it all became crystal clear—the Legion wanted to capture him!

434

Saturday, April 25
Desert One, Lesotho

While the EC-130H refueled, Bradford updated Pontowski on the threats his technicians had detected and warned him that heavy reinforcements were reaching the Iron Guard. Bradford glanced at his watch and sprinted across the ramp, climbing on board as the fourth engine spun to life. The Hercules taxied out and took off exactly seventeen minutes after landing.

Pontowski was still inside the communications van and wrote the takeoff time down as Waldo worked the radios. "Colonel, Kowalski has to beat feet. It's getting too hot."

"Hold her high and dry with the two Hogs," Pontowski told him. While Waldo found a safe area for her to orbit with the A-10s, Pontowski contacted de Royer on the secure radio and explained that without flares to light the ground and illuminate targets, his Warthogs needed direction from the Legion's forward air controllers. He ended with, "What's your situation?"

De Royer's reply was not reassuring. "The situation on the ground is fluid. We are advancing toward the south but encountering heavy resistance. There is a probing action on our northern perimeter by commando units. An enemy prisoner identified two commandos, the Wynberg and Tugela, and says more are arriving from the north. Can you interdict their arrival?"

Pontowski told Waldo to send Kowalski and the Hogs to the north and seal off the road leading to the main gate. "The flare ship and two Hogs will be on station in two minutes," he told de Royer.

"The housing area is isolated and quiet," de Royer said. "When the jamming resumes, have a Puma extract Bouchard." He broke the connection.

Since the Pumas did not have a secure radio, Pontowski sent a runner to get van der Roos. "I can't figure de Royer out," Pontowski told Standard while they waited. "He should be right here, not at the airfield."

"De Royer wants his own Dien Bien Phu," Standard said, recalling the defeat of the Foreign Legion at the hands of the Viet Minh in Indochina in 1954.

"The French got their asses kicked big time there," Pontowski said. "Why would he want to repeat that?"

Standard shook his head. "He's going to give the Legion one hell of a victory or one hell of a martyr."

Piet van der Roos burst into the communications van and Pontowski relayed de Royer's order to extract Bouchard. "I'll do it," van der Roos told him.

"What if you have to return fire?" Pontowski asked. He was really asking if van der Roos could shoot at other Afrikaners.

"No problem," van der Roos answered. "I've already made that decision."

"Colonel," Waldo interrupted. "Kowalski reports many vehicles moving on the road toward the Iron Gate. She's calling for everything we've got."

Saturday, April 25
Iron Gate, near Bloemfontein

The jamming was back. Strangely, it helped Beckmann in one respect, because he reverted to his backup systems of communications, which cut down the flow of needless information. But it also delayed his response to the changing situation. De Royer used that delay to get inside Beckmann's decision cycle. If Beckmann had trained his lower-ranking officers to act independently, they would have contained de Royer's attack and surrounded the legionnaires in short order.

Beckmann had ordered one lieutenant to hold his position at all costs, but the fast-moving legionnaires barely paused as they overran the lieutenant's platoon. That was when the lieutenant stopped talking to the command bunker and adopted the legionnaires' tactics. He ordered his men to scoot and shoot their way to safety and to regroup in the housing area.

Much to the lieutenant's surprise, it worked.

* * *

A runner reached Beckmann's bunker shortly after four in the morning and handed a message to a sergeant. The NCO read the message and forwarded it to Beckmann. The sergeant sat there for a moment, thinking. He had read every message that had come in and had a complete picture of the battle. Outside, the sound of gunfire was coming closer. Without a word, he grabbed his helmet and left.

Beckmann read the message, wadded it up, and threw it to the floor. A flare ship and four A-10s had cut the road leading to Iron Gate and stopped all traffic. The road was littered with burning hulks and the survivors were in desperate need of medical attention.

Part of Beckmann coldly analyzed the situation while his voices raged at him. The Iron Guard was cut off, but given time, the commandos would regroup and force their way through. The legionnaires could not hold Iron Gate for long. "But long enough to take you prisoner," a voice told him. The rational part of his mind calculated he had another four hours at the most. Sometime after sunrise, he reasoned, when the A-10s could roam at will above him and the gunners on the ridge lines butcher his men.

Another voice spoke to him and for the first time, he recognized the speaker. It was Erik, his brother. He listened and then picked up the telephone. But the line to the dispersal site was down. He scribbled a message and handed it to his communications officer. "This must go out at all costs. Send a runner and try to establish radio contact. You must not fail."

Before he left, he gave his last order. "Do not surrender."

MacKay's head hurt. The pain was a tiger, ripping and tearing at him. He fought the beast off and made his eyes focus. He was lying on the floor of the examination room, stripped naked, his hands tied behind his back. Plastic flexcuffs, he thought. Then he saw Ziba. She was also naked. But her hands were shackled in front of her.

"Why does he do this?" she asked. "Why doesn't he just . . ." Her voice trailed off in despair.

"Kill us and get it over with?" MacKay replied. "The mutha is crazy. He's gotta shred his victims first, strip away their dignity, show 'em that he's in control. The more you frustrate him, the more you gotta suffer." MacKay twisted his wrists back and forth, working the flexcuffs around until the slip clamp was against the plastic band. He worked his wrists, rubbing the clamp against the plastic, generating heat and weakening the plastic.

One of the guards came into the room, his face a blank. He grabbed Ziba's breasts, hard, and mouthed the word "nigger." The rage cocooned inside MacKay broke through and all the bonds that held him in check were gone. He flexed and jerked at the plastic flexcuffs as he came off the floor. The plastic clamp snapped and MacKay was on the guard. He drove a fist into his midriff and spun him around. He threw a choke hold around his neck and lifted the man off the floor, twisting and breaking his neck.

The other guard came through the door, his nine-millimeter automatic drawn, and fired. But his gun jammed. He was vaguely aware that MacKay was coming at him as he tried to clear the weapon. MacKay barreled into him. It was a classic blocking motion learned playing football, and MacKay drove the guard back against the wall. He drove his fist into the man's throat and the automatic clattered to the floor.

MacKay picked the pistol up and turned to Ziba. Her eyes were wide with fright; Beckmann was standing in the doorway, raising his pistol. Without thinking, MacKay whirled and threw his pistol, hitting Beckmann square in the face. He dropped the pistol he was holding and held his hands to his forehead.

MacKay was a blur as he came at Beckmann, his rage still building. Adrenaline coursed through him, driving him on. Beckmann went down. MacKay towered over him for a moment as a growling sound grew in his throat to a howl, ugly and primeval. He picked Beckmann up and threw him toward the stairs, skidding him across the floor. Beckmann started to move but MacKay drove a bare foot into his temple, stunning him. MacKay rolled the Afrikaner onto his back and propped the heel of Beckmann's left boot on the second step, raising his leg four inches off the floor. MacKay raised his foot high and stomped the top of Beckmann's knee, shattering it.

Beckmann's scream echoed up the stairs and down the

empty corridors, reaching the courtyard. MacKay grabbed Beckmann's right leg and dropped the foot on the step, extending that knee. MacKay stood over the prostrate body. Ziba's hands grabbed his right arm and pulled him back. For a moment they stood over the body of the prostrate Beckmann. Then she released MacKay's arm.

"I'm not going to kill you," MacKay told Beckmann. Then he stomped again.

The mauling the lieutenant had taken from the legionnaires had made him a very cautious man, and he made sure the survivors of his platoon were spread out and well concealed. "Lieutenant," a sergeant whispered. "There." He pointed to a dark area between two houses. The lieutenant froze. Then he saw it—two figures moving silently in the night. One was carrying a bundle over his shoulders in a fireman's carry. "It's the kaffir," the NCO whispered. They all knew who MacKay was.

The lieutenant motioned for the sergeant to follow them.

The legionnaire crouched at the back door of the Slavins' house saw the movement first through his night-vision goggles. "Colonel Bouchard," he whispered, "someone is coming this way." Bouchard moved next to him and waited. Night-vision goggles have a very narrow field of view and flatten depth perception, but the model the legionnaires were wearing gave them excellent detail.

"It's okay," Bouchard said, recognizing MacKay. He held the door open to let them in.

MacKay dropped his bundle and collapsed to the kitchen floor, gasping for breath. "Who is that?" Bouchard said, motioning at the figure on the floor.

"Beckmann," MacKay said.

The platoon was moving toward the Slavins' house when they heard the sound of the helicopter. The lieutenant waited for it to come into sight, hoping it belonged to the Iron Guard. When he saw it was a Puma, he ordered his men to open fire.

For a moment the Puma hovered, defying the hail of

gunfire as bullets cut through the cargo compartment and into the overhead engine bays. One of the door gunners was hit and crumpled to the deck while the other kept raking the night with his 7.62-millimeter machine gun. Piet van der Roos pulled on the collective as the dying helicopter autorotated to earth.

The helicopter burst into flames, and for the first time, the lieutenant felt the rush of victory. He shouted for his men to cease fire to conserve ammunition. Nothing happened. He shouted again as the sergeant next to him crumpled to the ground. He was vaguely aware of figures running from the burning helicopter as more rounds cut into the night around him, pounding at his men. They were in another firefight. But with whom?

The lieutenant fell to the ground and rolled behind a tree. Muzzle flashes were coming from the house where the kaffirs had gone. It was too much, first the legionnaires, now two kaffirs. He yelled at his men to start an envelopment. It was a tactic they had practiced many times.

The helicopter crew piled through the door and suddenly, it was silent. Van der Roos was the last in, dragging his wounded door gunner. "He'll live," a legionnaire said. He quickly bandaged the wounded American.

Bouchard stood back from a window and looked outside, scanning the night with his NVGs. He saw movement. They only had seconds. "Where is the Legion?" he asked.

"At the airfield," van der Roos replied.

Bouchard told MacKay to lead the way and take everyone to the airfield. Four of his legionnaires would go with them to help carry the wounded American, Beckmann, and the children. He looked over at a bearded NCO. "You and me, Willi?"

"This is why we came, Colonel," the NCO answered with a heavy German accent. They were the rear guard.

Why are they doing this, van der Roos wondered. Was it to save their comrades? Or was it for a more important reason? All his questions and doubts vanished as he stood there.

"Go," Bouchard ordered.

MacKay ran through the house and led the group out the

patio doors. The legionnaires fanned out and cleared a corridor. Bouchard had read the developing situation correctly and they were unopposed.

Bouchard handed Willi an AA-52 light machine gun and grabbed a sack of forty-millimeter grenades. Much to his surprise van der Roos was dragging four ammunition belts of 7.5-millimeter ammo for the AA-52 into the room. "You brought them," he said, "so let's use them."

Before Bouchard could order him to follow the others, gunfire cut into the house, driving them to the floor. Willi returned fire with the AA-52 and Bouchard lobbed the forty-millimeter grenades into the night as quickly as he could load them into the grenade launcher mated to his assault rifle. The bark of a MAT-49 echoed from another room. Van der Roos returned with four more belts of ammunition for the AA-52. Suddenly, it was silent. The firepower coming from the house had totally surprised the lieutenant, and he had to regroup. "Who is in the other room?" Bouchard demanded.

"The Zulu," van der Roos answered. He wasn't the only one fighting for his country. Like van der Roos, Ziba had stayed behind.

"Merde," Bouchard growled.

"They will try another side next time," Willi said. He crawled across the floor dragging the AA-52. The twenty-pound weapon could put out a massive amount of firepower and cut cars in half. But it was also a target. Van der Roos grabbed an assault rifle and followed him, still dragging the heavy ammo belts.

The night exploded in a living hell as the platoon opened fire, sending hundreds of rounds into the cement-block house. But the Afrikaner penchant for solid construction saved the defenders. If the house had been of wood construction the firefight would have lasted about twenty seconds. Again, the AA-52's field of fire commanded the fight and forced the lieutenant to move his men. Willi moved with them and van der Roos stayed behind to hold that side of the house.

By now, the lieutenant was certain he had only four or five legionnaires trapped in the house and he could sense victory—as soon as he could take out the machine gun. A corporal brought up an RPG-7, the Soviet-built rocket-propelled grenade that could penetrate six inches of steel armor. The lieutenant ordered a probing action and sacrificed two men to fix the new location of the AA-52.

The probing action heated up and Willi shouted for more ammo. Van der Roos was in the hall moving toward him when the RPG exploded. The concussion knocked him out. He came to as someone crawled past. It was Ziba, dragging the AA-52 into the kitchen. "He's dead," she said. Van der Roos moved like a robot and followed her, dragging an ammunition belt. But this was the last one.

The house was full of smoke and he could smell a fire burning. Through the smoke, he could see Ziba tying a bandage around Bouchard's chest. One look and van der Roos knew the Frenchman was dying. "Put it there," Bouchard said, pointing to the door. Ziba understood and shoved the muzzle of the machine gun out the door. A hail of gunfire cut across the house, sending concrete chips and dust over them. Ziba loaded the last belt.

MacKay moved fast and they were clear of the housing area in seven minutes. He stopped when he saw the airfield. He had gotten them there, now a legionnaire would have to take them through the lines. In the distance, he could hear the firefight going on at the house. The professional soldier in him was in overdrive and he mentally gave Bouchard and the sergeant another three to five minutes at the max. A legionnaire joined him. "We had to give Beckmann another shot of morphine," the legionnaire said. "His knees are killing him."

"I hope so," MacKay grunted. "But keep him alive. That mutha is gonna stand trial." He looked around and did a head count. Ziba and van der Roos were missing. "I'm going back," MacKay growled. He had come too far to lose Ziba now. The legionnaire threw MacKay a MAT-49 and an ammo pouch. MacKay was up and running, retracing his steps.

The gunfire raking the house slowed, then died. Bouchard motioned van der Roos to join him. "You and the woman . . . go."

442

"We're surrounded," van der Roos replied.

Bouchard shook his head and pointed to the other side of the house, in the direction of the burning helicopter. "Go that way, it will be okay." He had not lost his situational awareness and had the measure of his opponents. They were being enveloped, not encircled. Otherwise, the attackers would be caught in their own crossfire. "I will count to ten. When I start firing, run." The two did as he said and crawled out of the room. Bouchard raised his gloved hand in salute and started to count.

Bouchard was wrong. The Afrikaner lieutenant was fairly certain the ammunition cooking off in the burning Puma would seal that quadrant of the envelopment. But rather than take a chance, he had left a lance corporal and a private behind. They saw Ziba and van der Roos the moment they broke from the house, and opened fire.

The ground kicked up around them and they ran faster. Ziba was still carrying the MAT-49 and she swung it around, firing as she ran. Another burst of gunfire cut into them and van der Roos put on a burst of speed, outdistancing Ziba, running toward the waiting shadows and safety. He heard a scream and looked over his shoulder. Ziba was down. She was on the ground, crawling forward, still dragging the MAT-49 after her. Two more bullets hit her.

Van der Roos skidded to a halt and fell to the ground as he reversed direction. He ran for Ziba. More gunfire and he went down. He rolled on the ground, drawing his automatic. He fired and emptied the clip as he reached Ziba. He grabbed her MAT-49 and fired as he dragged her to her feet.

MacKay came out of the shadows and saw the two Africans stumbling across the open area. He opened fire, trying to give them cover. Again, Ziba fell to the ground.

Ziba looked up at van der Roos. "Go," she gasped in Zulu.

"We do this together," he said in Afrikaans, reaching for her.

A long burst of gunfire cut into them.

CHAPTER
27

Saturday, April 25
Iron Gate, near Bloemfontein

De Royer paced the bunker as the reports came in. They only confirmed what he could hear outside—silence. Resistance was collapsing and the Iron Guard was surrendering. Only a few isolated pockets were holding out. He removed his helmet and flak vest and donned a blue beret. He issued orders to the colonel and left.

Itzig Slavin stood up when he saw de Royer walk into the hangar. "Thank you, sir. My family . . ." The right words eluded Slavin and he could not say more. De Royer shook his hand and looked at the man lying on the ground—Beckmann.

De Royer had done what he came for, and by rescuing Slavin, he had taken Prime away from Beckmann. For a moment, he wondered if Slavin had discovered cold nuclear fusion. If not, he decided, perhaps in the future. A feeling of satisfaction swept over him. Now it was time to end it. He turned to the woman. "Miss Darnell, there are many things here you need to see before we withdraw."

Sam was tired and wanted to collapse on the big pile of parachutes in the corner and sleep for a week. "How long do I have?" she asked.

"I'm not sure," he told her. "You will be escorted. They will take you where it is safe and will bring you back when it is time to leave."

"Thank you," Sam told him. She grabbed her camera and followed the four legionnaires detailed to take her around the base.

Saturday, April 25
Desert One, Lesotho

"Relay the message to Sparky," Pontowski told Waldo.

The captain stepped on the transmit button on the floor and made the radio call. "Sparky, Desert One. Strangle all jamming. Repeat, strangle jamming."

"Why did de Royer order the jamming stopped?" Standard asked, perplexed by the decision to stop jamming the Iron Guard's communications.

"So what's left of the Iron Guard's command and control system can surrender," Pontowski answered. Where had he learned that? Then he remembered: when he had attended Squadron Officers' School as a junior captain. What else had he forgotten that de Royer was reteaching him?

"Sir," Waldo said, "the last of the Hogs are recovering now."

"Turn them and get them back on status," Pontowski told him.

"They're a bunch of tired jocks," Waldo reminded him.

Pontowski knew it was the truth. How much more could he push them? It was time to find out. "Let's go say 'howdy' to the troops," he told Standard. He grabbed his personal radio as he left.

The two men walked the line, stopping at each revetment to speak to the pilot. Waldo was right, they were exhausted. He had been pushing them since early Friday morning and some of them had flown six sorties in the last twenty-four hours. Six *combat* sorties, he corrected himself. He knew what that meant and the toll it took on an individual. Thank God I haven't lost any more pilots on this phase of the operation, he told himself. Then it hit him hard. He had lost a C-130 crew. How could he forget that so easily? It won't happen again, he promised himself.

They found Maggot sitting on the ground, his back

against a revetment wall. "How's it going?" Pontowski asked him.

"I'm really bushed," he admitted, not getting up.

As they talked, a vague itch at the back of Pontowski's mind demanded a scratching. He remembered the last time it had happened. He had ignored it and Tango Leonard and Tanya Perko had died. Not this time. "Maggot, I need to put two Hogs in a CAP and the rest on five-minute alert."

Maggot stood up. As long as Pontowski was asking, he would do it. "Sounds fair to me, Boss."

"Not you. Who's in the best shape to fly?"

Maggot thought for a few moments. Technically, by the regulations, they should have all been in crew rest. But combat didn't work that way. "You, Waldo, and Bag," he answered.

Pontowski stood there, thinking. He wanted to fly, to do the mission. But that wasn't his job anymore. De Royer had tried to tell him that early on, that he was too close to operations. His job was to decide what to do, when it would be done, and who would do it. Pontowski keyed his radio. "Waldo, you're up. Get your gear. I want you and Bag to fly a CAP. You've got the lead. Launch ASAP."

But why did de Royer let me be the airborne mission commander? he wondered. Then it came to him. The critical decision to abort or continue the attack had to be made on the spot by someone who understood air operations, which Pontowski did. In this particular case, that also meant sharing the danger.

Standing in the early morning dark, cold, tired, and hungry, he finally understood de Royer. "I'll be damned," he muttered to himself. The critical decision to withdraw from Iron Gate had to be made by someone who understood ground operations. De Royer was where he had to be to make the right decision at the right time.

De Royer did not have a martyr complex; he did not want his own Dien Bien Phu. He was sharing the risk when he could and leading by example. Pontowski grinned at Maggot. "Come on, let's get something to eat. You get to play mission director."

"Ah, no," Maggot groaned. Pontowski knew how he felt.

Saturday, April 25
Iron Gate, near Bloemfontein

Sam was standing outside the command bunker. She hit the record button as two legionnaire sappers rigged the heavy blast door with explosives. What was left of Beckmann's staff was barricaded inside and refused to surrender. The sappers moved away, stringing wire behind them. An explosion blew the door open and knocked the sappers to the ground. "That came from inside," a legionnaire told her. Sam recorded it all and breathed easier when the sappers got up and dusted themselves off.

"They sealed themselves in," the same legionnaire said.

"Are they still alive?" she asked.

The legionnaire shrugged. "Probably. Do you want to see the gallows next?" She nodded, half-afraid of what was coming. Her escort led her into the security compound. The gallows was still standing in the courtyard. *"Mon Dieu,"* one of the legionnaires whispered.

"Down here," another legionnaire shouted, leading her into Interrogation. Nothing in Sam's experience had prepared her for the next five minutes. Her hands shook as a legionnaire explained what she was recording. Finally, she couldn't take any more and ran up the stairs.

"Show the world what the Afrikaners are," a legionnaire told her.

Piet van der Roos is an Afrikaner, Sam thought. He isn't like this and his family are decent, caring people—like most of the Afrikaners I've met. This is the lunatic fringe, the haters at work. "This could happen anywhere," she told the legionnaire. "Anywhere," she repeated for emphasis. That was the story she would tell.

The legionnaire's radio crackled. "The general wants to see you in the weapons storage area," he said.

Sam knew she had the story of the year as she followed de Royer through the underground tunnels. "Without Doctor Slavin, we would have never found this," the general explained in English. He walked on, his voice never changing inflection. Sam stayed as close as she could so her shotgun mike could record what he was saying. A sergeant opened the heavy armored steel doors to a weapons bay. "These are nerve gas canisters."

"What are you going to do with them?" Sam asked.

"Rig them with explosive charges, seal the bunkers, and blow them up," de Royer said.

"Can I document it?" she asked.

"Certainly."

Sam jammed a fresh battery pack and cassette into her camera.

Saturday, April 25
Near Bloemfontein, South Africa

Lee Bradford was a tired man when he glanced at his watch. It's morning, he thought. He sat at his console in the rear of the EC-130H and sipped at a cup of coffee, thinking what his crew had done. What a shame, he thought. No one will ever know. But that was the world of ECM. Still, he felt good. "Colonel," a radio technician said over the intercom, "we're picking up radio traffic on a tactical net. Should we jam it?"

Bradford came alert. A tactical net was used to scramble fighters. He hit a toggle switch and listened. Two Aeros were being scrambled. "Jam it," he shouted. "Source?"

"The command bunker," the radio technician told him.

"Where are the Aeros launching from?"

The radio technician gave him the coordinates. "Colonel, I speak a little Russian," the technician said. "Before we started jamming, the pilots were talking to each other about wearing gas masks."

Saturday, April 25
Desert One, Lesotho

Bradford's voice was on every frequency. "Attention all aircraft. Two bandits are approaching from the north. They are configured for NBC. Repeat, they are configured for NBC." He gave the launch site coordinates and fell silent.

Maggot was sitting at the mission director's position in the communications van and leaned forward, almost yelling into his boom mike. "Waldo, copy all?"

"Rog," Waldo replied, much calmer. "Jettisoning now." The two Warthogs jettisoned their bomb loads and turned to the north to search for the intruders. Waldo told Bag to take the lead since he had two Sidewinder missiles and a full load of thirty-millimeter rounds. Waldo only had the cannon and 542 rounds in the ammo drum.

Honor the threat! Pontowski thought. Those Aeros have to be carrying nerve gas. Even with gas masks, how many can survive a chemical attack without MOPP suits? How many wounded and innocent civilians will die? "We've got five Hogs sitting on the ramp," Pontowski said to Maggot. "Scramble them into defense CAPs over de Royer." He let Maggot work the scramble, and, four minutes later, the first two A-10s were airborne. He checked the time. It was fifteen minutes flying time to Iron Gate. Too long.

"Colonel," Maggot said, "the first shuttle is landing." A C-130 was on short final with the wounded. De Royer was pulling out.

"Use all three C-130s and send the Pumas in. They can help." Pontowski stepped outside. It was light and the sun was above the horizon.

"Find 'em, Waldo," he muttered.

Saturday, April 25
Near Bloemfontein, South Africa

Waldo was a man with a problem. He was flying an aircraft that had been built for killing tanks and close air support of troops in contact with the enemy. It was not an air superiority fighter designed for seeking out other aircraft and shooting them down. Yet that was exactly what he had to do. And he only had two sets of eyeballs to do it with: his and Bag's.

The two pilots split apart and entered separate patterns

with Bag slightly farther to the north and more to the west. They hoped that would put Bag closer to the intruders and give them maximum visual coverage over a wide area. The patterns they were flying were oriented east to west and resembled long, very narrow figure-eights so they would always be turning to the north. It didn't work, for what they gained in visual coverage, they lost in mutual support.

The two Aeros were on the deck and flying down a broad valley when they saw the distinctive planform of a Warthog turning above them. It was Bag turning back to the east. More often than not, aerial combat is a matter of exploiting an opportunity. The Russian in the lead Aero simply reefed around hard to the left, pulled his nose up, and fell in behind and below Bag Talbot. He sweetened the shot by closing the distance between them. He even had time to double-check his switches.

Automatically, Bag did a belly check and rolled to the left to see what was below him and at his six-o'clock position. Most fighter pilots never see the other fighter or missile that kills them. Bag did.

Waldo saw the explosion. "Bag!" he shouted over the radio. There was no answer. Then he saw the Aero. Incredibly, the pilot was doing a victory roll. Another Aero came up and joined on the victor as they headed south. Waldo's face froze. He firewalled the throttles and made the radio call. "Two bandits twenty-four miles north, inbound, eight hundred feet." Then, "They splashed Bag. I'm engaged." Bradford answered him. There was no one to help and Waldo had four minutes to catch the Aeros and kill them.

Geometry, altitude, and speed were in Waldo's favor. He was on one leg of a triangle converging on the Aeros, which were flying down the other leg. But Waldo's leg was shorter. He was also above them. Going downhill is one thing the Warthog does very well, and Waldo swapped his altitude for speed. The Aeros were cruising at 280 knots, conserving fuel, and Waldo was at 380 and accelerating when they saw him.

The Aeros turned into Waldo, trying to generate an overshoot. But Waldo wasn't having it. He turned with them, hard to the left, creating an over G on the Hog. For a fraction of a second, luck was on Waldo's wing. The lead Aero pilot tightened up his turn and loaded his airframe with five *G*s. Other than bleeding off airspeed, it was a normal maneuver. But the gas mask he was wearing slipped under the *G* force and partially blinded him. Instinctively, he eased off the turn as Waldo fell in behind.

The three jets were in a tight Lufbery four hundred feet above the ground with Waldo sandwiched in the middle. He didn't care. He kept his turn coming as his airspeed bled off. The lead Aero was in the pipper and Waldo mashed the trigger. The cannon fired six rounds and luck switched sides. A round coming out of the ammo drum on the feed links was not properly seated in the holding tabs. The thirty-millimeter round hit the breech cockeyed and exploded.

Waldo's first round missed the Aero, the second hit the right wing root, and the last three missed. The depleted uranium slug that hit the Aero's wing did not explode but the energy from the high muzzle velocity tore the wing off the fuselage. The Aero twisted to the right, into its missing wing, as it hit the ground.

The speed of what happened next defied the imagination and took about as long as reading this sentence. But Waldo made it happen. The explosion in the A-10's gun bay had ruptured the hydraulic system and its controls were rapidly bleeding away. Waldo rolled out and jerked his throttles full aft. He pulled back on the stick, slowing his Hog, and hesitated for a fraction of a second as the Aero on his tail rapidly closed. When he saw that the Aero was passing on his right, he gave the Hog full right aileron. The Aero was there as the A-10 rolled, crashing into it.

Luck was absolutely neutral as the laws of physics and the work of Fairchild's engineers took over. The A-10 was heavier and built like the tanks it was meant to destroy. It survived the midair collision, the Aero didn't, and Waldo had his fourth kill, one short of becoming an ace. Now all he had to do was stay alive.

Saturday, April 25
Iron Gate, near Bloemfontein

The legionnaires found MacKay sitting beside the two bodies. He slowly stood as de Royer and one of the sergeants who had parachuted in with Bouchard approached. "General, this is the man I told you about," the sergeant said.

MacKay came to attention and saluted. "Colonel John MacKay, United States Army."

De Royer returned his salute. "Are these the South Africans who stayed behind?"

MacKay's voice was strained with emotion and his words came in short, rapid bursts. "Yes, sir. But I was too late." He motioned at two other bodies on the far side of the grassy area. "I got them. The others . . . stormed the house. They left . . . when it got light."

De Royer looked around. "Was it worth it?" MacKay asked. The general didn't answer. They stood there for a moment, not speaking. Then MacKay spun around and walked away.

"We found Colonel Bouchard in the house," a sergeant said. De Royer followed the sergeant and stepped over the rubble of what had been a wall and into the kitchen of Slavin's house. Bouchard was lying face down on the floor in a pool of blood. A MAT-49 submachine gun was next to him and the bodies of two soldiers were crumpled in the doorway. The AA-52 was on its side, empty. De Royer bent and examined the bag with forty-millimeter grenades. It was empty.

Bouchard had given a good account of himself.

Gently, de Royer rolled Bouchard over. A voice behind him said, "Sergeant Willi Storch is in the other room."

"Get him," was all de Royer said. He adjusted Bouchard's flak vest. Well, my friend, de Royer thought. How many did you hold off?

Slowly, he removed the black glove from Bouchard's left hand. He touched the ugly burn scars that covered the skeletal outline of what had been a hand. Still, it had

452

functioned, a tribute to Bouchard's perseverance in recovering from the burns that had almost killed him.

De Royer stood up and drew himself to attention. He saluted Bouchard, holding the glove in his own left hand.

Saturday, April 25
Desert One, Lesotho

The ramp was packed with four hundred legionnaires, five Warthogs, and two C-130s. Only the Pumas, Kowalski, and Waldo were missing. Pontowski stepped out of the comm van and walked past the first-aid tent where two French doctors and four nurses were performing medical miracles. Set farther back was another tent. This one held fourteen body bags.

Standard joined him. "Is that the last C-130?" he asked Pontowski, pointing to a C-130 on landing rollout.

"That's it. De Royer and his command element should be on board." They watched as the C-130 taxied clear of the runway and pulled into the parking area.

Standard shook his head. "They are gonna have my ass when they find out the French have been here."

Pontowski wanted to ask who the "they" were. Instead, "One hell of a forward operating location you got here. You could fight a war from here."

"That was the idea when we built it," Standard told him. He laughed. Knowing Gengha Dung, she would send the Department of Defense an itemized statement for the use of Desert One. "Wait until you see the bill."

A helicopter flew over and settled to the ground. One more to go, Pontowski thought. The Pumas were extracting the legionnaires who had been holding the ridge lines. They had been the first to go in and were the last to come out. The C-130's engines were spinning down and a tall figure was marching across the ramp toward him. It was de Royer.

Pontowski saluted. "Well done, sir."

"Have all aircraft recovered?" de Royer asked.

"Two Pumas are inbound and there's Waldo. He's still burning off fuel."

"Why doesn't he land?" Standard asked.

"Because I wouldn't let him." Pontowski replied. This was going to take some explaining. "He's lost his hydraulics and is in manual reversion. The book says to eject but he wants to recover the jet. There's a damn good chance he'll auger in on landing and close the runway. So he's holding and burning off fuel until everyone else is down."

"Why don't you just order him to eject?" Standard said.

"I suggested it," Pontowski said. "But it's his decision." De Royer nodded, agreeing with him. Pontowski keyed his personal radio. "Maggot, tell Waldo he can land."

"Roger that," Maggot answered.

A Puma came in and landed as they waited, each lost in his own thoughts. Standard broke the silence. "General de Royer, did you destroy the base?"

"No."

"Did you turn it over to someone?" Standard asked.

"Yes."

This is like pulling teeth, Standard thought. "To who, sir?"

"A commando," de Royer said. The two men stared at the Frenchman, not believing what they had just heard. A smile played at de Royer's lips but he suppressed it. "I gave it back with instructions to use it properly."

"But why?" Standard asked.

"Who else was I to give it to? It is their base. Besides, we have Beckmann."

"Oh, my God," Standard muttered. "How? Who?"

"Your man, MacKay, captured him," de Royer replied.

"Where is MacKay?" Standard asked.

De Royer shook his head. "He walked away."

The last Puma approached, hovered, and settled to the ground. Pontowski's head nodded in relief when he saw Sam get off, still carrying her camera. His eyes followed her as she walked toward them and he felt a pang of regret at the way things had turned out. But that was life. He was surprised when de Royer saluted her. Then he remembered the time on the ramp at Andrews when the general had saluted Sergeant Patricia Owens's parents in the same way.

"Thank you, General," Sam said. She looked at Pontowski. "I wanted to be on the last helicopter out."

"I'm pleased that you got your wish, Miss Darnell," Pontowski replied.

"It's Sam, Colonel." Was she laughing at him? She looked around. "What are you waiting for?"

He pointed. "For that." Waldo was entering downwind.

"Come on, you mutha," Waldo muttered as sweat poured down his face. He was tired after flying in manual reversion for almost two hours and talking to himself helped. But he understood why Pontowski wouldn't let him land.

What had Pontowski said? "Jettison that puppy, Waldo. I got lots of Hogs, only one you."

"Sorry, Colonel," Waldo said to himself. "That's the standard line. I'm giving this one back to you." But that was also the standard response. "Landing Gear Alternate Extension," he muttered, going through the emergency drill to lower the gear. He pulled on the gear handle and dropped it. "Two in the green," he muttered. The main gear was down and locked but the nose gear was still up. He bounced the aircraft to move things along but that didn't help.

He increased airspeed and pulled two Gs, trying to break the nose gear free. "What the hell!" The explosion in the gun bay had jammed the nose gear doors, and nothing Waldo could do broke it free.

"What now?" Maybe it was time to eject. "No way. I nursed you this far. And I'm flying on fumes anyway." It was true. The fuel gauge read empty. He turned final.

Maggot was standing beside Pontowski as Waldo came across the approach end of the runway. "Shit-oh-dear," he mumbled. Sam raised her camera and focused on the jet. "Why didn't he punch out?" Maggot asked. He knew the answer because he would have done exactly what Waldo was doing. But it was different when it was another jock.

Instinctively, Sam followed the A-10 as it touched down on its main gear. She held her breath.

Waldo held the nose up as long as he could. Then it dropped. The snout of the Warthog, the muzzle of the Avenger cannon, dug into the concrete, absorbing the forward momentum of the fighter. The forces were transmitted back along the cannon, which had the strength to resist them, and into the fuel bays behind the cockpit. But no airframe could take that kind of punishment. The Warthog's back broke as it pitch-poled straight ahead, over its nose and onto its back. It skidded down the runway tail first, on top of the canopy, sending a wave of sparks and shredded Plexiglas to each side. Finally, it spun completely around and came to a halt, pointing back up the runway.

Men were running toward the A-10 as Sam zoomed in on the cockpit. She could see Waldo hanging in his shoulder straps with his head bent forward and the top of his helmet resting against concrete. "He's trapped!" she shouted.

"The ejection seat!" Pontowski shouted. "It saved him." The top of the ACES-II ejection seat was acting like a pillar and holding the pilot's head off the runway.

A bright flash mushroomed, enveloping the Warthog and driving the men back. The flames grew into a cloud. Then just as suddenly, the flames were gone. Sam's camera recorded a dark figure crawling out of the cockpit and running for all he was worth.

"A flash fire," Maggot said. There wasn't enough fuel left to sustain the fire once it ignited.

"There goes the world's luckiest SOB," Pontowski muttered.

Sam turned her camera on Pontowski and caught the relief in his face. "I don't know about that," she said, making a promise she intended to keep.

EPILOGUE

Friday, May 1
Cape Town, South Africa

MacKay found his seat in the first-class section of the Boeing 747-400. The white South African Airways steward came by and smiled. "It's nineteen hours to New York. If there's anything I can do to make your flight more comfortable, please ask."

"A pillow and a blanket," MacKay answered. "I'm really tired."

"You're an American?" the steward asked as he got a pillow and a blanket from the overhead compartment. MacKay nodded an answer. "Were you in South Africa long?"

"Just a few days," he lied, falling easily into his cover story. "Business." *Will I ever know the full truth of it?* he thought.

"I hope you enjoyed your stay and will come back," the steward said, moving on.

MacKay settled into the deep leather seat and felt the tension drain away as the turbofan engines came to life and they taxied to the runway. He turned to the window as the big airliner climbed into the late-afternoon sky, passing to the north of Table Mountain. He could see the coast stretching down to the Cape of Good Hope and ahead of them, the clear blue of the South Atlantic. He was going home.

But no matter where he went, Ziba would be with him.

Wednesday, May 6
The White House, Washington, D.C.

Cyrus Piccard was in an unbelievably good mood when he entered Carroll's office. "Germany!" He was almost shouting. "Can you believe it? They want Beckmann tried by the International Criminal Tribunal in The Hague. The neo-Axis advancing the concept of universal jurisdiction! The world never ceases to amaze me."

Bill Carroll smiled at the old man and looked at Mazie. His voice was going and it was difficult to speak.

"Germany misread the situation," Mazie said. "Prime was too much of a temptation and they went after it. That's why they backed Beckmann. Unfortunately, that also meant backing his dream of an Afrikaner homeland. It was simply a matter of showing them the error of their ways. Now they're scrambling to mend their political fences."

"Who accomplished that miracle?" Piccard asked.

"Mazie," Carroll said.

It was one of the few times that Cyrus Piccard was at a loss for words. "I must know," he finally managed, "does cold fusion work?"

Mazie shook her head. "Not yet. Doctor Slavin claims he can get ignition without an explosion. Unfortunately, he gets an uncontrollable meltdown. He thinks he can solve the problem in ten or twenty years. Our scientists aren't so sure."

Mazie is ready, Carroll thought.

Carroll's secretary knocked at the door. "Your wife is here, Mr. Carroll." Mary came through the door dressed in warmups. The two Secret Service agents Carroll had run countless miles with were right behind her. But that was over, in his past. The two men were also dressed in warmups and running shoes.

Carroll stared in horror at the wheelchair Wayne Adams

and Chuck Stanford were pushing. It was a specially designed sports chair with a headrest. "From us," Adams said.

"We're going for a run," Stanford announced.

Mary looked at her husband. "Get in the chair, Bill."
Carroll didn't move. "You only have to do it once," she
said. Silence. Slowly, the national security advisor pulled
himself up and sat in the wheelchair. It fit him like a glove,
and Mary fastened the seat belt.

Without a word, Adams pushed him out the door with
Mary and Stanford right behind. They walked briskly out of
the White House, never slowing. When they reached Ellipse
Road, Adams started to run, pushing Carroll. It wasn't a
sprint, but it was a hard run, well under six minutes a mile.
When Adams couldn't maintain the pace, Mary took over.
They never slowed. Then Stanford took over as they raced
around the Mall.

Tourists stared in wonder as an agent on a mountain bike
cleared a path for them. Carroll lay back in the chair and
felt the wind whip at his face.

For a few moments, he was at peace with his world.

Wednesday, May 27
Aubagne, France

The Legion's band marched into position before the
Monument aux Morts. Muffled drums beat the cadence as
four companies of the 2nd Régiment Étranger Parachutiste
moved forward to the ready line. General Charles de Royer
stood with the commander of the Legion on the reviewing
stand, his back ramrod straight and his tan uniform devoid
of medals. On a small table in front of him a glass case held
a black glove destined for the Legion's museum.

The ceremony played out with precision as La Légion
Étrangère honored its dead. Fourteen names were read off,
not by rank but by the order in which they died. That was
the Legion. A salute was fired and the 2nd REP passed in
review. The band marched off and the ceremony was over.
The TV cameras were turned off and the reporters returned
to their cars.

Little Matt held on to his father's hand. "I remember him from the United Nations," he said. "He looks taller outside with that funny hat."

"It's called a kepi, good buddy," Pontowski said.

"Will I be as tall as him when I grow up?"

Pontowski smiled. "I don't think so."

Elizabeth Gordon joined them. "Congratulations on your promotion, General. Sam told me the Senate finally confirmed your nomination."

"Thank you," he said, not telling her that he was as surprised as Congresswoman Nevers. He had never expected the secretary of defense to make good on his promise.

"I never had a chance to thank you."

"There's nothing to thank me for," Pontowski replied.

"For inviting us to the ceremony," she added. "I'm glad we came."

They looked at each other, trying to be polite. "I thought your special on the Iron Guard was outstanding," Pontowski said. "I understand you swept the ratings."

"It was Sam's special, not mine," she admitted. Silence. "Will there ever be peace between us?" she asked.

Can anyone keep the peace when there is no peace to begin with? Pontowski wondered. "I doubt it," he replied.

"It's between you and me," she said. "Not you and Sam."

Pontowski accepted the truth. "There's someone I'd like you to meet," he told his son, taking his hand.

"She's by the cars," Gordon called as they walked away.

ACKNOWLEDGMENTS

I owe a debt of gratitude to the many people who gave unsparingly of their time, knowledge, and advice to make this book happen. Without the help and encouragement of my wife, Sheila, and my son, Eric, I would have lost my way countless times. Major Jim Preston of the 442nd Fighter Wing (AFRES) was always there when I needed a dose of reality, advice, and help.

Charles D. Poe, a linguistic researcher par excellence, helped with the fine-tuning of terminology, ideas, and pointing out sources that proved invaluable in creating a realistic scenario.

Others contributed significantly: Dr. Michael Spieth for his help in understanding Lou Gehrig's disease, Lauri Mighton-Kain for her insights into TV reporting, Rob Barnes for the help with nuclear attack submarines, Derek Greeff for sharing his experiences as a Parabet in the South African Defense Force, and Lieutenant Colonel Paul Woodford, USAF, for an introduction to the world of Hashing.

Ken and Marcia Fritz helped with their unfailing good humor and support. Marcia's insights into South Africa, not to mention accounting, came at a critical time. Jimmy Ntintili of Face to Face tours in Johannesburg promised me the "good, the bad, and ugly" of life in Soweto. He also showed me the beautiful.

Lieutenant Commanders Dan Hendricks and Richard Rieckenberg, USN, gave me a quick education in nuclear energy on board the USS *Nimitz* and an appreciation of

ACKNOWLEDGMENTS

what goes on below the glamour of the flight deck. On the Air Force side, Captains Paul Heye, Jr., and E. T. King II, along with Technical Sergeant Lyle Inscho, proved again what a grand old lady the C-130 Hercules is. And in the process they showed me how far forward the 37th ALS, the Blue Tail Flies, was leaning in support of Operation Provide Promise in Bosnia. But that is a story in itself.

Finally, my portrayal of the problems of command only hints at what goes on behind the scenes. Colonel James H. Kyle, USAF (Retired), reveals the reality and agony of command better than any work of fiction in his book *The Guts to Try*.

GLOSSARY

AA-52: French-made 7.5-millimeter light machine gun, weighs twenty pounds, with eight hundred rounds per minute cyclic rate of fire. An excellent weapon.

ACT: Air combat tactics, dogfighting.

Adjudant Offisier: A warrant officer.

ALS: Amyotrophic lateral sclerosis, Lou Gehrig's disease. ALS is a motor neuron disease that affects mostly men and causes a degeneration in the nerves controlling the muscles. The cause is unknown and there is no cure.

ANC: African National Congress. The oldest political party in South Africa and the first black political movement of its kind in Africa. It cuts across tribal lines and played a major role in the defeat of apartheid.

Apartheid: Afrikaans for "separateness" or "apartness." It became the official policy of South Africa in 1948 in order to give whites economic, political, and social control of the country.

AWB: Afrikaanse Weerstandsbeweging, a neo-Nazi, white supremacist group that believes in the use of force. Its military arm is the Iron Guard. The AWB considers the Ku Klux Klan a liberal organization.

Azanian: The Azanian People's Organization is a pan-African political movement that believes there is a need for cathartic violence to overcome the brutalization Africans have suffered under apartheid.

Bandit: Any aircraft positively identified as hostile.

GLOSSARY

BDU: Battle dress uniform. The latest name given to the uniform worn in battle.

CAP: Combat air patrol. A protective umbrella of fighters with the specific mission of finding and destroying enemy aircraft.

CBU-58: Cluster bomb unit. The CBU-58 contains 650 baseball-sized bomblets, each of which explodes into 260 fragments. Inside each bomblet are two 5-grain titanium incendiary pellets. It is a quantum jump over napalm and has the advantage of being a politically correct weapon.

COIC: Combined operations intelligence center. It brings command, communications, control, intelligence, and operations together under one roof.

DCI: The director of central intelligence. The individual in charge of all U.S. intelligence agencies and functions. Also heads the CIA.

Fission: The process in which a neutron strikes the nucleus of an atom, splits it into fragments, and releases several neutrons, radiation, and heat.

Fusion: The opposite of fission. Two hydrogen nuclei collide, fuse, and create a new nucleus. The result is a form of helium, radiation, and large amounts of heat.

GPS: Global positioning system. A satellite-based navigation system that provides extremely accurate positioning of aircraft, ships, and individuals. Current receivers are the size of a hand-held scientific calculator and are getting smaller. Very cosmic and available to the public.

IG: Inspector General. A military organization that investigates complaints and conducts inspections.

Inkatha: The Zulu-based political party in South Africa. It is the rival of the ANC and is located mostly in Kwa-Zulu/Natal Province.

ISA: Intelligence Support Agency. One of the "boys in the basement" of the Pentagon. The ISA was formed during the Reagan administration under the Department of the Army to bypass the restrictions placed on the CIA for covert operations. It was effective and its current status is unknown.

GLOSSARY

Koevoet: Literally "crowbar" in Afrikaans. It was an elite counterterrorist unit operating on the Namibian-Angolan border during the 1980s. Now disbanded.

Kommandant: A lieutenant colonel.

Kukri: A South African variant of the earlier Sidewinder air-to-air missile.

Laager: A defensive circle of wagons used by voortrekkers to fight off hostile tribes. The laager became the symbol of Afrikaner resistance to political change.

LZ: Landing zone.

Mark-82 AIR: Air inflatable retarded. A five-hundred-pound bomb that can be employed at low altitudes. Its fall is retarded by the balute, an inflatable balloon/parachute that deploys behind it and slows the bomb's descent, allowing the delivery aircraft to escape the bomb's blast.

MAT-49: French-made nine-millimeter submachine gun comparable to others in its class. Empty weight of seven pounds and fires at six hundred rounds per minute.

MOPP: Mission operative protection posture. The protective suit and equipment worn to counter chemical warfare. It is very hot and cumbersome.

NVG: Night-vision goggles.

PRC-103: The latest small survival radio used by air crews. It can be integrated with the LARS (lightweight recovery system) to provide a discrete beacon, coding, and homing. The homing feature is accurate to a few feet.

ROE: Rules of engagement. Normally, a collection of very good ideas designed to keep fighter pilots alive. The ROE get screwed up when politicians think they've got a clue and make inputs.

SAR: Search and rescue.

Sidewinder: The AIM-9, or air intercept missile. It is infrared-guided, and the latest versions are guaranteed to water a bandit's eyeballs.

STU-III: A portable, key-activated, plug-in-anywhere telephone that scrambles telephone conversations.

Tomahawk: A twenty-foot-long sea- or land-launched cruise missile. The latest models have a one-thousand-

GLOSSARY

mile range and can deliver a one-thousand-pound warhead with extreme accuracy.

Tsotsis: The vicious young black township gang members who lead a life of violent street crime.

Twin Gun: A twin-barreled twenty-millimeter antiaircraft artillery system manufactured by Rheinmetall of Dusseldorf. It has an excellent fire-control system and a 1,000-rounds-per-minute cyclic rate of fire per barrel. The actual rate of fire is limited by the 550-round ammunition box per barrel.

VLS: Vertical Launch System. The vertical launch tubes for the Tomahawk cruise missile located in the bow of *Los Angeles*–class attack submarines.

Voortrek: The migration of the trekboers (seminomadic Dutch cattle herders) in the 1830s to avoid English rule in South Africa. They were called voortrekkers and their fierce spirit of independence and stubbornness has become the symbol of the modern Afrikaner.